Robert Michael Ballantyne

The floating Light of the Goodwin sands; a Tale

Robert Michael Ballantyne

The floating Light of the Goodwin sands; a Tale

ISBN/EAN: 9783337024376

Printed in Europe, USA, Canada, Australia, Japan

Cover: Foto ©Andreas Hilbeck / pixelio.de

More available books at **www.hansebooks.com**

THE FLOATING LIGHT

OF

THE GOODWIN SANDS.

A Tale.

By R. M. BALLANTYNE,

AUTHOR OF "ERLING THE BOLD;" "DEEP DOWN;" "THE LIFEBOAT;"
"THE LIGHTHOUSE;" "FIGHTING THE FLAMES;" ETC.

With Illustrations by the Author.

PHILADELPHIA:
CLAXTON, REMSEN & HAFFELFINGER,
819 & 821 MARKET STREET.
1871.

PREFACE.

THIS tale, reader—if you read it through—will give you some insight into the condition, value, and vicissitudes of the light-vessels, or floating lighthouses, which guard the shores of this kingdom, and mark the dangerous shoals lying off some of our harbours and roadsteads. It will also convey to you—if you don't skip—a general idea of the life and adventures of some of the men who have manned these interesting and curious craft in time past, as well as give you some account of the sayings and doings of several other personages more or less connected with our coasts. May you read it with pleasure and profit, and—"may your shadow never be less."

I gratefully express my acknowledgment and tender my best thanks to the Elder Brethren of the Trinity House, to whose kindness I am indebted for having been permitted to spend a week on board the Gull-stream light-vessel, one of the three floating-lights which mark the Goodwin Sands; and to Robin Allen, Esq., Secretary to the Trinity House, who has kindly furnished me with valuable books, papers, and information. I have also gratefully to tender my best thanks to Captain Vaile, District Superintendent under the Trinity House at Ramsgate, for the ready and extremely kind manner in which he afforded me every facility for visiting the various light-vessels and buoys of his district, and for observing the nature and duties of the service.

To the master of the Gull, whose "bunk" I occupied while he was on shore—to Mr. John Leggett, the mate, who was in command during the period of my visit— and to the men of the "Floating-light" I have to offer my heartfelt thanks for not only receiving me with generous hospitality, but for treating me with hearty goodwill during my pleasant sojourn with them in their interesting and peculiar home.

My best thanks, for much useful and thrilling information, are due to Mr. Isaac Jarman, the coxswain, and Mr. Fish, the bowman, of the Ramsgate Lifeboat—men who may be said to carry their lives continually in their hands, and whose profession it is to go out at the call of duty and systematically grapple with Death and rob him of his prey. To the Harbour Master, and Deputy Harbour Master at Ramsgate, I am also indebted for information and assistance, and to Mr. Reid, the master of the Aid steam-tug which attends upon, and shares the perils of, the Lifeboat.

R. M. BALLANTYNE.

EDINBURGH, 1870.

CONTENTS.

vi

CONTENTS.

LIST OF ILLUSTRATIONS.

THE FLOATING LIGHT OF THE GOODWIN SANDS:

A TALE.

CHAPTER I.

PARTICULAR INQUIRIES.

A LIGHT—clear, ruddy and brilliant, like a huge carbuncle—uprose one evening from the deep, and remained hovering about forty feet above the surface, scattering its rays far and wide, over the Downs to Ramsgate and Deal, along the coast towards Dover, away beyond the North Foreland, across the Goodwin Sands, and far out upon the bosom of the great North Sea.

It was a chill November evening, when this light arose, in the year—well, it matters not what year. We have good reasons, reader, for shrouding this point in mystery. It may have been recently; it may have been "long, long ago." We don't intend to tell. It was not the first time of that light's

A

appearance, and it certainly was not the last. Let it suffice that what we are about to relate did happen, sometime or other within the present century.

Besides being cold, the evening in question was somewhat stormy—"gusty," as was said of it by a traveller with a stern visage and remarkably keen grey eyes, who entered the coffee-room of an hotel which stood on the margin of Ramsgate harbour facing the sea, and from the upper windows of which the light just mentioned was visible.

"It is, sir," said the waiter, in reply to the "gusty" observation, stirring the fire while the traveller divested himself of his hat and greatcoat.

"Think it's going to blow hard?" inquired the traveller, planting himself firmly on the hearth-rug, with his back to the fire, and his thumbs hooked into the armholes of his waistcoat.

"It may, sir, and it may not," answered the waiter, with the caution of a man who has resolved, come what may, never to commit himself. "Sometimes it comes on to blow, sir, w'en we don't look for it; at other times it falls calm w'en we least expects it. I don't pretend to understand much about the weather myself, sir, but I shouldn't wonder if it *was* to come on to blow 'ard. It ain't an uncommon thing at Ramsgate, sir."

The traveller, who was a man of few words, said "Humph!" to which the waiter dutifully replied

"Yessir," feeling, no doubt, that the observation was too limited to warrant a lengthened rejoinder.

The waiter of the Fortress Hotel had a pleasant, sociable, expressive countenance, which beamed into a philanthropic smile as he added,—

"Can I do anything for you, sir?"

"Yes—tea," answered the traveller with the keen grey eyes, turning, and poking the fire with the heel of his boot.

"Anything *with* it, sir?" asked the waiter with that charmingly confident air peculiar to his class, which induces one almost to believe that if a plate of elephant's foot or a slice of crocodile's tail were ordered it would be produced, hot, in a few minutes.

"D'you happen to know a man of the name of Jones in the town?" demanded the traveller, facing round abruptly.

The waiter replied that he had the pleasure of knowing at least seven Joneses in the town.

"Does one of the seven deal largely in cured fish and own a small sloop?" asked the traveller.

"Yessir, he do, but he don't live in Ramsgate; he belongs to Yarmouth, sir, comes 'ere only now and then."

"D'you know anything about him?"

"No, sir, he don't frequent this 'otel."

The waiter said this in a tone which showed that he deemed that fact sufficient to render Jones altogether unworthy of human interest; "but I believe," he added slowly, "that he is said to 'ave plenty of money, bears a bad character, and is rather fond of his bottle, sir."

"You know nothing more?"

"Nothing, sir."

"Ham and eggs, dry toast and shrimps," said the keen-eyed traveller in reply to the reiterated question.

Before these viands were placed on the table the brief twilight had passed away and darkness enshrouded land and sea. After they had been consumed the traveller called for the latest local paper, to which he devoted himself for an hour with unflagging zeal—reading it straight through, apparently, advertisements and all, with as much diligence as if it were a part of his professional business to do so. Then he tossed it away, rang the bell, and ordered a candle.

"I suppose," he said, pointing towards the sea, as he was about to quit the room, "that that is the floating light?"

"It is one of 'em, sir," replied the waiter. "There are three lights on the sands, sir; the Northsan 'ead, the Gull-stream, and the Southsan 'ead. That one, sir, is the Gull."

"How far off may it be?"

"About four miles, sir."

" What is the mate's name ?"

" Welton, sir, John Welton."

" Is he aboard just now ?"

" Yessir, it's the master's month ashore. The master and mate 'ave it month an' month about, sir —one month afloat, next month ashore ; but it seems to me, sir, that they have 'arder work w'en ashore than they 'ave w'en afloat—lookin' after the Trinity stores, sir, an' goin' off in the tender to shift and paint the buoys an' such like ; but then you see, sir, w'en it's their turn ashore they always gits home to spend the nights with their families, sir, w'ich is a sort of compensation, as it were,—that's where it is, sir."

" Humph ! d' you know what time it is slack water out there in the afternoon just now ?"

" About three o'clock, sir."

" Call me at nine to-morrow ; breakfast at half-past ; beefsteaks, coffee, dry toast. Good-night."

" Yessir—good-night, sir—No. 27, sir, first floor, left-hand side."

No. 27 slammed his door with that degree of violence which indicates a stout arm and an easy conscience. In less than quarter of an hour the keen grey eyes were veiled in slumber, as was proved unmistakeably to the household by the sounds that proceeded from the nose to which these eyes belonged.

It is not unfrequently found that strength of mind, vigour of body, high colour, and a tremendous appetite are associated with great capacity for snoring. The man with the keen grey eyes possessed all these qualities, as well as a large chin and a firm mouth, full of very strong white teeth. He also possessed the convenient power of ability to go to sleep at a moment's notice and to remain in that felicitous condition until he chose to awake. His order to be "called" in the morning had reference merely to hot water; for at the time of which we write men were still addicted to the ridiculous practice of shaving—a practice which, as every one knows, is now confined chiefly to very old men—who naturally find it difficult to give up the bad habit of a lifetime—and to little boys, who *erroneously* suppose that the use of a sharp penknife will hasten Nature's operations.

Exactly at nine o'clock, a knock at the door and " Ot water, sir," sounded in the ears of No. 27. At half-past nine precisely No. 27 entered the coffee-room, and was so closely followed by the waiter with breakfast that it seemed as if that self-sacrificing functionary had sat up all night keeping the meal hot in order to testify, by excessive punctuality, the devotion of his soul to duty.

The keen-eyed man had a keen appetite, if one might judge from appearances in such a matter. A thick underdone steak that overwhelmed his plate appeared to melt away rapidly from before him. Potatoes he disposed of in two bites each; small ones were immolated whole. Of mustard he used as much as might have made a small-sized plaster; pepper he sowed broadcast; he made no account whatever of salt, and sugar was as nothing before him. There was a peculiar crash in the sound produced by the biting of his toast, which was suggestive at once of irresistible power and thorough disintegration. Coffee went down in half-cup gulps; shrimps disappeared in shoals, shells and all; and —in short, his proceedings might have explained to an intelligent observer how it is that so many men grow to be exceedingly fat, and why it is that hotel proprietors cannot afford to lower their apparently exorbitant charges. The waiter, standing modestly by, and looking on with solemn interest, mentally attributed the traveller's extraordinary powers and high health to the fact that he neither smoked nor drank. It would be presumptuous in us to hazard a speculation on this subject in the face of an opinion held by one who was so thoroughly competent to judge.

Breakfast over, the keen-eyed man put on his hat and overcoat and sallied forth to the harbour, where he spent the greater part of the forenoon in loitering about, inspecting the boats—particularly the

lifeboat—and the shipping with much interest, and
entering into conversation with the boatmen who
lounged upon the pier. He was very gracious to
the coxswain of the lifeboat—a bluff, deep-chested,
hearty, neck-or-nothing sort of man, with an intelligent eye, almost as keen as his own, and a
manner quite as prompt. With this coxswain he
conversed long about the nature of his stirring and
dangerous duties. He then made inquiry about
his crew: how many men he had, and their circumstances ; and, by the way, whether any of them
happened to be named Jones. One of them was so
named, the coxswain said—Tom Jones. This led
the traveller to ask if Tom Jones owned a small
sloop. No, he didn't own a sloop, not even a boat.
Was there any other Jones in the town who owned
a small sloop and dealt largely in cured fish? Yes
there was, and he was a regular gallow's-bird, if all
reports were true, the coxswain told him.

The traveller did not press the subject long.
Having brought it up as it were incidentally, he
dismissed it carelessly, and again concentrated his
attention and interest on the lifeboat.

To all the men with whom he conversed this
bluff man with the keen grey eyes put the same
question, and he so contrived to put it that it
seemed to be a matter of comparatively little interest to him whether there was or was not a man

of the name of Jones in the town. Nevertheless, he gained all the information about Jones that he desired, and then, hiring a boat, set out for the floating light.

The weather, that had appeared threatening during the night, suddenly became calm and fine, as if to corroborate the statement of the waiter of the Fortress Hotel in regard to its uncertainty ; but knowing men in oilcloth sou'westers and long boots gave it as their opinion that the weather was not to be trusted. Fortunately for the traveller, it remained trustworthy long enough to serve his purpose. The calm permitted his boat to go safely alongside of the light-ship, and to climb up the side without difficulty.

The vessel in which he found himself was not by any means what we should style clipper-built—quite the reverse. It was short for its length, bluff in the bows, round in the stern, and painted all over, excepting the mast and deck, of a bright red colour, like a great scarlet dragon, or a gigantic boiled lobster. It might have been mistaken for the first attempt in the ship-building way of an infatuated boy, whose acquaintance with ships was founded on hearsay, and whose taste in colour was violently eccentric. This remarkable thing had one immense mast in the middle of it, supported by six stays, like the Norse galleys of old, but it had no yards; for, although the sea was indeed its home, and it incessantly braved the fury of the storm, diurnally cleft the waters of flood and ebb-tide, and gallantly breasted the billows of ocean all the year round, it had no need of sails. It never advanced an inch on its course, for it had no course. It never made for any port. It was never either homeward or outward bound. No streaming eyes ever watched its departure; no beating hearts ever hailed its return. Its bowsprit never pointed either to "Green-land's icy mountains, or India's coral strand," for it had no bowsprit at all. Its helm was never swayed to port or starboard, although it *had* a helm, because the vessel turned submissive with the tides, and its rudder, being lashed hard and fast amidships—like most weather-cocks—couldn't move. Its doom was to tug perpetually, day and night, from year to year, at a gigantic anchor which would not let go, and to strain at a monster chain-cable which would not snap—in short, to strive for ever, like Sisyphus, after something which can never be attained.

A sad destiny, some may be tempted to exclaim. No, reader, not so sad as it appears. We have presented but one side of the picture. That curious, almost ridiculous-looking craft, was among the aristocracy of shipping. Its important office stamped it with nobility. It lay there, conspicuous in its royal colour, from day to day and year to year, to mark the fair-way between the white cliffs of Old England and the outlying shoals—distinguished in daylight by a huge ball at its mast-head, and at night by a magnificent lantern with argand lamps and concave reflectors, which shot its rays like lightning far and wide over the watery waste, while, in thick weather, when neither ball nor light could be discerned, a sonorous gong gave its deep-toned warning to the approaching mariner, and let him know his position amid the surrounding dangers. Without such warnings by night and by day, the world would suffer the loss of thousands of lives and untold millions of gold. Indeed the mere absence of such warnings for one stormy night would certainly result in loss irreparable to life and property. As well might Great Britain dispense with her armies as with her floating lights! That boiled-lobster-like craft was also, if we may be allowed to say so, stamped with magnanimity, because its services were disinterested and universal. While other ships were sailing grandly to their ports in all their canvas panoply, and swelling with the pride of costly merchandise within, each unmindful of the other, *this* ship remained floating there, destitute of cargo, either rich or poor, never in port, always on service, serene in all the majesty of her one settled self-sacrificing purpose—to guide the converging navies of the world safely past the dangerous shoals that meet them on their passage to the world's greatest port, the Thames, or to speed them safely thence when outward-bound. That unclipperly craft, moreover, was a gallant vessel, because its post was one of danger. When other ships fled on the wings of terror—or of storm trysails—to seek refuge in harbour and roadstead, this one merely lengthened her cable—as a knight might shake loose the reins of his war-horse on the eve of conflict—and calmly awaited the issue, prepared to let the storm do its worst, and to meet it with a bold front. It lay right in the Channel, too, "i' the imminent deadly breach," as it were, prepared to risk encounter with the thousands of ships, great and small, which passed to and fro continually ;— to be grazed and fouled by clumsy steersmen, and to be run into at night by unmanageable wrecks or derelicts ; ready for anything in fact—come weal come woe, blow high blow low—in the way of duty, for this vessel was the Floating Light that marked the Gull-stream off the celebrated and fatal Goodwin Sands.

CHAPTER II.

. THE FLOATING LIGHT BECOMES THE SCENE OF FLOATING SURMISES
AND VAGUE SUSPICIONS.

It must not be supposed, from what has been said, that the Gull Lightship was the only vessel of the kind that existed at that time. But she was a good type of the class of vessels (numbering at present about sixty) to which she belonged, and, both as regarded her situation and duties, was, and still is, one of the most interesting among the floating lights of the kingdom.

When the keen-eyed traveller stepped upon her well-scrubbed deck, he was courteously received by the mate, Mr. John Welton, a strongly-built man above six feet in height, with a profusion of red hair, huge whiskers, and a very peculiar expression of countenance, in which were united calm self-possession, coolness, and firmness, with great good-humour and affability.

"You are Mr. Welton, I presume?" said the traveller abruptly, touching his hat with his forefinger in acknowledgment of a similar salute from the mate.

"That is my name, sir."

"Will you do me the favour to read this letter?" said the traveller, selecting a document from a portly pocket-book, and presenting it.

Without reply the mate unfolded the letter and quietly read it through, after which he folded and returned it to his visitor, remarking that he should be happy to furnish him with all the information he desired, if he would do him the favour to step down into the cabin.

"I may set your mind at rest on one point at once," observed the stranger, as he moved towards the companion-hatch, "my investigations have no reference whatever to yourself."

Mr. Welton made no reply, but a slight look of perplexity that had rested on his brow while he read the letter cleared away.

"Follow me, Mr. Larks," he said, turning and descending the ladder sailor-fashion—which means crab-wise.

"Do you happen to know anything," asked Mr. Larks, as he prepared to follow, "about a man of the name of Jones? I have come to inquire particularly about him, and about your son, who, I am told—"

The remainder of the sentence was lost in the cabin of the floating light. Here, with the door and skylight shut, the mate remained closeted for a long time in close conference with the keen-eyed man, much to the surprise of the two men who constituted the watch on deck, because visitors of any kind to a floating light were about as rare as snowflakes in July, and the sudden advent of a visitor, who looked and acted mysteriously, was in itself a profound mystery. Their curiosity, however, was only gratified to this extent, that they observed the stranger and the mate through the skylight bending earnestly over several newspapers spread out before them on the cabin table.

In less than an hour the keen-eyed man re-appeared on deck, bade the mate an abrupt good-bye, nodded to the men who held the ropes for him, descended into the boat, and took his departure for the shore whence he had come.

By this time the sun was beginning to approach the horizon. The mate of the floating light took one or two turns on the deck, at which he gazed earnestly, as if his future destiny were written there. He then glanced at the compass and at the vessel's bow, after which he leant over the side of the red-dragon, and looked down inquiringly at the flow of the tide. Presently his attention was fixed on the shore, behind which the sun was about to set, and, after a time, he directed a stern look towards the sky, as if he were about to pick a quarrel with that part of the universe, but thinking better of it, apparently, he unbent his brows, let his eyes fall again on the deck, and muttered to himself, " H'm ! I expected as much."

What it was that he expected, Mr. John Welton never told from that day to this, so it cannot be recorded here, but, after stating the fact, he crossed his arms on his broad chest, and, leaning against the stern of his vessel, gazed placidly along the deck, as if he were taking a complacent survey of the vast domain over which he ruled.

It was an interesting kingdom in detail. Leaving out of view all that which was behind him, and which, of course, he could not see, we may remark that, just before him stood the binnacle and compass, and the cabin skylight. On his right and left the territory of the quarter-deck was seriously circumscribed, and the promenade much interfered with, by the ship's boats, which, like their parent, were painted red, and which did not hang at the davits, but, like young lobsters of the kangaroo type, found shelter within their mother, when not at sea on their own account. Near to them were two signal-carronades. Beyond the skylight rose the bright brass funnel of the cabin chimney, and the winch, by means of which the lantern was hoisted. Then came another skylight, and the companion-hatch about the centre of the deck. Just beyond this stood the most important part of the vessel—the lantern-house. This was a circular wooden structure, above six feet in diameter, with a door and small windows. Inside was the lantern—the beautiful piece of costly mechanism for which the light-ship, its crew, and its appurtenances were maintained. Right through the centre of this house rose the thick unyielding mast of the vessel. The lantern, which was just a little less than its house, surrounded this mast and travelled upon it. Beyond this the capital of the kingdom, the eye of the monarch was arrested by another bright brass funnel, which was the chimney of the galley-fire, and indicated the exact position of the abode of the crew, or—to continue our metaphor—the populace, who, however, required no such indicator to tell of their existence or locality, for the chorus of a "nigger" melody burst from them, ever and anon, through every opening in the decks, with jovial violence, as they sat, busily engaged on various pieces of work below. The more remote parts of this landscape—or light-scape, if we may be allowed the expression—were filled up with the galley-skylight, the bitts, and the windlass, above which towered the gong, and around which twined the two enormous chain cables. Only one of these, however, was in use—that, with a single mushroom-anchor, being sufficient to hold the ship securely against tide and tempest.

In reference to this we may remark in passing

that the cable of a floating light is frequently renewed, and that the chafing of the links at the
hawse-hole is distributed by the occasional paying
out or hauling in of a few yards of chain—a process
which is styled "easing the nip."

"Horroo! me hearty, ye're as clain as a lady's
watch," exclaimed a man of rugged form but pleasant
countenance, as he issued from the small doorway of
the lantern-house with a bundle of waste in one
hand and an oil-can in the other.

This was one of the lamplighters of the light-ship
—Jerry MacGowl—a man whose whole soul was, so
to speak, in that lantern. It was his duty to clip
and trim the wicks, and fill the lamps, and polish the
reflectors and brasses, and oil the joints and wheels
(for this was a revolving—in other words a flashing
light), and clean the glasses and windows. As there
were nine lights to attend to, and get ready for
nightly service, it may be easily understood that the
lamplighter's duty was no sinecure.

The shout of Jerry recalled the king from his contemplation of things in general to the lantern in
particular.

"All ready to hoist, Jerry?" inquired Mr. Welton, going forward.

"All ready, sir," exclaimed the man, looking at
his handiwork with admiration, and carefully removing a speck of dust that had escaped his notice

from one of the plate-glass windows; "An't she a purty thing now?—baits the best Ginaiva watch as iver was made. Ye might ait yer supper off her floor and shave in the reflictors."

"That's a fact, Jerry, with no end of oil to your salad too," said Mr. Welton, surveying the work of the lamplighter with a critical eye.

"True for ye," replied Jerry, "an' as much cotton waste as ye like without sinful extravagance."

"The sun will be down in a few minutes," said the mate, turning round and once more surveying the western horizon.

Jerry admitted that, judging from past experience, there was reason to believe in the probability of that event; and then, being of a poetical temperament, he proceeded to expatiate upon the beauty of the evening, which was calm and serene.

"D'ye know, sir," he said, gazing towards the shore, between which and the floating light a magnificent fleet of merchant-men lay at anchor waiting for a breeze—each vessel reflected clearly in the water along with the dazzling clouds of gold that towered above the setting sun—"D'ye know, sir, I niver sees a sky like that but it minds me o' the blissid green hills an' purty lakes of owld Ireland, an' fills me buzzum wid a sort of inspiration till it feels fit a'most to bust."

"You should have been a poet, Jerry," observed

the mate, in a contemplative tone, as he surveyed the shipping through his telescope.

"Just what I've often thought mesilf, sir," replied Jerry, wiping his forehead with the bunch of waste—"many a time I've said to mesilf, in a thoughtful mood—

> Wan little knows what dirty clo'es
>   May kiver up a poet ;
> What fires may burn an' flout an' skurn,
>   An' no wan iver know it."

"That's splendid, Jerry; but what's the meanin' of 'skurn?'"

"Sorrow wan of me knows, sir, but it conveys the idee somehow; don't it, now?"

"I'm not quite sure that it does," said the mate, walking aft and consulting his chronometer for the last time, after which he put his head down the hatchway and shouted, "Up lights!" in a deep sonorous voice.

"Ay, ay, sir," came the ready response from below, followed by the prompt appearance of the other lamplighter and the four seamen who composed the crew of the vessel. Jerry turned on his heel, murmuring, in a tone of pity, that the mate, poor man, "had no soul for poethry."

Five of the crew manned the winch; the mate and Jerry went to a block-tackle which was also connected with the lifting apparatus. Then the order to hoist was given, and immediately after, just

as the sun went down, the floating light went up,—
a modest yet all-important luminary of the night.
Slowly it rose, for the lantern containing it weighed
full half a ton, and caused the hoisting chain and
pulleys to groan complainingly. At last it reached
its destination at the head of the thick part of the
mast, but about ten or fifteen feet beneath the ball.
As it neared the top, Jerry sprang up the chain-
ladder to connect the lantern with the rod and pinion
by means of which, with clockwork beneath, it was
made to revolve and "flash" once every third of a
minute.

Simultaneously with the ascent of the Gull
light there arose out of the sea three bright stars on
the nor'-eastern horizon, and another star in the
south-west. The first were the three fixed lights
of the lightship that marked the North sandhead;
the latter was the fixed light that guarded the South
sandhead. The Goodwin sentinels were now placed
for the night, and the commerce of the world might
come and go, and pass those dreaded shoals, in
absolute security.

Ere long the lights of the shipping in the Downs
were hung out, and one by one the lamps on shore
shone forth—those which marked the entrance of
Ramsgate harbour being conspicuous for colour and
brilliancy—until the water, which was so calm as to
reflect them all, seemed alive with perpendicular

streams of liquid fire; land and sea appearing to be
the subjects of one grand illumination. A much
less poetical soul than that of the enthusiastic lamplighter might have felt a touch of unwonted inspiration on such a night, and in such a scene. The
effect on the mind was irresistibly tranquillizing.
While contemplating the multitudes of vessels that
lay idle and almost motionless on the glassy water,
the thought naturally arose that each black hull enshrouded human beings who were gradually sinking
into rest—relaxing after the energies of the past day
—while the sable cloak of night descended, slowly
and soothingly, as if God were spreading His hand
gently over all to allay the fever of man's busy day-
life and calm him into needful rest.

The watch of the floating light having been set,
namely, two men to perambulate the deck—a strict
watch being kept on board night and day—the rest
of the crew went below to resume work, amuse themselves, or turn in as they felt inclined.

While they were thus engaged, and darkness was
deepening on the scene, Welton stood on the quarter-
deck observing a small sloop that floated slowly
towards the lightship. Her sails were indeed set,
but no breath of wind bulged them out; her onward
progress was caused by the tide, which had by that
time begun to set with a strong current to the north-
ward. When within about a cable's length, the

rattle of her chain told that the anchor had been let go. A few minutes later, a boat was seen to push off from the sloop and make for the lightship. Two men rowed it and a third steered. Owing to the force of the current they made the vessel with some difficulty.

"Heave us a rope," cried one of the men, as they brushed past.

"No visitors allowed aboard," replied Mr. Welton sternly; catching up, nevertheless, a coil of rope.

"Hallo! father, surely you've become very unhospitable," exclaimed another voice from the boat.

"Why, Jim, is that you, my son?" cried the mate, as he flung the coil over the side.

The boatmen caught it, and next moment Jim stood on the deck—a tall strapping young seaman of twenty or thereabouts—a second edition of his father, but more active and lithe in his motions.

"Why you creep up to us, Jim, like a thief in the night. What brings you here, lad, at such an hour?" asked Mr. Welton, senior, as he shook hands with his son.

"I've come to have a talk with 'ee, father. As to creeping like a thief, a man must creep with the tide when there's no wind, d'ye see, if he don't come to an anchor. 'Tis said that time and tide wait for no man; that bein' so, I have come to see you now that I've got the chance. That's where it is. But I can't stay long, for old Jones will—"

"What!" interrupted the mate with a frown, as he led his son to the forepart of the vessel, in order to be out of earshot of the watch, " have 'ee really gone an' shipped with that scoundrel again, after all I've said to 'ee?"

"I have, father," answered the young man with a perplexed expression; "it is about that same that I've come to talk to 'ee, and to explain—"

"You have need to explain, Jim," said the mate sternly, "for it seems to me that you are deliberately taking up with bad company; and I see in you already one o' the usual consequences; you don't care much for your father's warnings."

" Don't say that, father," exclaimed the youth earnestly, "I am sure that if you knew—stay; I'll send back the boat, with orders to return for me in an hour or so."

Saying this he hurried to the gangway, dismissed the boat, and returned to the forepart of the vessel, where he found his father pacing the deck with an anxious and somewhat impatient air.

"Father," said Jim, as he walked up and down beside his sire, " I have made up my mind that it is my duty to remain, at least a little longer, with Jones, because—"

"Your duty!" interrupted the mate in surprise.

"James!" he added, earnestly, "you told me not long ago that you had taken to attending the prayer-meetings at the sailors' chapel when you could manage it, and I was glad to hear you say so, because I think that the man who feels his need of the help of the Almighty, and acts upon his feeling, is safe to escape the rocks and shoals of life—always supposin' that he sails by the right chart—the Bible; but tell me, does the missionary, or the Bible, teach that it is any one's duty to take up with a swearing, drinking scoundrel, who is going from bad to worse, and has got the name of being worthy of a berth in Newgate?"

"We cannot tell, father, whether all that's said of Morley Jones be true. We may have our suspicions, but we can't prove t'em; and there's no occasion to judge a man too soon."

"That may be so, Jim, but that is no reason why you should consort with a man who can do you no good, and will certainly do 'ee much harm, when you 've no call for to do so. Why do 'ee stick by him—that's what I want to know—when everybody says he 'll be the ruin of you? And why do 'ee always put me off with vague answers when I git upon that subject? You did not use to act like that, Jim. You were always fair an' aboveboard in your young days. But what's the use of askin'? It's plain that bad company has done it, an' my only wonder is, how *you* ever come to play the hypocrite to that extent, as to go to the prayer-meeting and make believe you 've turned religious."

There was a little bitterness mingled with the tone of remonstrance in which this was said, which appeared to affect the young man powerfully, for his face crimsoned as he stopped and laid his hand on his father's shoulder.

" Whatever follies or sins I may have committed," he said, solemnly, " I have not acted a hypocrite's part in this matter. Did you ever yet find me out, father, tellin' you a lie ?"

" Well, I can't say I ever did," answered the mate with a relenting smile, " 'xcept that time when you skimmed all the cream off the milk and cap-sized the dish and said the cat done it, although you was slobbered with it from your nose to your toes—but you was a *very* small fellow at that time, you was, and hadn't got much ballast aboard nor begun to stow your conscience."

" Well, father," resumed Jim with a half-sad smile, " you may depend upon it I am not going to begin to deceive you now. My dear mother's last words to me on that dreary night when she died,— ' Always stick to the *truth*, Jim, whatever it may cost you,'—have never been forgotten, and I pray God they never may be. Believe me when I tell you that I never join Morley in any of his sinful doings, especially his drinking bouts. You know that I am a total abstainer—"

"No, you 're not," cried Mr. Welton, senior; "you don't abstain totally from bad company, Jim, and it 's that I complain of."

" I never join him in his drinking bouts," repeated Jim, without noticing the interruption; "and as he never confides to me any of his business transactions, I have no reason to say that I believe them to be unfair. As I said before, I may suspect, but suspicion is not knowledge; we have no right to condemn him on mere suspicion."

"True, my son; but you have a perfect right to steer clear of him on mere suspicion."

"No doubt," replied Jim, with some hesitation in his tone, "but there are circumstances—"

"There you go again with your 'circumstances,'" exclaimed Welton senior with some asperity; "why don't you heave circumstances overboard, rig the pumps and make a clean breast of it? Surely it 's better to do that than let the ship go to the bottom!"

"Because, father, the circumstances don't all belong to myself. Other people's affairs keep my tongue tied. I do assure you that if it concerned only myself, I would tell you everything; and, indeed, when the right time comes, I promise to tell you all—but in the meantime I— I—"

"Jim," said Mr. Welton, senior, stopping suddenly

and confronting his stalwart son, "tell me honestly, now, isn't there a pretty girl mixed up in this business ?"

Jim stood speechless, but a mantling flush, which the rays of the revolving light deepened on his sunburnt countenance, rendered speech unnecessary.

"I knew it," exclaimed the mate, resuming his walk and thrusting his hands deeper into the pockets of his coat, "it never was otherwise since Adam got married to Eve. Whatever mischief is going you 're sure to find a woman underneath the *very* bottom of it, no matter how deep you go ! If it wasn't that the girls are at the bottom of everything good as well as everything bad, I 'd be glad to see the whole bilin of 'em made fast to all the sinkers of all the buoys along the British coast and sent to the bottom of the North Sea."

"I suspect that if that were done," said Jim, with a laugh, "you 'd soon have all the boys on the British coast making earnest inquiries after their sinkers ! But after all, father, although the girls are hard upon us sometimes, you must admit that we couldn't get on without 'em."

"True for ye, boy," observed Jerry MacGowl, who, coming up at that moment, overheard the conclusion of the sentence. "It 's mesilf as superscribes to that same. Haven 't the swate creeturs led me the life of a dog, turned me inside out like an owld stockin',

trod me in the dust as if I was benaith contimpt
an' riven me heart to mortial tatters, but I couldn't
get on widout 'em nohow for all that. As the pote
might say, av he only knowd how to putt it in proper verse :——

> ' Och, woman dear, ye darlin',
> It 's I would iver be
> Yer praises caterwaulin'
> In swaitest melodee ! ' "

"Mind your own business, Jerry," said the mate,
interrupting the flow of the poet's inspiration.

"Sure it 's that same I'm doin', sir," replied the
man, respectfully touching his cap as he advanced
towards the gong that surrounded the windlass and
uncovered it. "Don't ye see the fog a-comin' down
like the wolf on the fold, an' ain't it my dooty to
play a little tshune for the benefit o' the public ?"

Jerry hit the instrument as he spoke and drowned
his own voice in its sonorous roar. He was driven
from his post, however, by Dick Moy, one of the
watch, who, having observed the approaching fog
had gone forward to sound the gong, and displayed
his dislike to interference by snatching the drumstick out of Jerry's hand and hitting him a smart
blow therewith on the top of his head.

As further conversation was under the circumstances impossible, John Welton and his son retired to the cabin, where the former detailed to the
latter the visit of the strange gentleman with the

keen grey eyes, and the conversation that had passed between them regarding Morley Jones. Still the youth remained unmoved, maintaining that suspicion was not proof, although he admitted that things now looked rather worse than they had done before.

While the father and son were thus engaged, a low moaning wail and an unusual heave of the vessel caused them to hasten on deck, just as one of the watch put his head down the hatch and shouted,

"A squall, sir, brewing up from the nor'-east."

CHAPTER III.

A DISTURBED NIGHT; A WRECK AND AN UNEXPECTED RESCUE.

THE aspect of the night had completely changed. The fog had cleared away; heavy clouds rolled athwart the sky; a deeper darkness descended on the shipping at anchor in the Downs, and a gradually increasing swell caused the Gull to roll a little and tug uneasily at her cable. Nevertheless the warning light at her mast-head retained its perpendicular position in consequence of a clever adaptation of mechanism on the principle of the universal joint.

With the rise of the swell came the first rush of the squall.

"If they don't send the boat at once, you'll have to spend the night with us, Jim," said the mate, looking anxiously in the direction of the sloop belonging to Morley Jones, the dark outlines of which could just be seen looming of a deeper black against the black sky.

"It's too late even now," returned Jim in an

anxious tone ; "the boat, like everything else about the sloop, is a rotten old thing, and would be stove against the side in this swell, slight though it be as yet. But my chief trouble is, that the cables are not fit to hold her if it comes on to blow hard."

For some time the wind increased until it blew half a gale. At that point it continued steady, and as it gave no indication of increasing, John Welton and his son returned to the cabin, where the latter amused himself in glancing over some of the books in the small library with which the ship was furnished, while the sire busied himself in posting up the ship's log for the day.

For a considerable time they were silent, the one busily engaged writing, the other engrossed with a book. At last Mr. Welton senior heaved a deep sigh, and said, while he carefully dotted an *i* and stroked a *t*,—

"It has always been my opinion, Jim, that when boys are bein' trained for the sea, they should be taught writing in a swing or an omnibus, in order to get 'em used to do it in difficult circumstances. There she goes again," he added, referring to a lurch of the vessel which caused the tail of a *y* to travel at least two inches out of its proper course. "Now, that job's done. I'll turn in for a spell, and advise you to do the same, lad."

"No, I'll go on deck and have a talk with Dick

Moy. If the gale don't increase I 'll perhaps turn in, but I couldn't sleep just now for thinkin' o' the sloop."

"Please yourself, my son, an' you 'll please me," replied the mate with a smile which ended in a yawn as he opened the door of a small sleeping berth, and disappeared into its recesses.

James Welton stood for a few minutes with his back to the small fireplace, and stared meditatively at the cabin lamp.

The cabin of the floating light was marvellously neat and immaculately clean. There was evidence of a well-ordered household in the tidiness with which everything was put away in its proper place, even although the fair hand of woman had nothing to do with it, and clumsy man reigned paramount and alone! The cabin itself was very small —about ten feet or so in length, and perhaps eight in width. The roof was so low that Jim could not stand quite erect because of the beams. The grate resembled a toy, and was of brass polished so bright that you might have used it for a looking-glass ; the fire in it was proportionately small, but large enough for the place it had to warm. A crumb or speck of dust could scarce have been found on the floor with a microscope,—and no wonder, for whenever John Welton beheld the smallest symptom of such a blemish he seized a brush and shovel and swept it away. The books in the little library at the stern were neatly arranged, and so were the cups, plates, glasses, salt-cellars, spoons, and saucers, in the little recess that did duty as a cupboard. In short, order and cleanliness reigned everywhere.

And not only was this the case in the cabin, but in every department of the ship. The bread-lockers, the oil-room next to the cabin, the galley where the men lived—all were scrupulously clean and everything therein was arranged with the method and precision that one is accustomed to expect only on board a man-of-war. And, after all, what is a floating light but a man-of-war? Its duty is, like that of any three-decker, to guard the merchant service from a dangerous foe. It is under command of the Trinity Corporation—which is tantamount to saying that it is well found and handled—and it does battle continually with the storm. What more could be said of a man-of-war? The only difference is that it does its work with less fuss and no noise!

After warming himself for a short time, for the night had become bitterly cold, Jim Welton put on one of his sire's overcoats and went on deck, where he had a long walk and talk with Dick Moy, who gave it as his opinion that " it was a wery cold night," and said that he " wouldn't be surprised if it wor to come on to blow 'arder before mornin'."

Dick was a huge man with a large expanse of good-

natured visage, and a tendency to make all his statements with the solemnity of an oracle. Big and
little men, like large and small dogs, have usually a
sympathetic liking for each other. Dick Moy's chief
friend on board was little Jack Shales, who was the
life of the ship, and was particularly expert, as were
also most of his mates, in making, during hours of
leisure, beautiful workboxes and writing-desks with
inlaid woods of varied colours, which were sold at a
moderate price on shore, in order to eke out the
monthly wage and add to the comforts of wives and
little ones at Ramsgate. It may be added that Jack
Shales was unquestionably the noisiest man on board.
He had a good voice ; could sing, and *did* sing, from
morning till night, and had the power of uttering a
yell that would have put to shame the wildest warrior
among the Cherokee savages ! ·

Jack Shales kept watch with Moy that night, and
assisted in the conversation until a sudden snow
storm induced young Welton to bid them good-night
and retire below.

"Good-night," said Shales, as Jim's head was dis-
appearing down the hatchway, "stir up the fire and
keep yourself warm."

"That's just what I mean to do," replied Jim ;
"sorry I can't communicate some of the warmth to
you."

"But you can think of us," cried Jack, looking

down the hatchway, "you can at least pity us poor babes out here in the wind and snow!"

"Shut up, Jack!" said Moy with a solemn growl, "wot a tremendous jaw you've got w'en you let loose! Why, wot are 'ee starin' at now? 'Ave 'ee seed a ghost?"

"No, Dick," said Shales, in a tone of voice from which every vestige of jocularity had disappeared; "look steady in the direction of the South sandhead light and—see! ain't that the flash of a gun?"

"It looks like it. A wreck on the sand, I fear," muttered Dick Moy, putting up both hands to guard his eyes from the snow-flakes that were driven wildly about by the wind, which had by that time increased to a furious gale.

For a few minutes the two men stood gazing intently towards the south-west horizon. Presently a faint flash was seen, so faint that they could not be certain it was that of a signal-gun. In a few minutes, however, a thin thread of red light was seen to curve upwards into the black sky.

"No mistake now," cried Jack, leaping towards the cabin skylight, which he threw up, and bending down, shouted—"South sandhead light is firing, sir, and sending up rockets!"

The mate, who was at the moment in the land of dreams, sprang out of them and out of his bunk, and stood on the cabin floor almost before the sentence was finished. His son, who had just drawn the blanket over his shoulders, and given vent to the first sigh of contentment with which a man usually lays his head on his pillow for the night, also jumped up, drew on coat, nether garments, and shoes, as if his life depended on his speed, and dashed on deck. There was unusual need for clothing that night, for it had become bitterly cold, a coat of ice having formed even on the salt-water spray which had blown into the boats. They found Dick Moy and Jack Shales already actively engaged—the one loading the lee gun, the other adjusting a rocket to its stick. A few hurried questions from the mate elicited all that it was needful to know. The flash of the gun from the South sandhead lightship, about six miles off, had been distinctly seen a third time, and a third rocket went up just as Welton and his son gained the deck, indicating that a vessel had struck upon the fatal Goodwin Sands. The report of the gun could not be heard, owing to the gale carrying the sound to leeward, but the bright line of the rocket was distinctly visible. At the same moment the flaring light of a burning tar-barrel was observed. It was the signal of the vessel in distress just on the southern tail of the sands.

By this time the gun was charged and the rocket in position.

"Look alive, Jack, fetch the poker!" cried the mate as he primed the gun.

Jack Shales dived down the companion-hatch, and in another moment returned with a red-hot poker, which the mate had thrust into the cabin fire at the first alarm. He applied it in quick succession to the gun and rocket. A blinding flash and deafening crash were followed by the whiz of the rocket as it sprang with a magnificent curve far away into the surrounding darkness.

This was their answer to the South sandhead light, which, having fired three guns and sent up three rockets to attract the attention of the Gull, then ceased firing. It was also their first note of warning to the look-out on the pier of Ramsgate harbour. Of the three light-ships that guarded the sands, the Gull lay nearest to Ramsgate; hence, whichever of the other two happened to send up signals, the Gull had to reply and thenceforward to continue repeating them until the attention of the Ramsgate look-out should be gained, and a reply given.

"That's a beauty," cried the mate, referring to the rocket; "fetch another, Jack; sponge her well out, Dick Moy, we'll give 'em another shot in a few minutes."

Loud and clear were both the signals, but four and a half miles of distance and a fresh gale neutralized their influence. The look-out on the pier did not observe them. In less than five minutes the gun and rocket were fired again. Still no answering signal came from Ramsgate.

"Load the weather gun this time," cried the mate, "they'll have a better chance of seeing the flash of that."

Jack obeyed, and Jim Welton, having nothing to do but look on, sought shelter under the lee of the weather bulwarks, for the wind, according to Dick Moy, "was blowin' needles and penknives."

The third gun thundered forth and shook the floating light from stem to stern, but the rocket struck the rigging and made a low wavering flight. Another was therefore sent up, but it had scarcely cut its bright line across the sky when the answering signal was observed—a rocket from Ramsgate pier!

"That's all right now; *our* duty's done," said the mate, as he went below, and, divesting himself of his outer garments, quietly turned in, while the watch, having sponged out and re-covered the guns, resumed their active perambulation of the deck.

James Welton, however, could not calm down his feelings so easily. This was the first night he had ever spent in a light-ship; the scene was therefore quite new to him, and he could not help feeling somewhat disappointed at the sudden termination of the noise and excitement. He was told that the

Ramsgate lifeboat could not be out in less than an hour, and it seemed to his excited spirit a terrible thing that human lives should be kept so long in jeopardy. Of course he began to think, "Is it not possible to prevent this delay?" but his better sense whispered to him that excited spirits are not the best judges in such matters, although it cannot be denied that they have an irresistible tendency to judge. There was nothing for it, however, but to exercise philosophic patience, so he went below and turned in, as sailors have it, "all standing," to be ready when the lifeboat should make its appearance.

The young sailor's sleep was prompt and profound. It seemed to him but a few minutes after he had laid his head on the pillow when Jack Shale's voice again resounded in the cabin—

"Lifeboat close alongside, sir. Didn't see her till this moment. She carries no lights."

The Weltons, father and son, sprang out of their bunks a second time, and, minus coat, hat, and shoes, scrambled on deck just in time to see the Broadstairs lifeboat rush past before the gale. She was close under the stern, and rendered spectrally visible by the light of the lantern.

"What are you firing for?" shouted the coxswain of the boat.

"Ship on the sands, bearing south," roared Jack Shales at the full pitch of his stentorian voice.

There was no time for more, for the boat did not pause in her meteor-like flight. The question was asked and answered as she passed with a magnificent rush into darkness. The reply had been heard, and the lifeboat shot, straight as an arrow, to the rescue.

Reader, we often hear and read of such scenes, but we can tell you from experience that vision is necessary to enable one to realize the full import of all that goes on. There was a strange thrill at the heart of young Welton when he saw the familiar blue-and-white boat leaping over the foaming billows. Often had he seen it in model and in quiescence in its boat-house, ponderous and almost ungainly; but now he saw it for the first time in action, as if endued with life. So, we fancy, warriors might speak of our heavy cavalry as *we* see them in barracks and as *they* saw them at Alma.

Again all was silent and unexciting on board the Gull; but, not many minutes later, the watch once more shouted down the skylight,—

"Tug's in sight, sir."

It was afterwards ascertained that a mistake had been made in reference to the vessel that had signalled. Some one on shore had reported that the guns and rockets had been seen flashing from the *North* sandhead vessel, whereas the report should have been, "from the vessel at the *South* sandhead." The single word was all-important. It had the effect of sending the steam-tug Aid (which always attends upon the Ramsgate lifeboat) in the wrong direction, involving much loss of time. But we mention this merely as a fact, not as a reproof. Accidents will happen, even in the best regulated families. The Ramsgate lifeboat service is most admirably regulated; and for once that an error of this kind can be pointed out, we can point to dozens —ay, hundreds—of cases in which the steamer and lifeboat have gone, straight as the crow flies, to the rescue, and have done good service on occasions when all other lifeboats would certainly have failed; so great is the value of steam in such matters.

On this occasion, however, the tug appeared somewhat late on the scene, and hailed the Gull. When the true state of the case was ascertained, her course was directed aright, and full steam let on. The Ramsgate boat was in tow far astern. As she passed, the brief questions and answers were repeated for the benefit of the coxswain, and Jim Welton observed that every man in the boat appeared to be crouching down on the thwarts except the coxswain, who stood at the steering tackles. No wonder. It is not an easy matter to sit up in a gale of wind, with freezing spray, and sometimes green seas, sweeping over one! The men were doubtless wide-awake and listening, but, as far as vision went, that boat was manned by ten oilskin coats and sou'-westers !

A few seconds carried them out of sight, and so great was the power of steam that, despite the loss of time, they reached the neighbourhood of the wreck as soon as the Broadstairs' boat, and found that the crew of the stranded vessel had already been saved, and taken ashore by the Deal lifeboat.

It may be as well to observe here, that although in this case much energy was expended unnecessarily, it does not follow that it· is frequently so expended. Often, far too often, all the force of lifeboat service on that coast is insufficient to meet the demands on it. The crews of the various boats in the vicinity of the Goodwin Sands are frequently called out more than once in a night, and they are sometimes out all night, visiting various wrecks in succession. In all this work the value of the steamtug is very conspicuous, for it can tow its boat again and again to windward of a wreck, and renew the effort to save life in cases where, devoid of such aid, lifeboats would be compelled to give in after the failure of their first attempt, in consequence of their being driven helplessly to leeward

But we have forestalled our narrative. The drama, as far as the Gull-Light was concerned, ended that night with the disappearance of the tug and lifeboat. It was not until several days afterwards that her

crew learned the particulars of the wreck in connection with which they had acted so brief but so important a part.

Meanwhile, Dick Moy, who always walked the
deck with a rolling swagger, with his huge hands
thrust deep into his breeches' pockets when there
was nothing for them to do, said to Jim Welton
"he'd advise 'im to go below an' clap the dead-
lights on 'is peepers."

Jim, approving the advice, was about to descend
to the cabin, when he was arrested by a sharp cry
that appeared to rise out of the waves.

"Wot iver is that?" exclaimed Dick, as they all
rushed to the port bow of the vessel and looked over
the side.

"Something in the water," cried Jack Shales,
hastily catching up a coil of rope and throwing it
overboard with that promptitude which is peculiar
to seamen.

"Why, _he_ can't kitch hold on it; it's only a
dog," observed Dick Moy.

All uncertainty on this point was cleared away,
by a loud wail to which the poor animal gave vent,
as it scraped along the ship's hull, vainly endeavouring to prevent itself from being carried past by the
tide.

By this time they were joined by the mate and
the rest of the crew, who had heard the unwonted

sounds and hurried on deck. Each man was eagerly suggesting a method of rescue, or attempting to carry one into effect, by means of a noose or otherwise, when Mr. Welton, senior, observed that Mr. Welton, junior, was hastily tying a rope round his waist.

"Hallo! Jim," he cried, "surely you don't mean to risk your life for a dog?"

"There's no risk about it, father. Why should I leave a poor dog to drown when it will only cost a ducking at the worst? You know I can swim like a cork, and I ain't easily cooled down."

"You shan't do it if I can prevent," cried the mate, rushing at his reckless son.

But Jim was too nimble for him. He ran to the stern of the vessel, leaped on the bulwarks, flung the end of the coil of rope among the men, and shouting "Hold on taut, boys!" sprang into the sea.

The men did "hold on" most powerfully; they did more, they hauled upon the rope, hand over hand, to a "Yo-heave-ho!" from Jerry MacGowl, which put to shame the roaring gale, and finally hauled Jim Welton on board with a magnificent Newfoundland dog in his arms, an event which was greeted with three enthusiastic cheers!

CHAPTER IV.

A NEW CHARACTER INTRODUCED.

THE gale was a short-lived one. On the following morning the wind had decreased to a moderate breeze, and before night the sea had gone down sufficiently to allow the boat of Mr. Jones's sloop to come alongside of the floating light.

Before Jim Welton bade his friends good-bye, he managed to have an earnest and private talk with each of them. Although he had never been connected with the Gull, he had frequently met with the men of that vessel, and, being one of those large-hearted sympathetic men who somehow worm themselves into the affection and confidence of most of their friends and comrades, he had something particular to say to each, either in reference to wives and families on shore, or to other members of that distracting section of the human family which, according to Mr. Welton senior, lay at the foundation of all mischief.

But young Welton did not confine himself to

temporal matters. It has already been hinted that he had for some time been in the habit of attending prayer-meetings, but the truth was that he had recently been led by a sailor's missionary to read the Bible, and the precious Word of God had been so blessed to his soul, that he had seen his own lost condition by nature, and had also seen, and joyfully accepted, Jesus Christ as his all-sufficient Saviour. He had come to "know the truth," and "the truth had set him free;" free, not only from spiritual death and the power of sin, but free from that unmanly shame which, alas! too often prevents Christians from taking a bold stand on the Lord's side.

The young sailor had, no doubt, had severe inward conflicts, which were known only to God and himself, but he had been delivered and strengthened, for he was not ashamed of Christ in the presence of his old comrades, and he sought by all the means in his power to draw them to the same blessed Saviour.

"Well, good-bye, Jim," said Mr. Welton, senior, as his son moved towards the gangway, when the boat came alongside, "all I've got to say to 'ee, lad, is, that you're on dangerous ground, and you have no right to shove yourself in the way of temptation."

"But I don't *shove* myself, father; I think I am led in that way. I may be wrong, perhaps, but such is my belief."

"You'll not forget that message to my mother," whispered a sickly-looking seaman, whose strong-boned frame appeared to be somewhat attenuated by disease.

"I'll not forget, Rainer. It's likely that we shall be in Yarmouth in a couple of days, and you may depend upon my looking up the old woman as soon after I get ashore as possible."

"Hallo! hi!" shouted a voice from below, "wot's all the hurry?" cried Dick Moy, stumbling hastily up on deck while in the act of closing a letter which bore evidence of having been completed under difficulties, for its form was irregular, and its back was blotted. "Here you are, putt that in the post at Yarmouth, will 'ee, like a good fellow?"

"Why, you've forgotten the address," exclaimed Jim Welton in affected surprise.

"No, I 'aven't. There it is hall right on the back."

"What, that blot?"

"Ay, that's wot stands for Mrs. Moy," said Dick, with a good-natured smile.

"Sure now," observed Jerry MacGowl, looking earnestly at the letter, "it do seem to me, for all the world, as if a cat had drawed his tail across it after stumblin' over a ink-bottle."

"Don't Mrs. Moy live in Ramsgate?" inquired Jim Welton.

"Of course she do," replied Dick.

"But I'm not going there; I'm goin' to Yarmouth," said Jim.

"Wot then?" retorted Dick, "d''ee suppose the clerk o' the post-office at Yarmouth ain't as well able to read as the one at Ramsgate, even though the writin' *do* be done with a cat's tail? Go along with 'ee."

Thus dismissed, Jim descended the side and was quickly on board the sloop Nora to which he belonged.

On the deck of the little craft he was received gruffly by a man of powerful frame and stern aspect, but whose massive head, covered with shaggy grey curling hair, seemed to indicate superior powers of intellect. This was Morley Jones, the master and owner of the sloop.

"A pretty mess you've made of it; I might have been in Yarmouth by this time," he said, testily.

"More likely at the bottom of the sea," answered Jim, quietly, as he went aft and looked at the compass—more from habit than from any desire to receive information from that instrument.

"Well, if I had been at the bottom o' the sea, what then? Who's to say that I mayn't risk my life if I see fit? It's not worth much," he said, gloomily.

"You seem to forget that in risking your own life you risk the lives of those who sail along with you," replied Jim, with a bold yet good-humoured look at the skipper.

"And what if I do risk their lives?—they ain't worth much, either, *I*'m sure?"

"Not to you, Morley, but worth a good deal to themselves, not to mention their wives and families and friends. You know well enough that if I had wished ever so much to return aboard last night your boat could not have got alongside the Gull for the sea. Moreover, you also know that if you had attempted to put to sea in such weather, this leaky tub, with rotten sails and running gear, would have been a wreck on the Goodwin sands before now, and you and I, with the two men and the boy, would have been food for the gulls and fishes."

"Not at all," retorted Jones, "there's not much fear of our lives here. The lifeboat crews are too active for that; and as to the sloop, why, she's insured you know for her full value—for more than her value, indeed."

Jones said this with a chuckle and a sly expression in his face, as he glanced meaningly at his companion.

"I know nothing about your insurance or your cargo, and, what's more, I don't want to know," said Jim, almost angrily. "You've been at Square-Tom again," he added, suddenly laying his hand upon the shoulder of his companion and looking earnestly into his eyes.

It was now Jones's turn to be angry, yet it was

evident that he made an effort to restrain his feelings, as he replied, " Well, what if I have ?   It's one
thing for you to advise me to become a teetotaller,
and it's quite another thing for me to agree to do it.
I tell you again, as I've often told you before, Jim
Welton, that *I don't mean to do it*, and I'm not
going to submit to be warned and reasoned with
by you, as if you was my grandfather.   I *know* that
drink is the curse of my life, and I know that it will
kill me, and that I am a fool for giving way to it,
but it is the only thing that makes me able to
endure this life; and as for the next, I don't care
for it, and *I don't believe in it."*

"But your not believing in it does not make it
less certain," replied Jim, quietly, but without any
approach to solemnity in his tone or look, for he
knew that his companion was not in a mood just
then to stand such treatment.   " You remember the
story of the ostrich that was run down?   Finding
that it could not escape, it stuck its head in the
sand and thought that nobody saw it.   You may
shut your eyes, Morley, but facts remain facts for
all that."

"Shutting my eyes is just what I am *not* doing,"
returned Jones, flinging round and striding to the
other side of the deck ; then, turning quickly, he
strode back, and added, with an oath, "have I not
told you that I see myself, my position, and my pro-

spects, as clearly as you do, and that I intend to face them all, and take the consequences ? "

Jim Welton flushed slightly, and his eyes dilated, as he replied,—

"Have you not the sense to see, Morley Jones, that my remonstrances with you are at least disinterested ?   What would you think if I were to say to you, 'Go, drink your fill till death finds you at last wallowing on the ground like a beast, or worse than a beast; I leave you to your fate'?"   .

"I would think that Jim Welton had changed his nature," replied Jones, whose anger disappeared as quickly as it came.   "I have no objection to your storming at me, Jim.   You may swear at me as much as you please, but, for any sake, spare me your reasonings and entreaties, because they only rouse the evil spirit within me, without doing an atom of good; and don't talk of leaving me.   Besides, let me tell you, you are not so disinterested in this matter as you think.   There is some one in Yarmouth who has something to do with your interest in me."

The young man flushed again at the close of this speech, but not from a feeling of anger.   He dropt his eyes before the earnest though unsteady gaze of his half-tipsy companion, who burst into a loud laugh as Jim attempted some stammering reply.

"Come," he added, again assuming the stern aspect

which was natural to him, but giving Jim a friendly slap on the shoulder, "don't let us fall out, Jim; you and I don't want to part just now. Moreover, if we have a mind to get the benefit of the tide to-night, the sooner we up anchor the better, so we won't waste any more time talking."

Without waiting for a reply, Mr. Jones went forward and called the crew. The anchor was weighed, the sails were set, and the sloop Nora—bending over before the breeze, as if doing homage in passing her friend the Gull-Light—put to sea, and directed her course for the ancient town and port of Yarmouth.

CHAPTER V.

MORE NEW CHARACTERS INTRODUCED.

IF it be true that time and tide wait for no man, it is equally true, we rejoice to know, that authors and readers have a corresponding immunity from shackles, and are in nowise bound to wait for time or tide.

We therefore propose to leave the Gull-stream light, and the Goodwin sands, and the sloop Nora, far behind us, and, skipping a little in advance of Time itself, proceed at once to Yarmouth.

Here, in a snug parlour, in an easy chair, before a cheerful fire, with a newspaper in his hand, sat a bluff little elderly gentleman, with a bald head and a fat little countenance, in which benignity appeared to hold perpetual though amicable rivalry with fun.

That the fat little elderly gentleman was eccentric could scarcely be doubted, because he not only looked *over* his spectacles instead of through them, but also, apparently, read his newspaper upside down. A closer inspéction, however, would have shown that he was not reading the paper at all, but looking over the top of it at an object which accounted for much of the benignity, and some of the fun of his expression.

At the opposite side of the table sat a very beautiful girl, stooping over a book, and so earnestly intent thereon as to be evidently quite oblivious of all else around her. She was at that interesting age when romance and reality are supposed to be pretty equally balanced in a well-regulated female mind—about seventeen. Although not classically beautiful—her nose being slightly turned upward—she was, nevertheless, uncommonly pretty, and, as one of her hopeless admirers expressed it, "desperately loveable." Jet black ringlets—then in vogue—clustered round an exceedingly fair face, on which there dwelt the hue of robust health. Poor Bob Queeker, the hopeless admirer above referred to, would have preferred that she had been somewhat paler and thinner, if that had been possible; but this is not to be wondered at, because Queeker was about sixteen years of age at that time, and wrote sonnets to the moon and other celestial bodies, and also indulged in "lines" to various terrestrial bodies, such as the lily or the snowdrop, or something equally drooping or pale. Queeker never by any chance addressed the sun, or the red-rose, or anything else suggestive of health and vigour. Yet his melancholy soul could not resist Katie,—which was this angel's name,— because, although she was energetic, and vigorous, and matter-of-fact, not to say slightly mischievous, she was intensely sympathetic and tender in her feelings, and romantic too.   But her romance puzzled him.   There was something too intense about it for his taste.   If he had only once come upon her un- awares, and caught her sitting with her hands clasped, gazing in speechless adoration at the moon, or even at a street-lamp, in the event of its being thick weather at the time, his love for her would have been without alloy.

As it was, Queeker thought her "desperately love- able," and in his perplexity continued to write son- nets without number to the moon, in which efforts, however, he was singularly unsuccessful, owing to the fact that, after he had gazed at it for a consider- able length of time, the orb of night invariably adopted black ringlets and a bright sunny com- plexion.

George Durant—which was the name of the bald fat little elderly gentleman—was Katie's father. Looking at them, no one would have thought so, for Katie was tall and graceful in form; and her countenance, except when lighted up with varying emotion, was grave and serene.

As Mr. Durant looked at it just then, the gravity had deepened into severity; the pretty eyebrows frowned darkly at the book over which they bent, and the rosy lips represented a compound of pursing and pouting as they moved and muttered something inaudibly.

"What is it that puzzles you, Katie?" asked her father, laying down the paper.

"'Sh!" whispered Katie, without lifting her head; "seventeen, twenty-two, twenty-nine, thirty-six,—one pound sixteen;—no, I *can't* get it to balance. Did you ever know such a provoking thing?"

She flung down her pencil, and looked full in her father's face, where fun had, for the time, so thoroughly conquered and overthrown benignity, that the frown vanished from her brow, and the rosy lips expanded to join her sire in a hearty fit of laughter.

"If you could only see your own face, Katie, when you are puzzling over these accounts, you would devote yourself ever after to drawing *it*, instead of those chalk-heads of which you are so fond."

"No, I wouldn't, papa," said Katie, whose gravity quickly returned. "It's all very well for you to joke about it, and laugh at me, but I can tell you that this account *won't* balance; there is a two-and-sixpence wrong somewhere, and you know it has to be all copied out and sent off by the evening post to-morrow. I really can't understand why we are called upon to make so many copies of all the accounts and papers for that ridiculous Board of Trade;

I'm sure they have plenty of idle clerks of their own, without requiring us to slave as we do—for such a wretched salary, too!"

Katie shook her curls indignantly, as she thought of the unjust demands and inadequate remuneration of Government, and resumed her work, the frowning brows and pursed coral lips giving evidence of her immediate and total absorption in the accounts.

Old Mr. Durant, still holding the newspaper upside down, and looking over the top of it and of his spectacles at the fair accountant, thought in his heart that if the assembled Board, of which his daughter spoke in such contemptuous terms, could only behold her labouring at their books, in order to relieve her father of part of the toil, they would incontinently give orders that he should be thenceforth allowed a salary for a competent clerk, and that all the accounts sent up from Yarmouth should be bound in cloth of gold!

"Here it is, papa, I've got it!" exclaimed Katie, looking up with enthusiasm similar to that which might be expected in a youthful sportsman on the occasion of hooking his first salmon. "It was the two-and-sixpence which you told me to give to—"

At that moment the outer door bell rang.

"There's cousin Fanny, oh, I'm *so* glad!" exclaimed Katie, shutting up her books and clearing away a multitude of papers with which the table was lumbered; "she has promised to stay a week, and has come in time to go with me to the singing class this afternoon. She's a darling girl, as fond of painting and drawing almost as I am, and hates cats. Oh, I do so love a girl that doesn't like cats. Eh, pussy, shall I tread on your tail?"

This question was put to a recumbent cat which lay coiled up in earthly bliss in front of the fire, and which Katie had to pass in carrying her armful of books and papers to the sideboard drawer in which they were wont to repose. She put out her foot as if to carry her threat into execution.

"Dare!" exclaimed Mr. Durant, with whom the cat was a favourite.

"Well, then, promise that if Mr. Quecker comes to-night you won't let him stay to spoil our fun," said Katie, still holding her foot over the cat's unconscious tail.

As she spoke, one of the rather heavy account-books (which ought to have been bound in cloth of gold) slipped off the pile, and, as ill luck would have it, fell on the identical tail in question, the cat belonging to which sprang up with a fierce cater-waul in rampant indignation.

"Oh, papa, you *know* I didn't mean it."

Mr. Durant's eyes twinkled with amusement as he beheld the sudden change of poor Katie's expression to intense earnestness, but before he could reply the door was thrown open; "cousin Fanny" rushed in, the cat rushed out, the two young ladies rushed into each other's arms, and went in a species of ecstatic waltz up-stairs to enjoy the delights of a private interview, leaving Mr. Durant to sink into the arms of his easy chair and resume his paper— *this* time with the right side up !

Let it be understood that the old gentleman was employed in Yarmouth under one of the departments of the Board of Trade.   We refrain from entering into particulars as to which department, lest the vindictive spirit which was accredited to that branch of the Government by Miss Katie—who being a lady, must of course have been right—should induce it to lay hold of our estimable friend and make an example of him for permitting his independent daughter to expose its true character.   In addition to his office in this connection Mr. Durant also held the position of a retired merchant and ship-owner, and was a man of considerable wealth, although he lived in a quiet unostentatious way. In fact, his post under Government was retained chiefly for the purpose of extending his influence in his native town—for he counted himself a "bloater" —and enabling him to carry out more vigorously his schemes of Christian philanthropy.

Cousin Fanny Hennings was a "darling girl" in Katie's estimation, probably because she was her opposite in many respects, though not in all. In good-humour and affection they were similar, but Fanny had none of Katie's fire, or enthusiasm, or intellect, or mischief; she had, however, a great appreciation of fun, and was an inordinate giggler. Fat, fair, and fifteen, with flaxen curls, pink cheeks, and blue eyes, she was the *beau-idéal* of a wax-doll, and possessed about as much self-assertion as may be supposed to belong to that class of the doll-community which is constructed so as to squeak when squeezed. As Katie Durant squeezed her friend pretty often, both mentally and physically, cousin Fanny squeaked a good deal more than usual during her occasional visits to Yarmouth, and even after her return home to Margate, where she and her widowed mother dwelt—as Queeker poetically said —"in a cottage by the sea." It was usually acknowledged by all her friends that Fanny had increased her powers amazingly while absent, in so much that she learned at last to squeak on her own account without being squeezed at all.

After the cousins had talked in private until they had made themselves almost too late for the singing-class, they issued from the house and betook themselves to the temple of music, where some amazing pieces were performed by some thirty young vocalists of both sexes to their own entire satisfaction, and to the entire dissatisfaction, appar-

ently, of their teacher, whose chief delight seemed
to be to check the flow of gushing melody at a
critical point, and exclaim, "Try it again!" Being
ignorant of classical music we do not venture to
give an opinion on these points, but it is important
to state, as bearing on the subject in a sanitary
point of view, that all the pupils usually left the
class in high spirits, with the exception of Queeker,
who had a voice like a cracked tea-kettle, knew
no more about music than Katie's cat—which he
adored because it was Katie's—and who went to the
class, which was indebted for its discord chiefly to
him, wholly and solely because Katie Durant went
to it, and thus afforded him an opportunity of occasionally shaking hands with her.

On the present evening, however, being of a shy
disposition, he could not bring himself to face cousin
Fanny. He therefore left the hall miserable, and
went home with desperate intentions as to the moon.
Unfortunately that luminary was not visible, the
sun having just set, but from his bedroom window,
which commanded a view of the roadstead, he beheld the lantern of the St. Nicolas Gatt floating-
light, and addressed the following lines to it with all
the fervour incident to a hopeless affection :—

> " Why blaze, ye bright benignant beaming star,
> Guiding the homebound seaman from afar,
> Lighting the outbound wand'rer on his way,
> With all the lightsome perspicuity of day ?

Why not go out at once ! and let be hurl'd
Dark, dread, unmitigated darkness o'er the world !
Why should the heavenly constellations shine ?
Why should the weather evermore be fine ?
Why should this rolling ball go whirling round ?
Why should the noise of mirth and music sound ?
Why should the sparrow chirp, the blackbird sing,
The mountains echo, and the valleys ring,
With all that's cheerful, humorous, and glad,
Now that my heart is smitten and my brain gone mad ? "

Queeker fetched a long deep-drawn sigh at this point, the agony of intense composition being for a moment relaxed. Then, catching his breath and glaring, he went on in a somewhat gentler strain,—

"Forgive me, Floating-light, and you, ye sun,
Moon, stars, and elements of Nature, every one ;
I did but vent my misery and spleen
In utt'ring words of fury that I hardly mean.
At least I do in part—but hold ! why not ?—
Oh ! cease ye fiendish thoughts that rage and plot
To bring about my ruin. Hence ! avaunt !
Or else in pity tell me what you want.
I cannot live, and yet I would not die !
My hopes are blighted ! Where, oh whither shall I fly ?
'Tis past ! I'll cease to dally with vain sophistry,
And try the virtue of a calm philosophy."

The effect of composition upon Queeker was such that when he had completed his task he felt greatly tranquillized, and, having shut up his portfolio, formed the sudden resolution of dropping in upon the Durants to tea.

Meantime, and before the love-sick youth had begun the lines above quoted, Katie and her cousin walked home by a road which conducted them close past the edge of those extensive sandy plains called the Denes of Yarmouth. Here, at the corner of a quiet street, they were arrested by the sobbing of a little boy who sat on a railing by the roadside, swaying himself to and fro in an agony of grief.

Katie's sympathetic heart was instantly touched. She at once went up to the boy, and made earnest inquiries into the cause of his distress.

"Please, ma'am," said the boy, "I 've lost a shillin', and I can't find it nowheres. Oh, wot ever shall I do? My mother gave it me to give with two other bobs to my poor sick brother whom I 've comed all this way to see, and there I 've gone an' lost it, an' I 'll 'ave to lay out all night in the cold, for I dursn't go to see 'im without the money—boo, hoo!"

"Oh, how *very* unfortunate!" exclaimed Katie with real feeling, for the boy, whose soul was thus steeped to all appearance in woe unutterable, was very small, and very dirty and ragged, and had an extremely handsome intelligent face, with a profusion of wild brown curls. "But I can make that up to you, poor boy," she added, drawing out her purse, "here is a shilling for you. Where do you live?"

"At Ramsgate, ma'am."

"At Ramsgate?" exclaimed Katie in surprise, "why, how did you manage to get here?"

"I come in a lugger, ma'am, as b'longs to a friend o' ourn. We 've just arrived, an' we goes away agin to-morrow."

A SMALL DECEIVER.—Page 64.

" Indeed ! That will give you little time to see your sick brother. What is the matter with him ?"

" Oh, he's took very bad, ma'am. I'm sorry to say he's bad altogether, ma'am. Bin an' run'd away from 'ome. A'most broke his mother's 'eart, he has, an' fall'd sick here, he did."

The small boy paused abruptly at this point, and looked earnestly in Katie's kind and pitiful face.

" Where does your brother live ?" asked Katie.

The small boy looked rather perplexed, and said that he couldn't rightly remember the name of the street, but that the owner of the lugger "know'd it." Whereat Katie seemed disappointed, and said she would have been so glad to have visited him, and given him such little comforts as his disease might warrant.

" Oh, ma'am," exclaimed the small boy, looking wistfully at her with his large blue eyes, " *wot* a pity I've forgot it ! The doctor ordered 'im wine too—it was as much as 'is life was worth not to 'ave wine, —but of course they couldn't afford to git 'im wine— even cheap wine would do well enough, at two bob or one bob the bottle. If you was to give me two bob—shillins I mean, ma'am—I'd git it for 'im to-night."

Katie and her cousin conversed aside in low tones for a minute or two as to the propriety of complying with this proposal, and came to the conclusion

E

that the boy was such a nice outspoken honest-like
fellow, that it would do no harm to risk that sum in
the circumstances. Two shillings were therefore
put into the boy's dirty little hand, and he was
earnestly cautioned to take care of it, which he
earnestly, and no doubt honestly, promised to do.

" What is your name, boy ?" asked Katie, as she
was about to leave him.

" Billy—Billy Towler, ma'am," answered the
urchin, pulling his forelock by way of respectful
acknowledgment, " but my friends they calls me
Walleye, chiefly in consikence o' my bein' wery
much the rewerse of blind, ma'am, and niver capable
of bein' cotched in a state o' slumber at no time."

This reply had the effect of slightly damaging
the small boy's character for simplicity in Katie's
mind, although it caused both herself and her companion to laugh.

" Well, Billy," she said, opening her card-case,
" here is my card—give it to your sick brother, and
when he sends it to me with his address written on
the back of it I'll call on him."

" Thankee, ma'am," said the small boy.

After he had said this, he stood silently watching
the retiring figure of his benefactress, until she was
out of sight, and then dashing round the corner of a
bye-street which was somewhat retired, he there
went off into uncontrollable fits of laughter—slapped

his small thighs, held his lean little sides with both hands, threw his ragged cap into the air, and in various other ways gave evidence of ecstatic delight. He was still engaged in these violent demonstrations of feeling when Morley Jones—having just landed at Yarmouth, and left the sloop *Nora* in charge of young Welton—came smartly round the corner, and, applying his heavy boot to the small boy's person, kicked him into the middle of the road.

CHAPTER VI.

THE TEMPTER AND THE TEMPTED.

"WHAT are ye howlin' there for, an' blockin' up the Queen's highway like that, you precious young villain?" demanded Morley Jones.

"An' wot are you breakin' the Queen's laws for like that?" retorted Billy Towler, dancing into the middle of the road and revolving his small fists in pugilistic fashion. "You big hairy walrus, I don't know whether to 'ave you up before the beaks for assault and battery or turn to an' give 'ee a good lickin'."

Mr. Jones showed all his teeth with an approving grin, and the small boy grinned in return, but still kept on revolving his fists, and warning the walrus to "look hout and defend hisself if he didn't want his daylights knocked out or his bows stove in!"

"You're a smart youth, you are," said Jones.

"Ha! you're afraid, are you? an' wants to make friends, but I won't 'ave it at no price. Come on, will you?"

Jones, still grinning from ear to ear, made a rush at the urchin, who, however, evaded him with such ease that the man perceived he had not the smallest chance of catching him.

"I say, my lad," he asked, stopping and becoming suddenly grave, " where d' you come from ?"

"I comes from where I b'longs to, and where I'm agoin' back to w'en it suits me."

"Very good," retorted Jones, "and I suppose you don't object to earn a little money in an easy way ?"

"Yes, I do object," replied Billy ; "it ain't worth my while to earn a *little* money in any way, no matter how easy ; I never deals in small sums. A fi' pun' note is the lowest figur' as I can stoop to."

"You'll not object, however, to a gift, I daresay," remarked Jones, as he tossed a half-crown towards the boy.

Billy caught it as deftly as a dog catches a bit of biscuit, looked at it in great surprise, tossed it in the air, bit its rim critically, and finally slid it into his trousers pocket.

"Well, you know," he said slowly, "to obleege a *friend*, I'm willin' to accept."

"Now then, youngster, if I'm willing to trust that half-crown in your clutches, you may believe I have got something to say to 'ee worth your while listenin' to ; for you may see I'm not the man to give it to 'ee out o' Christian charity."

"That's true," remarked Billy, who by this time had become serious, and stood with his hands in his pockets, still, however, at a respectful distance.

"Well, the fact is," said Mr. Jones, "that I've bin lookin' out of late for a smart lad with a light heart and a light pocket, and that ain't troubled with much of a conscience."

"That's me to a tee," said Billy promptly; "my 'art's as light as a feather, and my pocket is as light as a maginstrate's wisdom. As for conscience, the last beak as I wos introdooced to said I must have bin born without a conscience altogether; an' 'pon my honour I think he wos right, for I never felt it yet, though I've often tried—'xcept once, w'en I'd cleaned out the pocket of a old ooman as was starin' in at a shop winder in Cheapside, and she fainted dead away w'en she found it out, and her little grand-darter looked so pale and pitiful that I says to myself, 'Hallo! Walleye, you've bin to the wrong shop this time; go an' put it back, ye young dog;' so I obeyed orders, an' slipped back the purse while pretendin' to help the old ooman. It wos risky work, though, for a bobby twigged me, and it was only my good wind and tough pair o' shanks that saved me. Now," continued the urchin, knitting his brows as he contemplated the knotty point, "I've had my doubts whether that wos conscience, or a sort o' nat'ral weakness pecooliar to my constitootion. I 've half a mind to call on the Bishop of London on the point one o' these days."

"So, you 're a city bird," observed Jones, admiringly.

"Ah, and I can see that you 're a provincial one," replied Billy, jingling the half-crown against the silver in his pocket.

"What brings you so far out of your beat, Wall-eye?" inquired Jones.

"Oh, I 'm on circuit just now, makin' a tower of the provinces. I tried a case just before you came up, an' made three shillins out of it, besides no end o' promises—which, unfort'nately, I can't avail myself of—from a sweet young lady, with such a pleasant face, that I wished I could adopt her for a darter. But that 's an expensive luxury, you see; can't afford it yet."

"Well, youngster," said Jones, assuming a more grave yet off-hand air, "if you choose to trust me, I 'll put you in the way of makin' some money without much trouble. It only requires a little false swearing, which I daresay you are used to."

"No, I ain't," retorted the urchin indignantly; "I never tells a lie 'xcept w'en I can't help it. *Then*, of course, a feller *must* do it!"

"Just so, Walleye, them 's my sentiments. Have you got a father?"

"No, nor yet a mother," replied Billy. "As far

as I'm aweer of, I wos diskivered on the steps of a city work'us, an' my first impressions in this life wos the knuckles of the old woman as banged me up. The governor used to talk a lot o' balderdash about our bein' brought up ; but I knows better. I wos banged up ; banged up in the mornins, banged to meals, and banged to bed ; banged through thick and thin, for everything an' for nothin', until I banged myself out o' the door one fine mornin', which I banged arter me, an' 'ave bin bangin' about, a gen'lem'n at large, ever since."

"Ha! got no friends and nothin' to do?" said Morley Jones.

"Jis so."

"Well, if you have a mind to take service with me, come along an' have a pot o' beer."

The man turned on his heel and walked off to a neighbouring public-house, leaving the small boy to follow or not as he pleased, and apparently quite indifferent as to what his decision might be.

Billy Towler—*alias* Walleye—looked after him with an air of uncertainty. He did not like the look of the man, and was about to decide against him, when the jingle of the half-crown in his pocket turned the scale in his favour. Running after him, he quietly said, "I'm your man," and then began to whistle, at the same time making an abortive effort to keep step with his long-limbed employer, who said nothing in reply, but, entering a public-house, ordered two pots of beer. These, when produced, he and his little companion sat down to discuss in the most retired box in the place, and conversed in low tones.

"What was it brought you to Yarmouth, Wall-eye?" asked Mr. Jones.

"Call me Billy," said the boy, "I like it better."

"Well, Billy—and, by the way, you may call me Morley—my name's Jones, but, like yourself, I have a preference. Now, then, what brought you here?"

"H'm, that involves a story—a hanecdote, if I may so speak," replied this precocious youngster with much gravity. "You see, some time arter I runn'd away from the work'us, I fell'd in with an old gen'lem'n with a bald head an' a fat corpus. Do 'ee happen to know, Mr. Morley, 'ow it is that bald heads an' fat corpuses a'most always go together?"

Morley replied that he felt himself unable to answer that difficult question; but supposed that as good-humour was said to make people fat, perhaps it made them bald also.

"I dun know," continued Billy; "anyhow, this old gen'lem'n he took'd a fancy to me, an' took'd me home to his 'otel; for he didn't live in London —wos there only on a wisit at the time he felled in love with me at first sight. Well, he give me a splendacious suit of noo clo'es, an 'ad me put to a

school, where I soon larned to read and write; an'
I do b'lieve wos on the highroad to be Lord Mayor
of London, when the old schoolmaster died, before
I'd bin two year there, an' the noo un wos so fond
o' the bangin' system that I couldn't stand it, an' so
bid 'em all a tender farewell, an' took to the streets
agin. The old gen'lem'n he comed three times from
Yarmouth, where he belonged, for to see me arter I
wos put to the school, an' I had a sort o' likin' for
him, but not knowin' his name, and only been aweer
that he lived at Yarmouth, I thought I'd have no
chance o' findin' him. Over my subsikint career
I'll draw a wail; it's enough to say I didn't like
either it or my pals, so I made up my mind at last
to go to Yarmouth an' try to find the old gen'lem'n
as had adopted me—that's what he said he'd done
to me. W'en I'd prigged enough o' wipes to pay
my fare down, I comed away,—an' here I am."

"Have you seen the old gentleman?" asked
Morley, after a pause.

"No, only just arrived this arternoon."

"And you don't know his name, nor where he
lives?"

"No."

"And how did you expect to escape bein' nabbed
and put in limbo as a vagrant?" inquired Morley.

"By gittin' employment, of coorse, from some
respectable gen'lem'n like yourself, an' then runnin'

away from 'im w'en I 'd diskivered the old chap wi' the bald head."

Morley Jones smiled grimly.

" Well, my advice to you is," he said, " to fight shy of the old chap, even if you do discover him. Depend upon it the life you would lead under his eye would be one of constant restraint and worry. He 'd put you to school again, no doubt, where you 'd get banged as before—a system I don't approve of at all—and be made a milksop and a flunkey, or something o' that sort—whereas the life you 'll lead with me will be a free and easy rollikin' manly sort o' life. Half on shore and half at sea. Do what you like, go where you will,—when business has bin attended to—victuals and clothing free gratis, and pocket-money enough to enable you to enjoy yourself in a moderate sort of way. You see I 'm not goin' to humbug you. It won't be all plain sailin', but what is a man worth if he ain't fit to stand a little rough-and-tumble ? Besides, rough work makes a fellow take his ease with all the more zest. A life on the ocean wave one week, with hard work, and a run on shore the next week, with just enough to do to prevent one wearyin'. That 's the sort o' thing for you and me, Billy, eh boy ?" exclaimed the tempter, growing garrulous in his cups, and giving his small victim a pat on the shoulder, which, although meant to be a facetious touch, well-nigh unseated him.

Billy Towler recovered himself, however, and received it as it was meant, in perfect good humour. The beer had mounted to his own little brain, and his large eyes glowed with more than natural light as he sat gazing into his companion's rugged face, listening with delight to the description of a mode of life which he thought admirably suited to his tastes and capabilities.   He was, however, a shrewd little creature.   Sad and very rough experience of life had taught him to be uncommonly circumspect for his years.

"What's your business, Morley?" he demanded eagerly.

"I've a lot of businesses," said Mr. Jones with a drunken leer, "but my principal one is fishcuring. I'm a sort of shipowner too.   Leastwise I've got two craft—one bein' a sloop, the other a boat. Moreover, I charter no end of vessels, an' do a good deal in the insurance way.   But you'll understand more about these things all in good time, Billy.   I live, while I'm at home, in Gravesend, but I've got a daughter and a mother livin' at Yarmouth, so I may say I've got a home at both places.   It's a convenient sort o' thing, you see,—a town residence and a country villa, as it were.   Come, I'll take you to the villa now, and introduce 'ee to the women."

So saying, this rascal paid for the poison he had been administering in large doses to himself and his apprentice, and, taking Billy's dirty little hand in his large horny fist, led him towards the centre of the town.

Poor Billy little knew the nature of the awful gulf of sin and misery into which he was now plunging with a headlong hilarious vivacity peculiarly his own. He was, indeed, well enough aware of the fact that he was a thief, and an outcast from society, and that he was a habitual breaker of the laws of God and man, but he was naturally ignorant of the extent of his guilt, as well as of the certain and terrible end to which it pointed, and, above all, he had not the most remote conception of the almost hopeless slavery to which he was doomed when once fairly secured in the baleful net which Morley Jones had begun to twine around him.

But a higher Power was leading the poor child in a way that he knew not—a way that was little suspected by his tempter—a way that has been the means of snatching many and many a little one from destruction in time past, and that will certainly save many more in time to come—as long as Christian men and women band together to unite their prayers and powers for the rescue of perishing souls.

Traversing several streets with unsteady gait—for he was now much the worse of drink—Mr. Jones led his willing captive down one of those

innumerable narrow streets, or passages, termed
"rows," which bear some resemblance to the "closes"
of the Scottish capital.   In width they are much
the same, but in cleanliness there is a vast difference,
for whereas the *closes* of the northern capital are
notorious for dirt, the *rows* of Yarmouth are celebrated for their neat tidy aspect.   What the cause
of the neatness of the latter may be we cannot tell,
but we can bear the testimony of an eye-witness to
the fact that—considering the class of inhabitants
who dwell in them, their laborious lives and limited
means—the *rows* are wondrously clean.   Nearly all
of them are paved with pebbles or bricks.   The
square courts opening out of them on right and left,
although ridiculously small, are so thoroughly scoured
and swept that one might roll on their floors with
white garments and remain unsoiled.   In each court
may be observed a water-bucket and scrubbing-brush
wet, usually, from recent use, also a green painted
box-garden of dimensions corresponding to the court,
full of well-tended flowers.   Almost every door has
a wooden or stone step, and each step is worn and
white with repeated scrubbings—insomuch that one
is irresistibly led to suspect that the "Bloaters"
must have a strong infusion of the Dutch element
in their nature.

Emerging at the lower end of the row, Mr. Jones
and his small companion hastened along the centre

of a narrow street which led them into one of much wider dimensions, named Friar's Lane. Proceeding along this for some time, they diverged to the right into another of the rows not far from the old city-wall, at a place where one of the massive towers still rears its rugged head as a picturesque ruin. The moon sailed out from under a mass of clouds at this point, giving to objects the distinctness of daylight. Hitherto Billy Towler had retained some idea of the direction in which he was being led, but this last turn threw his topographical ideas into utter confusion.

"A queer place this," he remarked, as they emerged from the narrowest passage they had yet traversed into a neat, snug, and most unexpected little square, with a garden in the middle of it, and a flagstaff in one corner.

"Adam-and-Eve gardens, they call it," said Mr. Jones; "we're pretty nigh home now."

"I wonder they didn't call it Eden at once," observed Billy; "it would have been shorter and comes to the same thing."

"Here we are at last," said Mr. Jones, stumbling against a small door in one of the network of rows that surrounded this Yarmouth paradise. "Hope the women are in," he added, attempting to lift the latch, but, finding that the door was locked, he hammered at it with foot and fist violently.

" Hallo ! " shouted the deep voice of a man within.

" Hallo, indeed ! Who may *you* be ? " growled Mr. Jones with an angry oath. " Open the door, will you ? "

. The door was opened at once by James Welton, who stood aside to let the other pass.

" Oh ! it's you, is it ? " said Mr. Jones. " Didn't recognise your voice through the door. I thought you couldn't have got the sloop made snug so soon. Well, lass, how are 'ee ; and how's the old ooman ? "

As the man made these inquiries in a half-hearty voice, he advanced into a poorly-furnished apartment, so small and low that it seemed a couple of sizes too small for him, and bestowed a kiss first upon the cheek of his old mother, who sat cowering over the fire, but brightened up on hearing his voice, and then upon the forehead of his daughter Nora, the cheerfulness of whose greeting, however, was somewhat checked when she observed the intoxicated state of her father.

Nora had a face which, though not absolutely pretty, was intensely winsome in consequence of an air of quiet womanly tenderness which surrounded it as with a halo. She was barely eighteen, but her soft eyes possessed a look of sorrow and suffering which, if not natural to them, had, at all events, become habitual.

" Who is this little boy, father ? " she said, turning towards Billy Towler, who still stood in the doorway a silent but acute observer of all that went on.

"Oh, that? why—a—that's my noo 'prentice just come down from Gravesend. He's been helpin' for some time in the 'hang'" (by which Mr. Jones meant the place where his fish were cured), "and I'm goin' to take him to sea with me next trip. Come in, Billy, and make yourself at home."

The boy obeyed with alacrity, and made no objection to a cup of tea and slice of bread and butter which Nora placed before him—supper being just then in progress.

"You'd better get aboard as soon as may be," said Jones to Jim Welton somewhat sternly. "I didn't expect you to leave the sloop to-night."

"And I didn't intend to leave her," replied Jim, taking no notice of the tone in which this was said; "but I thought I'd come up to ask if you wished me to begin dischargin' early to-morrow morning."

"No, we're not going to discharge," returned Jones.

"Not going to discharge!" echoed Jim in surprise.

"No. I find that it's not worth while discharging any part of the cargo here. On the contrary, I mean to fill up with bloaters and run over with

F

them to the coast of France; so you can go and
stow the top tier of casks more firmly, and get ready
for the noo ones.   Good-night."

The tone in which this was said left no excuse for
Jim to linger, so he bade the household good-night
and departed.

He had not gone far, however, when he was arrested by the sound of a light footstep.   It was that
of Nora, who had followed him.

"Nora!" exclaimed the young sailor in surprise,
returning quickly and taking one of the girl's hands
in both of his.

"Oh, Jim!" said Nora, with a look and tone of
earnest entreaty, "don't, don't forsake him just
now—if the love which you have so often pro-
fessed for me be true, don't forsake him, I beseech
you."

Jim protested in the most emphatic terms that
he had no intention of forsaking anybody, and made
a great many more protestations, in the midst of
which there were numerous ardent and more or
less appropriate references to hearts that never
deserted their colours, sheet-anchors that held on
through thick and thin, and needles that pointed,
without the smallest shadow of variation, to the
pole.

"But what makes you think I'm going to leave
him?" he asked, at the end of one of those flights.

"Because he is so rough to 'ee, Jim," replied the girl, leaning her head on her lover's shoulder; "he spoke so gruff even now, and I thought you went away huffed. Oh, Jim, you are the only one that has any influence over him—"

"Not the only one," returned Jim, quietly smoothing the fair girl's hair with his hard strong hand.

"Well, the only *man*, at any rate," continued Nora, "especially when he is overcome with that dreadful drink. Dear Jim, you won't forsake him, will you, even though he should insult, even though he should *strike* you?"

"No, never! Because he is your father, Nora, I'll stick by him in spite of all he can say or do to me, and try, God helping me, to save him. But I cannot stick by him if—"

"If what?" asked the girl anxiously, observing that he hesitated.

"If he does anything against the laws," said Jim in a low voice. "It isn't that I'm afraid of my good name—I'd even let that go, for *your* sake, if by so doing I could get him out of mischief; and as long as I know nothing against him *for certain*, I'll stand by him. But if he does fall, and I come to know it, I *must* leave him, Nora, because I won't be art and part in it. I could no longer go on my knees to pray for him if I did that, Nora. Moreover, if anything o' that sort should happen, I must leave the country, because he'd be sure to be caught and tried, and I will never stand witness against *your* father if I can avoid it by fair means."

Poor Nora hung her head as she asked in a low voice if Jim really thought her father was engaged in illegal practices.

" I can't say that I do," replied the youth earnestly. " Come, cheer up, dearest Nora. After all, it is chiefly through reports that my suspicions have been aroused, and we all know how easy it is for an enemy to raise an evil report. But, Nora, I wish you had not bound me to secrecy as to my reason for sticking by your father. Why should I not say boldly that it's all for love of you ?"

"Why should you wish to give any reason at all, Jim, and above all, *that* reason ?" asked Nora, looking up with a blush.

" Because," said the youth, with a perplexed look, "my secrecy about the matter has puzzled my father to such an extent that his confidence in me is entirely shaken. I have been all my life accustomed to open all my heart to him, and now, without rhyme or reason, as he thinks, I have suddenly gone right round on the other tack, and at the same time, as he says, I have taken up with doubtful company. Now, if—"

The sound of approaching footsteps here brought the interview to an abrupt close. Nora ran back to her poor home, and Jim Welton, directing his steps towards the harbour, returned on board the little sloop which had been named after the girl of his heart.

CHAPTER VII.

TREATS OF QUEEKER AND OTHERS—ALSO OF YOUTHFUL JEALOUSY,
LOVE, POETRY, AND CONFUSION OF IDEAS.

RETURNING, now, to the moon-struck and Katie-smitten Queeker, we find that poetic individual walking disconsolately in front of Mr. George Durant's mansion.

In a previous chapter it has been said that, after composing his celebrated lines to the lantern of the floating light, he resolved to drop in upon the Durants about tea-time—and well did Queeker know their tea-time, although, every time he went there uninvited, the miserable hypocrite expressed surprise at finding them engaged with that meal, and said he had supposed they must have finished tea by that time !

But, on arriving at the corner of the street, his fluttering heart failed him. The thought of the cousin was a stumbling-block which he could not surmount. He had never met her before ; he feared that she might be witty, or sarcastic, or sharp in some way or other, and would certainly make game of him in the presence of Katie. He had observed this cousin narrowly at the singing-class, and had been much impressed with her appearance; but whether this impression was favourable or unfavourable was to him, in the then confused state of his feelings, a matter of great uncertainty. Now that he was about to face her, he felt convinced that she must be a cynic, who would poison the mind of Katie against him, and no power within his unfortunate body was capable of inducing him to advance and raise the knocker.

Thus he hung in torments of suspense until nine o'clock, when, in a fit of desperation, he rushed madly at the door and committed himself by hitting it with his fist.

His equanimity was not restored by its being opened by Mr. Durant himself.

" Queeker !" exclaimed the old gentleman in surprise; "come in, my dear sir; did you stumble against the door? I hope you haven't hurt yourself?"

" Not at all—a—no, not at all; the fact is, I ran up the steps rather hastily, and—how do you do, Miss Durant? I hope you are *quite* well?"

Poor Queeker said this and shook hands with as much earnestness as if he had not seen Katie for five years.

"Quite well, thank you. My cousin, Fanny Hennings—Mr. Queeker."

Fanny bowed and Mr. Queeker bowèd, and, with a flushed countenance, asked her about the state of her health with unnatural anxiety.

"Thank you, Mr. Squeeker, I am very well," replied Fanny.

The unhappy youth would have corrected her in regard to his name, but hesitated and missed the opportunity, and when, shortly afterwards, while engaged in conversation with Mr. Durant, he observed Fanny giggling violently in a corner by herself, he felt assured that Katie had kindly made the correction for him.

The announcement of supper relieved him slightly, and he was beginning to calm down over a piece of bread and cheese when the door-bell rang. Immediately after a heavy foot was heard in the passage, the parlour door was flung open, the maid announced Mr. Hall, and a tall elegant young man entered the room. His figure was slender, but his chest was deep and his shoulders were broad and square. An incipient moustache of fair hair floated like a summer cloud on his upper lip, which expanded with a hearty smile as he advanced towards Mr. Durant and held out his hand.

"You have forgotten me, I fear," he said.

"Forgotten you!" exclaimed the old gentleman,

starting up and seizing the young man's hand, which he shook violently—"forgotten Stanley Hall—little Stanney, as I used to call you? Man, how you *are* grown, to be sure. What a wonderful change!"

"For the worse, I fear!" exclaimed the youth, laughing.

"Come, no fishing for compliments, sir. Let me introduce you to my daughter Katie, my niece Fanny Hennings, and my young friend Queeker. Now, then, sit down, and make yourself at home; you're just in time; we've only just begun; ring the bell for another plate, Katie. How glad I am to see you, Stanney, my boy—I can't call you by any other than the old name, you see. How did you leave your father, and what brings you here? Come, out with it all at once. I declare you have quite excited me."

Well was it for poor Queeker that every one was too much occupied with the new comer to pay any attention to him, for he could not prevent his visage from betraying something of the feelings which harrowed up his soul. The moment he set eyes on Stanley Hall, mortal jealousy—keen, rampant, virulent jealousy of the worst type—penetrated every fibre of his being, and turned his heart to stone! We cannot afford space to detail the various shades of agony, the degrees of despair, through which this unfortunate young man passed during that evening.

A thick volume would not suffice to contain it all. Language is powerless to express it. Only those who have similarly suffered can conceive it.

Of course, we need scarcely add that there was no occasion for jealousy. Nothing was further from the mind of Stanley than the idea of falling in love with Katie. Nevertheless, politeness required that he should address himself to her occasionally. At such times, Queeker's soul was stabbed in an unutterable manner. He managed to command himself, notwithstanding. To his credit, be it said, that he refrained from using the carving-knife. He even joined with some show of interest (of course hypocritical) in the conversation.

Stanley Hall was not only good-looking, but good-humoured, and full of quiet fun and anecdote, so that he quickly ingratiated himself with all the members of the family.

"D' you know it makes me feel young again to hear these old stories about your father's college-life," said Mr. Durant. " Have some more cheese, Stanney—you look like a man who ought to have a good appetite—fill your glass and pass the bottle—thanks. Now, how comes it that you have turned up in this out-of-the-way part of the world? By-the-bye, I hope you intend to stay some time, and that you will take up your quarters with me? You can't imagine how much pleasure it would give me to have the son of my old companion as a guest for some time. I'm sure that Katie joins me heartily in this hope."

Queeker's spirit sank with horror, and when Katie smilingly seconded her father's proposal, his heart stood still with dismay. Fanny Hennings, who had begun to suspect that there was something wrong with Queeker, put her handkerchief to her mouth, and coughed with what appeared to be unreasonable energy.

"I regret," said Stanley (and Queeker's breath came more freely), "that my stay must necessarily be short. I need not say that it would afford me the highest pleasure to accept your kind invitation" (he turned with a slight bow to Katie, and Queeker almost fainted), "but the truth is, that I have come down on a particular piece of business, in regard to which I wish to have your advice, and must return to London to-morrow or next day at furthest."

Queeker's heart resumed its office.

"I am sorry to hear that—very sorry. However, you shall stay to-night at all events; and you shall have the best advice I can give you on any subject you choose to mention. By the way, talking of advice, you're an M.D. now, I fancy?"

"Not yet," replied Stanley. "I am not quite fledged, although nearly so, and I wish to go on a voyage before completing my course."

"Quite right, quite right—see a little of life first, eh? But how comes it, Stanney, that you took kindly to the work at last, for, when I knew you first you could not bear the idea of becoming a doctor?"

"One's ideas change, I suppose," replied the youth, with a smile,—"probably my making the discovery that I had some talent in that direction had something to do with it."

"H'm; how did you make that discovery, my boy?" asked the old gentleman.

"That question can't easily be answered except by my inflicting on you a chapter of my early life," replied Stanley, laughing.

"Then inflict it on us without delay, my boy. I shall delight to listen, and so, I am sure, will Katie and Fanny. As to my young friend Queeker, he is of a somewhat literary turn, and may perhaps throw the incidents into verse, if they are of a sufficiently romantic character!"

Katie and Fanny declared they would be charmed to hear about it, and Queeker said, in a savagely jesting tone, that he was so used to things being inflicted on him, that he didn't mind—rather liked it than otherwise!

"But you must not imagine," said Stanley, "that I have a thrilling narrative to give you. I can merely relate the two incidents which fixed my destiny in regard to a profession. You remember, I daresay, that my heart was once set upon going to sea. Well, like most boys, I refused to listen to advice on that point, and told my father that I should never make a surgeon—that I had no taste or talent for the medical profession. The more my father tried to reason me out of my desire, the more obstinate I became. The only excuse that I can plead is that I was very young, very ignorant, and very stupid. One day, however, I was left in the surgery with a number of dirty phials to wash—my father having gone to visit a patient at a short distance, when our servant came running in, saying that there was a cab at the door with a poor boy who had got his cheek badly cut. As I knew that my father would be at home in less than quarter of an hour, I ordered him to be brought in. The poor child—a little delicate boy—was very pale, and bleeding profusely from a deep gash in the cheek, made accidentally by a knife with which he had been playing. The mouth was cut open almost to the ear. We laid him on a sofa, and I did what I could to stop the flow of blood. I was not sixteen at the time, and, being very small for my age, had never before felt myself in a position to offer advice, and indeed I had not much to offer. But one of the bystanders said to me while we were looking at the child,—

"'What do you think should be done, sir?'

" The mere fact of being asked my opinion gratified my vanity, and the respectful ' sir ' with which the question concluded caused my heart to beat high with unwonted emotion. It was the first time I had ever been addressed gravely as a man; it .was a new sensation, and I think may be regarded as an era in my existence.

" With much gravity I replied that of course the wound ought to be sewed up.

"'Then the sooner it's done the better, I think,' said the bystander, 'for the poor child will bleed to death if it is allowed to go on like that.'

" A sudden resolution entered into my mind. I stroked my chin and frowned, as if in deep thought, then, turning to the man who had spoken, said,— ' It ought certainly to be done with as little delay as possible ; I expect my father to return every minute ; but as it is an urgent case, I will myself undertake it, if the parents of the child have no objection.'

"'Seems to me, lad,' remarked a country fellow, who had helped to carry the child in, ' that it beant a time to talk o' parients objectin' w'en the cheeld's blood'n to deth. Ye'd better fa' to work at once— if 'ee knows how.'

" I cast upon this man a look of scorn, but made no reply. Going to the drawer in which the surgical instruments were kept, I took out those that suited my purpose, and went to work with a degree of coolness which astonished myself. I had often seen my father sew up wounds, and had assisted at many an operation of the kind, so that, although altogether unpractised, I was not ignorant of the proper mode of procedure. The people looked on with breath-less interest. When I had completed the operation, I saw my father looking over the shoulders of the people with an expression of unutterable sur-prise not unmingled with amusement. I blushed deeply, and began some sort of explanation, which, however, he cut short by observing in an off-hand manner, that the thing had been done very well, and the child had better be carried into my bedroom and left there to rest for some time. He thus got the people out of the surgery, and then, when we were alone, told me that I was a born surgeon, that he could not have done it much better himself, and, in short, praised me to such an extent that I felt quite proud of my performance."

Queeker, who had listened up to this point with breathless attention, suddenly said,—

"D' you mean to say that you *really* did that?"

"I do," replied Stanley with an amused smile.

"Sewed up a mouth cut all the way to the ear?" ·

"Yes."

"With a—a— "

"With a needle and thread," said Stanley.

Queeker's powers of utterance were paralysed. He

looked at the young doctor with a species of awe-stricken admiration. Jealousy, for the time, was in abeyance.

" This, then, was the beginning of your love for the profession ?" said Mr. Durant.

" Undoubtedly it was, but a subsequent event confirmed me in my devotion to it, and induced me to give up all thoughts of the sea. The praise that I had received from my father—who was not usually lavish of complimentary remarks—made me am-bitious to excel in other departments of surgery, so I fixed upon the extraction of teeth as my next step in the profession. My father had a pretty large practice in that way. We lived, as you remember, in the midst of a populous rural district, and had frequent visits from farm servants and labourers with heads tied up and lugubrious faces.

" I began to fit myself for duty by hammering big nails into a block of wood, and drawing them out again. This was a device of my own, for I wished to give my father another surprise, and did not wish to betray what I was about, by asking his advice as to how I should proceed. I then extracted the teeth from the jaw-bones of all the sheep's-heads that I could lay hands on ; after a good deal of practice in this way, I tried to tempt our cook with an offer of five shillings to let me extract a back tooth which had caused her a great deal of suffering at intervals for many months; but she was a timid woman, and would not have allowed me for five guineas, I believe, even to look into her mouth. I also tried to tempt our small stable-boy with a similar sum. He was a plucky little fellow, and, although there was not an unsound tooth in his head, agreed to let me draw one of the *smallest* of his back teeth for seven and sixpence if it should come out the first pull, and sixpence for every extra rug! I thought the little fellow extravagant in his demands, but, rather than lose the chance, submitted. He sat down quite boldly on our operating chair, but grew pale when I advanced with the instrument; when I tried to open his mouth, he began to whimper, and finally, struggling out of my grasp, fled. I afterwards gave him sixpence, however, for affording me, as I told him, so much pleasurable anticipation.

"After this I cast about for another subject, but failed to procure a live one. It occurred to me, however, that I might try my hand on two skeletons that hung in our garret, so I got their heads off without delay, and gradually extracted every tooth in their jaws. As there were about sixty teeth, I think, in each pair, I felt myself much improved before the jaws were toothless. At last, I resolved to take advantage of the first opportunity that should offer, during my father's absence, to practise on the living subject. It was not long before I had a chance.

"One morning my father went out, leaving me in the surgery, as was his wont. I was deeply immersed in a book on anatomy, when I heard a tremendous double rap—as if made with the head of a stick—at the outer door, and immediately after the question put in the gruff bass voice of an Irishman, 'Is the dactur within?'

"A tremendous growl of disappointment followed the reply. Then, after a pause, 'Is the assistant within?' This was followed by a heavy tread in the passage, and, next moment, an enormous man, in very ragged fustian, with a bronzed hairy face, and a reaping-hook under his arm, stood in the surgery, his head almost touching the ceiling.

"'Sure it's niver the dactur's assistant ye are?' he exclaimed, with a look of surprise.

"I rose, drew myself up, and, endeavouring to look very solemn, said that I was, and demanded to know if I could do anything for him.

"'Ah, then, it's a small assistant ye are, anyhow,' he remarked; but stopped suddenly and his huge countenance was convulsed with pain, as he clapped his hand to his face, and uttered a groan, which was at least three parts composed of a growl.

"'Hooroo! whirr-r-hach! musha, but it's like the cratur 'o' Vesoovious all alive—o—in me head. Av it don't split up me jaw—there—ha—och!'

"The giant stamped his foot with such violence

that all the glasses, cups, and vials in the room rang again, and, clapping both hands over his mouth, he bent himself double in a paroxysm of agony.

"I felt a strange mixture of wild delight and alarm shoot through me. The chance had come in my way, but in anticipating it I had somehow always contemplated operating on some poor boy or old woman. My thoughts had never depicted such a herculean and rude specimen of humanity. At first, he would not believe me capable of extracting a tooth; but I spoke with such cool self-possession and assurance—though far from feeling either—that he consented to submit to the operation. For the sake of additional security, I seated him on the floor, and took his head between my knees; and I confess that when seated thus, in such close proximity to his rugged as well as massive head, gazing into the cavern filled with elephantine tusks, my heart almost failed me. Far back, in the darkest corner of the cave, I saw the decayed tooth—a massive lump of glistening ivory, with a black pit in the middle of it. Screwing up my courage to the utmost, I applied the key. The giant winced at the touch, but clasped his hard hands together—evidently prepared for the worst. I began to twist with right good-will. The man roared furiously, and gave a convulsive heave that almost upset myself and the big chair, and disengaged the key!

"'Oh, come,' said I, remonstratively, 'you ought to stand it better than that! why, the worst of it was almost over.'

"'Was it, though?' he inquired earnestly, with an upward glance, that gave to his countenance in that position a hideous aspect. 'Sure it had need be, for the worst baits all that iver I dramed of. Go at it again, me boy.'

"Resolving to make sure work of it next time, I fixed the key again, and, after getting it pretty tight —at which point he evidently fancied the worst had been again reached—I put forth all my strength in one tremendous twist.

"I failed for a moment to draw the tusk, but I drew forth a prolonged roar, that can by no means be conceived or described. The Irishman struggled. I held on tight to his head with my knees. The chair tottered on its legs. Letting go the hair of his head, I clapped my left hand to my right, and with both arms redoubled the strain. The roar rose into a terrible yowl. There was a crash like the rending of a forest tree. I dropped the instrument, sprang up, turned the chair on the top of the man, and cramming it down on him rushed to the door, which I threw open, and then faced about.

"There was a huge iron pestle lying on a table near my hand. Seizing it, I swayed it gently to and fro, ready to knock him down with it if he should rush at me, or to turn and fly, as should seem most advisable. I was terribly excited, and a good deal alarmed as to the possible consequences, but managed with much difficulty to look collected.

"The big chair was hurled into a corner as he rose sputtering from the floor, and holding his jaws with both hands.

"'Och! ye spalpeen, is that the way ye trait people?'

"'Yes,' I replied in a voice of forced calmness, 'we usually put a restraint on strong men like you, when they're likely to be violent.'

"I saw the corners of his eyes wrinkle a little, and felt more confidence.

"'Arrah, but it's the jawbone ye've took out, ye goormacalluchscrowl!'

"'No, it isn't, it's only the tooth,' I replied, going forward and picking it up from the floor.

"The amazement of the man is not to be described. I gave him a tumbler of water, and, pointing to a basin, told him to wash out his mouth, which he did, looking at me all the time, however, and following me with his astonished eyes, as I moved about the room. He seemed to have been bereft of the power of speech; for all that he could say after that was, 'Och! av yer small yer cliver!'

"On leaving he asked what was to pay. I said that I'd ask nothing, as he had stood it so well; and

he left me with the same look of astonishment in
his eyes and words of commendation on his lips."

"Well, that *was* a tremendous experience to begin
with," said Mr. Durant, laughing; "and so it made
you a doctor?"

"It helped. When my father came home I presented him with the tooth, and from that day to this
I have been hard at work; but I feel a little seedy
just now from over-study, so I have resolved to try
to get a berth as surgeon on board a ship bound for
India, Australia, China, or South America; and, as
you are a shipowner and old friend, I thought it
just possible you might be not only willing but able
to help me to what I want."

"And you thought right, Stanney, my boy," said
the old gentleman heartily; "I have a ship going to
sail for India in a few weeks, and we have not yet
appointed a surgeon. You shall have that berth if
it suits you."

At this point they were interrupted by the entrance of a servant maid with the announcement
that there was a man in the lobby who wished to
see Mr. Durant.

"I'll be back shortly," said the old gentleman to
Stanley as he rose; "go to the drawing-room, girls,
and give Mr. Hall some music. You'll find that my
Katie sings and plays very sweetly, although she
won't let me say so. Fanny joins her with a fine

contralto, I believe, and Queeker, too, he sings—a—
a what is it, Queeker ?—a bass or a baritone—eh ?"

Without waiting for a reply, Mr. Durant left the
room, and found Morley Jones standing in the lobby
hat in hand.

The old gentleman's expression changed instantly,
and he said with much severity—

" Well, Mr. Jones, what do *you* want ?"

Morley begged the favour of a private interview for
a few minutes.   After a moment's hesitation, Mr.
Durant led him into his study.

" Another loan, I suppose ?" said the old gentleman, as he lit the gas.

" I had expected to have called to pay the last
loan, sir," replied Mr. Jones somewhat boldly, " but
one can't force the market.   I have my sloop down
here loaded with herrings, and if I chose to sell at a
loss, could pay my debt to you twice over; but
surely it can scarcely be expected of me to do that.
I hear there is a rise in France just now, and mean to
run over there with them.   I shall be sure to dis-
pose of 'em to advantage.   On my return, I 'll pay
your loan with interest."

Morley Jones paused, and Mr. Durant looked at
him attentively for a few seconds.

" Is this all you came to tell me ?"

" Why, no sir, not exactly," replied Jones, a little
disconcerted by the stern manner of the old gentle-

man. "The sloop is not quite filled up, she could stow a few more casks, but I have been cleaned out, and unless I can get the loan of forty or fifty pounds—"

"Ha! I thought so. Are you aware, Mr. Jones, that your character for honesty has of late been called in question?"

"I am aware that I have got enemies," replied the fish-merchant coldly. "If their false reports are to be believed to my disadvantage, of course I cannot expect—"

"It is not my belief in their reports," replied Mr. Durant, "that creates suspicion in me, but I couple these reports with the fact that you have again and again deceived me in regard to the repayment of the loans which you have already received at various times from me."

"I can't help ill-luck, sir," said Morley with a downcast look. "If men's friends always deserted them at the same time with fortune there would be an end of all trade."

"Mr. Jones," said the other decidedly, "I tell you plainly that you are presumptuous when you count me one of your *friends*. Your deceased brother, having been an old and faithful servant of mine, was considered by me a friend, and it is out of regard to his memory alone that I have assisted *you*. Even now, I will lend you the sum you ask, but be assured it is the last you shall ever get from me. I distrust you, sir, and I tell you so—flatly."

While he was speaking the old gentleman had opened a desk. He now sat down and wrote out a cheque, which he handed to his visitor, who received it with a grim smile and a curt acknowledgment, and instantly took his leave.

Mr. Durant smoothed the frown from his brow, and returned to the drawing-room, where Katie's sweet voice instantly charmed away the memory of the evil spirit that had just left him.

The table was covered with beautiful pencil sketches and chalk-heads and water-colour drawings in various stages of progression—all of which were the production of the same fair, busy, and talented little hand that copied the accounts for the Board of Trade, for love instead of money, without a blot, and without defrauding of dot or stroke a single *i* or *t*!

Queeker was gazing at one of the sketches with an aspect so haggard and savage that Mr. Durant could not refrain from remarking it.

" Why, Queeker, you seem to be displeased with that drawing,.eh? What's wrong with it?"

" Oh, ah!" exclaimed the youth, starting, and becoming very red in the face—" no, not with the drawing, it is beautiful—*most* beautiful, but I—in —fact I was thinking, sir, that thought sometimes leads us into regions of gloom in which—where—

one can't see one's way, and *ignes fatui* mislead or
—or—"

" Very true, Queeker," interrupted the old gentleman, good-humouredly ; " thought is a wonderful
quality of the mind—transports us in a moment
from the Indies to the poles; fastens with equal
facility on the substantial and the impalpable;
gropes among the vague generalities of the abstract,
and wriggles with ease through the thick obscurities
of the concrete—eh, Queeker ? Come, give us a
song, like a good fellow."

" I never sing—I *cannot* sing, sir," said the youth,
hurriedly.

" No ! why, I thought Katie said you were attending the singing-class."

The fat cousin was observed here to put her handkerchief to her mouth and bend convulsively over a
drawing.

Queeker explained that he had just begun to
attend, but had not yet attained sufficient confidence
to sing in public.   Then, starting up he suddenly
pulled out his watch, exclaimed that he was quite
ashamed of having remained so late, shook hands
nervously all round, and, rushing from the house,
left Stanley Hall in possession of the field !

Now, the poor youth's state of mind is not easily
accounted for.   Stanley, being a close observer, had
at an early part of the evening detected the cause

of Queeker's jealousy, and, being a kindly fellow, sought, by devoting himself to Fanny Hennings, to relieve his young friend; but, strange to say, Queeker was *not* relieved! This fact was a matter of profound astonishment even to Queeker himself, who went home that night in a state of mind which cannot be adequately described, sat down before his desk, and, with his head buried in his hands, thought intensely.

"Can it be," he murmured in a sepulchral voice, looking up with an expression of horror, "that I love them *both*? Impossible. Horrible! Perish the thought—yes (seizing a pen)

> Perish the thought
> Which never ought
> To be,
> Let not the thing

(thing—wing—bing—ping—jing—ring—ling—ting —cling—dear me, what a quantity of words with little or no meaning there are in the English language!—what *will* rhyme with—ah! I have it— sting—)

> Let not the thing
> Reveal its sting
> To me!"

Having penned these lines, Queeker heaved a deep sigh—cast one long lingering gaze on the moon, and went to bed.

CHAPTER VIII.

THE SLOOP NORA—MR. JONES BECOMES COMMUNICATIVE, AND BILLY
TOWLER, FOR THE FIRST TIME IN HIS LIFE, THOUGHTFUL.

A DEAD calm, with a soft, golden, half-transparent
mist, had settled down on Old Father Thames,
when, early one morning, the sloop Nora floated
rather than sailed towards the mouth of that celebrated river, bent, in the absence of wind, on creeping out to sea with the tide.

Jim Welton stood at the helm, which, in the
circumstances, required only attention from one of
his legs, so that his hands rested idly in his coat
pockets. Morley Jones stood beside him.

"So you managed the insurance, did you?" said
Jim in a careless way, as though he put the question
more for the sake of saying something than for any
interest he had in the matter.

Mr. Jones, whose eyes and manner betrayed the
fact that even at that early hour he had made
application to the demon-spirit which led him cap-

tive at its will, looked suspiciously at his questioner,
and replied,—

"Well, yes, I've managed it."

"For how much?" inquired Jim.

"For £300."

Jim looked surprised. "D'ye think the herring
are worth that?" he asked.

"No, they ain't, but there's some general cargo
besides as 'll make it up to that, includin' the value
o' the sloop, which I've put down at £100. Moreover, Jim, I have named you as the skipper. They
required his name, d'ye see, and as I'm not exactly
a seafarin' man myself, an' wanted to appear only
as the owner, I named you."

"But that was wrong," said Jim, "for I'm *not* the
master."

"Yes, you are," replied Morley, with a laugh. "I
make you master now. So, pray, Captain Welton,
attend to your duty, and be civil to your employer.
There's a breeze coming that will send you foul o'
the Maplin light if you don't look out."

"What's the name o' the passenger that came
aboard at Gravesend, and what makes him take a
fancy to such a craft as this?" inquired Jim.

"I can answer these questions for myself," said
the passenger referred to, who happened at that
moment to come on deck. "My name is Stanley
Hall, and I have taken a fancy to the Nora chiefly

because she somewhat resembles in size and rig a
yacht which belonged to my father, and in which I
have had many a pleasant cruise.   I am fond of the
sea, and prefer going to Ramsgate in this way rather
than by rail   I suppose you will approve my preference of the sea?" he added, with a smile.

"I do, indeed," responded Jim.   "The sea is my
native element.   I could swim in it as soon a'most
as I could walk, and I believe that—one way or
other, in or on it—I have had more to do with it
than with the land."

"You are a good swimmer, then, I doubt not?"
said Stanley.

"Pretty fair," replied Jim, modestly.

"Pretty fair!" echoed Morley Jones, "why, he's
the best swimmer, I'll be bound, in Norfolk—ay, if
he were brought to the test I do b'lieve he'd turn
out to be the best in the kingdom."

On the strength of this subject the two young
men struck up an acquaintance, which, before they
had been long together ripened into what might
almost be styled a friendship.   They had many
sympathies in common.   Both were athletic; both
were mentally as well as physically active, and,
although Stanley Hall had the inestimable advantage of a liberal education, Jim Welton possessed
a naturally powerful intellect, with a capacity for
turning every scrap of knowledge to good use.

Their conversation was at that time, however, cut short by the springing up of a breeze, which rendered it necessary that the closest attention should be paid to the management of the vessel among the numerous shoals which rendered the navigation there somewhat difficult.

It may be that many thousands of those who annually leave London on voyages, short and long—of profit and pleasure—have very little idea of the intricacy of the channels through which they pass, and the number of obstructions which, in the shape of sandbanks, intersect the mouth of the Thames at its junction with the ocean. Without pilots, and an elaborate well-considered system of lights, buoys, and beacons, a vessel would be about as likely to reach London from the ocean, or *vice versa*, in safety, as a man who should attempt to run through an old timber-yard blindfold would be to escape with unbroken neck and shins. Of shoals there are the East and West Barrows, the Nob, the Knock, the John, the Sunk, the Girdler, and the Long sands, all lying like so many ground-sharks, quiet, unobtrusive, but very deadly, waiting for ships to devour, and getting them too, very frequently, despite the precautions taken to rob them of their costly food.

These sand-sharks (if we may be allowed the expression) separate the main channels, which are named respectively the Swin or King's channel, on

the north, and the Prince's, the Queen's, and the
South channels, on the south.   The channel through
which the Nora passed was the Swin, which, though
not used by first-class ships, is perhaps the most
frequented by the greater portion of the coasting
and colliery vessels, and all the east country craft.
The traffic is so great as to be almost continuous;
innumerable vessels being seen in fine weather passing to and fro as far as the eye can reach.   To mark
this channel alone there was, at the time we write
of, the Mouse light-vessel, at the western extremity
of the Mouse sand; the Maplin lighthouse, on the
sand of the same name; the Swin middle light-
vessel, at the western extremity of the Middle and
Heaps sand; the Whittaker beacon, and the Sunk
light-vessel on the Sunk sand—besides other beacons
and numerous buoys.   When we add that floating
lights and beacons cost thousands and hundreds of
pounds to build, and that even buoys are valued in
many cases at more than a hundred pounds each,
besides the cost of maintenance, it may be conceived
that the great work of lighting and buoying the
channels of the kingdom—apart from the light-*house*
system altogether—is one of considerable expense,
constant anxiety, and vast national importance.   It
may also be conceived that the Elder Brethren of
the Corporation of Trinity House—by whom, from
the time of Henry VIII. down to the present day,

that arduous duty has been admirably performed—
hold a position of the highest responsibility.

It is not our intention, however, to trouble the
reader with further remarks on this subject at this
point in our tale. In a future chapter we shall add
a few facts regarding the Trinity Corporation, which
will doubtless prove interesting ; meanwhile we have
said sufficient to show that there was good reason
for Jim Welton to hold his tongue and mind his
helm.

When the dangerous navigation was past, Mr.
Jones took Billy Towler apart, and, sitting down
near the weather gangway, entered into a private and
confidential talk with that sprightly youngster.

"Billy, my boy," he said, with a leer that was
meant to be at once amiable and patronizing, "you
and I suit each other very well, don't we?"

Billy, who had been uncommonly well treated by
his new master, thrust his hands into the waistband
of his trousers, and, putting his head meditatively on
one side, said in a low voice,—

"H'm—well, yes, you suit me pretty well."

The respectable fish-curer chuckled, and patted
his protégé on the back. After which he proceeded
to discuss, or rather to detail, some matters which,
had he been less affected by the contents of Square-
Tom, he might have hesitated to touch upon.

"Yes," he said, "you'll do very well, Billy

You 're a good boy and a sharp one, which, you see, is exactly what I need. There are a lot o' small matters that I want you to do for me, and that couldn't be very well done by anybody else; 'cause, d' ye see, there ain't many lads o' your age who unite so many good qualities."

"Very true," remarked Billy, gravely nodding his head—which, by the way, was now decorated with a small straw hat and blue ribbon, as was his little body with a blue Guernsey shirt, and his small legs with white duck trousers of approved sailor cut.

"Now, among other things," resumed Morley, "I want you to learn some lessons."

Billy shook his head with much decision.

"That won't go down, Mister Jones. I don't mean for to larn no more lessons. I've 'ad more than enough o' that. Fact is I *consider* myself edicated raither 'igher than usual. Can't I read and write, and do a bit o' cypherin'? Moreover, I knows that the world goes round the sun, w'ich is contrairy to the notions o' the haincients, wot wos rediklous enough to suppose that the sun went round the world. And don't I know that the earth is like a orange, flattened at the poles? though I don't b'lieve there *is* no poles, an' don't care a button if there was. That's enough o' jogrify for my money; w'en I wants more I 'll ax for it."

"But it ain't that sort o' lesson I mean, Billy,"

said Mr. Jones, who was somewhat amused at the indignant tone in which all this was said. "The lesson I want you to learn is this: I want you to git off by heart what you and I are doin', an' going to do, so that if you should ever come to be questioned about it at different times by different people, you might always give 'em the same intelligent answer,—d' ye understand?"

"Whew!" whistled the boy, opening his eyes and showing his teeth; "beaks an' maginstrates, eh?"

"Just so. And remember, my boy, that you and I have been doin' one or two things together of late that makes it best for both of us to be very affectionate to, and careful about, each other. D' ye understand that?"

Billy Towler pursed his little red lips as he nodded his small head and winked one of his large blue eyes. A slight deepening of the red on his cheeks told eloquently enough that he *did* understand that.

The tempter had gone a long way in his course by that time. So many of the folds of the thin net had been thrown over the little thoughtless victim, that, light-hearted and defiant though he was by nature, he had begun to experience a sense of restraint which was quite new to him.

"Now, Billy," continued Jones, "let me tell you that our prospects are pretty bright just now. I

have effected an insurance on my sloop and cargo
for £300, which means that I've been to a certain
great city that you and I know of, and paid into a
company—we shall call it the Submarine Insurance
Company—a small sum for a bit of paper, which
they call a policy, by which they bind themselves
to pay me £300 if I should lose my ship and cargo.
You see, my lad, the risks of the sea are very great,
and there's no knowing what may happen between
this and the coast of France, to which we are bound
after touching at Ramsgate.   D'ye understand?"

Billy shook his head, and with an air of perplexity said that he "wasn't quite up to that dodge
—didn't exactly see through it."

"Supposin'," said he, "you does lose the sloop
an' cargo, why, wot then?—the sloop an' cargo cost
somethin', I dessay?"

"Ah, Billy, you're a smart boy—a knowing young
rascal," replied Mr. Jones, nodding approval; "of
course they cost something, but therein lies the
advantage.   The whole affair, sloop an' cargo, ain't
worth more than a few pounds; so, if I throw it all
away, it will be only losing a few pounds for the
sake of gaining three hundred.   What think you
of that, lad?"

" I think the Submarine Insurance Company
must be oncommon green to be took in so easy,"
replied the youngster with a knowing smile.

"They ain't exactly green either, boy, but they know that if they made much fuss and bother about insuring they would soon lose their customers, so they often run the risk of a knowin' fellow like me, and take the loss rather than scare people away. You know, if a grocer was in the habit of carefully weighing and testing with acid every sovereign he got before he would sell a trifle over the counter, —if he called every note in question, and sent up to the bank to see whether it wasn't a forgery, why, his honest customers wouldn't be able to stand it. They'd give him up. So he just gives the sovereign a ring and the note a glance an' takes his chance. So it is in some respects with insurance companies. They look at the man and the papers, see that all's right, as well as they can, and hope for the best. That's how it is."

"Ha! they must be jolly companies to have to do with. I'd like to transact some business with them submarines," said the boy, gravely.

"And so you shall, my lad, so you shall," cried Mr. Jones with a laugh; "all in good time. Well, as I was saying, the cargo ain't worth much; it don't extend down to the keel, Billy, by no means; and as for the sloop—she's not worth a rope's-end. She's as rotten as an old coffin. It's all I've been able to do to make her old timbers hold together for this voyage."

Billy Towler opened his eyes very wide at this, and felt slightly uncomfortable.

"If she goes down in mid-channel," said he, "it strikes me that the submarines will get the best of it, 'cause it don't seem to me that you're able to swim eight or ten miles at a stretch."

"We have a boat, Billy, we have a boat, my smart boy."

Mr. Jones accompanied this remark with a wink and a slight poke with his thumb in the smart boy's side, which, however, did not seem to have the effect of reassuring Billy, for he continued to raise various objections, such as the improbability of the sloop giving them time to get into a boat when she took it into her head to go down, and the likelihood of their reaching the land in the event of such a disaster occurring during a gale or even a stiff breeze. To all of which Mr. Jones replied that he might make his mind easy, because he (Jones) knew well what he was about, and would manage the thing cleverly.

"Now, Billy, here's the lesson that you've got to learn. Besides remembering everything that I have told you, and only answering questions in the way that I have partly explained, and will explain more fully at another time, you will take particular note that we left the Thames to-day all right with a full cargo—Jim Welton bein' master, and one passenger bein' aboard, whom we agreed to put ashore at Ramsgate. That you heard me say the vessel and cargo were insured for £300, but were worth more, and that I said I hoped to make a quick voyage over and back. Besides all this, Billy, boy, you'll keep a sharp look-out, and won't be surprised if I should teach you to steer, and get the others on board to go below. If you should observe me do anything while you are steering, or should hear any noises, you'll be so busy with the tiller and the compass that you'll forget all about *that*, and never be able to answer any questions about such things at all. Have I made all that quite plain to you?"

"Yes, captain; hall right."

Billy had taken to styling his new employer captain, and Mr. Jones did not object.

"Well, go for'ard and take a nap. I shall want you to-night perhaps; it may be not till to-morrow night."

The small boy went forward, as he was bid, and, leaning over the bulwark of the Nora, watched for a long time the rippling foam that curled from her bows and slid quietly along her black hull, but Billy's thoughts were not, like his eyes, fixed upon the foam. For the first time in his life, perhaps, the foundling outcast began to feel that he was running in a dangerous road, and entertained some misgivings that he was an uncommonly wild, if not wicked, fellow. It is not to be supposed that his perceptions on this subject were very clear, or his meditations unusually profound, but it is certain that, during the short period of his residence in the school of which mention has been made, his conscience had been awakened and partially enlightened, so that his precociously quick intelligence enabled him to arrive at a more just apprehension of his condition than might have been expected,—considering his years and early training.

We do not say that Billy's heart smote him. That little organ was susceptible only of impressions of jollity and mischief. In other respects—never having been appealed to by love—it was as hard as a small millstone. But the poor boy's anxieties were aroused, and the new sensation appeared to add a dozen years to his life. Up to this time he had been accustomed to estimate his wickednesses by the number of days, weeks, or months of incarceration that they involved—" a wipe," he would say, " was so many weeks," a "silver sneezing-box," or a "gold ticker," in certain circumstances, so many more; while a "crack," i.e., a burglary (to which, by the way, he had only aspired as yet) might cost something like a trip over the sea at the Queen's expense; but it had never entered into the head of the small transgressor of the law to meditate such an awful deed as the sinking of a ship, involving as it did the possibility of murder and suicide, or hanging if he should escape the latter contingency.

Moreover, he now began to realize more clearly the fact that he had cast in his lot with a desperate man, who would stick at nothing, and from whose clutches he felt assured that it would be no easy matter to escape. He resolved, however, to make the attempt the first favourable opportunity that should offer; and while the resolve was forming in his small brain his little brows frowned sternly at the foam on the Nora's cutwater. When the resolve was fairly formed, fixed, and disposed of, Billy's brow cleared, and his heart rose superior to its cares. He turned gaily round. Observing that the seaman, who with himself and Jim Welton composed the crew of the sloop, was sitting on the heel of the bowsprit half asleep, he knocked his cap off, dived down the fore-hatch with a merry laugh, flung himself into his berth, and instantly fell asleep, to dream of the dearest joys that had as yet crossed his earthly path—namely, his wayward wanderings, on long summer days, among the sunny fields and hedgerows of Hampstead, Kensington, Finchley, and other suburbs of London.

CHAPTER IX.

MR. JONES TAKES STRONG MEASURES TO SECURE HIS ENDS, AND INTRO-
DUCES BILLY AND HIS FRIENDS TO SOME NEW SCENES AND INCIDENTS.

AGAIN we are in the neighbourhood of the Goodwin sands. It is evening. The sun has just gone
down. The air and sea are perfectly still. The
stars are coming out one by one, and the floating
lights have already hoisted their never-failing signals.

The Nora lies becalmed not far from the Goodwin
buoy, with her sails hanging idly on the yards.
Bill Towler stands at the helm with all the aspect
and importance of a steersman, but without any
other duty to perform than the tiller could have
performed for itself. Morley Jones stands beside
him with his hands in his coat pockets, and Stanley
Hall sits on the cabin skylight gazing with interest
at the innumerable lights of the shipping in the
roadstead, and the more distant houses on shore.
Jim Welton, having been told that he will have to
keep watch all night, is down below taking a nap,
and Grundy, having been ordered below to attend to

some trifling duty in the fore part of the vessel, is also indulging in slumber.

Long and earnestly and anxiously had Morley Jones watched for an opportunity to carry his plans into execution, but as yet without success. Either circumstances were against him, or his heart had failed him at the push. He walked up and down the deck with uncertain steps, sat down and rose up frequently, and growled a good deal—all of which symptoms were put down by Stanley to the fact that there was no wind.

At last Morley stopped in front of his passenger and said to him,—

" I really think you 'd better go below and have a nap, Mr. Hall. It's quite clear that we are not goin' to have a breeze till night, and it may be early morning when we call you to go ashore ; so, if you want to be fit for much work to-morrow, you 'd better sleep while you may."

" Thank you, I don't require much sleep," replied Stanley ; " in fact, I can easily do without rest at any time for a single night, and be quite able for work next day. Besides, I have no particular work to do to-morrow, and I delight to sit at this time of the night and watch the shipping. I 'm not in your way, am I ?"

" Oh, not at all, not at all," replied the fish-merchant, as he resumed his irregular walk.

This question was prompted by the urgency with which the advice to go below had been given.

Seeing that nothing was to be made of his passenger in this way, Morley Jones cast about in his mind to hit upon another expedient to get rid of him, and reproached himself for having been tempted by a good fare to let him have a passage.

Suddenly his eye was attracted by a dark object floating in the sea a considerable distance to the southward of them.

" That's lucky," muttered Jones, after examining it carefully with the glass, while a gleam of satisfaction shot across his dark countenance; " could not have come in better time. Nothing could be better."

Shutting up the glass with decision, he turned round, and the look of satisfaction gave place to one of impatience as his eye fell on Stanley Hall, who still sat with folded arms on the skylight, looking as composed and serene as if he had taken up his quarters there for the night. After one or two hasty turns on the deck, an idea appeared to hit Mr. Jones, for he smiled in a grim fashion, and muttered, " I'll try that, if the breeze would only come."

The breeze appeared to have been waiting for an invitation, for one or two " cat's-paws" ruffled the surface of the sea as he spoke.

" Mind your helm, boy," said Mr. Jones suddenly;

" let her away a point ; so, steady. Keep her as she
goes ; and, harkee " (he stooped down and whispered),
" *when I open the skylight* do you call down, ' breeze
freshenin', sir, and has shifted a point to the
west'ard.' "

" By the way, Mr. Hall," said Jones, turning
abruptly to his passenger; " you take so much interest
in navigation that I should like to show you a new
chart I 've got of the channels on this part of the
coast. Will you step below ?"

" With pleasure," replied Stanley, rising and following Jones, who immediately spread out on the
cabin table one of his most intricate charts,—which,
as he had expected, the young student began to
examine with much interest,—at the same time
plying the other with numerous questions.

" Stay," said Jones, " I 'll open the skylight—don't
you find the cabin close ?"

No sooner was the skylight opened than the small
voice of Billy Towler was heard shouting,—

" Breeze freshenin', sir, and has shifted a pint to
the west'ard."

" All right," replied Jones ;—" excuse me, sir, I 'll
take a look at the sheets and braces and see that all 's
fast—be back in a few minutes."

He went on deck, leaving Stanley busy with the
chart.

" You 're a smart boy, Billy. Now do as I tell

'ee, and keep your weather eye open. D'ye see that bit o' floating wreck a-head? Well, keep straight for that and *run right against it.* I'll trust to 'ee, boy, that ye don't miss it."

Billy said that he would be careful, but resolved in his heart that he *would* miss it!

Jones then went aft to a locker near the stern, whence he returned with a mallet and chisel, and went below. Immediately thereafter Billy heard the regular though slight blows of the mallet, and pursed his red lips and screwed up his small visage into a complicated sign of intelligence.

There was very little wind, and the sloop made slow progress towards the piece of wreck although it was very near, and Billy steered as far from it as he could without absolutely altering the course.

Presently Jones returned on deck and replaced the mallet and chisel in the locker. He was very warm and wiped the perspiration frequently from his fore-head. Observing that the sloop was not so near the wreck as he had expected, he suddenly seized the small steersman by the neck and shook him as a terrier dog shakes a rat.

"Billy," said he, quickly, in a low but stern voice, "it's of no use. I see what you are up to. Your steerin' clear o' that won't prevent this sloop from bein' at the bottom in quarter of an hour, if not sooner! If you hit it you may save yourself and

me a world of trouble. It's so much for your own
interest, boy, to hit that bit of wreck, *that I'll trust
you again.*"

So saying, Jones went down into the cabin, apolo-
gized for having kept Stanley waiting so long, said
that he could not leave the boy at the helm alone
for more than a few minutes at a time, and that he
would have to return on deck immediately after he
had made an entry on the log slate.

Had any one watched Morley Jones while he was
making that entry on the log slate, he would have
perceived that the strong man's hand trembled excessively, that perspiration stood in beads upon his
brow, and that the entry itself consisted of a number
of unmeaning and wavering strokes.

Meanwhile Billy Towler, left in sole possession of
the sloop, felt himself in a most unenviable state of
mind. He knew that the crisis had arrived, and the
decisive tone of his tyrant's last remark convinced
him that it would be expedient for himself to obey
orders. On the other hand, he remembered that he
had deliberately resolved to throw off his allegiance,
and as he drew near the piece of wreck, he reflected
that he was at that moment assisting in an act which
might cost the lives of all on board.

Driven to and fro between doubts and fears, the
poor boy kept changing the course of the sloop in a
way that would have soon rendered the hitting of

the wreck an impossibility, when a sudden and rather sharp puff of wind caused the Nora to bend over, and the foam to curl on her bow as she slipped swiftly through the water.   Billy decided at that moment to *miss* the wreck when he was close upon it, and for that purpose deliberately and smartly put the helm hard a-starboard.

Poor fellow, his seamanship was not equal to his courage !   So badly did he steer, that the very act which was meant to carry him past the wreck, thrust him right upon it !

The shock, although a comparatively slight one, was sufficiently severe to arouse the sleepers, to whom the unwonted sensation and sound carried the idea of sudden disaster.   Jim and Grundy rushed on deck, where they found Morley Jones already on the bulwarks with a boat-hook, shouting for aid, while Stanley Hall assisted him with an oar to push the sloop off what appeared to be the topmast and cross-trees of a vessel, with which she was entangled.

Jim and Grundy each seized an oar, and, exerting their strength, they were soon clear of the wreck.

"Well," observed Jim, wiping his brow with the sleeve of his coat, " it 's lucky it was but a light top-mast and a light breeze, it can't have done us any damage worth speaking of."

"I don't know that," said Jones.   "There are often iron bolts and sharp points about such wreckage that don't require much force to drive 'em through a ship's bottom. Take a look into the hold, Jim, and see that all's right."

Jim descended into the hold, but immediately returned, exclaiming wildly,—

"Why, the sloop's sinkin'! Lend a hand here if you don't want to go down with her," he cried, leaping towards the boat.

Stanley Hall and Grundy at once lent a hand to get out the boat, while the fish-merchant, uttering a wild oath, jumped into the hold as if to convince himself of the truth of Jim's statement. He returned quickly, exclaiming,—

"She must have started a plank. It's rushing in like a sluice. Look alive, lads; out with her!"

The boat was shoved outside the bulwarks, and let go by the run; the oars were flung hastily in, and all jumped into her as quickly as possible, for the deck of the Nora was already nearly on a level with the water. They were not a minute too soon. They had not pulled fifty yards from their late home when she gave a sudden lurch to port and went down stern foremost.

To say that the party looked aghast at this sudden catastrophe, would be to give but a feeble idea of the state of their minds. For some minutes they could do nothing but stare in silence at the few feet of the Nora's topmast which alone remained above water as a sort of tombstone to mark her ocean grave.

When they did at length break silence, it was in short interjectional remarks, as they resumed the oars.

Mr. Jones, without making a remark of any kind, shipped the rudder; the other four pulled.

"Shall we make for land?" asked Jim Welton, after a time.

"Not wi' the tide running like this," answered Jones; "we'll make the Gull, and get 'em to take us aboard till morning. At slack tide we can go ashore."

In perfect silence they rowed towards the floating light, which was not more than a mile distant from the scene of the disaster. As the ebb tide was running strong, Jim hailed before they were close alongside—"Gull, ahoy! heave us a rope, will you?"

There was instant bustle on board the floating light, and as the boat came sweeping past a growl of surprise was heard to issue from the mate's throat as he shouted, "Look out!"

A rope came whirling down on their heads, which was caught and held on to by Jim.

"All right, father," he said, looking up.

"All wrong, I think," replied the sire, looking down. "Why, Jim, you always turn up like a bad shilling, and in bad company too. Where ever have you come from this time ?"

"From the sea, father. Don't keep jawin' there, but help us aboard, and you'll hear all about it."

By this time Jones had gained the deck, followed by Stanley Hall and Billy. These quickly gave a brief outline of the disaster, and were hospitably received on board, while Jim and Grundy made fast the tackles to their boat, and had it hoisted inboard.

"You won't require to pull ashore to-morrow," said the elder Mr. Welton, as he shook his son's hand. "The tender will come off to us in the morning, and no doubt the captain will take you all ashore."

"So much the better," observed Stanley, "because it seems to me that our boat is worthy of the rotten sloop to which she belonged, and might fail to reach the shore after all !"

"Her owner is rather fond of ships and boats that have got the rot," said Mr. Welton, senior, looking with a somewhat stern expression at Morley Jones, who was in the act of stooping to wring the water out of the legs of his trousers.

"If he is," said Jones, with an equally stern glance at the mate, "he is the only loser—at all events the chief one—by his fondness."

"You're right," retorted Mr. Welton sharply ; "the loss of a kit may be replaced, but there are

some things which cannot be replaced when lost.
However, you know your own affairs best. Come
below, friends, and have something to eat and
drink."

After the wrecked party had been hospitably
entertained in the cabin with biscuit and tea, they
returned to the deck, and, breaking up into small
parties, walked about or leaned over the bulwarks in
earnest conversation. Jack Shales and Jerry Mac-
Gowl took possession of Jim Welton, and, hurrying
him forward to the windlass, made him there
undergo a severe examination and cross-questioning
as to how the sloop Nora had met with her disaster.
These were soon joined by Billy Towler, to whom
the gay manner of Shales and the rich brogue of
MacGowl were irresistibly attractive.

Jim, however, proved to be much more reticent
than his friends deemed either necessary or agreeable. After a prolonged process of pumping, to
which he submitted with much good humour and
an apparent readiness to be pumped quite dry, Jerry
MacGowl exclaimed,—

" Och, it ain't of no use trying to git no daiper.
Sure we 've sounded 'im to the bottom, an' found
nothin' at all but mud."

" Ay, he 's about as incomprehensible as that
famous poet you 're for ever givin' us screeds of.
What 's 'is name—somebody's *son* ?"

"Tenny's son, av coorse," replied Jerry; but he ain't incomprehensible, Jack; he's only too daip for a man of or'nary intellick. His thoughts is so awful profound sometimes that the longest deep-sea lead line as ever was spun can't reach the bottom of 'em. It's only such oncommon philosophers as Dick Moy there, or a boardin'-school miss (for extremes meet, you know, Jack), that can rightly make him out."

"Wot's that you're sayin' about Dick Moy?" inquired that worthy, who had just joined the group at the windlass.

"He said you was a philosopher," answered Shales.

"You're another," growled Dick, bluntly, to MacGowl.

"Faix, that's true," replied Jerry; "there's two philosophers aboord of this here light, an' the luminous power of our united intellicks is so strong that I've had it in my mind more than wance to suggest that if they wos to hoist you and me to the masthead together, the Gull would git on first-rate without any lantern at all."

"Not a bad notion that," said Jack Shales. "I'll mention it to the superintendent to-morrow, when the tender comes alongside. P'raps he'll report you to the Trinity House as being willin' to serve in that way without pay, for the sake of economy."

"No, not for economy, mate," objected Dick Moy.

"We can't afford to do dooty as lights without increased pay. Just think of the intellektooal force required for to keep the lights agoin' night after night."

"Ay, and the amount of the doctor's bill," broke in MacGowl, "for curin' the extra cowlds caught at the mast-head in thick weather."

"But we wouldn't go up in thick weather, stoopid," said Moy,—"wot ud be the use? Ain't the gong enough at sich times?"

"Och, to be sure. Didn't I misremember that? What a thing it is to be ready-witted, now! And since we are makin' sich radical changes in the floating-light system, what would ye say, boys, to advise the Boord to use the head of Jack Shales instead of a gong? It would sound splendiferous, for there ain't no more in it than an empty cask. The last gong they sint us down was cracked, you know, so I fancy that's considered the right sort; and if so, Jack's head is cracked enough in all conscience."

"I suppose, Jerry," said Shales, "if my head was appointed gong, you'd like that your fist should git the situation of drumstick."

"Stop your chaffin', boys, and let's catch some birds for to-morrow's dinner," said one of the men who had been listening to the conversation." "There's an uncommon lot of 'em about to-night, an' it seems to me if the fog increases we shall have more of 'em."

"Ho—o—o—!

> "'Sich a gittin' up stairs, and
> A playin' on the fiddle,'"

sang Jack Shales, as he sprang up the wire-rope ladder that led to the lantern, round which innumerable small birds were flitting, as if desirous of launching themselves bodily into the bright light.

"What is that fellow about?" inquired Stanley Hall of the mate, as the two stood conversing near the binnacle.

"He's catching small birds, sir. We often get a number in that way here. But they ain't so numerous about the Gull as I've seen them in some of the other lightships. You may find it difficult to believe, but I do assure you, sir, that I have caught as many as five hundred birds with my own hand in the course of two hours."

"Indeed! what sort of birds?"

"Larks and starlings chiefly, but there were other kinds amongst 'em. Why, sir, they flew about my head and round the lantern like clouds of snowflakes. I was sittin' on the lantern just as Shales is sittin' now, and the birds came so thick that I had to pull my sou'-wester down over my eyes, and hold up my hands sometimes before my face to protect myself, for they hit me all over. I snapped at 'em, and caught 'em as fast as I could use my hands— gave their heads a screw, and crammed 'em into my pockets. In a short time the pockets were all as full as they could hold—coat, vest, and trousers. I had to do it so fast that many of 'em wasn't properly killed, and some came alive agin, hopped out of my pockets, and flew away."

At that moment there arose a laugh from the men as they watched their comrade, who happened to be performing a feat somewhat similar to that just described by the mate.

Jack Shales had seated himself on the roof of the lantern. This roof being opaque, he and the mast, which rose above him, and its distinctive ball on the top, were enveloped in darkness. Jack appeared like a man of ebony pictured against the dark sky. His form and motions could therefore be distinctly seen, although his features were invisible. He appeared to be engaged in resisting an attack from a host of little birds which seemed to have made up their minds to unite their powers for his destruction; the fact being that the poor things, fascinated by the brilliant light, flew over, under, and round it, with eyes so dazzled that they did not observe the man until almost too late to sheer off and avoid him. Indeed, many of them failed in this attempt, and flew right against his head, or into his bosom. These he caught, killed, and pocketed, as fast as possible, until his pockets were full, when he descended to empty them.

"Hallo! Jack, mind your eye," cried Dick Moy, as his friend set foot on the deck, "there's one of 'em a-goin' off with that crooked sixpence you're so fond of."

Jack caught a starling which was in the act of wriggling out of his coat pocket, and gave it a final twist.

"Hold your hats, boys," he cried, hauling forth the game. "Talk of a Scotch moor—there's nothin' equal to the top of the Gull lantern for real sport!"

"I say, Jack," cried Mr. Welton, who, with Stanley and the others, had crowded round the successful sportsman, "there are some strange birds on the ball. Gulls or crows, or owls. If you look sharp and get inside, you may perhaps catch them by the legs."

Billy Towler heard this remark, and, looking up, saw the two birds referred to, one seated on the ball at the mast-head, the other at that moment sailing round it. Now it must be told, and the reader will easily believe it, that during all this scene Billy had looked on not only with intense interest, but with a wildness of excitement peculiar to himself, while his eyes flashed, and his small hands tingled with a desire to have, not merely a finger, but, all his ten fingers, in the pie. Being only a visitor, however, and ignorant of everybody and everything connected with a floating light, he had modestly held his tongue and kept in the background. But he could no

longer withstand the temptation to act. Without
uttering a word, he leaped upon the rope-ladder of
the lantern, and was half way up it before any one
observed him, determined to forestall Jack Shales.
Then there was a shouting of " Hallo ! what is that
scamp up to ?" " Come down, you monkey !" "He 'll
break his neck!"   " Serve him right !"   " Hi! come
down, will 'ee ?" and similar urgent as well as complimentary expressions, to all of which Billy turned a
deaf ear.   Another minute and he stood on the roof of
the lantern, looking up at the ball and grasping the
mast, which rose—a bare pole—twelve or fifteen feet
above him.

"Och! av the spalpeen tries that," exclaimed
Jerry MacGowl, "it 'll be the ind of 'im intirely."

Billy Towler did try it.   Many a London lamp-
post had he shinned up in his day.   The difference
did not seem to him very great.   The ball, he observed, was made of light bands or lathes arranged
somewhat in the form of lattice-work.   It was full
six feet in diameter, and had an opening in the
under part by which a man could enter it.   Through
the lozenge-shaped openings he could see two enormous ravens perched on the top.   Pausing merely
for a second or two to note these facts and recover
breath, he shinned up the bare pole like a monkey,
and got inside the ball.

The spectators on deck stood in breathless suspense and anxiety, unable apparently to move; but when they saw Billy clamber up the side of the ball like a mouse in a wire cage, put forth his hand, seize one of the ravens by a leg and drag it through the bars to him, a ringing cheer broke forth, which was mingled with shouts of uncontrollable laughter.

The operation of drawing the ill-omened bird through the somewhat narrow opening against the feathers, had the double effect of ruffling it out to a round and ragged shape, very much beyond its ordinary size, and of rousing its spirit to ten times its wonted ferocity, insomuch that, when once fairly inside, it attacked its captor with claw, beak, and wing furiously. It had to do battle, however, with an infant Hercules. Billy held on tight to its leg, and managed to restrain its head and wings with one arm, while with the other he embraced the mast and slid down to the lantern; but not before the raven freed its head and one of its wings, and renewed its violent resistance.

On the lantern he paused for a moment to make the captive more secure, and then let his legs drop over the edge of the lantern, intending to get on the rounds of the ladder, but his foot missed the first one. In his effort to regain it he slipped. At that instant the bird freed his head, and with a triumphant "caw!" gave Billy an awful peck on the nose. The result was that the poor boy fell

back. He could not restrain a shriek as he did so,
but he still kept hold of the raven, and made a wild
grasp with his disengaged hand. Fortunately he
caught the ladder, and remained swinging and
making vain efforts to hook his leg round one of the
ropes.

"Let go the bird!" shouted the mate, rushing
underneath the struggling youth, resolved at all
hazards to be ready to break his fall if he should
let go.

"Howld on!" yelled Jerry MacGowl, springing
up the ladder—as Jack Shales afterwards said—like
a Chimpanzee maniac, and clutching Billy by the
neck.

"Ye may let go now, ye spalpeen," said Jerry, as
he held the upper half of Billy's shirt, vest, and jacket
in his powerful and capacious grasp, "I'll howld ye
safe enough."

At that moment the raven managed to free its
dishevelled wings, the fierce flapping of which it
added to its clamorous cries and struggles of indignation. Feeling himself safe, Billy let go his hold,
and used the freed hand to seize the raven's other
leg. Then the Irishman descended, and thus, amid
the riotous wriggles and screams of the dishevelled
bird, and the cheers, laughter, and congratulations of
his friends, our little hero reached the deck in safety.

But this was not the end of their bird-catching

on that memorable occasion. It was, indeed, the grand incident of the night—the culminating point, as it were, of the battle—but there was a good deal of light skirmishing afterwards. Billy's spirit, having been fairly roused, was not easily allayed. After having had a piece of plaister stuck on the point of his nose, which soon swelled up to twice its ordinary dimensions, and became bulbous in appearance, he would fain have returned to the lantern to prosecute the war with renewed energy. This, however, Mr. Welton senior would by no means permit, so the youngster was obliged to content himself with skirmishing on deck, in which he was also successful.

One starling he found asleep in the fold of a tarpaulin. Another he discovered in a snug corner under the lee of one of the men's coats, and both were captured easily. Then Dick Moy showed him a plan whereby he caught half a dozen birds in as many minutes. He placed a small hand-lantern on the deck, and spread a white handkerchief in front of it. The birds immediately swarmed round this so vigorously, that they even overturned the lantern once or twice. Finally, settling down on the handkerchief, they went to sleep. It was evident that the poor things had not been flying about for mere pleasure. They had been undoubtedly fascinated by the ship's glaring light, and had kept flying round it until nearly exhausted, insomuch that they fell asleep almost immediately after settling down on the handkerchief, and were easily laid hold of.

During the intervals of this warfare Mr. George Welton related to Billy Towler and Stanley Hall numerous anecdotes of his experience in bird-catching on board the floating lights. Mr. Welton had been long in the service, and had passed through all the grades; having commenced as a seaman, and risen to be a lamplighter and a mate—the position he then occupied. His office might, perhaps, be more correctly described as second master, because the two were *never* on board at the same time, each relieving the other month about, and thus each being in a precisely similar position as to command, though not so in regard to pay.

"There was one occasion," said the mate, "when I had a tough set-to with a bird, something like what you have had to-night, youngster. I was stationed at the time in the Newarp light-vessel, off the Norfolk coast. It happened not long after the light had gone up. I observed a very large bird settle on the roof of the lantern, so I went cautiously up, hopin' it would turn out a good one to eat, because you must know we don't go catchin' these birds for mere pastime. We're very glad to get 'em to eat; and I can assure you the larks make excellent pies. Well, I raised my head slowly above the lantern, and pounced on it. Instantly its claws went deep into my hands. I seized its neck, and tried to choke it; but the harder I squeezed, the harder it nipped, until I was forced to sing out for help. Leavin' go the neck, in order to have one hand free, I descended the ladder with the bird hanging to the other hand by its claws. I found I had no occasion to hold tight to *it*, for it held tight to *me!* Before I got down, however, it had recovered a bit, let go, and flew away, but took refuge soon after in the lantern-house on deck. Here I caught it a second time, and once more received the same punishment from its claws. I killed it at last, and then found, to my disgust, that it was a monster sparrow-hawk, and not fit for food!"

"Somethink floatin' alongside, sir," said Dick Moy, running aft at that moment and catching up a boat-hook, with which he made a dart at the object in question, and struck, but failed to secure it.

"What is it, Moy?" asked Mr. Welton.

"On'y a bit o' wreck, I think. It looked like a corp at first."

Soon after this most of the people on board the Gull went below and turned in, leaving the deck in charge of the regular watch, which, on that occasion, consisted of Dick and his friend Jack Shales. Jerry MacGowl kept them company for a time, being, as he observed, "sintimentally inclined" that night.

Stanley Hall, attracted by the fineness of the night, also remained on deck a short time after the others were gone.

"Do you often see dead bodies floating past?" he asked of Dick Moy,

"Not wery often, sir, but occasionally we does. You see, we're so nigh the Goodwin sands, where wrecks take place in the winter months pritty constant, that poor fellers are sometimes washed past us; but they ain't always dead. One night we heard loud cries not far off from us, but it was blowin' a gale, and the night was so dark we could see nothin'. We could no more have launched our boat than we could 'ave gone over the falls o' Niagary without capsizin'. When next the relief comed off, we heard that it was three poor fellers gone past on a piece of wreck."

"Were they lost?" inquired Stanley.

"No, sir, they warn't all of 'em lost. A brig saw 'em at daylight, but just as they wos being picked up, one wos so exhausted he slipped off the wreck an' wos drownded. 'Nother time," continued Moy, as he paced slowly to and fro, "we seed a corp float past, and tried to 'ook it with the boat-'ook, but missed it. It wos on its face, and we could see it 'ad on a belt and sheath-knife. There wos a bald spot on the 'ead, and the gulls wos peckin' at it, so we know'd it wos dead—wery likely a long time."

"There's a tight liftle craft," remarked Shales, pointing to a vessel which floated at no great dis-. tance off.

"W'ich d'ye mean?" asked Dick; for there were so many vessels, some at anchor and some floating past with the tide, like phantom ships, that it was not easy to make out which vessel was referred to; "the one wi' the shoulder-o'-mutton mains'l?"

"No; that schooner with the raking masts an' topsail?"

"Ah, that's a purty little thing from owld Ireland," returned Jerry MacGowl. "I'd know her anywhere by the cut of her jib. Av she would only spaik, she'd let ye hear the brogue."

"Since ye know her so well, Paddy, p'raps you can tell us what's her cargo?" said Jack Shales.

"Of coorse I can—it's fruit an' timber," replied Jerry.

"Fruit and timber!" exclaimed Stanley with a laugh; "I was not aware that such articles were exported from Ireland."

"Ah, sure they are, yer honour," replied Jerry. "No doubt the English, with that low spirit of jealousy that's pecooliar to 'em, would say it was brooms an' taties, but *we* calls it fruit and timber!"

"After that, Jerry, I think it is time for me to turn in, so I wish you both a good-night, lads."

"Good-night, sir, good-night," replied the men, as Stanley descended to his berth, leaving the watch to spin yarns and perambulate the deck until the bright beams of the floating light should be rendered unnecessary by the brighter beams of the rising sun.

CHAPTER X.

TREATS OF TENDER SUBJECTS OF A PECULIAR KIND, AND SHOWS HOW BILLY TOWLER GOT INTO SCRAPES AND OUT OF THEM.

THE fact that we know not what a day may bring forth, receives frequent, and sometimes very striking, illustration in the experience of most people. That the day may begin with calm and sunshine, yet end in clouds and tempest—or *vice versa*—is a truism which need not be enforced. Nevertheless, it is a truism which men are none the worse of being reminded of now and then. Poor Billy Towler was very powerfully reminded of it on the day following his night-adventure with the ravens ; and his master was taught that the best-laid plans of men, as well as mice, are apt to get disordered, as the sequel will show.

Next morning the look-out on board the Gull lightship reported the Trinity steam-tender in sight, off the mouth of Ramsgate harbour, and the ensign was at once hoisted as an intimation that she had been observed.

This arrangement, by the way, of hoisting a signal on board the floating lights when any of the Trinity yachts chance to heave in sight, is a clever device, whereby the vigilance of light-ship crews is secured, because the time of the appearing of these yachts is irregular, and, therefore, a matter of uncertainty. Every one knows the natural and almost irresistible tendency of the human mind to relax in vigilance when the demand on attention is continual—that the act, by becoming a mere matter of daily routine, loses much of its intensity. The crews of floating lights are, more than most men, required to be perpetually on the alert, because, besides the danger that would threaten innumerable ships should their vessels drift from their stations, or any part of their management be neglected, there is great danger to themselves of being run into during dark stormy nights or foggy days. Constant vigilance is partly secured, no doubt, by a sense of duty in the men; it is increased by the feeling of personal risk that would result from carelessness; and it is almost perfected by the order for the hoisting of a flag as above referred to.

The superintendent of the district of which Ramsgate is head-quarters, goes out regularly once every month in the tender to effect what is styled "the relief,"—that is, to change the men, each of whom passes two months aboard and one month on shore, while the masters and mates alternately have a month on shore and a month on board. At the same time he puts on board of the four vessels of which he has charge—namely, the *Goodwin*, the *Gull*, the *South-sandhead*, and the *Varne* light-ships,—water, coal, provisions, and oil for the month, and such stores as may be required; returning with the men relieved and the empty casks and cans, etc., to Ramsgate harbour. Besides this, the tender is constantly obliged to go out at irregular intervals—it may be even several times in a week—for the purpose of replacing buoys that have been shifted by storms—marking, with small green buoys, the spot where a vessel may have gone down, and become a dangerous obstruction in the "fair way"—taking up old chains and sinkers, and placing new ones—painting the buoys—and visiting the North and South Foreland lighthouses, which are also under the district superintendent's care.

On all of these occasions the men on duty in the floating lights are bound to hoist their flag whenever the tender chances to pass them within sight, on pain of a severe reprimand if the duty be neglected, and something worse if such neglect be of frequent occurrence. In addition to this, some of the Elder Brethren of the Trinity House make periodical visits of inspection to all the floating lights round the coasts of England; and this they do purposely at irregular times, in order, if possible, to catch the guardians of the coast napping ; and woe betide " the watch " on duty if these inspecting Brethren should manage to get pretty close to any light-ship without having received the salute of re- cognition ! Hence the men of the floating lights are kept ever on the alert, and the safety of the navigation, as far as human wisdom can do it, is secured.   Hence also, at whatever time any of our floating lights should chance to be visited by strangers, they, like our lighthouses, will invariably be found in perfect working order, and as clean as new pins, except, of course, during periods of general cleaning up or painting.

Begging pardon for this digression, we return to Billy Towler, whose delight with the novelty of his recent experiences was only equalled by his joyous anticipations of the stirring sea-life that yet lay before him.

The satisfaction of Mr. Jones, however, at the success of his late venture, was somewhat damped by the information that he would have to spend the whole day on board the tender.   The district super- intendent, whose arduous and multifarious duties required him to be so often afloat that he seemed to be more at home in the tender than in his own house ashore, was a man whose agreeable manners, and kind, hearty, yet firm disposition, had made him a favourite with every óne in the service. Immediately on his boarding the Gull, he informed the uninvited and unfortunate guests of that floating light that he would be very glad to take them ashore, but that he could not do so until evening, as, besides effecting "the relief," he meant to take advantage of the calm weather to give a fresh coat of paint to one or two buoys, and renew their chains and sinkers, and expressed a hope that the delay would not put them to much inconvenience.

Stanley Hall, between whom and the superintendent there sprang up an intimate and sympathetic friendship almost at first sight, assured him that so far from putting him to inconvenience it would afford him the greatest pleasure to spend the day on board. Billy Towler heard this arrangement come to with an amount of satisfaction which was by no means shared by his employer, who was anxious to report the loss of the Nora without delay, and to claim the insurance money as soon as possible. He judged it expedient, however, to keep his thoughts and anxieties to himself, and only vented his feelings in a few deep growls, which, breaking on the ears of Billy Towler, filled the heart of that youthful sinner with additional joy.

"Wot a savage he is!" said Dick Moy, looking at Jones, and addressing himself to Billy.

"Ah, ain't he just!" replied the urchin.

" Has he not bin good to 'ee ? " asked the big seaman, looking down with a kindly expression at the
small boy.

"Middlin'," was Billy's cautious reply.   "I say,
Neptune," he added, looking up into Dick's face,
" wot 's yer name ? "

"It ain't Neptune, anyhow," replied Dick. "That 's
wot we 've called the big black Noofoundland dog
you sees over there a-jumping about Jim Welton as
if he had falled in love with him."

" Why is it so fond of him ?" asked Billy.

Dick replied to this question by relating the incident of the dog's rescue by Jim.

" Werry interestin'.   Well, but wot *is* your name ?"
said Billy, returning to the point.

" Dick."

" Of course I know that ; I 've heerd 'em all call ye
that often enough, but I 'spose you 've got another?"

" Moy," said the big seaman.

" Moy, eh ?" cried Billy, with a grin, "that *is* a funny
name, but there ain't enough of it for my taste."

The conversation was interrupted at this point by
the superintendent, who, having been for many
years in command of an East Indiaman, was styled
" Captain." He ordered the mate and men whose
turn it was to be " relieved " to get into the tender
along · with the strangers.   Soon afterwards the
vessel steamed away over the glassy water, and

Billy, who had taken a fancy to the big lamplighter, went up to him and said,—

"Well, Dick Moy, where are we agoin' to just now?"

Dick pointed to a black speck on the water, a considerable distance ahead of them.

"We're agoin' to that there buoy, to lift it and put down a noo un."

"Oh, that's a boy, is it? and are them there boys too?" asked Billy, looking round at the curious oval and conical cask-like things, of gigantic proportions, which lumbered the deck and filled the hold of the tender.

"Ay, they're all buoys."

"None of 'em girls?" inquired the urchin gravely.

"No, none of 'em," replied Dick with equal gravity, for to him the joke was a very stale one.

"No? that's stoopid now; I'd 'ave 'ad some of 'em girls for variety's sake—wot's the use of 'em?" asked the imp, who pretended ignorance, in order to draw out his burly companion.

"To mark the channels," replied Dick. "We puts a red buoy on one side and a checkered buoy on t'other, and if the vessels keeps atween 'em they goes all right—if not, they goes ashore."

"H'm, that's just where it is now," said Billy. "If *I* had had the markin' o' them there channels I'd 'ave put boys on one side an' girls on t'other all the way up to London—made a sort o' country dance of it, an' all the ships would 'ave gone up the middle an' down agin, d' ye see ?"

" Port, port a little," said the captain at that moment.

" Port it is, sir," answered Mr. Welton, senior, who stood at the wheel.

The tender was now bearing down on one of the numerous buoys which mark off the channels around the Goodwin sands, and it required careful steering in order to avoid missing it on the one hand, or running into it on the other. A number of men stood on the bow of the vessel, with ropes and boat-hooks, in readiness to catch and make fast to it. These men, with the exception of two or three who formed the permanent crew of the tender, were either going off to "relieve" their comrades and take their turn on board the floating lights, or were on their way to land, having been "relieved"—such as George Welton the mate, Dick Moy, and Jerry MacGowl. Among them were several masters and mates belonging to the light-vessels of that district —sedate, grave, cheerful, and trustworthy men, all of them—who had spent the greater part of their lives in the service, and were by that time middle-aged or elderly, but still, with few exceptions, as strong and hardy as young men.

Jerry, being an unusually active and powerful

fellow, took a prominent part in all the duties that devolved on the men at that time.

That these duties were not light might have been evident to the most superficial observer, for the buoys and their respective chains and sinkers were of the most ponderous and unwieldy description.

Referring to this, Stanley Hall said, as he stood watching the progress of the work, "Why, captain, up to this day I have been in the habit of regarding buoys as trifling affairs, not much bigger or more valuable than huge barrels or washing-tubs, but now that I see them close at hand, and hear all you tell me about them, my respect increases wonderfully."

" It will be increased still more, perhaps," replied the captain, "when I tell you the cost of some of them. Now, then, MacGowl, look out—are you ready?"

" All ready, sir."

" Port a little—steady."

" Steady !" replied Mr. Welton.

"Arrah! howld on—och! stiddy—heave—hooray!" cried the anxious Irishman as he made a plunge at the buoy which was floating alongside like a huge iron balloon, bumping its big forehead gently, yet heavily, against the side of the tender, and, in that simple way conveying to the mind of Stanley an idea of the great difficulty that must attend the shifting of buoys in rough weather. .

The buoy having been secured, an iron hook and

chain of great strength were then attached to the ring in its head.   The chain communicated with a powerful crane rigged up on the foremast, and was wrought by a steam windlass on deck.

"You see we require strong tackle," said the captain to Stanley, while the buoy was being slowly raised. "That buoy weighs fully three-quarters of a ton, and cost not less, along with its chain and sinker, than £150, yet it is not one of our largest. We have what we call monster buoys, weighing considerably more than a ton, which cost about £300 apiece, including a 60-fathom chain and a 30-cwt. sinker. ·Those medium-sized ones, made of wood and hooped like casks, cost from £80 to £100 apiece without appendages.   Even that small green fellow lying there, with which I intend to mark the Nora, if necessary, is worth £25, and as there are many hundreds of such buoys all round the kingdom, you can easily believe that the guarding of our shores is somewhat costly."

"Indeed it must be," answered Stanley; "and if such insignificant-looking things cost so much, what must be the expense of maintaining floating lights and lighthouses ?"

"I can give you some idea of that too," said the captain—"

"Look out !" exclaimed the men at that moment.

"Och ! be aisy," cried Jerry, ducking as he spoke,

and thus escaping a blow from the buoy, which would have cracked his head against the vessel's side like a walnut.

" Heave away, lad ! "

The man at the windlass obeyed. The irresistible steam-winch caused the huge chain to grind and jerk in its iron pulley, and the enormous globular iron buoy came quietly over the side, black here and brown there, and red-rusted elsewhere; its green beard of sea-weed dripping with brine, and its sides grizzled with a six-months' growth of barnacles and other shell-fish.

It must not be supposed that, although the engine did all the heavy lifting, the men had merely to stand by and look on. In the mere processes of capturing the buoy and making fast the chains and hooks, and fending off, etc., there was an amount of physical effort—straining and energizing—on the part of the men, that could scarcely be believed unless seen. Do not fancy, good reader, that we are attempting to make much of a trifle in this description. Our object is rather to show that what might very naturally be supposed to be trifling and easy work, is, in truth, very much the reverse.

The buoy having been lifted, another of the same size and shape, but freshly painted, was attached to the chain, tumbled over the side, and left in its place. In this case the chain and sinker did not require renewing, but at the next visited it was found that buoy, chain, and sinker had to be lifted and renewed.

And here again, to a landsman like Stanley, there was much to interest and surprise. . If a man, ignorant of such matters, were asked what he would do in the event of his having to go and shift one of those buoys, he might probably reply, "Well, I suppose I would first get hold of the buoy and hoist it on board, and then throw over another in its place;" but it is not probable that he would reflect that this process involved the violent upturning of a mass of wood or metal so heavy that all the strength of the dozen men who had to struggle with it was scarce sufficient to move gently even in the water; that, being upturned, an inch chain had to be unshackled—a process rendered troublesome, owing to the ponderosity of the links which had to be dealt with, and the constrained position of the man who wrought,—and that the chain and sinker had to be hauled out of the sand or mud into which they had sunk so much, that the donkey-engine had to strain until the massive chains seemed about to give way, and the men stood in peril of having their heads suddenly cut open.

Not to be too prolix on this subject, it may be said, shortly, that when the chain and sinker of the next buoy were being hauled in, a three-inch rope snapped and grazed the finger of a man, fortunately

taking no more than a little of the skin off, though
it probably had force enough to have taken his hand
off if it had struck him differently. Again they
tried, but the sinker had got so far down into the
mud that it would not let go. The engine went at
last very slowly, for it was applying almost the
greatest strain that the chains could bear, and the
bow of the tender was hauled considerably down into
the sea. The men drew back a little, but, after a few
moments of suspense, the motion of the vessel gradually loosened the sinker and eased the strain.

" There she goes, handsomely," cried the men, as
the engine again resumed work at reasonable speed.

" We sometimes lose chains and sinkers altogether in that way," remarked Dick Moy to Billy,
who stood looking on with heightened colour and
glowing eyes, and wishing with all the fervour of
his small heart that the whole affair would give way,
in order that he might enjoy the *tremendous* crash
which he thought would be sure to follow.

" Would it be a great loss ?" he asked.

"It would, a wery great un," said Dick ; " that there
chain an' sinker is worth nigh fifty or sixty pound."

While this work was being done, the captain was
busy with his telescope, taking the exact bearings
of the buoy, to ascertain whether or not it had shifted
its position during the six months' conflict with tide
and tempest that it had undergone since last being

overhauled. Certain buildings on shore coming into line with other prominent buildings, such as steeples, chimneys, and windmills, were his infallible guides, and these declared that the buoy had not shifted more than a few feet. He therefore gave the order to have the fresh buoy, with its chain and sinker, ready to let go.

The buoy in question,—a medium one about eight feet high, five feet in diameter, and conical in shape—stood at the edge of the vessel, like an extinguisher for the biggest candle that ever was conceived in the wildest brain at Rome. Its sinker, a square mass of cast-iron nearly a ton in weight, lay beside it, and its two-inch chain, every link whereof was eight or ten inches long, and made of the toughest malleable iron, was coiled carefully on the main-hatch, so that nothing should impede its running out.

" All ready ?" cried the captain, taking a final glance through the telescope.

" All ready, sir," replied the men, several of whom stood beside the buoy, prepared to lay violent hands on it, while two stood with iron levers under the sinker, ready to heave.

" Stand here, Billy, an' you 'll see it better," said Dick Moy, with a sly look, for Dick had by this time learned to appreciate the mischievous spirit of the urchin.

" Let go !" cried the captain.

SHIFTING THE BUOYS   P. 167

"Let go!" echoed the men.

The levers were raised; the thrust was given. Away went the sinker; overboard went the buoy; out went the chain with a clanging roar and a furious rush, and up sprang a column of white spray, part of which fell in-board, and drenched Billy Towler to the skin!

As well might Dick Moy have attempted to punish a pig by throwing it into the mud as to distress Billy by sousing him with water! It was to him all but a native element. In fact, he said that he believed himself to be a hamphiberous hanimal by nature, and was of the opinion that he should have been born a merman.

"Hooray! shower-baths free, gratis, for nothink!" he yelled, as soon as he had re-caught his breath. "Any more o' that sort comin'?" he cried, as he pulled off his shirt and wrung it.

"Plenty more wery like it," said Dick, cuhckling, "and to be had wery much on the same terms."

"Ah, if you'd only jine me—it would make it so much more pleasant," retorted the boy; "but it would take a deal more water to kiver yer huge carcase."

"That boy will either make a first-rate man, or an out-and-out villain," observed the captain to Stanley, as they stood listening to his chaffing remarks.

L

"He'll require a deal of taming," said Jim Welton, who was standing by; "but he's a smart, well-disposed little fellow as far as I know him."

Morley Jones, who was seated on the starboard bulwarks not far off, confided his opinion to no one, but he was observed to indulge in a sardonic grin, and to heave his shoulders as if he were agitated with suppressed laughter when this last remark was made.

The steamer meanwhile had been making towards another of the floating lights, alongside of which some time was spent in transferring the full water-casks, receiving the "empties," etc., and in changing the men. The same process was gone through with the other vessels, and then, in the afternoon, they returned towards Ramsgate harbour. On the way they stopped at one of the large buoys which required to be painted. The weather being suitable for that purpose, a boat was lowered, black and white paint-pots and brushes were put into her, and Jack Shales, Dick Moy, and Jerry MacGowl were told off to perform the duty. Stanley Hall also went for pastime, and Billy Towler slid into the boat like an eel, without leave, just as it pushed off.

"Get out, ye small varmint!" shouted Jerry; but the boy did not obey; the boat was already a few feet off from the vessel, and as the captain either did not see or did not care, Billy was allowed to go.

" You 'll only be in the way, an' git tired of yer life before we 're half done," said Dick Moy.

"Never mind, he shall keep me company," said Stanley, laughing. ".We will sit in judgment on the work as it proceeds—won't we, Billy ?"

" Well; sir," replied the boy, with intense gravity, " that depends on whether yer fine-hart edication has bin sufficiently attended. to ; but I 've no objection to give you the benefit o' my adwice if you gits into difficulties."

A loud laugh greeted this remark, and Billy, smiling with condescension, said he was gratified by their approval.

A few minutes sufficed to bring them alongside the buoy, which was one of the largest size, shaped like a cone, and painted in alternate stripes of white and black. It rose high above the heads of the men when they stood up beside it in the boat. It was made of timber, had a wooden ring round it near the water, and bore evidence of having received many a rude buffet from ships passing in the dark.

" A nice little buoy this," said Billy, looking at it with the eye and air of a connoisseur; " wot 's its name ? "

" The North Goodwin ; can't 'ee read ? don't 'ee see its name up there on its side, in letters as long as yerself?" said Jack Shales. as he stirred up the paint in one of the pots.

"Ah, to be sure; well, it might have bin named the Uncommon Good-win," said Billy, "for it seems to have seen rough service, and to have stood it well. Come, boys, look alive, mix yer colours an' go to work; England expecks every man, you know, for to do his dooty."

"Wot a bag of impudence it is!" said Dick Moy, catching the ring-bolt on the top of the buoy with the boat-hook, and holding the boat as close to it as possible, while his mates dipped their brushes in the black and white paint respectively, and began to work with the energy of men who know that their opportunity may be cut short at any moment by a sudden squall or increasing swell.

Indeed, calm though the water was, there was enough of undulation to render the process of painting one of some difficulty, for, besides the impossibility of keeping the boat steady, Dick Moy found that all his strength could not avail to prevent the artists being drawn suddenly away beyond reach of their object, and as suddenly thrown against it, so that their hands and faces came frequently into contact with the wet paint, and gave them a piebald appearance.

For some time Billy contented himself with looking on and chaffing the men, diversifying the amusement by an occasional skirmish with Stanley, who had armed himself with a brush, and was busy helping.

"It's raither heavy work, sir, to do all the judg-ment business by myself," he said. "There's that feller Shales, as don't know how a straight line should be draw'd. Couldn't ye lend me your brush, Jack? or p'raps Dick Moy will lend me his beard, as he don't seem to be usin' it just now."

"Here, Dick," cried Stanley, giving up his brush, "you've had enough of the holding-on business; come, I'll relieve you."

"Ay, that's your sort," said Billy; "muscle to the boat-'ook, an' brains to the brush." .

"Hold on tight, sir," cried Shales, as the boat gave a heavy lurch away from the buoy, while the three painters stood leaning as far over the gunwale as was consistent with safety, and stretching their arms and brushes towards the object of their solicitude.

Stanley exerted himself powerfully; a reactionary swell helped him too much, and next moment the three men went, heads, hands, and brushes, plung-ing against the buoy!

"Och! morther!" cried Jerry, one of whose black hands had been forced against a white stripe, and left its imprint there. "Look at that, now!"

"All right," cried Shales, dashing a streak of white over the spot.

"There's no preventing it," said Stanley, apolo-getically, yet laughing in spite of himself.

"I say, Jack, this is 'igh art, this is," observed

Moy, as he drew back to take another dip, "but I'm free to confess that I'd raither go courtin' the girls than painting the buoys."

"Oh! Dick, you borrowed that from me," cried Billy; "for shame, sir!"

"Well, well," observed Jerry, "it's many a time I've held on to a painter, but I niver thought to become wan. What would ye call this now—a landscape or a portrait?"

"I would call it a marine piece," said Stanley.

"How much, sir?" asked Dick Moy, who had got upon the wooden ring of the buoy, and was standing thereon attempting, but not very successfully, to paint in that position.

"A mareeny-piece, you noodle," cried Billy; "don't ye onderstand the genel'm'n wot's a sittin' on judgment on 'ee? A mareeny-piece is a piece o' mareeny or striped kaliko, w'ich is all the same, and wery poor stuff it is too. Come, I'll stand it no longer. I hold ye in sich contempt that I *must* look down on 'ee."

So saying, the active little fellow seized the boathook, and swung himself lightly on the buoy, the top of which he gained after a severe scramble, amid the indignant shouts of the men.

"Well, since you have gone up there, we'll keep you there till we are done."

"All right, my hearties," retorted Billy, in great

delight and excitement, as the men went on with their work.

Just then another heave of the swell drew the boat away, obliging the painters to lean far over the side as before, pointing towards their "pictur," as Jerry called it, but unable to touch it, though expecting every moment to swing within reach again. Suddenly Billy Towler—while engaged, no doubt, in some refined piece of mischief—slipped and fell backwards with a loud cry. His head struck the side of the boat in passing, as he plunged into the sea.

"Ah, the poor craitur!" cried Jerry MacGowl, immediately plunging after him.

Now, it happened that Jerry could not swim a stroke, but his liking for the boy, and the suddenness of the accident, combined with his reckless disposition, rendered him either forgetful of or oblivious to that fact. Instead of doing any good, therefore, to Billy, he rendered it necessary for the men to give their undivided attention to hauling his unwieldy carcase into the boat.

The tide was running strong at the time. Billy rose to the surface, but showed no sign of life. He was sinking again, when Stanley Hall plunged into the water like an arrow, and caught him by the hair.

Stanley was a powerful swimmer, but he could make no headway against the tide that was running to the southward at the time, and before the men had succeeded in dragging their enthusiastic but reckless comrade into the boat, Billy and his friend had been swept to a considerable distance. As soon as the oars were shipped, however, they were quickly overtaken and rescued.

Stanley was none the worse for his ducking, but poor Billy was unconscious, and had a large cut in his head, which looked serious. When he was taken on board the tender, and restored to consciousness, he was incapable of talking coherently. In this state he was taken back to Ramsgate and conveyed to the hospital.

There, in a small bed, the small boy lay for many weeks, with ample leisure to reflect upon the impropriety of coupling fun—which is right—with mischief—which is emphatically wrong, and generally leads to disaster. But Billy could not reflect, because he had received a slight injury to the brain, it was supposed, which confused him much, and induced him, as his attentive nurse said, to talk "nothing but nonsense."

The poor boy's recently-made friends paid him all the attention they could, but most of them had duties to attend to which called them away, so that, ere long, with the exception of an occasional visit from Mr. Welton of the Gull light, he was left entirely to the care of the nurses and house-surgeons, who were extremely kind to him.

Mr. Morley Jones, who might have been expected to take an interest in his *protégé*, left him to his fate, after having ascertained that he was in a somewhat critical condition, and, in any case, not likely to be abroad again for many weeks.

There was one person, however, who found out and took an apparently deep interest in the boy. This was a stout, hale gentleman, of middle age, with a bald head, a stern countenance, and keen grey eyes. He came to the hospital, apparently as a philanthropic visitor, inquired for the boy, introduced himself as Mr. Larks, and, sitting down at his bedside, sought to ingratiate himself with the patient. At first he found the boy in a condition which induced him to indulge chiefly in talking nonsense, but Mr. Larks appeared to be peculiarly interested in this nonsense, especially when it had reference, as it frequently had, to a man named Jones! After a time, when Billy became sane again, Mr. Larks pressed him to converse more freely about this Mr. Jones, but with returning health came Billy's sharp wit and caution. He began to be more circumspect in his replies to Mr. Larks, and to put questions, in his turn, which soon induced that gentleman to discontinue his visits, so that Billy Towler again found himself in what might with propriety have been styled his normal condition—absolutely destitute of friends.

But Billy was not so destitute as he supposed himself to be—as we shall see.

Meanwhile Morley Jones went about his special business. He reported the loss of the sloop Nora; had it advertised in the *Gazette;* took the necessary steps to prove the fact; called at the office of the Submarine Insurance Company, and at the end of three weeks walked away, chuckling, with £300 in his pocket!

In the satisfaction which the success of this piece of business induced, he opened his heart and mind pretty freely to his daughter Nora, and revealed not only the fact of Billy Towler's illness, but the place where he then lay. Until the money had been secured he had kept this a secret from her, and had sent Jim Welton on special business to Gravesend in order that he might be out of the way for a time, but, the motive being past, he made no more secret of the matter.

Nora, who had become deeply interested in the boy, resolved to have him brought up from Ramsgate to Yarmouth by means of love, not being possessed of money. The moment, therefore, that Jim Welton returned, she issued her commands that he should go straight off to Ramsgate, find the boy, and, by hook or crook, bring him to the " Garden of Eden," on pain of her utmost displeasure.

"But the thing an't possible," said Jim. "I haven't got money enough to do it."

"Then you must find money somehow, or make it," said Nora, firmly. "That dear boy *must* be saved. When he was stopping here I wormed all his secrets out of his little heart, bless it—"

"I don't wonder!" interrupted Jim, with a look of admiration.

"And what do you think?" continued the girl, not noticing the interruption, "he confessed to me that he had been a regular London thief! Now I am quite sure that God will enable me to win him back, if I get him here—for I know that he is fond of me—and I am equally sure that he will be lost if he is again cast loose on the world."

"God bless you, Nora; I'll do my best to fetch him to 'ee, even if I should have to walk to Ramsgate and carry him here on my shoulders; but don't you think it would be as well also to keep him— forgive me, dear Nora, I *must* say it—to keep him out of your father's way? He might teach him to drink, you know, if he taught him no worse, and that's bad enough."

Nora's face grew pale as she said—

"Oh, Jim, are you *sure* there is nothing worse that he is likely to teach him? My father has a great deal of money just now, I—I hope that—"

"Why, Nora, you need not think he stole it," said Jim hurriedly, and with a somewhat confused look; "he got it in the regular way from the Insurance

Company, and I couldn't say that there's anything absolutely wrong in the business; but—"

The young sailor stopped short and sighed deeply.

Nora's countenance became still more pale, and she cast down her eyes, but spoke not a word for some moments.

"You *must* bring the boy to me, Jim," she resumed, with a sudden start. "He may be in danger here, but there is almost certain ruin before him if he is left to fall back into his old way of life."

We need not trouble the reader with a detailed account of the means by which Jim Welton accomplished his object. Love prevailed—as it always did, always does, and always will—and ere many days had passed Billy Towler was once more a member of the drunkard's family, with the sweet presence of Nora ever near him, like an angel's wing overshadowing and protecting him from evil.

CHAPTER XI.

THE ANCIENT CORPORATION OF TRINITY HOUSE OF DEPTFORD STROND.

As landmarks—because of their affording variety, among other reasons—are pleasant objects of contemplation to the weary traveller on a long and dusty road, so landmarks in a tale are useful as resting-places. We purpose, therefore, to relieve the reader, for a very brief period, from the strain of mingled fact and fiction in which we have hitherto indulged—turn into a siding, as it were—and, before getting on the main line again, devote a short chapter to pure and unmitigated fact.

So much has been said in previous chapters, and so much has yet to be said, about the lights, and buoys, and beacons which guard the shores of Old England, that it would be unpardonable as well as ungracious were we to omit making special reference to the ancient CORPORATION OF TRINITY HOUSE OF DEPTFORD STROND, under the able management of which the whole of the important work has been devised and carried into operation, and is now most efficiently maintained.

It cannot be too urgently pressed upon un-nautical —especially young—readers, that the work which this Corporation does, and the duties which it performs, constitute what we may term *vital service*.

It would be too much, perhaps, to say that the life of the nation depends on the faithful and wise conduct of that service, but assuredly our national prosperity is intimately bound up with it. The annual list of ships wrecked and lives lost on the shores of the kingdom is appalling enough already, as every observant reader of the newspapers must know, but if the work of the Trinity House—the labours of the Elder Brethren—were suspended for a single year—if the lights, fixed and floating, were extinguished, and the buoys and beacons removed, the writer could not express, nor could the reader conceive, the awful crash of ruin, and the terrific cry of anguish that would sweep over the land from end to end, like the besom of destruction.

We leave to hard-headed politicians to say what, or whether, improvements of any kind might be made in connection with the Trinity Corporation. We do not pretend to be competent to judge whether or not that work might be *better* done. All that we pretend to is a certain amount of competency to judge, and right to assert, that it is *well* done, and one of

the easiest ways to assure one's-self of that fact is, to
go visit the lighthouses and light-vessels on the coast,
and note their perfect management; the splendid
adaptation of scientific discoveries to the ends they
are designed to serve; the thoroughness, the cleanliness, the beauty of everything connected with the
matériel employed; the massive solidity and apparent indestructibility of the various structures
erected and afloat; the method everywhere observ-
able; the perfect organization and the steady re-
spectability of the light-keepers—observe and note
all these things, we say, and it will be impossible to
return from the investigation without a feeling that
the management of this department of our coast
service is in pre-eminently able hands.

Nor is this to be wondered at, when we reflect
that the Corporation of Trinity House is composed
chiefly (the acting part of it entirely) of nautical
men—men who have spent their youth and man-
hood on the sea, and have had constantly to watch
and guard against those very rocks and shoals, and
traverse those channels which it is now their duty
to light and buoy.*

It has been sagely remarked by some philosopher,

* The service which the Corporation of Trinity House renders to
the coasts of England, is rendered to those of Scotland by the Com-
missioners of Northern Lights, and to those of Ireland by the Com-
missioners of Irish Lights—both, to some extent, under the supervision
of the Trinity House.

we believe—at least it might have been if it has not
—that everything must have a beginning. We
agree with the proposition, and therefore conclude
that the Corporation of Trinity House must have
had a beginning, but that beginning would appear
to be involved in those celebrated "mists of antiquity" which unhappily obscure so much that men
would give their ears to know now-a-days.

Fire—which has probably been the cause of more
destruction and confusion than all of the other
elements put together—was the cause of the difficulty
that now exists in tracing this ancient Corporation to
its origin, as will be seen from the following quota-
tion from a little " Memoir, drawn up the present
Deputy-Master, and printed for private distribution," which was kindly lent to us by the present
secretary of the House, and from which most of
our information has been derived.

" The printed information hitherto extant [in
regard to the Corporation of Trinity House]· is
limited to the charter of confirmation granted by
James II. (with the minor concession, by Charles II.,
of Thames Ballastage) and a compilation from the
records of the Corporation down to 1746, by its
then secretary, Mr. Whormby, supplemented by a
memoir drawn up, in 1822, by Captain Joseph
Cotton, then Deputy-master. But the *data* of these
latter are necessarily imperfect, as the destruction

by fire, in 1714, of the house in Water Lane had already involved a disastrous loss of documentary evidence, leaving much to be inferentially traced from collateral records of Admiralty and Navy Boards. These, however, sufficiently attest administrative powers and protective influence scarcely inferior to the scope of those departments."

More than a hundred years before the date of its original charter (1514) the Corporation existed in the form of a voluntary association of the "shipmen and mariners of England," to which reference is made in the charter as being an influential body of long standing even at that time, which protected maritime interests, and relieved the aged and indigent among the seafaring community, for which latter purpose they had erected an almshouse at Deptford, in Kent, where also were their headquarters. This society had inspired confidence and acquired authority to establish regulations for the navigation of ships and the government of seamen, which, by general consent, had been adopted throughout the service. It was, therefore, of tested and approved capacity, which at length resulted in the granting to it of a charter by Henry VIII. in 1514.

From this date the history proper of the Corporation of Trinity House of Deptford Strond begins. In the charter referred to it is first so named, and is described as " The Guild or Fraternity of the most

M

glorious and undividable Trinity of St. Clement."
The subsequent charter of James I., and all later
charters, are granted to "The Master, Wardens, and
Assistants of the Guild, Fraternity, or Brotherhood
of the most glorious and undivided Trinity, and of
St. Clement, in the parish of Deptford, in the county
of Kent." The grant of Arms to the Corporation
is dated 1573, and includes the motto, *Trinitas in
Unitate.*

Np reason can now be assigned for the application
of its distinctive title. The mere fact that the con-
-stitution of the guild included provision for the
maintenance of a chaplain, and for the conduct of
divine service in the parish church, is not, we think,
sufficient to account for it.

In the house or hall at Deptford, adjoining the
almshouses, the business of the Corporation was first
conducted. Afterwards, for the sake of convenient
intercourse with shipowners and others, in a house
in Ratcliffe ; next at Stepney, and then in Water
Lane, Tower Street. The tenement there falling into
decay—after having been twice burnt and restored
—was forsaken, and an estate was purchased on
Tower Hill, on which the present Trinity House was
built, from designs by Wyatt, in 1798.

A good idea of the *relative* antiquity of the Corporation may be gathered from the fact that about
the year 1520—six years after the date of the first

charter—the formation of the Admiralty and Navy
Boards was begun, and " on the consequent establishment of dockyards and arsenals, the Deptford
building-yard was confided to the direction of the
Trinity House, together with the superintendence of
all navy stores and provisions. So closely, indeed,
were the services related, that the first Master of the
Corporation, under the charter, was Sir Thomas
Spert, commander of the ' Henry Grace-à-Dieu,'
(our first man-of-war), and sometime Controller of
the Navy. The Corporation thus became, as it
were, the civil branch of the English Maritime
Service, with a naval element which it preserves to
this day."

Government records show that the Trinity Brethren
exercised considerable powers, at an early period, in
manning and outfitting the navy ; that they reported
on ships to be purchased, regulated the dimensions
of those to be built, and determined the proper com-
plement of sailors for each, as well as the armament
and stores. Besides performing its peaceful duties,
the Corporation was bound to render service at sea if
required, but, in consideration of such liability, the
Brethren and their subordinates were exempted from
land service of every kind. They have been frequently called upon to render service afloat, " and
notably upon two occasions—during the mutiny at
the Nore in 1797, when the Elder Brethren, almost

in view of the mutinous fleet, removed or destroyed every beacon and buoy that could guide its passage out to sea; and again in 1803, when a French invasion was imminent, they undertook and carried out the defences of the entrance to the Thames by manning and personally officering a cordon of fully-armed ships, moored across the river below Gravesend, with an adequate force of trustworthy seamen, for destruction, if necessary, of all channel marks that might guide an approaching enemy."

We cannot afford space to enter fully into the history of the Trinity Corporation. Suffice it to say that it has naturally been the object of a good deal of jealousy, and has undergone many searching investigations, from all of which it has emerged triumphantly. Its usefulness having steadily advanced with all its opportunities for extension, it received in 1836 "the culminating recognition of an Act of Parliament, empowering its executive to purchase of the Crown, and to redeem from private proprietors, their interests in all the coast-lights of England, thus bringing all within its own control. By Crown patents, granted from time to time, the Corporation was enabled to raise, through levy of tolls, the funds necessary for erection and maintenance of these national blessings; . . . and all surplus of revenue over expenditure was applied to the relief of indigent and aged mariners, their wives, widows,

and orphans." About 1853, the allowance to out-
pensioners alone amounted to upwards of £30,000 per
annum, and nearly half as much more of income,
derived from property held in trust for charitable
purposes, was applied to the maintenance of the
almshouses at Deptford and Mile-end, and to other
charitable uses for the benefit of the maritime
community.

The court or governing body of the Corporation
is now composed of thirty-one members, namely, the
Master, four Wardens, eight Assistants, and eighteen
Elder Brethren.   The latter are elected out of those
of the class of younger Brethren who volunteer, and
are approved as candidates for the office.   Eleven
members of this court of thirty-one are men of dis-
tinction—members of the Royal Family, Ministers
of State, naval officers of high rank, and the like.
The remainder—called Acting Brethren—are chiefly
officers of the mercantile marine, with a very few—
usually three—officers of Her Majesty's navy. .The
younger Brethren—whose number is unlimited—
are admissible at the pleasure of the court.   They
have no share in the management, but are entitled
to vote in the election of Master and Wardens.

The duties of the Corporation, as described in their
charters generally, were to " treat and conclude upon
all and singular articles anywise concerning the
science or art of mariners."   A pretty wide and some-

what indefinite range ! At the present time these duties are, as follows :—

To maintain in perfect working order all the light-houses, floating lights, and fog-signal stations on the coasts of England; and to lay down, maintain, renew, and modify all the buoys, beacons, and sea-signals; to regulate the supply of stores, the appoint-ment of keepers, and constantly to inspect the stations—a service which entails unremitting atten-tion upon the members, some of whom are always on duty, either afloat in the steam-vessels or on land journeys.

To examine and license pilots for a large portion of our coasts ; and to investigate generally into all matters relative to pilotage.

To act as nautical advisers with the Judge of the High Court of Admiralty, a duty which frequently engages some of the Brethren for considerable periods of time on intricate causes of the greatest import-ance.

To survey and inspect the channels of the Thames and the shoals of the North Sea, and other points of the coast at which shifting, scouring, growth or waste of sand may affect the navigation, and require to be watched and notified.

To supply shipping in the Thames with ballast.

The Elder Brethren have also to perform the duty of attending the Sovereign on sea-voyages.

In addition to all this, it has to superintend the distribution of its extensive charities, founded on various munificent gifts and legacies, nearly all given or left for the benefit of "poor Jack" and his relatives ; and to manage the almshouses ; also the affairs of the House on Tower Hill, and the engineering department, with its superintendence of new works, plans, drawings, lanterns, optical apparatus, etc.—the whole involving, as will be obvious to men who are acquainted with "business," a mass of detail which must be almost as varied as it is enormous.

The good influence of the operations of the Trinity House might be shown by many interesting instances. Here is one specimen ; it has reference to ballast-heaving :—

"Formerly the ballast, when laid in barge or lighter alongside the ship to be supplied, was heaved on board by men who were hired and paid by various waterside contractors, and subjected to great hardships, not only from the greed of their employers, but from a demoralizing system of payment through publicans and local harpies. These evils were altogether removed by the establishment of a Heavers' Office under control of the Trinity House, where men could attend for employment, and where their wages could be paid with regularity, and free from extortionate deduction."

Many more examples might be given, but were

we to indulge in this strain our chapter would far exceed its proper limits.

The light-vessels belonging to the Corporation are 43 in number : 38 in position and 5 in reserve to meet casualties.* Of lighthouses there are 76; sixty-one of which, built of brick, stone, or timber, are on shore ; eleven, of granite, are on outlying rocks ; and four, on iron piles, are on sandbanks. There are 452 buoys of all shapes and sizes on the coast, and half as many more in reserve, besides about 60 beacons of various kinds, and 21 storehouses in connection with them. Also 6 steam-vessels and 7 sailing tenders maintained for effecting the periodical relief of crews and keepers, shifting and laying buoys, etc.

The working staff which keeps the whole complex machinery in order, consists of 7 district superin-tendents, 11 local agents, 8 buoy-keepers, 21 store-keepers, watchmen, etc. ; 177 lighthouse-keepers, 427 crews of floating lights, 143 crews of steam and sailing vessels, and 6 fog-signal attendants—a total of 800 men.

Among the great and royal personages who have

* The floating lights of England are illuminated by means of lamps with metallic reflectors, on what is styled the catoptric system. The dioptric system, in which the rays of light are transmitted through glass, has been introduced into the floating lights of India by the Messrs. Stevenson, C.E., of Edinburgh. The first floating light on this system in India was shown on the Hoogly in 1865. Since then, seve-ral more dioptric lights have been sent to the same region, and also to Japan in 1869, and all reports agree in describing these lights as being eminently successful.

filled the office of Master of the Corporation of Trinity House, we find, besides a goodly list of dukes and earls—the names of (in 1837) the Duke of Wellington, (1852) H.R.H. Prince Albert, (1862) Viscount Palmerston, and (1866) H.R.H. the Duke of Edinburgh. The last still holds office, and H.R.H. the Prince of Wales heads the list of a long roll of titled and celebrated honorary Brethren of the Corporation.

We make no apology for the interpolation of this chapter, because if the reader has skipped it no apology is due, and if he has not skipped it, we are confident that no apology will be required.

CHAPTER XII.

STRANGE SIGHTS AND SCENES ON LAND AND SEA.

THE river Hoogly. Off Calcutta. Tropical vege-
tation on the shore. Glittering sunshine on the
water. Blue sky and fleecy clouds overhead.
Equally blue sky and fleecy clouds down below.
A world of sky and water, with ships and boats,
resting on their own inverted images, in the midst.
Sweltering heat everywhere. Black men revelling
in the sunshine. White men melting in the shade.
The general impression such, that one might almost
entertain the belief that the world has become
white-hot, and the end of time is about to be
ushered in with a general conflagration.

Such is the scene, reader, to which we purpose to
convey you.

The day was yet young when a large vessel shook
out her topsails, and made other nautical demonstrations of an intention to quit the solid land ere
long, and escape if possible from the threatened
conflagration.

" I wonder when those brutes will be sent off," said the first mate of the ship to the surgeon, who stood on the poop beside him.

"What brutes do you refer to?" asked the surgeon, who was no other than our young friend Stanley Hall.

" Why, the wild beasts, to be sure. Have you not heard that we are to have as passengers on the voyage home two leopards, an elephant, and a rhinoceros ?"

"Pleasant company ! I wonder what Neptune will say to that ?" said Stanley, with a laugh, as he walked forward to ask the opinion of the owner of the said Neptune. "I say, Welton, we are to have an elephant, a rhinoceros, and two leopards, on this voyage."

" Indeed ?"

" Yes, what will Neptune say to it ?"

" Oh, he won't mind, sir," replied Jim, patting the head of the large Newfoundland dog with grey paws which stood beside him.

Jim and Stanley had taken a fancy to each other when on board the Nora. The former had carried out a plan of going to sea, in order to be out of the way if he should happen to be wanted as a witness at the trial of Morley Jones, which event he felt certain must take place soon. He had made application to Stanley, who spoke to Mr. Durant about him,—the result being that Jim obtained a berth on board the ship Wellington, which stood A 1 at Lloyds. Hence we find him in the Hoogly.

"Neptune is a wise dog, sir," continued Jim; "he don't feel much put out by curious company, and is first-rate at taking care of himself. Besides, there is no jealousy in his nature. I suppose he feels that nobody can cut him out when he has once fairly established a friendship. I don't grudge the dive off the bulwarks of the old Gull, when I saved Neptune, I assure you."

"He was worth saving," remarked Stanley, stooping to pat the meek head of the dog.

"Yes, I heard last night of the expected passengers," pursued Jim, "and am now rigging up tackle to hoist 'em on board. I meant to have told you of 'em last night, but we got into that stiff argument about teetotalism, which put it completely out of my head."

"Ah, Welton, you'll never convince me that teetotalism is right," said Stanley, with a good-humoured laugh. "Not that I care much about wine or spirits myself, but as long as a man uses them in moderation they can do him no harm."

"So I thought once, sir," returned Jim, "but I have seen cause to change my mind. A healthy man can't use them in moderation, because *use* is *abuse*. Stimulants are only fit for weaklings and sick folk. As well might a stout man use crutches to help him to walk, as beer or brandy to help him to work; yet there are some strong young men so helpless that they can't get on at all without their beer or grog!"

"Come, I'll join issue with you on that point," said Stanley, eagerly, for he was very fond of an argument with Jim, who never lost his temper, and who always paid his opponent the compliment of listening attentively to what he had to say.

"Not just now," replied Jim, pointing towards the shore; "for yonder comes a boat with some of the passengers we were talking of."

"Is that tackle rigged, Welton?" shouted the mate.

"It is, sir," replied Jim.

"Then stand by, some of you, to hoist these leopards aboard."

When the little boat or dingy came alongside, it was observed that the animals were confined in a large wooden cage, through the bars of which they glared savagely at the half-dozen black fellows who conveyed them away from their native land. They seemed to be uncommonly irate. Perhaps the injustice done them in thus removing them against their will had something to do with it. Possibly the motion of the boat had deranged their systems. Whatever the cause, they glared and growled tremendously.

" Are you sure that cage is strong enough ?" asked the mate, casting a dubious look over the side.

" Oh yes, massa—plenty strong. Hould a Bengal tiger," said one of the black fellows, looking up with a grin which displayed a splendid double row of glittering teeth.

" Very well, get the slings on, Welton, and look sharp, bo's'n, for more company of the same kind is expected," said the mate.

The bo's'n—a broad, short, burly man, as a boat-swain always is and always ought to be, with, of course, a terrific bass voice, a body outrageously long, and legs ridiculously short—replied, " Ay, ay, sir," and gave some directions to his mates, who stood by the hoisting tackles.

At the first hoist the appearance of the cage justified the mate's suspicions, for the slings bent it in so much that some of the bars dropped out.

" Avast heaving," roared the boatswain. " Lower!"

Down went the cage into the dingy. The bars were promptly replaced, and the slings fastened in better position.

" Try it again, bo's'n," said the mate.

The order to hoist was repeated, and up went the cage a second time, but it bent as before, so that several bars again slipped out, leaving the leopards sufficient space to jump through if they chose.

" Lower !" yelled the mate.

The men obeyed promptly—rather too promptly ! The cage went down by the run into the boat, and with a crash fell asunder.

" Cut the rope !" cried the mate.

Jim Welton jumped into the chains, cut the painter, and the boat was swept away by the tide, which was running strong past the ship. At the same moment the black fellows went over the sides into the water like six black eels radiating from a centre, and away went the dingy with the leopards in possession, mounted on the débris of their prison, lashing their sides with their tails, and looking round in proud defiance of all mankind !

The crew of the boat, each of whom could swim like a frog, were soon picked up. Meanwhile, all on board the Wellington who had telescopes applied them to their eyes, and watched the progress of the dingy.

It chanced that the current set with considerable force towards the opposite side of the river, where lay an island on which was a public garden. There ladies and gentlemen in gay costume, as well as many natives and children, were promenading the shady walks, chatting pleasantly, listening to the sweet strains of music, enjoying the fragrance of scented flowers, with the jungle and its inhabitants very far indeed from their thoughts—except, per-chance, in the case of a group surrounding a young officer, who was, no doubt, recounting the manner in which he had potted a tiger on the occasion of his last day out with the Rajah of Bangalore, or some such dignitary!

Straight to the shores of this Eden-like spot the dingy drifted, and quietly did the leopards abide the result—so also did the deeply interested crew of the Wellington, who, of course, were quite unable to give any note of warning.

The little boat was seen to touch the shore, and the leopards were observed to land leisurely without opposition from the enemy.   Immediately after, something resembling a sensation was apparent in the garden.   The distance was too great to permit of sound travelling to the observers, but it lent enchantment to the view to the extent of rendering the human beings there like moving flowers of varied hue.   Presently there was a motion, as if a tornado had suddenly burst upon the flower-beds and scattered them right and left in dire confusion —not a few appearing to have been blown up into the trees!

That same day the crack shots and sportsmen of Calcutta went down to the usually peaceful islet and engaged in all the wild work of a regular hunt, and at eve the two leopards were seen, by interested observers in the Wellington, being conveyed away in triumph on a litter.

But, long before this happy consummation of the

day's sport in the garden, the remainder of the expected company had arrived alongside the Wellington, and the undaunted bo's'n—who declared himself ready on the shortest notice to hoist any living creature on board, from a sperm whale to a megatherium—tackled the elephant. The ponderous brute allowed itself to be manipulated with the utmost good-humour, and when carefully lowered on the deck it alighted with as much softness as if it had been shod with India-rubber, and walked quietly forward, casting a leer out of its small eyes at the mate, as if it were aware of its powers, but magnanimously forbore to use them to the disadvantage of its human masters. In passing it knocked off the bo's'n's hat, but whether this was done by accident or design has never been ascertained. At all events the creature made no apology.

If this passenger was easy-going and polite, the rhinoceros, which came next, was very much the reverse. That savage individual displayed a degree of perverse obstinacy and bad feeling which would have been deemed altogether inexcusable even in a small street-boy.

In the whites of its very small grey eyes wickedness sat enthroned. The end of its horns—for it had two on its nose—appeared to be sharpened with malignity, its thick lips quivered with anger, and its ridiculously small tail wriggled with passionate emotion, as if that appendage felt its insignificance, yet sought to obtrude itself on public notice.

To restrain this passenger was a matter of the utmost difficulty. To get him into the slings might have perplexed Hercules himself, but nothing could appall the bo's'n. The slings were affixed, the order to hoist was given by the mate, who had descended from the poop, and stood near the gangway. Up went the monster with a grunt, and a peculiar rigidity of body, which evidently betokened horror at his situation.

Being fully five tons in weight, this passenger had to be received on board with caution.

"Lower away," was given.

" Hold on," was added.

Both orders were obeyed, and the huge animal hung within three inches of the deck.

" Stand clear there, lads."

There was no occasion for that order. It had been anticipated.

" Lower," was again given.

The moment the feet of the creature touched the deck he dashed forward with ungovernable fury, broke the slings, overturned the bo's'n, who fortunately rolled into the port scuppers, and took possession of the ship, driving the men into the chains and up the rigging.

" Jump up !" shouted Jim Welton to the bo's'n.

"Here he comes aft!" yelled several of the men.

There was no need to warn the boatswain. He heard the thunder of the monster's feet, and sprang into the main rigging with an amount of agility that could hardly have been excelled by a monkey.

"Why, what are you all afraid of?" asked the captain of the ship, who had come on board with a number of passengers just before the occurrence of this incident.

"Come down here, sir, and you'll see," replied the mate, who was in the main-chains.

The captain declined with a smile, and advised the use of a lasso.

Immediately every man of the ship's crew became for the nonce a Mexican wild-horse tamer! Running nooses were made, and Jack, albeit unused to taking wild cattle on the prairies of America, was, nevertheless, such an adept at casting a coil of rope that he succeeded beyond the most sanguine expectation. The bo's'n was the first to throw a loop over the creature's front horn—cast a hitch over its foremast as he styled it—amid a deafening cheer. He was immediately pulled out of the rigging, and a second time lay wallowing in the port scuppers; but he cared nothing for that, being upheld by the glory of having succeeded in fixing the first noose. Soon after that Stanley Hall threw a noose over the creature's head, and Jim Welton fixed one on its

second horn—or, as the bo's'n said, round his mizzen.
In the course of half-an-hour the rhinoceros was so
completely entangled in the twisted ropes that he
seemed as though he were involved in a net. He
was finally captured, and led to a ponderous stall
that had been prepared for him between the fore and
main masts.

Soon afterwards the last of the human passengers
came on board. There were many of them. Officers
and their wives and children—some in health, some
in sickness. Old warriors returning home to repose
on their laurels. Young warriors returning home to
recruit their health, or to die. Women who went
out as wives returning as widows, and women who
went out as widows returning as wives. Some returning with fortunes made, a few returning with
fortunes broken; but all, old and young, healthy and
sick, rich and poor, hopeful and hopeless, glad at
the prospect of leaving the burning skies of India
behind, and getting out among the fresh breezes
of the open sea. Then the sails were set, and with
a light evening breeze the Wellington began her
voyage—homeward bound. . . .

Once again the scene changes. Blue skies are
gone. Grey clouds preponderate. In the Atlantic,
tossed by the angry billows, a large ship scuds before
the wind as though she were fleeing from the pur-
suit of a relentless enemy. She has evidently seen

rough and long service. Her decks have been swept by many a heavy sea; her spars have been broken and spliced. The foremast is sprung, the maintopgallant mast is gone, and the mizzen has been snapped off close by the deck. Her bulwarks are patched here and there, and her general appearance bears evidence of the tremendous power of Ocean.

It would be difficult in that weatherworn hull to recognise the trim full-rigged ship that left the Hoogly many months before.

It was not a recent gale that had caused all this damage. In the South Atlantic, several weeks before, she had encountered one of those terrific but short-lived squalls which so frequently send many of man's stoutest floating palaces to the bottom. Hence her half-wrecked condition.

The passengers on board the Wellington did not, however, seem to be much depressed by their altered circumstances. The fact was, they had become so used to rough weather, and had weathered so many gales, and reached their damaged condition by such slow degrees, that they did not realize it as we do, turning thus abruptly from one page to another. Besides this, although still some weeks' sail from the white cliffs of old England, they already began to consider the voyage as good as over, and not a few of the impatient among them had begun to pack up so as to be ready for going ashore. And how carefully were those preparations for landing made! With what interest the sandal-wood fans, and inlaid ivory boxes and elaborately carved chess-men and curious Indian toys, and costly Indian shawls were re-examined and repacked in more secure and carefully-to-be-remembered corners, in order that they might be got at quickly when eager little hands " at home—" Well, well, it is of no use to dwell on what was meant to be, for not one of those love-tokens ever reached its destination. All were swallowed up by the insatiable sea.

But let us not forestall. The elephant and rhinoceros were the only members of the community that had perished on the voyage. At first the elephant had been dreaded by many, but by degrees it won the confidence and affection of all. Houses innumerable had been built for it on deck, but the sagacious animal had a rooted antipathy to restraint. No sort of den, however strongly formed, could hold him long. The first structures were so ridiculously disproportioned to his strength as to be demolished at once. On being put into the first "house that Jack built," he looked at it demurely for at least five minutes, as if he were meditating on the probable intentions of the silly people who put him there, but neither by look nor otherwise did he reveal the conclusions to which he came. His in-

tentions, however, were not long of being made
known. He placed his great side against the den ;
there was a slow but steady rending of timbers, as
if the good ship herself were breaking up, a burst of
laughter from the men followed, and " Sambo " was
free. When the succeeding houses were built so
strong that his side availed not, he brought his
wonderful patience and his remarkable trunk to bear
on them, and picked them to pieces bit by bit.
Then ropes were tried, but he snapped weak ropes
and untied strong ones.

At last he was permitted to roam the decks at
perfect liberty, and it was a point of the greatest
interest to observe the neat way in which he picked
his steps over the lumbered decks, without treading
upon anything—ay, even during nights when these
decks in the tropical regions were covered with
sleeping men !

Everybody was fond of Sambo. Neptune doted
on him, and the children—who fed him to such an
extent with biscuits that the bo's'n said he would be
sartin' sure to die of appleplexy—absolutely adored
him. Even the gruff, grumpy, unsociable rhinoceros amiably allowed him to stroke its head with
his trunk.

Sambo troubled no one except the cook, but that
luxurious individual was so constantly surrounded
by a halo, so to speak, of delicious and suggestive

odours that the elephant could not resist the temptation to pay him frequent visits, especially when
dinner was being prepared.   One of his favourite
proceedings at such times was to put his trunk into
the galley, take the lid off the coppers, make a small
coil of the end of his proboscis, and therewith at one
sweep spoon out a supply of potatoes sufficient for
half-a-dozen men!   Of course the cook sought to
counteract such tendencies, but he had to be very
circumspect, for Sambo resented insults fiercely.

One day the cook caught his enemy in the very
act of clearing out the potato copper.   Enraged beyond endurance, he stuck his "tormentors" into
the animal's trunk.   With a shriek of rage Sambo
dashed the potatoes in the man's face, and made a
rush at him.   The cook fled to his sanctum and shut
the door.   There the elephant watched him for an
hour or more.   The united efforts, mental and physical, of the ship's crew failed to remove the indignant
creature, so they advised the cook to remain where
he was for some time.   He hit on the plan, however,
of re-winning the elephant's friendship.   He opened
his door a little and gave him a piece of biscuit.
Sambo took it.   What his feelings were no one could
tell, but he remained at his post.   Another piece of
biscuit was handed out.   Then the end of the injured proboscis was smoothed and patted by the
cook.   Another large piece of biscuit was adminis-

tered, and by degrees the cure was effected. Thus successfully was applied that grand principle which has accomplished so much in this wicked world, even among higher animals than elephants—the overcoming of evil with good!

Eventually Sambo sickened. Either the cold of the north told too severely on a frame which had been delicately nurtured in sunny climes, or Sambo had surreptitiously helped himself during the hours of night to something deleterious out of the paint or pitch pots. At all events he died, to the sincere regret of all on board—cook not excepted—and was launched overboard to glut the sharks with an unwonted meal, and astonish them with a new sensation.

Very dissimilar was the end of the rhinoceros. That bumptious animal retained its unamiable spirit to the last. Fortunately it did not possess the powers or sagacity of the elephant. It could not untie knots or pick its cage to pieces, so that it was effectually restrained during the greater part of the voyage; but there came a tempest at last, which assisted him in becoming free—free, not only from durance vile, but from the restraints of this life altogether. On the occasion referred to, the rudder was damaged, and for a time rendered useless, so that the good ship Wellington rolled to an extent that almost tore the masts out of her. Everything not firmly secured about the decks was washed overboard. Among other things, the rhinoceros was knocked so heavily against the bars of his crib that they began to give way.

At last the vessel gave a plunge and roll which seemed to many of those on board as though it must certainly be her last. The rhinoceros was sent crashing through the dislocated bars ; the ropes that held his legs were snapped like the cords wherewith Samson was bound in days of old, and away he went with the lurch of a tipsy man against the longboat, which he stove in.

"Hold on !" roared the bo's'n.

Whether this was advice to the luckless animal, or a general adjuration to everybody and everything to be prepared for the worst, we know not ; but instead of holding on, every one let go what he or she chanced to be holding on to at the moment, and made for a place of safety with reckless haste. The rhinoceros alone obeyed the order. It held on for a second or two in a most remarkable manner to the mainmast, but another lurch of the vessel cast it loose again ; a huge billow rolled under the stern ; down went the bow, and the brute slid on its haunches, with its fore legs rigid in front, at an incredible pace towards the galley. Just as a smash became imminent, the bow rose, the stern dropt, and away he went back again with equal speed, but in a more sidling attitude, towards the quarter-deck. Before that point was reached, a roll diverted him out of course and he was brought up by the main hatch, from which he rebounded like a billiard ball towards the starboard gangway. At this point he lost his balance, and went rolling to leeward like an empty cask. There was something particularly awful and impressive in the sight of this unwieldy monster being thus knocked about like a pea in a rattle, and sometimes getting into attitudes that would have been worthy of a dancer on the tight-rope, but the consummation of the event was not far off. An unusually violent roll of the ship sent him scrambling to starboard; a still more vicious roll checked and reversed the rush and dashed him against the cabin skylight. He carried away part of this, continued his career, went tail-foremost through the port bulwarks like a cannon-shot into the sea. He rose once, but, as if to make sure of her victory, the ship relentlessly fell on him with a weight that must have split his skull, and sent him finally to the bottom.

Strange to say, the dog Neptune was the only one on board that appeared to mourn the loss of this passenger. He howled a good deal that night in an unusually sad tone, and appeared to court sympathy and caresses more than was his wont from Jim Welton and the young people who were specially attached to him, but he soon became reconciled, alas! to the loss of his crusty friend.

The storms ceased as they neared the shores of England. The carpenter and crew were so energetic in repairing damages that the battered vessel began to wear once more something of her former trim aspect, and the groups of passengers assembled each evening on the poop, began to talk with ever-deepening interest of home, while the children played beside them, or asked innumerable questions about brothers, sisters, and cousins, whose names were as familiar as household words, though their voices and forms were still unknown.

The weather was fine, the sky was clear; warm summer breezes filled the sails, and all nature seemed to have sunk into a condition so peaceful as to suggest the idea that storms were past and gone for ever, when the homeward-bound ship neared the land. One evening the captain remarked to the passengers, that if the wind would hold as it was a little longer, they should soon pass through the Downs, and say good-bye to the sea breezes and the roll of the ocean wave.

CHAPTER XIII.

BOB QUEEKER COMES OUT VERY STRONG INDEED.

IT is both curious and interesting to observe the multitude of unlikely ways in which the ends of justice are ofttimes temporarily defeated. Who would have imagined that an old pump would be the cause of extending Morley Jones's term of villainy, of disarranging the deep-laid plans of Mr. Larks, of effecting the deliverance of Billy Towler, and of at once agonizing the body and ecstatifying the soul of Robert Queeker? Yet so it was. If the old pump had not existed—if its fabricator had never been born—there is every probability that Mr. Jones's career would have been cut short at an earlier period. That he would, in his then state of mind, have implicated Billy, who would have been transported along with him and almost certainly ruined; that Mr. Queeker would— but hold. Let us present the matter in order.

Messrs. Merryheart and Dashope were men of the

law, and Mr. Robert Queeker was a man of their
office—in other words, a clerk—not a "confidential"
one, but a clerk, nevertheless, in whose simple-
minded integrity they had much confidence.   Bob,
as his fellow-clerks styled him, was sent on a secret
mission to Ramsgate.   The reader will observe how
fortunate it was that his mission was *secret*, because
it frees us from the necessity of setting down here
an elaborate and tedious explanation as to how,
when, and where the various threads of his mission
became interwoven with the fabric of our tale.   Suffice it to say that the only part of his mission with
which we are acquainted is that which had reference
to two men—one of whom was named Mr. Larks,
the other Morley Jones.

Now, it so happened that Queeker's acquaintance,
Mr. Durant, had an intimate friend who dwelt near
a beautiful village in Kent.   When Queeker mentioned the circumstance of the secret mission which
called him to Ramsgate, he discovered that the old
gentleman was on the point of starting for this village,
in company with his daughter and her cousin Fanny.

"You'll travel with us, I hope, Queeker; our
roads lie in the same direction, at least a part of the
way, you know," said the hearty little old gentleman, with good-nature beaming in every wrinkle,
from the crown of his bald head to the last fold of
his treble chin; "it will be such a comfort to have

you to help me take care of the girls. And if you can spare time to turn aside for a day or two, I promise you a hearty welcome from my friend—whose residence, named Jenkinsjoy, is an antique paradise, and his hospitality unbounded. He has splendid horses, too, and will give you a gallop over as fine a country as exists between this and the British Channel. You ride, of course?"

Queeker admitted that he could ride a little.

"At least," he added, after a pause, "I used frequently to get rides on a cart-horse when I was a very little boy."

So it was arranged that Queeker should travel with them. Moreover, he succeeded in obtaining from his employers permission to delay for three days the prosecution of the mission—which, although secret, was not immediately pressing—in order that he might visit Jenkinsjoy. It was fortunate that, when he went to ask this brief holiday, he found Mr. Merryheart in the office. Had it been his mischance to fall upon Dashope, he would have received a blunt refusal and prompt dismissal—so thoroughly were the joys of that gentleman identified with the woes of other people.

But, great though Queeker's delight undoubtedly was on this occasion, it was tempered by a soul-harassing care, which drew forth whole quires of poetical effusions to the moon and other celestial bodies.

This secret sorrow was caused by the dreadful and astonishing fact, that, do what he would to the contrary, the weather-cock of his affections was veering slowly but steadily away from Katie, and pointing more and more decidedly towards Fanny Hennings! It is but simple justice to the poor youth to state that he loathed and abhorred himself in consequence.

"There am I," he soliloquized, on the evening before the journey began, " a monster, a brute, a lower animal almost, who have sought with all my strength to gain—perchance *have* gained—the innocent, trusting heart of Katie Durant, and yet, without really meaning it, but, somehow, without being able to help it, I am—*not* falling in love; oh! no, perish the thought! but, but—falling into something strangely, mysteriously, incomprehensibly, similar to— Oh! base ingrate that I am, is there no way; no back-door by which—?"

Starting up, and seizing a pen, at this point of irrepressible inspiration, he wrote, reading aloud as he set down the burning thoughts,—

> " Oh for a postern in the rear,
>   Where wretched man might disappear ;
>   And never more should seek her !
>
>   Fly, fly to earth's extremest bounds,

(Bounds, mounds, lounds, founds, kounds, downds, rounds, pounds, zounds !—hounds— ha ! hounds— I have it)—

> " Fly, fly to earth's extremest bounds,
> With huntsmen, horses, horns, and hounds ;
> And die !—dejected Queeker.

" I wonder," thought Queeker, as he sat biting the end of his quill—his usual method of courting inspiration, " I wonder if there is anything prophetic in these lines ! Durant said that his friend has splendid horses. They may, perhaps, be hunters ! Ha ! my early ambition, perchance, youth's fond dream, may yet be realized ! But let me not hope. Hope always tells a false as well as flattering tale *to me*. She has ever been, in my experience " (he was bitter at this point) " an incorrigible li— ahem ! story-teller."

Striking his clenched fist heavily on the table, Queeker rose, put on his hat, and went round to Mr. Durant's merely to inquire whether he could be of any service—not that he could venture to offer assistance in the way of packing, but there *might* be something, such as roping trunks, or writing and affixing addresses, in regard to which he might perhaps render himself useful.

" Why, Miss Durant," he said, on entering, " you are *always* busy."

" Am I ?" said Katie, with a smile, as she rose and shook hands.

" Yes, I—I—assure you, Miss Durant," said Queeker, bowing to Fanny, on whose fat pretty face there was a scarlet flush, the result either of

o

the suddenness of Queeker's entry, or of the suppression of her inveterate desire to laugh, "I assure you that it quite rouses my admiration to observe the ease with which you can turn your hand to anything. You can write out accounts better than any fellow in our office. Then you play and sing with so much ease, and I often find you making clothes for poor people, with pounds of tea and sugar in your pockets, besides many other things, and now, here you are painting like—like—one of the old masters !"

This was quite an unusual burst on the part of Queeker, who felt as though he were making some amends for his unfaithfulness in thus recalling and emphatically asserting the unquestionably good qualities of his lady-love. He felt as if he were honestly attempting to win himself back to his allegiance.

"You are very complimentary," said Katie, with a glance at her cousin, which threw that young lady into silent convulsions.

"Not at all," cried Queeker, forcing his enthusiasm up to white heat, and seizing a drawing, which he held up before him, in the vain attempt to shut Fanny out of his sight.

"Now, I call this most beautiful," he said, in tones of genuine admiration. "I *never* saw anything so sweet before."

"Indeed!" said Katie, who observed that the youth was gazing over the top of the drawing at her cousin. "I am so glad you like it, for, to say truth, I have felt disappointed with it myself, and papa says it is only so-so. Do point out to me its faults, Mr. Queeker, and the parts you like best."

She rose and looked over Queeker's shoulder with much interest, and took hold of the drawing to keep it firmly in its position.

There was an excessively merry twinkle in Katie's eyes as she watched the expression of Queeker's face when he exclaimed—

"Faults, Miss Durant, there are no—eh! why, what—"

"Oh you wicked, deceptive man, you've got it upside down!" said Katie, shaking her finger at the unhappy youth, who stammered, tried to explain—to apologize—failed, broke down, and talked unutterable nonsense, to the infinite delight of his fair tormentor.

As for Fanny, that Hebe bent her head suddenly over her work-basket, and thrust her face into it as if searching with microscopic intensity for something that positively refused to be found. All that we can safely affirm in regard to her is, that if her face bore any resemblance to the scarlet of her neck, the fact that her workbox did not take fire is little short of a miracle!

Fortunately for all parties Queeker inadvertently trod on the cat's tail, which resulted in a spurt so violent as to justify a total change of subject. Before the storm thus raised had calmed down, Mr. Durant entered the room.

At Jenkinsjoy Queeker certainly did meet with a reception even more hearty than he had been led to expect. Mr. Durant's friend, Stoutheart, his amiable wife and daughters and strapping sons, received the youthful limb of the law with that frank hospitality which we are taught to attribute "to Merrie England in the olden time." The mansion was old-fashioned and low-roofed, trellis-worked and creeper-loved ; addicted to oak panelling, balustrades, and tapestried walls, and highly suitable to ghosts of a humorous and agreeable tendency. Indeed it was said that one of the rooms actually *was* haunted at that very time ; but Queeker did not see any ghosts, although he afterwards freely confessed to having seen all the rooms in the house more or less haunted by fairy spirits of the fair sex, and masculine ghosts in buck-skins and top-boots ! The whole air and aspect of the neighbourhood was such that Queeker half expected to find a May-pole in the neighbouring village, sweet shepherdesses in straw hats, pink ribbons, and short kirtles in the fields, and gentle shepherds with long crooks, playing antique flageo-lets on green banks, with innocent-looking dogs beside them, and humble-minded sheep reposing in Arcadian felicity at their feet.

" Where does the meet take place to-day, Tom ?" asked Mr. Stoutheart senior of Mr. Stoutheart junior, while seated at breakfast the first morning after their arrival at Jenkinsjoy.

" At Curmersfield," replied young Stoutheart.

" Ah, not a bad piece of country to cross. You remember when you and I went over it together, Amy ?"

" We have gone over it so often together, papa," replied Amy, " that I really don't know to which occasion you refer."

" Why, that time when we met the hounds unexpectedly ; when you were mounted on your favourite Wildfire, and appeared to have imbibed some of his spirit, for you went off at a tangent, crying out, " Come along, papa !" and cleared the hedge at the roadside, crossed Slapperton's farm, galloped up the lane leading to Curmersfield, took the ditch, with the low fence beyond at Cumitstrong's turnip-field, in a flying leap—obliging me to go quarter of a mile round by the gate—and overtook the hounds just as they broke away on a false scent in the direction of the Neckornothing ditch."

" Oh yes, I remember," replied Amy with a gentle smile ; "it was a charming gallop. I wished to continue it, but you thought the ground would be

too much for me, though I have gone over it twice
since then in perfect safety.   You are far too timid,
papa."

Queeker gazed and listened in open-mouthed
amazement, for the young girl who acknowledged
in an offhand way that she had performed such tremendous feats of horsemanship was modest, pretty,
unaffected, and feminine.

"I wonder," thought Queeker, "if Fan— ah, I
mean Katie—could do that sort of thing?"

He looked loyally at Katie, but thought, dis-
loyally, of her cousin, accused himself of base unfaithfulness, and, seizing a hot roll, began to eat
violently.

"Would you like to see the meet, Mr. Queeker?"
said Mr. Stoutheart senior; " I can give you a good
mount.   My own horse, Slapover, is neither so elegant nor so high-spirited as Wildfire,.but he can go
over anything, and is quite safe."

A sensitive spring had been touched in the bosom
of Queeker, which opened a floodgate that set loose
an astonishing and unprecedented flow of enthusiastic eloquence.

"I shall like it of all things," he cried, with sparkling eyes and heightened colour.   " It has been my
ambition ever since I was a little boy to mount a
thoroughbred and follow the hounds.   I assure you
the idea of ' crossing country,' as it is called, I be-

lieve, and taking hedges, ditches, five-barred gates and everything as we go, has a charm for me which is absolutely inexpressible—"

Queeker stopped abruptly, because he observed a slight flush on Fanny's cheeks and a pursed expression on Fanny's lips, and felt uncertain as to whether or not she was laughing at him internally.

"Well said, Queeker," cried Mr. Stoutheart enthusiastically; "it's a pity you are a town-bred man. Such spirit as yours can find vent only in the free air of the country!"

"Amy, dear," said Katie, with an extremely innocent look at her friend, "do huntsmen in this part of England usually take 'everything as they go?' I think Mr. Queeker used that expression."

"N—not exactly," replied Amy, with a smile and glance of uncertainty, as if she did not quite see the drift of the question.

"Ah! I thought not," returned Katie with much gravity. "I had always been under the impression that huntsmen were in the habit of going *round* stackyards, and houses, and such things—not *over* them."

Queeker was stabbed—stabbed to the heart! It availed not that the company laughed lightly at the joke, and that Mr. Stoutheart said that he (Queeker) should realize his young dream, and reiterated the assurance that his horse would carry him over *any-*

thing if he only held tightly on and let him go. He had been stabbed by Katie—the gentle Katie—the girl whom he had adored so long—ha ! there was comfort in the word *had ;* it belonged to the past ; it referred to things gone by ; it rhymed with sad, bad, mad ; it suggested a period of remote antiquity, and pointed to a hazy future. As the latter thought rushed through his heated brain, he turned his eyes on Fanny, with that bold look of dreadful determination that marks the traitor when, having fully made up his mind, he turns his back on his queen and flag for ever !   But poor Queeker found little comfort in the new prospect, for Fanny had been gently touched on the elbow by Katie when she committed her savage attack ; and when Queeker looked at the fair, fat cousin, she was involved in the agonies of a suppressed but tremendous giggle.

After breakfast two horses were brought to the door. Wildfire, a sleek, powerful roan of large size, was a fit steed for the stalwart Tom, who, in neatly-fitting costume and Hessian boots, got into the saddle like a man accustomed to it. The other horse, Slap-over, was a large, strong-boned, somewhat heavy steed, suitable for a man who weighed sixteen stone, and stood six feet in his socks.

" Now then, jump up, Queeker," said Mr. Stout-heart, holding the stirrup.

If Queeker had been ,advised to vault upon the ridge-pole of the house, he could not have looked more perplexed than he did as he stood looking up at the towering mass of horse-flesh, to the summit of which he was expected to climb. However, being extremely light, and Mr. Stoutheart senior very strong, he was got into the saddle somehow.

"Where *are* the stirrups?" said Queeker, with a perplexed air, trying to look over the side of his steed.

"Why, they've forgot to shorten 'em," said Mr. Stoutheart with a laugh, observing that the irons were dangling six inches below the rider's toes.

This was soon rectified. Queeker's glazed leather leggings—which were too large for him, and had a tendency to turn round—were put straight; the reins were gathered up, and the huntsman rode away.

"All you've to do is to hold on," shouted Mr. Stoutheart, as they rode through the gate. "He is usually a little skittish at the start, but quiet as a lamb afterwards."

Queeker made no reply. His mind was brooding on his wrongs and sorrows; for Katie had quietly whispered him to take care and not fall off, and Fanny had giggled again.

"I *must* cure him of his foolish fancy," thought Katie as she re-entered the house, "for Fanny's

sake, if for nothing else ; though I cannot conceive
what she can see to like in him. There is no
accounting for taste !"

"I can at all events *die ;*"—thought Queeker,
as he rode along, shaking the reins and pressing his
little legs against the horse as if with the savage
intention of squeezing the animal's ribs together.

"There *was* prophetic inspiration in the lines !—
yes," he continued, repeating them,—

> "Fly, fly, to earth's extremest bounds,
> With huntsmen, horses, horn, and hounds,
> And die—dejected Queeker !

I'll change that—it shall be rejected Queeker *now.*"

For some time Tom Stoutheart and Queeker rode
over "hill and dale "—that is to say, they traversed
four miles of beautiful undulating and diversified
country at a leisurely pace, having started in good
time.

"Your father," observed Queeker, as they rode
side by side down a green lane, "said, I think, when
we started, that this horse was apt to be skittish at
the start. Is he difficult to hold in ?"

"Oh no," replied Tom, with a reassuring smile.
" He is as quiet and manageable as any man could
wish. He does indeed bounce about a little when
we burst away at first, and is apt then to get the
bit in his teeth ; but you've only to keep a tight
rein and he 'll go all right. His only fault is a habit

of tossing his head, which is a little awkward until you get used to it."

"Yes, I have discovered that fault already," replied Queeker, as the horse gave a practical illustration of it by tossing his enormous head back until it reached to within an inch of the point of his rider's nose. "Twice he has just touched my forehead. Had I been bending a little forward I suppose he would have given me an unpleasant blow."

"Rather," said Stoutheart junior. "I knew one poor fellow who was struck in that way by his horse and knocked off insensible. I think he was killed, but don't feel quite sure as to that."

"He has no other faults, I hope?" asked Queeker.

"None. As for refusing his leaps—he refuses nothing. He carries my father over anything he chooses to run him at, so it's not likely that he'll stick with a light-weight."

This was so self-evident that Queeker felt a reply to be unnecessary; he rode on, therefore, in silence for a few minutes, comforting himself with the thought that, at all events, he could die !

"I don't intend," said Queeker, after a few minutes' consideration, "to attempt to leap everything. I think that would be foolhardy. I must tell you, Mr. Stoutheart, before we get to the place of meeting, that I can only ride a very little, and have never attempted to leap a fence of any kind.

Indeed I never bestrode a real hunter before.   I shall
therefore content myself with following the hounds as
far as it is safe to do so, and will then give it up."

Young Stoutheart was a little surprised at the
modest and prudent tone of this speech, but he
good-naturedly replied,—

" Very well, I 'll guide you through the gates and
gaps. You just follow me, and you shall be all right,
and when you 've had enough of it, let me know."

Queeker and his friend were first in the field, but
they had not been there many minutes when one
and another and another red-coat came cantering
over the country, and ere long a large cavalcade
assembled in front of a mansion, the lawn of which
formed the rendezvous.   There were men of all sorts
and sizes, on steeds of all kinds and shapes—little men
on big horses, and big men on little horses ; men who
looked like " bloated aristocrats" before the bloating
process had begun, and men in whom the bloating
process was pretty far advanced, but who had no
touch of aristocracy to soften it.   Men who looked
healthy and happy, others who looked reckless and
depraved.   Some wore red-coats, cords, and tops—
others, to the surprise and no small comfort of
Queeker, who fancied that *all* huntsmen wore red
coats, were habited in modest tweeds of brown and
grey.   Many of the horses were sleek, glossy, and
fine-limbed, like racers; others were strong-boned and

rough. Some few were of gigantic size and rugged aspect, to suit the massive men who bestrode them. One of these in particular, a hearty, jovial farmer— and a relative of Tom's—appeared to the admiring Queeker to be big and powerful enough to have charged a whole troop of light dragoons single-handed with some hope of a successful issue. Ladies were there to witness the start, and two of the fair sex appeared ready to join the hunt and follow the hounds, while here and there little boys might be seen bent on trying their metal on the backs of Shetland ponies.

It was a stirring scene of meeting, and chatting, and laughing, and rearing, and curvetting, and fresh air, and sunshine.

Presently the master of the hounds came up with the pack at his heels. A footman of the mansion supplied all who desired it with a tumbler of beer.

"Have some beer?" said young Stoutheart, pointing to the footman referred to.

"No, thank you," said Queeker. "Will you?"

"No. I have quite enough of spirit within me. Don't require artificial stimulant," said the youth with a laugh. "Come now—we're off."

Queeker's heart gave a bound as he observed the master of the hounds ride off at a brisk pace followed by the whole field.

"I won't die yet. It's too soon," he thought, as he shook the reins and chirped to his steed.

Slapover did not require chirping. He shook his head, executed a mild pirouette on his left hind leg, and made a plunge which threatened first to leave his rider behind, and then to shoot him over his head. Queeker had been taken unawares, but he pressed his knees together, knitted his brows, and resolved not to be so taken again.

Whew! what a rush there was as the two or three hundred excited steeds and enthusiastic riders crossed the lawn, galloped through an open gate, and made towards a piece of rough ground covered with low bushes and bracken, through which the hounds were seen actively running as if in search of something. The bodies of the hounds were almost hidden, and Queeker, whose chief attention was devoted to his horse, had only time to receive the vague impression, as he galloped up, that the place was alive with white and pointed tails.

That first rush scattered Queeker's depression to the winds. What cared he for love, either successful or unrequited, now? Katie was forgotten. Fanny was to him little better than a mere abstraction. He was on a hunter! He was following the hounds! He had heard, or imagined he had heard, something like a horn. He was surprised a little that no one cried out "Tally-ho!" and in the wild excitement of his feelings thought of venturing on it himself, but the necessity of holding in Slapover with all the power of his arms, fortunately induced him to restrain his ardour.

. Soon after he heard a shout of some sort, which he tried to believe was " Tally-ho !" and the scattered huntsmen, who had been galloping about in all directions, converged into a stream. Following, he knew not and cared not what or whom, he swept round the margin of a little pond, and dashed over a neighbouring field.

From that point Queeker's recollection of events became a train of general confusion, with lucid points at intervals, where incidents of unusual interest or force arrested his attention.

The first of these lucid points was when, at the end of a heavy burst over a ploughed field, he came to what may be styled his first leap. His hat by that time had threatened so frequently to come off, that he had thrust it desperately down on his head, until the rim behind rested on the back of his neck. Trotting through a gap in a hedge into a road, young Stoutheart sought about for a place by which they might clamber up into the next field without going round by the gate towards which most of the field had headed.

" D! you think you could manage that ?" said Tom, pointing with the handle of his whip to a gap in the hedge, where there was a mound and a hollow with a *chevaux-de-frise* of cut stumps around, and a mass of thorn branches sufficiently thin to be broken through.

Queeker never looked at it, but gazing steadily in the face of his friend, said,—

" I 'll follow ! "

Stoutheart at once pushed his horse at it. It could not be called a leap. It was a mere scramble, done at the slowest possible pace. Wildfire gave one or two little bounds, and appeared to walk up perpendicularly on his hind legs, while Tom looked as if he were plastered against him with some adhesive substance ; then he appeared to drop perpendicularly down on the other side, his tail alone being visible.

" All right, come along," shouted Tom.

Queeker rode up to the gap, shut his eyes, gave a chirp, and committed himself to fate and Slapover. He felt a succession of shocks, and then a pause. Venturing to open his eyes, he saw young Stoutheart, still on the other side of the fence, laughing at him.

" You shouldn't hold so tight by the reins," he cried ; " you 've pulled him back into the road. Try it again."

Queeker once more shut his eyes, slacked the reins, and, seizing the pommel of the saddle, gave another chirp. Again there was a shock, which appeared to drive his body up against his head ; another which seemed to have all but snapped him off at the waist; then a sensation about his hat, as if a few wild-cats were attempting to tear it off, followed by a drop and a plunge, which threw him forward on his charger's neck.

"Dear me!" he exclaimed, panting, as he opened his eyes, "I had no idea the shock would have been so—so—shocking!"

Tom laughed; cried "Well done!" and galloped on. Queeker followed, his cheeks on fire, and per-spiration streaming from his brow.

"Now, then, here is an easy fence," cried Stout-heart, looking back and pointing to a part of the field where most of the huntsmen were popping over a low hedge, "will you try it?"

Queeker's spirit was fairly up.

"I'll try it!" he said, sternly.

"Come on then."

Stoutheart led the way gallantly, at full speed, and went over like an india-rubber ball. Queeker brought the handle of his riding-whip whack down on the flank of his astonished horse, and flew at the fence. Slapover took it with a magnificent bound. Queeker was all but left behind! He tottered, as it were, in the saddle; rose entirely out of it; came down with a crash that almost sent him over the horse's head, and gave him the probable sensations of a telescope on being forcibly shut up; but he held.

on bravely, and galloped up alongside of his companion, with a tendency to cheer despite his increased surprise at the extreme violence of the shocks to which his unaccustomed frame was being exposed.

After this our enthusiastic Nimrod went at everything, and feared nothing! Well was it for him that'he had arranged to follow Tom Stoutheart, else assuredly he would have run Slapover at fences which would have taxed the temerity even of that quadruped, and insured his destruction. Tom, seeing his condition, considerately kept him out of danger, and yet, being thoroughly acquainted with the country, managed to keep him well up with the hounds.

Towards the afternoon Queeker's fire began to abate. His aspect had become dishevelled. His hat had got so severely thrust down on his head, that the brim in front reposed on the bridge of his nose, as did the brim behind on the nape of his neck. His trousers were collected in folds chiefly about his knees, and the glazed leggings had turned completely round, presenting the calves to the front. But these were matters of small moment compared with the desperate desire he had to bring his legs together, if even for a moment of time! Sensations in various parts of his frame, which in the earlier part of the day had merely served to remind him that he was mortal, had now culminated into unquestionable aches and pains, and his desire to get off the back of Slapover became so intense, that he would certainly have given way to it had he not felt that in the event of his doing so there would be no possibility of his getting on again!

" Where are they all away to?" he asked in surprise, as the whole field went suddenly off helterskelter in a new direction.

" I think they've seen the fox," replied Stoutheart.

" Seen the fox! why, I forgot all about the fox! But—but haven't we seen it before? haven't we been after it *all day?*"

" No, we 've only got scent of it once or twice."

" Well, well," exclaimed Queeker, turning up his eyes, " I declare we have had as good fun as if we had been after the fox in full sight all the time!"

" Here is a somewhat peculiar leap," said Stoutheart, reining up as they approached a fence, on the other side of which was a high-road, " I 'll go first, to show you the way."

The peculiarity of the leap lay in the fact that it was a drop of about four feet into the road, which was lower, to that extent, than the field, and that the side of the road into which the riders had to drop was covered with scrubby bushes. To men accustomed to it this was a trifle. Most of the field had already taken it, though a few cautious riders had gone round by a gate.

When Queeker came to try it he felt uneasy—
sitting as he did so high, and looking down such a
precipice as it seemed to him.   However, he shut
his eyes, and courageously gave the accustomed
chirp, and Slapover·plunged down.   Queeker held
tight to the saddle, and although much shaken,
would have come out of the ordeal all right, had not
Slapover taken it into his head to make a second
spring over a low bush which stood in front of him.
On the other side of this bush there was an old
pump.   Queeker lost his balance, threw out his
arms, fell off, was hurled violently against the old
pump, and his right leg was broken !

A cart was quickly procured, and on trusses of
straw the poor huntsman was driven, sadly and
slowly, back to Jenkinsjoy, where he was tenderly
put to bed and carefully nursed for several weeks
by his hospitable and sympathizing friends.

Queeker bore his misfortune like a Stoic, chiefly
because it developed the great fact that Fanny
Hennings wept a whole night and a day after its
occurrence, insomuch that her fair face became so
swollen as to have lost much of its identity and all
its beauty—a fact which filled Queeker with hopes
so high that his recovery was greatly hastened by
the contented, almost joyous, manner in which he
submitted to his fate.

Of course Queeker's secret mission was, for the

time being, at an end ;—and thus it came to pass that an old pump, as we said at the beginning of this chapter, was the cause of the failure of several deep-laid plans, and of much bodily anguish and mental felicity to the youthful Nimrod.

Queeker's last observation before falling into a feverish slumber on the first night after his accident, was to the effect that fox-hunting was splendid sport —magnificent sport,—but that it appeared to him there was no occasion whatever for a fox. And ever after that he was wont to boast that his first and last day of fox-hunting, which was an unusually exciting one, had been got through charmingly without any fox at all. · It is even said that Queeker, descending from poetry,—his proper sphere,—to prose, wrote an elaborate and interesting paper on that subject, which was refused by all the sporting papers and journals to which he sent it ;—but, this not being certified, we do not record it, as a fact.

CHAPTER XIV.

WE turn now to a very different scene—the pier and harbour of Ramsgate. The storm-fiend is abroad. Thick clouds of a dark leaden hue drive athwart a sky of dingy grey, ever varying their edges, and rolling out limbs and branches in random fashion, as if they were fleeing before the wind in abject terror. The wind, however, is chiefly in the sky as yet. Down below there are only fitful puffs now and then, telling of something else in store. The sea is black, with sufficient swell on it to cause a few crested waves here and there to gleam intensely white by contrast. · It is early in the day, nevertheless there is a peculiar darkness in the atmosphere which suggests the approach of night. Numerous vessels in the offing are making with all speed for Ramsgate harbour, which is truly and deservedly named a " harbour of refuge," for already some two dozen ships of considerable size, and a large

fleet of small craft, have sought and found shelter
on a coast which in certain conditions of the wind
is fraught with danger. About the stores near the
piers, Trinity men are busy with buoys, anchors,
and cables ; elsewhere labourers are toiling, idlers
are loafing, and lifeboat-men are lounging about,
leaning on the parapets, looking wistfully out to sea,
with and without telescopes, from the sheer force of
habit, and commenting on the weather.   The broad,
bronzed, storm-battered coxswain of the celebrated
Ramsgate lifeboat, who seems to possess the power
of feeding and growing strong on hardship and exposure, is walking about at the end of the east pier,
contemplating the horizon in the direction of the
Goodwin Sands with the serious air of a man who
expects ere long to be called into action.

The harbour-master—who is, and certainly had
need be, a man of brain as well as muscle and energy,
to keep the conflicting elements around him in order
—moves about actively, making preparation for the
expected gale.

Early on the morning of the day referred to, Nora
Jones threaded her way among the stalls of the
marketplace under the town-hall, as if she were in
search of some one.   Not succeeding in her search,
she walked briskly along one of the main thorough-
fares of the town, and diverged into a narrow street,
which appeared to have retired modestly into a

corner in order to escape observation. At the farther
end of this little street, she knocked at the door of a
house, the cleanly appearance of which attested the
fact that its owner was well-doing and orderly.

Nora knocked gently; she did everything gently !

"Is Mrs. Moy at home?" she asked, as a very
bright little girl's head appeared.

No sooner was Nora's voice heard than the door
was flung wide open, and the little girl exclaimed,
" Yes, she 's at 'ome, and daddy too." She followed
up this assurance with a laugh of glee, and, seizing
the visitor's hand, dragged her into the house by
main force.

" Hallo, Nora, 'ow are 'ee, gal?" cried a deep bass
voice from the neighbourhood of the floor, where its
owner appeared to be smothered with children, for
he was not to be seen.

Nora looked down and beheld the legs and boots
of a big man, but his body and head were invisible,
being completely covered and held down by four
daughters and five sons, one of the former being a
baby, and one of the latter an infant.

Dick Moy, who was enjoying his month on shore,
rose as a man might rise from a long dive, flung
out his great right arm, scattered the children like
flecks of foam, and sat up with a beaming countenance, holding the infant tenderly in his left arm.
The baby had been cast under the table, where it

DICK MOY AT HOME.—Page 232.

lay, helpless apparently, and howling. It had passed the most tender period of life, and had entered on that stage when knocks, cuts, yells, and bruises are the order of the day.

" Glad to see you, Nora," said the man of the floating light, extending his huge hand, which the girl grasped and shook warmly. " You 'll excuse me not bein' more purlite. I 'm oppressed with child'n, as you see. It seems to me as if I 'd gone an' got spliced to that there 'ooman in the story-book wot lived in the shoe, an' had so many child'n she didn't know wot to do. If so, she knows wot to do now. She 's only got to hand 'em over to poor Dick Moy, an' leave him to suffer the consickences.—Ah, 'ere she comes."

Dick rose as he spoke, and handed a chair to Nora at the moment that his better, but lesser, half entered.

It must not be supposed that Dick said all this without interruption. On the contrary, he bawled it out in the voice of a bo'sn's mate, while the four daughters and five sons, including the baby and the infant, crawled up his legs and clung to his pockets, and enacted Babel on a small scale.

Mrs. Moy was a very pretty, tidy, cheerful little woman, of the fat, fair, and forty description, save that she was nearer thirty-five than forty. It was clear at a glance that she and Dick had been made

for each other, and that, had either married anybody
else, each would have done irreparable damage to
the other.

"Sit down, Nora. I'm so glad to see you. Come
to breakfast, I hope? we're just going to have it."

Mrs. Moy said this as if she really meant it, and
would be terribly disappointed if she met with a
refusal. Nora tried to speak, but Babel was too
much for her.

"Silence!" burst from Dick, as if a small cannon
had gone off in the room.

Babel was hushed.

"Mum's the word for *three minutes*," said Dick,
pointing to a huge Yankee clock which stood on the
chimney-piece, with a model frigate in a glass case,
and a painted sea and sky on one side of it, and a
model light-vessel in a glass case, and a painted sea
and sky on the other.

There was profound wisdom in this arrangement.
If Dick had ordered silence for an indefinite space
of time, there would have been discontent, approxi-
mating to despair, in Babel's bosom, and, therefore,
strong temptation to rebellion. But three minutes
embraced a fixed and known period of time. The
result was a desperate effort at restraint, mingled
with gleeful anticipation. The elder children who
could read the clock stared eagerly at the Yankee
time-piece; the younger ones who couldn't read the

clock, but who knew that the others could, stared
intently at their seniors, and awaited the signal.
With the exception of hard breathing, the silence
was complete; the baby being spell-bound by
example, and the feeble remarks of the infant—
which had been transferred to the arms of the eldest
girl—making no impression worth speaking of.

"You are very kind," said Nora, "I'll stay
breakfast with pleasure. Grandmother won't be up
for an hour yet, and father's not at home just
now."

"Werry good," said Dick, taking a short black
pipe out of his coat-pocket, "that's all right. And
.'ow do 'ee like Ramsgate, Nora, now you've had a
fair trial of it?"

"I think I like it better than Yarmouth; but
perhaps that is because we live in a more airy and
cheerful street. I would not have troubled you so
early, Mr. Moy—("'T ain't no trouble at all, Nora;
werry much the reverse")—but that I am anxious
to hear how you got on with poor Billy—"

At this point Babel burst forth with redoubled
fury. Dick was attacked and carried by storm; the
short black pipe was seized, and an old hat was
clapped on his head and thrust down over his eyes!
He gave in at once, and submitted with resignation.
He struck his colours, so to speak, without firing a
shot, and for full five minutes breasted the billows

of a sea of children manfully, while smart Mrs. Moy
spread the breakfast-table as quietly as if nothing
were going on, and Nora sat and smiled at them.

Suddenly Dick rose for the second time from his
dive, flung off the foam, tossed aside the baby,
rescued the infant from impending destruction, and
thundered " Silence! mum's the word for three
minutes more."

" That's six, daddy!" cried the eldest boy, whose
spirit of opposition was growing so strong that he
could not help indulging it, even against his own
interests.

" No," said Dick sternly.

" It was three minutes last time," urged the boy;
"an' you said three minutes *more* this time; three
minutes more than three minutes is six minutes,
ain't it?"

" Three minutes," repeated Dick, holding up a
warning finger.

Babel ceased; the nine pair of eyes (excepting
those of the infant) became fixed, and Nora proceeded—

" I wanted to hear how you got on with Billy.
Did they take him in at once? and what sort of
place is the Grotto? You see I am naturally anxious
to know, because it was a terrible thing to send a
poor boy away from his only friend among strangers
at such an age, and just after recovering from a bad

illness; but you know I could not do otherwise. It would have been his ruin to have—"

She paused.

"To have stopped where he was, I s'pose you would say?" observed Dick. "Well, I ain't sure o' that, Nora. It's quite true that the bad company he'd 'ave seen would 'ave bin against 'im; but to 'ave you for his guardian hangel might 'ave counteracted that. It would 'ave bin like the soda to the hacid, a fizz at first and all square arterwards. Hows'ever, that don't signify now, cos he's all right. I tuk him to the Grotto, the werry first thing arter I'd bin to the Trinity 'ouse, and seed him cast anchor there all right, and—"

Again Babel burst forth, and riot reigned supreme for five minutes more. At the end of that time silence was proclaimed as before.

"Now then," said Dick, "breakfast bein' ready, place the chairs."

The three elder children obeyed this order. Each member of this peculiar household had been "told off," as Dick expressed it, to a special duty, which was performed with all the precision of discipline characteristic of a man-of-war.

"That's all right; now go in and win," said Dick.

There was no occasion to appeal to the Yankee clock now. Tongues and throats as well as teeth and jaws were too fully occupied. Babel succumbed

for full quarter of an hour, during which period Dick
Moy related to Nora the circumstances connected
with a recent visit to London, whither he had been
summoned as a witness in a criminal trial, and to
which, at Nora's earnest entreaty, and with the boy's
unwilling consent, he had conveyed Billy Towler.
We say unwilling, because Billy, during his long
period of convalescence, had been so won by the
kindness of Nora, that the last thing in the world he
would have consented to bear was separation from
her; but, on thinking over it, he was met by this
insurmountable difficulty—that the last thing in the
world he would consent to do was to disobey her!
Between these two influences he went unwillingly
to London—for the sake of his education, as Nora
said to him—for the sake of being freed from the
evil influence of her father's example, as poor Nora
was compelled to admit to herself.

"The Grotto," said Dick, speaking as well as he
could through an immense mouthful of bacon and
bread, "is an institootion which I 'ave reason for to
believe desarves well of its country. It is an institootion sitooate in Paddington Street, Marylebone,
where homeless child'n, as would otherwise come to
the gallows, is took in an' saved—saved not only from
sin an' misery themselves, but saved from inflictin'
the same on society. I do assure *you*," said Dick,
striking the table with his fist in his enthusiasm,

so that the crockery jumped, and some of the children almost choked by reason of their food going down what they styled their " wrong throats"—" I do assure *you*, that it would 'ave done yer 'art good to 'ave seed 'm, as I did the day I went there, so clean and comf'r'able and 'appy—no mistake about that. Their 'appiness was genoo*ine*. Wot made it come 'ome to me was, that I seed there a little boy as I 'appened to know was one o' the dirtiest, wickedest, sharpest little willains in London —a mere spider to look at, but with mischief enough to fill a six-fut man to bu'stin'—an' there 'ee was, clean an' jolly, larnin' his lessons like a good un— an' no sham neither, cos 'e 'd got a good spice o' the mischief left, as was pretty clear from the way 'ee gave a sly pinch or pull o' the hair now an' again to the boys next him, an' drawed monkey-faces on his slate. But that spider, I wos told, could do figurin' like one o'clock, an' could spell like Johnson's Dictionairy.

"Well," continued Dick, after a few moments' devotion to a bowl of coffee, "I 'anded Billy Towler over to the superintendent, tellin' 'im 'ee wos a 'omeless boy as 'adn't got no parients nor relations, an' wos werry much in need o' bein' looked arter. So 'ee took 'im in, an' I bade him good-bye."

Dick Moy then went on to tell how that the superintendent of the Grotto showed him all over

the place, and told him numerous anecdotes regarding the boys who had been trained there ; that one
had gone into the army and become a sergeant, and
had written many long interesting letters to the institution, which he still loved as being his early and
only "home;" that another had become an artillery-
man ; another a man-of-war's man ; and another a
city missionary, who commended the blessed gospel
of Jesus Christ to those very outcasts from among
whom he had himself been plucked.   The superintendent also explained to his rugged but much interested and intelligent visitor that they had a flourishing
Ragged School in connection with the institution ;
also a Sunday-school and a "Band of Hope"—
which latter had been thought particularly necessary, because they found that many of the neglected
young creatures that came to them had already been
tempted and taught by their parents and by publicans to drink, so that the foundation of that dreadful craving disease had been laid, and those desires
had begun to grow which, if not checked, would
certainly end in swift and awful destruction.   One
blessed result of this was that the children had not
only themselves joined, but had in some instances
induced their drunken parents to attend the weekly
addresses.

All this, and a great deal more, was related by
Dick Moy with the wonted enthusiasm and energy

of his big nature, and with much gesticulation of his tremendous fist—to the evident anxiety of Nora, who, like an economical housewife as she was, had a feeling of tenderness for the crockery, even although it was not her own. Dick wound up by saying that if *he* was a rich man, "'ee'd give some of 'is super- floous cash to that there Grotto, he would."

"Perhaps you wouldn't," said Nora. "I've heard one rich man say that the applications made to him for money were so numerous that he was quite annoyed, and felt as if he was goin' to become bankrupt!"

"Nora," said Dick, smiting the table emphatically, "I'm not a rich man myself, an' wot's more, I never 'xpect to be, so I can't be said to 'ave no personal notions at all, d'ye see, about wot they feels; but I've also heerd a rich man give 'is opinion on that pint, and I've no manner of doubt that *my* rich man is as good as your'n—better for the matter of that; anyway he knowed wot was wot. Well, says 'ee to me, w'en I went an' begged parding for axin' 'im for a subscription to this 'ere werry Grotto —which, by the way, is supported by woluntary con- tribootions—'ee says, 'Dick Moy,' says 'ee, 'you've no occasion for to ax my parding,' says 'ee. ''Ere's 'ow it is. I've got *so* much cash to spare out of my hincome. Werry good; I goes an' writes down a list of all the charities. First of all comes the church

—which ain't a charity, by the way, but a debt owin' to the Lord—an' the missionary societies, an' the Lifeboat Institootion, an' the Shipwrecked Marriners' Society, and such like, which are the great *National* institootions of the country that *every* Christian ought to give a helpin' 'and to. Then there's the poor among one's own relations and friends; then the hospitals an' various charities o' the city or town in which one dwells, and the poor of the same. Well, arter that's all down,' says 'ee, 'I consider w'ich o' them ere desarves an' *needs* most support from me; an' so I claps down somethin' to each, an' adds it all up, an' wot is left over I holds ready for chance applicants. If their causes are good I give to 'em heartily; if not, I bow 'em politely out o' the 'ouse. That's w'ere it is,' says 'ee. 'An' do you know, Dick Moy,' says 'ee, 'the first time I tried that plan, and put down wot I thought a fair liberal sum to each, I wos amazed—I wos stunned for to find that the total wos so small and left so werry much of my spare cash yet to be disposed of, so I went over it all again, and had to double and treble the amount to be given to each. Ah, Dick,' says *my* rich man, 'if people who don't keep cash-books would only mark down wot they *think* they can afford to give away in a year, an' wot they *do* give away, they would be surprised. It's not always unwillingness to give that's the evil. Often it's ignorance o' what is actooally given—no account bein' kep'.'

"' Wot d'ye think, Dick,' *my* rich man goes on to say, ' there are some churches in this country which are dependent on the people for support, an' the contents o' the plates at the doors o' these churches on Sundays is used partly for cleanin' and lightin' of 'em ; partly for payin' their precentors, and partly for repairs to the buildins, and partly for helpin' out the small incomes of their ministers; an' wot d'ye think most c' the people—not many but *most* of 'cm—gives a week, Dick, for such important purposes ?'

"' I don' know, sir,' says I.

"' One penny, Dick,' says 'ee, ' which comes exactly to four shillins and fourpence a year,' says 'ee. ' An' they ain't paupers, Dick ! If they wos paupers, it wouldn't be a big sum for 'em to give out o' any pocket-money they might chance to git from their pauper friends, but they 're well-dressed people, Dick, and they seems to be well off ! Four an' fourpence a year ! think o' that—not to mention the deduction w'en they goes for a month or two to the country each summer. Four an' fourpence a year, Dick ! Some of 'em even goes so low as a halfpenny, which makes two an' twopence a year—£7, 11s. 8d. in a seventy-year *lifetime*, Dick, supposin' their liberality began to flow the day they wos born !'

"At this *my* rich man fell to laughing till I thought 'ee 'd a busted hisself; but he pulled up sudden, an' axed me all about the Grotto, and said it was a first-rate institootion, an' gave me a ten-pun' note on the spot. Now, Nora, *my* rich man is a friend o' yours—Mr. Durant, of Yarmouth, who came to Ramsgate a short time ago for to spend the autumn, an' I got introdooced to him through knowin' Jim Welton, who got aboord of one of his ships through knowin' young Mr. Stanley Hall, d' ye see ? That 's where it is."

After this somewhat lengthened speech, Dick Moy swallowed a slop-bowlful of coffee at a draught—he always used a slop-bowl—and applied himself with renewed zest to a Norfolk dumpling, in the making of which delicacy his wife had no equal.

"I believe that Mr. Durant is a kind good man," said Nora, feeding the infant with a crust dipped in milk, "and I am quite sure that he has got the sweetest daughter that ever a man was blessed with —Miss Katie ; you know her, I suppose ?"

"'Aven't seed 'er yet," was Dick's curt reply.

"She 's a dear creature," continued Nora—still doing her best to choke the infant—"she found out where I lived while she was in search of a sick boy in Yarmouth, who, she said, was the brother of a poor ragged boy named Billy Towler, she had once met with. Of course I had to tell her that Billy had been deceiving her and had no brother. Oh! you should have seen her kind face, Dick, when I told her this. I do think that up to that time she had lived under the belief that a young boy with a good-looking face and an honest look could not be a deceiver."

"Poor thing," said Dick, with a sad shake of the head, as if pitying her ignorance.

"Yes," continued Nora—still attempting to choke the infant—"she could not say a word at that time, but went away with her eyes full of tears. I saw her often afterwards, and tried to convince her there might be some good in Billy after all, but she was not easily encouraged, for her belief in appearances had got a shake that she seemed to find it difficult to get over. That was when Billy was lying ill in hospital. I have not seen much of her since then, she and her father having been away in London."

"H'm, I'm raither inclined to jine her in thinkin' that no good 'll come o' that young scamp. He's too sharp by half," said Dick with a frown. "Depend upon it, Nora, w'en a boy 'as gone a great length in wickedness there's no chance o' reclaimin' him."

"Dick," exclaimed Nora, with sudden energy, "depend upon it that *that's* not true, for it does not correspond with the Bible, which says that our

Lord came not to call the righteous but *sinners* to repentance."

"There's truth in *that*, anyhow," replied Dick, gazing thoughtfully into Nora's countenance, as if the truth had come home to him for the first time. What his further observations on the point might have been we know not, as at that moment the door opened and one of his mates entered, saying that he had come to go down with him to the buoy-store, as the superintendent had given orders that he and Moy should overhaul the old North Goodwin buoy, and give her a fresh coat of paint. Dick therefore rose, wiped his mouth, kissed the entire family, beginning with the infant and ending with "the missis," after which he shook hands with Nora and went out.

The storm which had for some time past been brewing, had fairly brewed itself up at last, and the wild sea was covered with foam. Although only an early autumn storm, it was, like many a thing out of season, not the less violent on that account. It was one of the few autumn storms that might have been transferred to winter with perfect propriety. It performed its work of devastation as effectively as though it had come forth at its proper season. On land chimney stacks and trees were levelled. At sea vessels great and small were dismasted and destroyed, and the east coast of the kingdom was strewn with wreckage and dead bodies. Full many a noble ship went down that night! Wealth that might have supported all the charities in London for a twelvemonth was sent to the bottom of the sea that night and lost for ever. Lives that had scarce begun and lives that were all but done, were cut abruptly short, leaving broken hearts and darkened lives in many a home, not only on the sea-caast but inland, where the sound of the great sea's roar is never heard. Deeds of daring were done that night, —by men of the lifeboat service and the coast-guard, —which seemed almost beyond the might of human skill and courage—resulting in lives saved from that same great sea—lives young and lives old—the salvation of which caused many a heart in the land, from that night forward, to bless God and sing for joy.

But of all the wide-spread and far-reaching turmoil; the wreck and rescue, the rending and relieving of hearts, the desperate daring, and dread disasters of that night we shall say nothing at all, save in regard to that which occurred on and in the neighbourhood of the Goodwin Sands.

CHAPTER XV.

A NIGHT OF WRECK AND DISASTER—THE GULL "COMES TO GRIEF."

WHEN the storm began to brew that night, George Welton, the mate of the floating light, walked the deck of his boiled-lobster-like vessel, and examined the sky and sea with that critical expression peculiar to seafaring men, which conveys to landsmen the reassuring impression that they know exactly what is coming, precisely what ought to be done, and certainly what will be the result of whatever happens !

After some minutes spent in profound meditation, during which Mr. Welton frowned inquiringly at the dark driving clouds above him, he said, "It'll be pretty stiff."

This remark was made to himself, or to the clouds, but, happening to be overheard by Jerry MacGowl, who was at his elbow, it was answered by that excellent man.

"True for ye ; it 'll blow great guns before midnight. The sands is showin' their teeth already."

The latter part of this remark had reference to brilliant white lines and dots on the seaward horizon, which indicated breakers on the Goodwin sands.

"Luk at that now," said Jerry, pointing to one of those huge clumsy vessels that are so frequently met with at sea, even in the present day, as to lead one to imagine that some of the shipbuilders in the time of Noah must have come alive again and gone to work at their old trade on the old plans and drawings. "Luk at that, now. Did iver ye see sitch a tub—straight up and down the side, and as big at the bow as the stern."

"She's not clipper built," answered the mate ; "they make that sort o' ship by the mile and sell her by the fathom,—cuttin' off from the piece just what is required. It don't take long to plaster up the ends and stick a mast or two into 'em."

"It 's in luck she is to git into the Downs before the gale breaks, and it 's to be hoped she has good ground-tackle," said Jerry.

The mate hoped so too in a careless way, and, remarking that he would go and see that all was made snug, went forward.

At that moment there came up the fore-hatch a yell, as if from the throat of a North American savage. It terminated in the couplet, tunefully sung—

> " Oh my ! oh my !
> O mammy, don't you let the baby cry !"

Jack Shales, following his voice, immediately after came on deck.

" Have 'ee got that work-box done ?" asked Jerry as his mate joined him.

" Not quite done yet, boy, but I'll get it finished after the lights are up. Duty first, pleasure afterwards, you know."

" Come now, Jack, confess that you're makin' it for a pretty girl."

" Well, so I am, but it ain't for my own pretty girl. It's for that sweet little Nora Jones, who came lately to live in Ramsgate. You see I know she's goin' to be spliced to Jim Welton, and as Jim is a good sort of fellow, I want to make this little gift to his future bride."

The gift referred to was a well-made work-box, such as the men of the floating light were at that time, and doubtless still are, in the habit of constructing in leisure hours. It was beautifully inlaid with wood of various kinds and colours, and possessed a mark peculiarly characteristic of floating-light boxes and desks, namely, two flags inlaid on the lid—one of these being the Union Jack. Most of the men on board displayed much skill and taste in the making of those boxes and desks, although they were all self-taught, and wrought with very simple tools in a not very commodious workshop.

"A great change from yesterday in the look o' things, Jerry," observed Shales, surveying the Downs, where, despite the stiff and ever increasing breeze amounting almost to a gale, numerous little pilot-boats were seen dancing on the waves, showing a mere shred of canvas, and looking out for a job. "Yesterday was all sunshine and calm, with pleasure-boats round us, and visitors heaving noospapers aboard. To-day it's all gloom, with gales brewin' and pilots bobbin' about like Mother Cary's chickens."

"That's true, Jack," replied Jerry, whose poetic soul was fired by the thought :—

> "'Timpest an' turmoil to-day,
>   With lots o' salt-wather an' sorrow.
> Blue little waves on the say,
>   An' sunny contintment to-morrow.'

That's how it is, Jack, me boy, all the world over—even in owld Ireland hersilf; an' sure if there's pace to be found on earth it's there it's to be dis-kivered."

"Right, Jerry, peace is *to be* discovered there, but I'm afraid it's in a very distant future as yet," said Jack with a laugh.

"All in good time," retorted Jerry.

"Up lights!" called the mate down the hatch-way.

"Ay, ay, sir," came in chorus from below.

Desks and boxes were thrust aside, the winch was manned, and the weighty lantern mounted slowly to its nocturnal watch-tower.

Its red eye flashed upon a dark scene. The gloom of approaching night was deepened by the inky clouds that obscured the sky. Thick fog banks came sweeping past at intervals; a cold north-easterly gale conveyed a wintry feeling to the air. Small thick rain fell in abundance, and everything attested the appropriateness of Jerry MacGowl's observation, that it was "dirty weather intirely."

The floating light was made snug—in other words, prepared for action—by having a good many more fathoms of her chain veered out, in order that she might strain less and swing more freely. Loose articles were secured or stowed away. Hatches were battened down, and many other little nautical arrangements made which it would require a seaman to understand as well as to describe in detail.

As the evening advanced the gale increased in violence tenfold, and darkness settled down like an impenetrable pall over land and sea. The roar of breakers on the Goodwin Sands became so loud that it was sometimes heard on board the Gull-light above the howling of the tempest. The sea rose

so much and ran so violently among the conflicting
currents caused by wind, tide, and sand-banks,
that the Gull plunged, swooped, and tore at her
cable so that the holding of it might have appeared
to a landsman little short of miraculous. Hissing
and seething at the opposition she offered, the larger
waves burst over her bows, and swept the deck
from stem to stern; but her ample scuppers dis-
charged it quickly, and up she rose again, dripping
from the flood, to face and fight and foil each succeeding billow.

High on the mast, swaying wildly to and fro, yet
always hanging perpendicular by reason of a simple
mechanism, the lantern threw out its bright beams,
involving the vessel and the foam-clad boiling sea
in a circle of light which ended in darkness profound, forming, as it were, a bright but ghostly
chamber shut in with walls of ebony, and revealing,
in all its appalling reality, the fury of the sea.
What horrors lay concealed in the darkness beyond
no one could certainly know; but the watch on
board the Gull could form from past experience a
pretty good conception of them, as they cowered
under the lee of the bulwarks and looked anxiously
out to windward.

Anxiously! Ay, there was cause for anxiety
that night. The risk of parting from their cable was
something, though not very great; but the risk of

being run down by passing or driving ships during intervals of fog was much greater, and the necessity of looking out for signals of distress was urgent.

It was a night of warfare, and the battle had begun early. Mr. Welton's record of the earlier part of that day in the log ran thus :—

"At 4 A.M. calm, with misty rain; at 8, wind south-east, light breeze. At noon, west-south-west, fresh breeze and rain. At 4 P.M., wind south-west, fresh gale and heavy rain. A large fleet anchored in the Downs. A schooner was seen to anchor in a bad place about this time. At 7, wind still increasing. The watch observed several vessels part from their anchors and proceed to Margate Roads. At 7.30 the wind flew into the nor'-nor'-west, and blew a hurricane."

These were the first mutterings of the fight that had begun.

It was now about a quarter to eight P.M. Jerry and his friend Shales were cowering behind the bulwark on the starboard bow, gazing to windward, but scarce able to keep their eyes open owing to wind and spray. Suddenly a large object was seen looming into the circle of light.

"Stand by!" roared Jerry and Jack, with startling vigour, as the one leaped towards the tiller, the other to the companion-hatch; "a vessel bearing down on our hawse!"

The mate and men rushed on deck in time to see a large ship pass close to the bow of the Gull. Jack had cast loose the tiller, because, although in ordinary circumstances the helm of a light-vessel is of no use, this was one of the few occasions in which it could be of service.   The rush of the tide past a ship at anchor confers upon it at all times, except during " slack water" (*i.e.*, when the tide is on the turn), the power of steering, so that she can be made to sheer swiftly to port or starboard, as may be required.   But for this power, floating lights would undoubtedly be run into more frequently than they are.

The danger being over, the helm was again made fast amidships, but as several vessels were soon after seen sweeping past—two or three of them burning tar-barrels and "flare-lights" for assistance, it became evident that there would be little or no rest for any one on board that night.   The mate put on his oiled coat, trousers, boots, and sou'wester, and remained on deck.

Between eight and nine o'clock a schooner was seen approaching.   She came out of surrounding darkness like a dim phantom, and was apparently making the attempt to go to windward of the floating light.   She failed, and in a moment was bearing down with terrible speed right upon them.

" Starboard your helm !" shouted the mate, at the

same moment springing to the tiller of his own
vessel.

The steersman of the driving vessel fortunately
heard and obeyed the order, and she passed—but
shaved the bow of the Gull so closely that one of
the men declared he could easily have jumped aboard
of her.

Again, at nine o'clock, there was a stir on board
the floating light, for another vessel was seen driving
towards her. This one was a brig. The foremast was
gone, and the remains of a tar-barrel were still
burning on her deck, but as none of the crew could
be seen, it was conjectured that some other ship
must have run foul of her, and they had escaped on
board of it. All hands were again called, the tiller
was cast loose, a wide sheer given to the Gull, and
the brig went past them at about the distance of a
ship-length. She went slowly by, owing, it was
afterwards ascertained, to the fact that she had
ninety fathoms of cable trailing from her bows. She
was laden with coal, and when the Deal boatmen
picked her up next day, they found the leg of a man
on her deck, terribly mutilated, as if it had got
jambed somehow, and been wrenched off! But no
one ever appeared to tell the fate of that vessel's
crew.

Shortly before ten, two tar-barrels were observed
burning in a north-easterly direction. These proved

to be the signals of distress from a ship and a barque, which were dragging their anchors. They gradually drove down on the north part of the sands; the barque struck on a part named the Goodwin Knoll, the ship went on the North sandhead.

Now the time for action had come. The Goodwin light-vessel, being nearest to the wrecks, fired a signal-gun and sent up a rocket.

"There goes the *Goodwin !*" cried the mate; "load the starboard gun, Jack."

He ran down himself for a rocket as he spoke, and Jerry ran to the cabin for the red-hot poker, which had been heating for some time past in readiness for such an event.

"A gun and a flare to the south-east'ard, sir, close to us," shouted Shales, who had just finished loading, as the mate returned with the rocket and fixed it in position.

"Where away, Jack?" asked the mate hastily, for it now became his duty to send the rocket in the direction of the new signals, so as to point out the position of the wreck to the lifeboat-men on shore.

"Due south-east, sir; there they go again," said Jack, "not so close as I thought. South sandhead vessel signalling now, sir."

There was no further need for questions. The flash of the gun was distinctly seen, though the

R

sound was not heard, owing to the howling of the hurricane, and the bright flare of a second tar-barrel told its own tale, while a gun and rocket from the floating light at the South sandhead showed that the vessel in distress had been observed by her.

"Fire!" cried the mate.

Jerry applied the poker to the gun, and the scene which we have described in a former chapter was re-enacted;—the blinding flash, the roar, and the curved line of light across the black sky; but there was no occasion that night to repeat the signals. Everywhere along the coast the salvors of life and property were on the alert—many of them already in action, out battling in midnight darkness with the raging sea. The signal was at once replied to from Ramsgate.

Truly it was a dreadful night; one of those tremendous hurricanes which visit our shores three or four times it may be in a century, seeming to shake the world to its foundations, and to proclaim with unwonted significance the dread power of Him who created and curbs the forces of nature.

But the human beings who were involved in the perils of that night had scant leisure, and little inclination, perchance, to contemplate its sublimity. The crew of the Gull light were surrounded by signals of disaster and distress. In whichever direction they turned their eyes burning tar-barrels and other flaring lights were seen, telling their dismal tale of human beings-in urgent need of assistance or in dire extremity.

Little more than an hour before midnight another craft was observed driving down on the hawse of the Gull. There was greater danger now, because it happened to be near the turn of the tide, or "slack water," so that the rudder could not be used to advantage. All hands were once more turned out, and as the vessel drew near Mr. Welton hailed her, but got no reply.

"Let go the rudder-pendants!" cried the mate as he shipped the tiller.

The order was promptly obeyed, and the helm shoved hard a-port, but there was no responsive sheer. The sea was at the time currentless. Another moment and the vessel, which was a large deserted brig, struck the floating light on the port-bow, and her fore shrouds caught the fluke of the spare anchor which projected from the side.

"An axe, Jerry; look alive!"

Jerry required no spur; he bounded forward, caught up an axe, and leaped with it into the chains of the vessel, which had already smashed part of the Gull's bulwarks and wrenched the iron band off the cat-head.

"Cut away everything," cried the mate, who observed that the decks of the brig were full of

water, and feared that she might be in a sinking
condition.

The other men of the Gull were busy with boat-
hooks, oars, and fenders, straining every nerve to
get clear of this unwelcome visitor, while Jerry
dealt the shrouds a few telling blows which quickly
cut them through, but, in sweeping past, the main-
topsail yard-arm of the brig went crashing into the
lantern.   Instantly the lamps were extinguished,
and the bright beams of the floating light were
gone!   The brig then dropt astern and was soon
lost to view.

This was a disaster of the most serious nature—
involving as it did the absence of a light, on the
faithful glow of which the fate of hundreds of vessels
might depend.   Fortunately, however, the extreme
fury of the gale had begun to abate; it was therefore probable that all the vessels which had not
already been wrecked had found ports of shelter, or
would now be able to hold on to their anchors and
weather the storm.

But floating-lights are not left without resource
in a catastrophe such as this.   In the book of Regulations for the Service it is ordered that, in circumstances of this kind, two red lights are to be shown,
one at the end of the davit forward, the other on a
stanchion beside the ensign staff aft, and likewise a
red flare light is to be shown every quarter of an

hour. Accordingly, while some of the men lit and fixed up the red lanterns, Jerry MacGowl was told off to the duty of showing the red flares, or, as he himself expressed it, "settin' oft a succession o' fireworks, which wos mightily purty, no doubt, an' would have bin highly entertainin' if it had been foin weather, and a time of rejoycin'!"

Meanwhile the lantern was lowered, and it was found that the only damage done had been the shattering of one of its large panes of glass. The lamps, although blown out, had not been injured. The men therefore set vigorously to work to put in a spare pane, and get the light once more into working order.

Leaving them, then, at this important piece of work, let us turn aside awhile and follow the fortunes of the good ship Wellington on that terrible night of storm and disaster.

When the storm was brewing she was not far from the Downs, but the baffling winds retarded her progress, and it was pitch dark when she reached the neighbourhood of the Goodwin sands. Nevertheless those on board of her did not feel much uneasiness, because a good pilot had been secured in the channel.

The Wellington came bowling along under close-reefed topsails. Stanley Hall and Jim Welton stood leaning over the taffrail, looking down into the black foam-streaked water. Both were silent, save that now and then Jim put down his hand to pat a black muzzle that was raised lovingly to meet it, and whispered, " We shall be home to-morrow, Neptune, —cheer up, old boy !"

But Jim's words did not express all his thoughts. If he had revealed them fully he would have described a bright fireside in a small and humble but very comfortable room, with a smiling face that rendered sunshine unnecessary, and a pair of eyes that made gaslight a paltry flame as well as an absolute extravagance. That the name of this cheap, yet dear, luminary began with an *N* and ended with an *a*, is a piece of information with which we think it unnecessary to trouble the reader.

Stanley Hall's thoughts were somewhat on the same line of rail, if we may be allowed the expression ; the chief difference being that *his* luminary beamed in a drawing-room, and sang and played and painted beautifully—which accomplishments, however, Stanley thought, would have been sorry trifles in themselves had they not been coupled with a taste for housekeeping and domestic economy, and relieving as well as visiting the poor, and Sabbath-school teaching ; in short, every sort of " good work," besides an unaccountable as well as admirable *penchant* for pitching into the Board of Trade, and for keeping sundry account-books in such a neat and methodical way that there remains a lasting blot on that Board in the fact of their not having been bound in cloth of gold !

Ever since his first visit to Yarmouth, Stanley had felt an increasing admiration for Katie Durant's sprightly character and sterling qualities, and also increasing pity for poor Bob Queeker, who, he thought, without being guilty of very egregious vanity, had no chance whatever of winning such a prize. The reader now knows that the pity thus bestowed upon that pitiful fox-hunting turncoat was utterly thrown away.

"I don't like these fogs in such dangerous neighbourhood," observed Jim Welton, as a fresh squall burst upon the ship and laid it over so much that many of the passengers thought she was going to capsize. "We should be getting near the floating lights of the Goodwin sands by this time."

"Don't these lights sometimes break adrift?" asked Stanley, "and thus become the cause of ships going headlong to destruction?"

"Not often," replied Jim. "Considering the constancy of their exposure to all sorts of weather, and the number of light-vessels afloat, it is amazin' how few accidents take place. There has been nothing of the kind as long as I can remember anything about the service, but my father has told me of a case where one of the light-vessels that marked a channel at the mouth of the Thames once broke adrift in a heavy gale. She managed to bring up again with her spare anchor, but did not dare to show her light, being out of her proper place, and therefore, a false guide. The consequence was that eight vessels, which were making for the channel, and counted on seeing her, went on the sands and were lost with nearly all hands."

" If that be so it were better to have lighthouses, I think, than lightships," said Stanley.

" No doubt it would, where it is possible to build 'em," replied Jim, "but in some places it is supposed to be impossible to place a lighthouse, so we must be content with a vessel. But even lighthouses are are not perfectly secure. I know of one, built on piles on a sand-bank, that was run into by a schooner and carried bodily away. Accidents will happen, you know, in the best regulated families ; but it seems to me that we don't hear of a floating-light breakin' adrift once in half a century—while, on the other hand, the good that is done by them is beyond all calculation."

The young men relapsed into silence, for at that moment another fierce gust of wind threw the ship over almost on her beam-ends. Several of the male passengers came rushing on deck in alarm, but the captain quieted them, and induced them to return to the cabin to reassure the ladies, who, with the children, were up and dressed, being too anxious to think of seeking repose.

It takes courts of inquiry,—formed of competent men, who examine competent witnesses and have the counsel of competent seamen,—many days of anxious investigation to arrive at the precise knowledge of the when, how, and wherefore of a wreck. We do not, therefore, pretend to be able to say whether it was the fault of the captain, the pilot, the man at the lead, the steersman, the look-out, or the weather, that the good ship Wellington met her doom. All that we know for certain is, that she sighted the southern light-vessel some time before midnight during the great gale, that she steered what was supposed to be her true course, and that, shortly after, she struck on the tail of the sands.

Instantly the foremast went by the board, and the furious sea swept over the hull in blinding cataracts, creating terrible dismay and confusion amongst nearly all on board.

The captain and first mate, however, retained their coolness and self-possession. Stanley and Jim also, with several of the officers on board, were cool and self-possessed, and able to render good service. While Stanley loaded a small carronade, young Welton got up blue lights and an empty tar-barrel. These were quickly fired. The South sandhead vessels immediately replied, the Gull, as we have seen, was not slow to answer, and thus the alarm was transmitted to the shore while the breakers that rushed over the Goodwins like great walls of snow, lifted the huge vessel like a cork and sent it crashing down, again and again, upon the fatal sands.

CHAPTER XVI.

GETTING READY FOR ACTION.

LET us turn back a little at this point, and see how the watchers on Ramsgate pier behaved themselves on that night of storm and turmoil. At the end of the east pier of Ramsgate harbour there stands a very small house, a sort of big sentry-box in fact, of solid stone, which is part and parcel of the pier itself—built not only *on* it but *into* it, and partially sheltered from the full fury of wind and sea by the low parapet-wall of the pier. This is the east pier watch-house; the marine residence, if we may so express it, of the coxswain of the lifeboat and his men. It is their place of shelter and their watch-tower; their nightly resort, where they smoke the pipe of peace and good fellowship, and spin yarns, or take such repose as the nature of their calling will admit of. This little stone house had need be strong, like its inmates, for, like them, it is frequently called upon to brave the utmost fury of the elements

—receiving the blast fresh and unbroken from the North Sea, as well as the towering billows from the same.

This nocturnal watch-tower for muscular men and stout hearts, small though it be, is divided into two parts, the outer portion being the sleeping-place of the lifeboat men. It is a curious little box, full of oilskin coats and sou'wester caps and sea-boots, and bears the general aspect of a house which had been originally intended for pigmies, but had got inhabited by giants, somehow, by mistake. Its very diminutive stove stands near to its extremely small door, which is in close proximity to its unusually little window. A little library with a scanty supply of books hangs near the stove-pipe, as if the owners thereof thought the contents had become somewhat stale, and required warming up to make them more palatable. A locker runs along two sides of the apartment, on the coverings of which stand several lanterns, an oil-can, and a stone jar, besides sundry articles with an extremely seafaring aspect, among which are several pairs of the gigantic boots before referred to—the property of the coxswain and his mates. The cork lifebelt, or jacket of the coxswain, hangs near the door. The belts for use by the other men are kept in an outhouse down among the recesses of the pier near the spot to which the lifeboat is usually brought to embark her crew. Only five of the lifeboat men, called harbour boatmen, keep watch in and around the little stone house at nights. The rest are taken from among the hardy coast boatmen of the place, and the rule is—"first come first served"—when the boat is called out. There is never any lack of able and willing hands to man the Ramsgate lifeboat.

Near the low ceiling of the watch-house several hammocks are slung, obliging men to stoop a little as they move about. It is altogether a snug and cozy place, but cannot boast much of the state of its atmosphere when the fire is going, the door shut, and the men smoking!

On the night of the storm that has already been described in our last chapter, the coxswain entered the watch-house, clad in his black oilskin garments, and glittering with salt-water from top to toe.

"There will be more work for us before long, Pike," he said, flinging off his coat and sou'-wester, and taking up a pipe, which he began to fill; "it looks blacker than ever in the nor'-east."

Pike, the bowman of the boat, who was a quiet man, vigorous in action, but of few words, admitted that there was much probability of their services being again in demand, and then, rising, put on his cap and coat, and went out to take a look at the night.

Two other men sat smoking by the little stove,

and talking in lazy tones over the events of the day,
which, to judge from their words, had been already
stirring enough.

Late the night before—one of them said, for the
information of the other, who appeared to have just
arrived, and was getting the news—the steam-tug
and lifeboat had gone out on observing signals from
the Gull, and had been told there was a wreck on
the sands; that they had gone round the back of the
sands, carefully examining them, as far as the east
buoy, encountering a heavy ground swell, with
much broken sea, but saw nothing; that they had
then gone closer in, to about seven fathoms of water,
when the lifeboat was suddenly towed over a log—
as he styled it, a baulk—of timber, but fortunately
got no damage, and that they were obliged to return
to harbour, having failed to discover the wreck,
which probably had gone to pieces before they got
out to the sands; so they had all their trouble for
nothing. The man—appealing by look to the coxswain, who smoked in silence, and gazed sternly
and fixedly at the fire, as if his mind were wandering
far away—went on to say, further, that early that
morning they had been again called out, and were
fortunate enough to save the crew of a small
schooner, and that they had been looking out for
and expecting another call the whole day. For the
truth of all which the man appealed again by look

to the coxswain, who merely replied with a slight nod, while he continued to smoke in silence, leaning his elbows on his knees, with his strong hands clasped before him, sailor fashion, and gazing gravely at the fire. It seemed as if he were resting his huge frame after the recent fatigues to which it had been exposed, and in anticipation of those which might be yet in store.

Just then the little door opened quickly, and Pike's dripping head appeared.

"I think the Gull is signalling," he said, and vanished.

The coxswain's sou'wester and coat were on as if by magic, and he stood beside his mate at the end of the pier, partly sheltered by the parapet wall.

They both clung to the wall, and gazed intently out to sea, where there was just light enough to show the black waves heaving wildly up against the dark sky, and the foam gleaming in lurid patches everywhere. The seas breaking in heavy masses on the pier-head drenched the two men as they bent their heads to resist the roaring blast. If it had been high water, they could not have stood there for a moment. They had not been there long before their constant friend, the master of the steam-tug, joined them. Straining their eyes intently in the direction of the floating-light, which appeared like a little star tossed on the far-off horizon, they observed

a slight flash, and then a thin curved line of red fire
was seen to leap into the chaos of dark clouds.

"There she goes!" cried the coxswain.

"An' no mistake," said Pike, as they all ran to
get ready for action.

Few and to the point were the words spoken.
Each man knew exactly what was to be done. There
was no occasion to rouse the lifeboat men on such a
night. The harbour-master had seen the signal, and,
clad in oilskins like the men, was out among them
superintending. The steam-tug, which lies at that
pier with her fires lighted and banked up, and her
water hot, all the year round, sounded her shrill
whistle and cast loose. Her master and mate were
old hands at the perilous work, and lost no time,
for wreck, like fire, is fatally rapid. There was no
confusion, but there was great haste. The lifeboat
was quickly manned. Those who were most active
got on the cork lifebelts and leaped in; those who
were less active, or at a greater distance when the
signal sounded, had to remain behind. Eleven stalwart men, with frames inured to fatigue and cold,
clad in oiled suits, and with lifebelts on, sat on the
thwarts of the lifeboat, and the coxswain stood on
a raised platform in her stern, with the tiller-ropes
in his hands. The masts were up, and the sails
ready to hoist. Pike made fast the huge hawser
that was passed to them over the stern of the steam-

tug, and away they went, rushing out right in the teeth of the gale.

No cheer was given,—they had no breath to spare for sentimental service just then. There was no one, save the harbour-master and his assistant with a few men on duty, to see them start, for few could have ventured to brave the fury of the elements that night on the spray-lashed pier. In darkness they left ; into darkness most appalling they plunged, with nothing save a stern sense of duty and the strong hope of saving human life to cheer them on their way.

S

CHAPTER XVII.

THE BATTLE.

AT first the men of the lifeboat had nothing to do but hold on to the thwarts, with the exception, of course, of the coxswain, whose energies were taxed from the commencement in the matter of steering the boat, which was dragged through the waves at such a rate by the powerful tug that merely to hold on was a work of some difficulty. Their course might much more truly be said to have been under than over the waves, so constantly did these break into and fill the boat. But no sooner was she full than the discharging tubes freed her, and she rose again and again, buoyant as a cork.

Those who have not seen this desperate work can form but a faint conception of its true character. Written or spoken words may conjure up a pretty vivid picture of the scene, the blackness of the night, and the heaving and lashing of the waves, but words cannot adequately describe the shriek of

the blast, the hiss and roar of breakers, and they
cannot convey the feeling of the weight of tons of
falling water, which cause the stoutest crafts of
human build to reel and quiver to their centres.

The steam-tug had not to contend with the ordinary straightforward rush of a North Sea storm.
She was surrounded and beset by great boiling
whirlpools and spouting cross-seas. They struck her
on the bow, on the side, on the quarter, on the stern.
They opened as if to engulf her. They rushed at
as if to overwhelm her. They met under her,
thrusting her up, and they leaped into her, crush-
ing her down. But she was a sturdy vessel; a
steady hand was at the wheel, and her weather-
beaten master stood calm and collected on the
bridge.

It is probable that few persons who read the
accounts of lifeboat service on the Goodwin sands
are aware of the importance of the duties performed
and the desperate risks run by the steam-tug.
Without her powerful engines to tow it to windward
of the wrecks the lifeboat would be much, very
much, less useful than it is. In performing this
service the tug has again and again to run into
shallow water, and steer, in the blackest nights, amid
narrow intricate channels, where a slight error of
judgment on the part of her master—a few fathoms
more to the right or left—would send her on the

sands, and cause herself to become a wreck and an object of solicitude to the lifeboat crew. " Honour to whom honour is due " is a principle easy to state, but not always easy to carry into practice. Every time the steam-tug goes out she runs her full share of the imminent risk ;—sometimes, and in some respects, as great as that of the lifeboat herself, for, whereas, a touch upon the sand, to which it is her duty to approach *as near as possible*, would be the death-warrant of the tug, it is, on the other hand, the glorious prerogative of the lifeboat to be almost incapable of destruction, and her peculiar privilege frequently to go " slap on and right over " the sands with slight damage, though with great danger. That the death-warrant just referred to has not been signed, over and over again, is owing almost entirely to the courage and skill of her master and mate, who possess a thorough and accurate knowledge of the intricate channels, soundings, and tides of those dangerous shoals, and have spent many years in risking their lives among them. Full credit is usually given to the lifeboat, though *not too much* by any means, but there is not, we think, a sufficient appreciation of the services of the steam-tug. She may be seen in the harbour any day, modestly doing the dirty work of hauling out the dredge-boats, while the gay lifeboat floats idly on the water to be pointed out and admired by summer visitors—thus unfairly, though unavoidably, are public favours often distributed!

Observe, reader, we are far from holding up these two as rivals. They are a loving brother and sister. Comparatively little could be done in the grand work of saving human life without the mighty strength of the "big brother;" and, on the other hand, nothing at all could be done without the buoyant activity and courage of the "little sister." Observe, also, that although the lifeboat floats in idleness, like a saucy little duck, in time of peace, her men, like their mates in the "big brother," are hard at work like other honest folk about the harbour. It is only when the sands "show their teeth," and the floating lights send up their signals, and the storm-blast calls to action, that the tug and boat unite, and the men, flinging down the implements of labour, rise to the dignity of heroic work with all the pith and power and promptitude of heroes.

As they ploughed through the foam together, the tug was frequently obliged to ease-steam and give herself time to recover from the shock of those heavy cross seas. Suddenly a bright flaring light was observed in the vicinity of a shoal called the *Break*, which lies between the Goodwins and the shore. It went out in a few seconds, but not before the master of the tug had taken its bearings and altered his course. At the same time signal-guns and rockets were observed, both from the North sandhead light-vessel and the Gull, and several flaring lights were also seen burning on or near the Goodwin sands.

On nearing the *Middle Break*, which was easily distinguishable from the surrounding turmoil by the intensity of its roar as the seas rolled over it, the coxswain of the lifeboat ordered the sail to be hoisted and the tow-rope slipped. Pike, who was a thoroughly intelligent and sympathetic bowman, had all in readiness; he obeyed the order instantly, and the boat, as if endued with sudden life, sprang away on its own account into the broken water.

Broken water! who but a lifeboat-man can conceive what that means?—except, indeed, those few who have been saved from wreck. A chaos of white water, rendered ghostly and grey by darkness. No green or liquid water visible anywhere; all froth and fury, with force tremendous everywhere. Rushing rivers met by opposing cataracts; bursting against each other; leaping high in air from the shock; falling back and whirling away in wild eddies,—seeking rest, but finding none! Vain indeed must be our attempt to describe the awful aspect, the mad music, the fearful violence of "broken water" on the Break!

In such a sea the boat was tossed as if she were a chip; but the gale gave her speed, and speed gave her quick steering power. She leaped over the foam, or dashed through it, or staggered under it, but always rose again, the men, meanwhile, holding on for life. Pike was ready in the bow, with an arm tightly embracing the bollard, or strong post, round which the cable runs. The coxswain's figure, towering high in the stern, with the steering tackles in his hands, leaned forward against a strong strap or band fixed across the boat to keep him in position.

They made straight for the spot where the flare light had been seen. At first darkness and thick spray combined prevented them from seeing anything, but in a few minutes ·a dark object was seen looming faintly against the sky, and the coxswain observed with anxious concern that it lay not to leeward, but to windward of him.

"Out oars! down with the sail!" he shouted.

His voice was very powerful, but it was swept away, and was only heard by those nearest to him. The order was instantly obeyed, however; but the gale was so heavy and the boat so large that headway could not be made. They could see that the wreck was a small vessel on her beam-ends. Being to leeward, they could hear despairing cries distinctly, and four or five human beings were seen clinging to the side. The lifeboat men strained till their sinews wellnigh cracked; it seemed doubtful whether they had advanced or not, when suddenly an unusually large wave fell in thunder on the Break; it rushed over the shallows with a foaming head, caught the boat on its crest and carried it far away to leeward.

Sail was again made. A box near the coxswain's feet was opened, and a blue-light taken out. There was no difficulty in firing this. A sharp stroke on its butt lighted the percussion powder within, and in a moment the scene was illumined by a ghastly glare, which brought out the blue and white boat distinctly, and gave corpse-like colour to the faces of the men. At the same time it summoned the attendant steamer.

In a few minutes the tug ran down to her; the tow-rope was taken on board, and away went the brother and sister once more to windward of the wreck; but now no wreck was to be seen! They searched round the shoal in all directions without success, and finally were compelled to come to the conclusion that the same sea which had carried the boat to leeward had swept the wreck away.

With sad hearts they now turned towards the Goodwins, but the melancholy incident they had just witnessed was soon banished from their minds by the urgent signals for aid still seen flaring in all directions. For the nearest of these they made at full speed. On their way, a dark object was seen to sweep past them across their stern as if on the wings of the wind. It was the Broadstairs lifeboat, which had already done good service that night, and was bent on doing more. Similarly occupied were the lifeboats of Deal, Walmer, and other places along the coast. A Deal lugger was also seen. The hardy beachmen of Kent fear no storm. They run out in all weathers to succour ships in distress, and much good service do they accomplish, but their powers are limited. Like the steam-tugs, they can hover around the sands in heavy gales, and venture gingerly near to them; but thus far, and no farther, may they go. They cannot, like the noble lifeboats, dash right into the caldron of surf, and dare the sands and seas to do their worst!

The lifeboat men felt cheered, no doubt, to know that so many able hands were fighting around them in the same battle, but they had little time to think on such things; the work in hand claimed their exclusive attention—as it must now claim ours.

One vessel was seen burning three very large flare lights. Towards this the steamer hastened, and when as near as prudence would permit her to approach the Goodwin sands—something less than quarter of a mile—the hawser was again slipped, sail was made on the lifeboat, and she once more entered. the broken water alone.

Here, of course, being more exposed, it was still more tremendous than on the Break. It was a little after midnight when they reached the sands, and made the discovery that they were on the wrong side of them. The tide was making, however, and in a short time there was sufficient water to enable the boat to run right over; she struck many times, but, being tough, received no serious damage. Soon they drew near the wreck, and could see that she had sunk completely, and that the crew were clinging to the jibboom.

When about fifty yards to windward, the anchor was let go, the lifeboat veered down towards the wreck, and with much difficulty they succeeded in taking off the whole crew of seven men. Signalizing the tug with another blue-light, they ran to leeward into deep water, and were again taken in tow; the saved men being with some difficulty put on board the tug. They were Dutchmen; and the poor master of the lost vessel could find no words sufficiently forcible to express his gratitude to the coxswain of the lifeboat. When he afterwards met him on shore, he wrung his hand warmly, and, with tears in his eyes, promised never to forget him. " Me never tinks of you," said he (meaning the reverse), "so long's I live; me tell the King of Holland!"

It is but just to add that the poor fellow faithfully redeemed his ill-expressed promise, and that the coxswain of the lifeboat now possesses a medal presented to him by the King of Holland in acknowledgment of his services on that occasion.

But the great work óf that night still remained to be done. Not far from the light-vessel a flare-light was seen burning brightly. It seemed to be well tended, and was often renewed. Towards this the tug now steered with the little sister in tow. They soon came near enough to observe that she was a large ship, going to pieces on the sands.

Slipping the cable once more, the lifeboat gallantly dashed into the thickest of the fight, and soon got within hail of the wreck.

Then it was that, for the first time, a ray of hope entered the hearts of the passengers of the luckless Wellington, and then it was that Jim Welton and Stanley Hall, with several young officers, who had kept the tar-barrels burning so briskly for so many hours, despite the drenching seas, sent up a loud thrilling cheer, and announced to the terror-stricken women and children that *the lifeboat was in sight!*

What a cry for those who had been for three hours dashing on the sands, expecting every moment that the ship would break up! The horrors of their situation were enhanced by the novelty of their sensations! All of us can realize to some extent, from hearsay and from paintings, what is meant by billows bursting high over ships' mast-heads and washing everything off the decks, but who that has not experienced it can imagine what it is to see gigantic yards being whipped to and fro as a light cane might be switched by a strong man, to see top-masts snapping like pipe-stems, to hear stout ropes cracking like pliant whipcord, and great sails flapping with thunder-claps or bursting into shreds? Above all, who can realize the sensation caused by one's abode being lifted violently with every surge and dropped again with the crashing weight of two thousand tons, or being rolled from side to side so that the floor on which one stands alternates between the horizontal and perpendicular, while one's frame each time receives a shock that is only too much in dread harmony with the desperate condition of the mind?

"The lifeboat in sight!" Who at such a time would not pray God's best blessing on the lifeboat, on the stalwart men who man it, and on the noble Society which supports it?

Certain it is that many a prayer of this kind was ejaculated on board the Wellington that night, while the passengers re-echoed the good news, and hurriedly went on deck. But what an awful scene of dreary desolation presented itself when they got there! The flares gave forth just enough light to make darkness visible—ropes, masts, yards, sails, everything in indescribable confusion, and the sea breaking over all with a violence that rendered it extremely difficult to maintain a footing even in the most sheltered position.

Fortunately by this time the vessel had been beaten sufficiently high on the shoal to prevent the terrible rolling to which she had been at first subjected; and as the officers and seamen vied with each other in attentions to the women and children, these latter were soon placed in comparative security, and awaited with breathless anxiety the arrival of the boat.

In order to keep the flare-lights burning all kinds of materials had been sacrificed. Deluged as they were continually by heavy seas, nothing but the most inflammable substances would burn. Hence, when their tar-barrels were exhausted, Stanley Hall and his assistants got hold of sheets, table-cloths, bedding, and garments, and saturated these with paraffine oil, of which, fortunately, there happened to be a large quantity on board. They now applied themselves with redoubled diligence to the construction and keeping alight of these flares, knowing well that the work which remained to be done before all should be rescued, was of a nature requiring time as well as care and courage.

On rushed the lifeboat through the broken water. When almost within hail, the coxswain heard the roar of an unusually heavy sea rushing behind him.

" Let go the fore-sheet," he shouted, " and hold on for your lives."

The wave—a billow broken to atoms, yet still retaining all its weight and motive force—overwhelmed the boat and passed on. Before she had quite recovered, another sea of equal size engulfed her, and as she had been turned broadside on by the first, the second caught her in its embrace and carried her like the wind bodily to leeward. Her immense breadth of beam prevented an upset, and she was finally launched into shallower water, where the sand had only a few feet of sea above it. She had been swept away full quarter of a mile in little more than a minute! Here the surf was like a boiling caldron, but there was not depth enough to admit of heavy seas.

The same sea that swept away the boat carried the fore and main masts of the Wellington by the board, and extinguished all her lights.

The boat drove quite two miles to leeward before the tug got hold of her again. To have returned to the wreck against wind and tide alone, we need scarcely repeat, would have been impossible, but with the aid of the tug she was soon towed to her old position and again cast loose.

Once more she rushed into the fight and succeeded in dropping anchor a considerable distance to windward of the wreck, from which point she veered down under her lee, but so great was the mass of broken masts, spars, and wreckage—nothing being now left but parts of the mizzen and bowsprit—that the coxswain was obliged to pay out 117 fathoms of cable to keep clear of it all.

The difficulty and danger of getting the boat alongside now became apparent to the people on the wreck, many of whom had never dreamed of such impediments before, and their hopes sank unreasonably low, just as, before, they had been raised unduly high.

With great difficulty the boat got near to the port quarter of the ship, and Pike stood up ready in the bow with a line, to which was attached a loaded cane, something like a large life-preserver.

"Heave!" shouted the coxswain.

The bowman made a deliberate and splendid cast; the weighted cane fell on the deck of the ship, and was caught by Jim Welton, who attached a hawser to it. This was drawn into the boat, and in a few seconds she was alongside. But she was now in great danger! The wild waters that heaved, surged, and leaped under the vessel's lee threatened to dash the boat in pieces against her every moment, and it was only by the unremitting and strenuous exertions of the men with boat-hooks, oars, and fenders that this was prevented. Now the boat surged up into the chains as if about to leap on board the ship; anon it sank into a gulf of spray, or sheered wildly to leeward, but by means of the hawser and cable, and a "spring" attached to the latter, she was so handled that one and another of the crew of the wreck were taken into her.

The first saved was a little child. It was too small and delicate to be swung over the side by a rope, so the captain asked Jim Welton, as being the most agile man in the ship and possessed of super-abundant animal courage, to take it in his arms and leap on board. Jim agreed at once, handed over the care of his flare-lights to one of the men, and prepared for action. The poor child, which was about a year old, clung to its mother's neck with terror, and the distracted woman—a soldier's widow —could scarce be prevailed on to let the little one out of her arms.

"Oh, let me go with him," she pleaded most earnestly, "he is all that is left to me."

"You shall follow immediately; delay may be death," said the captain, kindly, as he drew the child gently but firmly from her grasp.

It was securely bound to Jim's broad bosom by means of a shawl. Watching his opportunity when the boat came surging up on the crest of a billow almost to his feet, and was about to drop far down into the trough of the sea, the young sailor sprang from the side and was caught in the outstretched arms of the lifeboat men.

It had occurred to Stanley Hall, just before this

happened, that there was every probability of some
of the passengers falling overboard during the process of being transferred to the boat. Stanley was
of a somewhat eccentric turn of mind, and seldom allowed his thoughts to dissipate without taking action
of some kind. He therefore got into the mizzen chains
and quietly fastened a rope round his waist, the
other end of which he tied to a stanchion.

" You 'll get crushed by the boat there," cried the
captain, who observed him.

" Perhaps not," was the reply.

He stood there and watched Jim Welton as he
leaped. The mother of the child, unable to restrain
herself, climbed on the bulwarks of the vessel.
Just as she did so the boat surged up again,—so
close that it required but a short step to get into her.
Some of the passengers availed themselves of the
chance—the poor widow among-them. She sprang
with a cry of joy, for she saw her child's face at the
moment as they unbound him from Jim's breast,
but she sprang short. Little wonder that a woman
should neglect to make due allowance for the quick
swooping of the boat! Next moment she was in
the boiling foam. A moment later and she was in
Stanley Hall's grasp, and both were swept violently
to leeward, but the rope brought them up. Despite
darkness and turmoil the quick-eyed coxswain and
his mate had noted the incident. Pike payed

T

out the hawser, the coxswain eased off the spring; away went the boat, and next moment Pike had Stanley by the hair. Short was the time required for their strong arms to pull him and his burden in-board; and, oh! it was a touching sight to witness the expressions of the anxious faces that were turned eagerly towards the boat, and glared pale and ghastly in the flaring light, as her sturdy crew hauled slowly up, hand over hand, and got once more under the vessel's lee.

No sooner were they within reach than another impatient passenger leaped overboard. This was Jim's faithful dog Neptune! Watching his time with the intelligence of a human being, he sprang, with much greater precision and vigour than any human being could have done, and, alighting on Pike's shoulders, almost drove that stout boatman into the bottom of the boat.

Soon the boat was as full as it could hold. All the women and children had been got into her, and many of the male passengers, so that there was no room to move; still there remained from twenty to thirty people to be rescued. Seeing this, Jim seized Neptune by the neck and flung him back into the wreck. Catching a rope that hung over the side, he also swung himself on board, saying,—

"You and I must sink or swim together, Nep! Shove off, lads, and come back as soon as you can."

The hawser was slipped as he spoke ; the lifeboat was hauled slowly but steadily to windward up to her anchor. Tons of water poured over her every moment, but ran through her discharging tubes, and, deeply loaded though she was, she rose buoyant from each immersion like an invincible sea-monster.

When the anchor was reached, a small portion of the foresail was set, and then, cutting the cable with one blow of a hatchet, away they went like the scudding foam right over the boiling shallows on the spit of sand.

" Hand out a blue-light there," cried the coxswain.

A sharp blow caused the blue-fire to flare up and shed a light that fell strong as that of the full moon on the mingled grave, pale, stern, and terrified faces in the lifeboat.

" Safe !" muttered one of the crew.

" Safe ?" was echoed in surprise, no doubt, from several fluttering hearts.

As well might that have been said to the hapless canoe-man rushing over the Falls of Niagara as to the inexperienced ones there, while they gazed, horror-struck, on the tumult of mad waters in that sudden blaze of unearthly light. Their faith in a trust-worthy and intelligent boatman was not equal to their faith in their own eyes, backed by ignorance ! But who will blame them for lack of faith in the circumstances ? Nevertheless, they *were* safe. The watchful master of the tug,—laying-to off the deadly banks, now noting the compass, now casting the lead, anon peering into the wild storm,—saw the light, ran down to it, took the rescued ones on board, and, having received from the coxswain the information that there were "more coming," sent them down into his little cabin, there to be refreshed and comforted, while the lifeboat sheered off again, and once more sprang into the "broken water." So might some mighty warrior spur from the battle-field charged with despatches of the highest import bearing on the fight, and, having delivered his message, turn on his heel and rush back into the whirling tide of war to complete the victory which had been so well begun!

Once more they made for the wreck, which was by that time fast breaking up. Running right before the wind in such an awful gale, it was necessary to make the men crowd aft in order to keep the boat's head well out of the water. On this occasion one or two of the seamen of the Wellington, who had been allowed inadvertently to remain in the boat, became alarmed, for the seas were rolling high over the gunwale on each side, and rushing into her with such force as to make it a difficult matter to avoid being washed out. It was a new sensation to these men to rush thus madly between two walls of foam eight or ten feet high! They glanced backward, where another wall of foaming water seemed to be curling over the stern, as if about to drop inboard. The coxswain observed their looks, and knew their feelings. He knew there was no lack of courage in them, and that a little experience would change their minds on this point.

"Never look behind, lads," he cried; "look ahead; always look right ahead."

"Ay, Geordy," remarked one of the men,—a Scotchman,—to his mate, "it's rum sailin' this is. I thocht we was a' gaun to the bottom; but nae doot the cox'n kens best. It's a wonderfu' boat!"

Having so said, the sedate Scot dismissed his anxieties, and thereafter appeared to regard the surrounding chaos of water with no other feelings than philosophic interest and curiosity.

On nearing the wreck the second time, it was found that the tide had fallen so low that they could scarcely get alongside. Three times they struck on the shoal; on the third occasion the mizzen-mast and sail were blown out of the boat. They managed to drop anchor, however, and to veer down under the port bow of the Wellington, whence the anxious survivors threw ropes to them, and, one after another, leaped or swung themselves into the boat. But they were so long about it that before all had been got out the coxswain was obliged to drop to leeward to prevent being left aground. In spite of this, the boat got fast, and now they could neither advance to the wreck for the nine men who still remained in her, nor push off to rejoin the tug.

The space between the boat and vessel was crossed by such a continuous rush of broken water that for a time it was impossible to attempt anything, but as the tide fell the coxswain consulted with his bowman, and both agreed to venture to wade to the wreck, those on board having become so exhausted as to be unable or unwilling to make further effort to save themselves.

Acting on this resolve they with one of their men sprang into the raging surf and staggered to the wreck, where they induced two of the crew to leap overboard and brought them safely to the boat. Others of the lifeboat crew then joined them and four more were rescued.*

The tide had been at its lowest when this desperate work was begun,—before it was finished it had turned. This, coupled with the fact that they had all been nearly swept away during the last effort, and that there was a fresh burst of violence in the gale, induced them to wait until the tide should rise. When it did so sufficiently, they hauled and shoved the boat alongside, and the captain, who was one of the three remaining men, made a desperate spring,

* The coxswain—Mr. Isaac Jarman—who has rendered heroic service in the Ramsgate Lifeboat during the last ten years, has been personally instrumental in saving between four and five hundred lives.

THE LIFEBOAT RESCUE.—Page 294.

but missed the boat and was whirled away. Pike made a grasp at him but missed. The coxswain seized a life-buoy and hurled it towards him. It fell within his reach, and it was supposed that he had caught it, but they could not be certain. The boat was now afloat and bumping violently. If they had cut the cable in order to rescue the captain, which they could by no means make sure of doing, the improbability of being able to return in time to save the two remaining men would have been very great. It seemed to be life or death in either case, so they stuck by the wreck.

It was grey dawn now, and the wreckage was knocking against and around them to such an extent that the coxswain began to fear for the safety of his boat. Yet he was loath to leave the men to perish.

"Jump now, lads!" he cried, sheering up alongside, "it's your last chance. It's death to all of us if we stop longer here!"

The men sprang together. One gained the side of the boat and was saved, the other was swept away. He made frantic efforts to gain the boat, but before his companion had been got inboard he was out of sight, and although the cable was promptly cut and the sail set he could not be found. The boat was then run down along the sands in search of the captain. The coxswain knew well from experience that he must certainly have been swept by the current in the same direction as the wreckage. He therefore followed this, and in a short time 'had the inexpressible satisfaction and good fortune to find the captain. He had caught the life-buoy, and having managed to get it under his arms had floated about for the greater part of an hour. Though nearly dead he was still sensible, and, after being well chafed and refreshed with a little rum from the coxswain's case-bottle—provided for occasions of this sort—he recovered.

The great work of the lifeboat had now been accomplished, but they could not feel that it had been thoroughly completed without one more effort being made to save the lost man. They therefore ran still farther down the sand in the direction where he had been last seen. They followed the drift of wreckage as before. Presently the bowman uttered a thrilling shout, for, through the turmoil of dashing spray, he saw the man clinging to a spar!

So unexpected was this happy event that the whole crew involuntarily gave vent to a ringing cheer, although, in the circumstances, and considering the nature of their exhausting work and the time they had been exposed to it, one might have supposed them incapable of such a burst of enthusiasm.

In a few moments he was rescued, and now, with light hearts, they ran for the tug, which was clearly visible in the rapidly increasing daylight. They did not put off time in transferring the saved men to the steamer. The big hawser,—their familiar bond of attachment,—was made fast to them, and away went that noble big brother and splendid little sister straight for Ramsgate harbour.*

But the work of that wild night was not yet finished. On their way home they fell in with a schooner, the foretopmast and bowsprit of which were gone. As she was drifting towards the sands they hailed her. No reply being made, the lifeboat was towed alongside, and, on being boarded, it was found that she was a derelict. Probably she had got upon the sands during the night, been forsaken by her crew in their own boat—in which event there was small chance of any being saved—and had drifted off again at the change of the tide.

Be that as it might, six lifeboat men were put on board. Finding no water in her, they slipt her two cables, which were hanging from the bow, a rope was made fast to the steamer, and she was taken in tow.

---

* If the reader should desire to know something more of the history of the celebrated Ramsgate lifeboat, which, owing to its position, opportunities, and advantages, has had the most stirring career of all the lifeboat fleet, we advise the perusal of a work (at present in the press, if it be not already published) named *Storm Warriors, or the Ramsgate Lifeboat and the Goodwin Sands*, by the Rev. John Gilmore, whose able and thrilling articles on the lifeboat-service in *Macmillan's Magazine* are well known.

It was drawing towards noon when they neared the harbour. Very different indeed was the aspect of things there then from what it had been when they went out on their errand of mercy thirteen hours before. Although the gale was still blowing fresh it had moderated greatly. The black clouds no longer held possession of the sky, but were pierced, scattered, and gilded, as they were rolled away, by the victorious sun. The sea still raged and showed its white "teeth" fiercely, as if its spirit had been too much roused to be easily appeased; but blue sky appeared in patches everywhere; the rain had ceased, and the people of the town and visitors swarmed out to enjoy the returning sunshine, inhale the fresh sea-breeze, and await, anxiously, the return of the lifeboat—for, of course, every one in the town was aware by that time that she had been out all night.

When, at length, the smoke of the "big brother" was observed drawing near, the people flocked in hundreds to the piers and cliffs. Wherever a point of vantage was to be had, dozens of spectators crowned it. Wherever a point of danger was to be gained, daring spirits—chiefly in the shape of small boys—took it by storm, in absolute contempt of the police. "Jacob's Ladder"—the cliff staircase—was crowded from top to bottom. The west pier was rendered invisible to its outer extremity by human beings. The east pier, as far as it was dry, was covered by the fashion and beauty—as well as by the fishy and tarry—of the town. Beyond the point of dryness it was more or less besieged by those who were reckless, riotous, and ridiculously fond of salt-water spray. The yards and shrouds· of the crowded and much damaged shipping in the harbour were manned, and the windows of the town that commanded the sea were filled with human faces. An absolute battery of telescopes, like small artillery, was levelled at the approaching tug. Everywhere were to be seen and heard evidences of excitement, anxiety, and expectation.

It was not long before it was announced that flags were seen flying at the mast-heads of the tug and lifeboat—a sure evidence that a rescue had been successfully accomplished. This caused many a burst of cheering from the crowds, as the fact and its import became gradually known. But these were as nothing compared with the cheers that arose when the steamer, with the lifeboat and the schooner in tow, drew near, and it could be seen that there were many people on board—among them women and children. When they finally surged past the pier-head on the crest of a tremendous billow, and swept into the harbour under a vast shower of spray that burst over the pier and rose above the mast-heads of the shipping within—as if to pour a libation on the gallant crews—then a succession of cheers, that cannot be described, welcomed the victors and re-echoed from the chalk-cliffs, to be caught up and sent out again and again in thrilling cadence on the mad sea, which had thus been plundered of its booty and disappointed of its prey !

Scarfs and hats and kerchiefs and hands were waved in wild enthusiasm, strangely mingled with tender pity, when the exhausted women and children and the worn-out and battered lifeboat-men were landed. Many cheered, no doubt, to think of the strong hearts and invincible courage that dwelt in the breasts of Britain's sons ; while others,—tracing things at once to their true source,—cheered in broken tones, or were incompetent to cheer at all, when they thought with thankfulness of Britain's faith in the Word of God, which, directly or indirectly, had given that courage its inspiration, and filled those hearts with fire.

CHAPTER XVIII.

SHOWS THAT THERE ARE NO EFFECTS WITHOUT ADEQUATE CAUSES.

THERE were not a few surprising and unexpected meetings that day on Ramsgate pier. Foremost among the hundreds who pressed forward to shake the lifeboat-men by the hand, and to sympathize with and congratulate the wrecked and rescued people, was Mr. George Durant. It mattered nothing to that stout enthusiast that his hat had been swept away into hopeless destruction during his frantic efforts to get to the front, leaving his polished head exposed to the still considerable fury of the blast and the intermittent violence of the sun; and it mattered, if possible, still less that the wreck turned out to be one of his own vessels; but it was a matter of the greatest interest and amazement to him to find that the first man he should meet in the crowd and seize in a hearty embrace, was his young friend, Stanley Hall.

"What, Stanney!" he exclaimed in unmitigated surprise; "is it—can it be? Prodigious sight!"

The old gentleman could say no more, but continued for a few seconds to wring the hands of his young friend, gaze in his face, and vent himself in gusts of surprise and bursts of tearful laughter, to the great interest and amusement of the bystanders.

Mr. Durant's inconsistent conduct may be partly accounted for and excused by the fact that Stanley had stepped on the pier with no other garments on than a pair of trousers and a shirt, the former having a large rent on the right knee, and the latter being torn open at the breast, in consequence of the violent removal of all the buttons when its owner was dragged into the lifeboat. As, in addition to this, the young man's dishevelled hair did duty for a cap, and his face and hands were smeared with oil and tar from the flare-lights which he had assisted to keep up so energetically, it is not surprising that the first sight of him had a powerful effect on Mr. Durant.

"Why, Stanney," he said at length, "you look as if you were some strange sea-monster just broke loose from Neptune's menagerie !"

Perhaps this idea had been suggested by the rope round Stanley's waist, the cut end of which still dangled at his side, for Mr. Durant took hold of it inquiringly.

"Ay, sir," put in the coxswain, who chanced to be near him, "that bit of rope is a scarf of honour. He saved the life of a soldier's widow with it."

There was a tendency to cheer on the part of the bystanders who heard this.

"God bless you, Stanney, my boy! Come and get dressed," said the old gentleman, suddenly seizing his friend's arm and pushing his way through the crowd, "come along; oh, don't talk to me of the ship. I know that it's lost; no matter—*you* are saved. And do *you* come along with us Wel—Wel —what's the name of—? Ah! Welton—come; my daughter is here somewhere. I left her near the parapet. Never mind, she knows her way home."

Katie certainly was there, and when, over the heads of the people—for she had mounted with characteristic energy on the parapet, assisted by Queeker and accompanied by Fanny Hennings—she beheld Stanley Hall in such a plight, she felt a disposition to laugh and cry and faint all at once. She resisted the tendency, however, although the expression of her face and her rapid change of colour induced Queeker with anxious haste to throw out his arms to catch her.

"Ha!" exclaimed Queeker, "*I knew it!*"

What Queeker knew he never explained. It may have had reference to certain suspicions entertained in regard to the impression made by the young student on Katie the night of their first meeting; we cannot tell, but we know that he followed up the exclamation with the muttered remark, "It was fortunate that I pulled up in time."

Herein Queeker exhibited the innate tendency of the human heart to deceive itself. That furious little poetical fox-hunter had, by his own confession, felt the pangs of a guilty conscience in turning, just because he could not help it, from Katie to Fanny, yet here he was now basely and coolly taking credit to himself for having "pulled up in time!"

"Oh, look at the *dear* little children!" exclaimed Fanny, pointing towards a part of the crowd where several seamen were carrying the rescued and still terrified little ones in their strong arms, while others assisted the women along, and wrapped dry shawls round them.

"How dreadful to think," said Katie, making a hard struggle to suppress her agitation, "that all these would have been lost but for the lifeboat ; and how wonderful to think that some of our own friends should be among them!"

"Ay, there be many more besides these saved last night, miss," remarked a sturdy old boatman who chanced to be standing beside her. "All along the east coast the lifeboats has bin out, miss, you may be sure ; and they don't often shove off without bringin' somethin' back to show for their pains, though they don't all 'ave steamers for to tug 'em out. There's the Broadstairs boat, now ; I've jist

heerd she was out all night an' saved fifteen lives ;
an' the Walmer and Deal boats has fetched in a lot,
- I believe, though we han't got particklers yet."

Besides those whom we have mentioned as gazing
with the crowd at the arrival of the lifeboat, Morley
Jones, and Nora, and Billy Towler were there.
Jones and Billy had returned from London together
the night before the storm, and, like nearly every
one else in the town, had turned out to witness the
arrival of the lifeboat.

Dick Moy also was there, and that huge lump of
good-nature spent the time in making sagacious remarks and wise comments on wind and weather,
wrecks and rescues, in a manner that commanded
the intense admiration of a knot of visitors who
happened to be near him, and who regarded him as
a choice specimen—a sort of type—of the British
son of Neptune.

"This is wot *I* says," observed Dick, while the
people were landing, " so long as there 's 'ope, 'old on.
Never say die, and never give in ; them 's my sentiments. 'Cause why ? no one never knows wot may
turn up. If your ship goes down ; w'y, wot then ?
Strike out, to be sure. P'r'aps you may be picked
up afore long. If sharks is near, p'r'aps you may
be picked down. You can never tell. If you gets
on a shoal, wot then ? w'y, stick to the ship till a
lifeboat comes off to 'ee. Don't never go for to take

U

to your own boats. If you do—capsize, an' Davy
Jones's locker is the word. If the lifeboat can't git
alongside; w'y, wait till it can. If it can't; w'y, it
can only be said that it couldn't. No use cryin'
over spilt milk, you know. Not that I cares for
milk. It don't keep at sea, d'ye see; an's only fit
for babbys. If the lifeboat capsizes; w'y, then,
owin' to her parfection o' build, she rights again, an'
you, 'avin' on cork jackets, p'r'aps, gits into 'er by
the lifelines, all handy. If you 'aven't got no cork
jackets on, w'y, them that has 'll pick 'ee up. If not,
it's like enough you'll go down. But no matter,
you've did yer best, an' man, woman, or child can
do no more. You can only die once, d'ye see?"

Whether the admiring audience did or did not see
the full force of these remarks, they undoubtedly saw
enough in the gigantic tar to esteem him a marvel
of philosophic wisdom. Judging by their looks that
he was highly appreciated, it is just possible that
Dick Moy might have been tempted to extend his
discourse, had not a move in the crowd showed a
general tendency towards dispersion, the rescued
people having been removed, some to the Sailor's
Home, others to the residences of hospitable people
in the town.

Now, it must not be imagined that all these cha-
racters in our tale have been thus brought together,
merely at our pleasure, without rhyme or reason,

and in utter disregard of the law of probabilities. By no means.

Mr. Robert Queeker had started for Ramsgate, as the reader knows, on a secret mission, which, as is also well known, was somewhat violently interrupted by the sporting tendencies of that poetical law-clerk; but no sooner did Queeker recover from his wounds than—with the irresistible ardour of a Wellington, or a Blucher, or a bull-dog, or a boarding-school belle—he returned to the charge, made out his intended visit, set his traps, baited his lines, fastened his snares, and whatever else appertained to his secret mission, so entirely to the satisfaction of Messrs. Merryheart and Dashope, that these estimable men resolved, some time afterwards, to send him back again to the scene of his labours, to push still further the dark workings of his mission. Elate with success the earnest Queeker prepared to go. Oh, what joy if *she* would only go with him!

"And why not?" cried Queeker, starting up when this thought struck him, as if it had struck him too hard and he were about to retaliate,—"Why not? *That* is the question."

He emphasized *that* as if all other questions, Hamlet's included, sank into insignificance by contrast.

"Only last night," continued Queeker to himself, still standing bolt upright in a frenzy of inspiration, and running his fingers fiercely through his hair, so as to make it stand bolt upright too—"only last night I heard old Durant say he could not make up his mind where to go to spend the autumn this year. Why not Ramsgate? why not Ramsgate?

"Its chalky cliffs, and yellow sand,
    And rides, and walks, and weather,
Its windows, which a view command
    Of everything together.

"Its pleasant walks, and pretty shops,
    To fascinate the belles,
Its foaming waves, like washing-slops,
    To captivate the swells.

"Its boats and boatmen, brave and true,
    Who lounge upon the jetty,
And smile upon the girls too—
    At least when they are pretty.

"Oh! Ramsgate, where in all the earth,
    Beside the lovely sea,
Can any town of note or worth
    Be found to equal thee?

Nowhere!" said Queeker, bringing his fist down on the table with a force that made the ink leap, when he had finished these verses—verses, however, which cost him two hours and a profuse perspiration to produce.

It was exactly a quarter to eight P.M. by the Yarmouth custom-house clock, due allowance being made for variation, when this "Nowhere!" was uttered, and it was precisely a quarter past nine P.M. that day week when the Durants drove up to the door of the Fortress Hotel in Ramsgate, and ordered beds and tea,—so powerful was the influence of a great mind when brought to bear on Fanny Hennings, who exercised irresistible. influence over the good-natured Katie, whose power over her indulgent father was absolute !

Not less natural was the presence, in Ramsgate, of Billy Towler. We have already mentioned that, for peculiarly crooked ends of his own, Morley Jones had changed his abode to Ramsgate—his country abode, that is. His headquarters and town department continued as before to flourish in Gravesend, in the form of a public-house, which had once caught fire at a time, strange to say, when the spirit and beer casks were all nearly empty, a curious fact which the proprietor alone was aware of, but thought it advisable not to mention when he went to receive the £200 of insurance which had been effected on the premises a few weeks before ! It will thus be seen that Mr. Jones's assurance, in the matter of dealing with insurance, was considerable.

Having taken up his temporary abode, then, in Ramsgate, and placed his mother and daughter therein as permanent residents, Mr. Jones commenced such a close investigation as to the sudden disappearance of his ally Billy, that he wormed out of the unwilling but helpless Nora not only what had become of him, but the name and place of his habitation. Having accomplished this, he dressed himself in a blue nautical suit with brass buttons, took the morning train to London, and in due course presented himself at the door of the Grotto, where he requested permission to see the boy Towler.

The request being granted, he was shown into a room, and Billy was soon after let in upon him.

"Hallo ! young Walleye, why, what ever has come over you?" he exclaimed in great surprise, on observing that Billy's face was clean, in which condition he had never before seen it, and his hair brushed, an extraordinary novelty; and, most astonishing of all, that he wore unragged garments.

Billy, who, although outwardly much altered, had apparently lost none of his hearty ways and sharp intelligence, stopped short in the middle of the room, thrust both hands deep into his trousers pockets, opened his eyes very wide, and gave vent to a low prolonged whistle.

"What game may *you* be up to ?" he said, at the end of the musical prelude.

"You are greatly improved, Billy," said Jones, holding out his hand.

"I'm not aweer," replied the boy, drawing back "as I've got to thank *you* for it."

"Come, Billy, this ain't friendly, is it, after all I've done for you ?" said Jones, remonstratively; "I only want you to come out an' 'ave a talk with me about things, an' I'll give 'ee a swig o' beer or whatever you take a fancy to. You ain't goin' to show the white feather and become a milksop, are you?"

"Now, look here, Mister Jones," said the boy, with an air of decision that there was no mistaking, as he retreated nearer to the door; "I don't want for to have nothin' more to do with *you*. I've see'd much more than enough of 'ee. You knows me pretty well, an' you knows that wotiver else I may be, I ain't a hippercrite. I knows enough o' your doin's to make you look pretty blue if I like, but for reasons of my own, wot you've got nothink to do with, I don't mean to peach. All I ax is, that you goes your way an' let me alone. That's where it is. The people here seem to 'ave got a notion that I've got a soul as well as a body, and that it ain't 'xactly sitch a worthless thing as to be never thought of, and throw'd away like an old shoe. They may be wrong, and they may be right, but I'm inclined to agree with 'em. Let me tell 'ee that *you* 'ave did more than anybody else to show me the evil of wicked ways, so you needn't stand there grinnin' like a rackishoot wi' the toothache. I've jined the Band of Hope, too, so I don't want none o' your beer nor nothin' else, an' if you offers to lay hands on me, I'll yell out like a she-spurtindeel, an' bring in the guv'nor, wot's fit to wollop six o' you any day with his left hand."

This last part of Billy's speech was made with

additional fire, in consequence of Morley Jones taking a step towards him in anger.

"Well, boy," he said, sternly, "hypocrite or not, you've learned yer lesson pretty pat, so you may do as you please. It's little that a chip like you could do to get me convicted on anything you've seen or heard as yet, an' if ye did succeed, it would only serve to give yourself a lift on the way to the gallows. But it wasn't to trouble myself about you and your wishes that I came here for (the wily rascal assumed an air and tone of indifference at this point); if you had only waited to hear what I'd got to say, before you began to spit fire, you might have saved your breath. The fact is that my Nora is very ill—so ill that I fear she stands a poor chance o' gittin' better. I'm goin' to send her away on a long sea voyage. P'r'aps that may do her good; if not, it's all up with her. She begged and prayed me so earnestly to come here and take you down to see her before she goes, that I could not refuse her—particularly as I happened to have business in London anyhow. If I'd known how you would take it, I would have saved myself the trouble of comin'. However, I'll bid you good-day now."

"Jones," said the boy earnestly, "that's a lie."

"Very good," retorted the man, putting on his hat carelessly, "I'll take back that message with your compliments—eh?"

"No; but," said Billy, almost whimpering with anxiety, " is Nora *really* ill ?"

" I don't wish you to come if you don't want to," replied Jones; "you can stop here till doomsday for me. But do you suppose I'd come here for the mere amusement of hearing you give me the lie ?"

" I'll go !" said Billy, with as much emphasis as he had previously expressed on declining to go.

The matter was soon explained to the manager of the Grotto. Mr. Jones was so plausible, and gave such unexceptionable references, that it is no disparagement to the penetration of the superintendent of that day to say that he was deceived. The result was, as we have shown, that Billy ere long found his way to Ramsgate.

When Mr. Jones introduced him ceremoniously to Nora, he indulged in a prolonged and hearty fit of laughter. Nora gazed at Billy with a look of intense amazement, and Billy stared at Nora with a very mingled expression of countenance, for he at once saw through the deception that had been practised on him, and fully appreciated the difficulty of his position—his powers of explanation being hampered by a warning, given him long ago by his friend Jim Welton, that he must be careful how he let Nora into the full knowledge of her father's wickedness.

CHAPTER XIX.

CONFIDENCES AND CROSS PURPOSES.

KATIE DURANT, sitting with a happy smile on her fair face, and good-will in her sweet heart to all mankind—womankind included, which says a good deal for her—was busy with a beautiful sketch of a picturesque watermill, meditating on the stirring scene she had so recently witnessed, when a visitor was announced.

"Who can it be?" inquired Katie; "papa is out, you know, and no one can want me."

The lodging-house keeper, Mrs. Cackles, smiled at the idea of no one wanting Katie, knowing, as she did, that there were at least twenty people who would have given all they were worth in the world to possess her, either in the form of wife, sister, daughter, friend, governess, or companion.

"Well, miss, she do wants you, and says as no one else will do."

"Oh, a lady, please show her in, Mrs. Cackles."

"Well, she ain't a lady, either, though I've seen

many a lady· as would give their weight in gold to be like her."

So saying the landlady departed, and in a few seconds introduced Nora.

" Miss Jones !" cried Katie, rising with a pleased smile and holding out her hand; "this is a very unexpected pleasure."

"Thank you, Miss Durant. I felt sure you would remember me," said Nora, taking a seat, "and I also feel sure that you will assist me with your advice in a matter of some difficulty, especially as it relates to the boy about whose sick brother you came to me at Yarmouth some time ago—you remember ?"

" Oh ! Billy Towler," exclaimed Katie, with animation; " yes, I remember ; you are right in expecting me to be interested in him. Let me hear all about it."

Hereupon Nora gave Katie an insight into much of Billy Towler's history, especially dwelling on that part of it which related to his being sent to the Grotto, in the hope of saving him from the evil influences that were brought to bear upon him in his intercourse with her father.

" Not," she said, somewhat anxiously, "that I mean you to suppose my dear father teaches him anything that is wicked ; but his business leads him much among bad men—and— they drink and smoke, you know, which is very bad for a young boy to see; and many of them are awful swearers. Now, poor Billy has been induced to leave the Grotto and to come down here, for what purpose I don't know; but I am *so* disappointed, because I had hoped he would not have got tired of it so soon; and what distresses me most is, that he does not speak all his mind to me; I can see that, for he is very fond of me, and did not use to conceal things from me—at least I fancied not. The strange thing about it too is, that he says he is willing to return to the Grotto immediately, if I wish it."

"I am very *very* sorry to hear all this," said Katie, with a troubled air; "but what do you propose to do, and how can I assist you?—only tell me, and I shall be so happy to do it, if it be in my power."

"I really don't know how to put it to you, dear Miss Durant, and I could not have ventured if you had not been so very kind when I met you in Yarmouth; but—but your father owns several vessels, I believe, and—and—you will excuse me referring to it, I know—he was so good as to get a situation on board of the Wellington—which has so unfortunately been wrecked—for a young—a—a young —man; one of those who was saved—"

"Yes, yes," said Katie, quickly, thinking of Stanley Hall, and blushing scarlet; "I know the young gentleman to whom you refer; well, go on."

" Well," continued Nora, thinking of Jim Welton, and blushing scarlet too, "that young man said to me that he felt sure if I were to make application to Mr. Durant through you, he would give Billy a situation in one of his ships, and so get him out of harm's way."

"He was right," said Katie, with a somewhat puzzled expression; "and you may rely on my doing what I can for the poor boy with papa, who is always happy to help in such cases; but I was not aware that Mr. Hall knew either you or Billy."

" Mr. Hall!" exclaimed Nora, in surprise.

" Did you not refer to him just now?"

"No, miss; I meant James Welton."

" Oh!" exclaimed Katie, prolonging that monosyllable in a sliding scale, ranging from low to high and back to low again, which was peculiarly suggestive; "I beg your pardon, I quite misunderstood you; well, you may tell Mr. Welton that I will befriend Billy to the utmost of my power."

The door opened as she spoke, and cousin Fanny entered.

" Katie, I've come to tell you that Mr. Queek——"

She stopped short on observing Nora, who rose hastily, thanked Katie earnestly for the kind interest she had expressed in her little friend, and took her leave.

"This is a very interesting little incident, Fan," said Katie with delight when they were alone; "quite a romancelet of real life.   Let me see; here is a poor boy—the boy who deceived us, you remember—whom bad companions are trying to decoy into the wicked meshes of their dreadful net, and a sweet young girl, a sort of guardian angel as it were, comes to me and asks my aid to save the boy, and have him sent to sea.   Isn't it delightful?   Quite the ground-work of a tale—and might be so nicely illustrated," added Katie, glancing at her drawings. "But forgive me, Fan; I interrupted you.   What were you going to tell me?"

"Only that Mr. Queeker cannot come to tea to-night, as he has business to attend to connected with his secret mission," replied Fanny.

"How interesting it would be," said Katie, musing, "if we could only manage to mix up this mission of Mr. Queeker's in the plot of our romance; wouldn't it?   Come, I will put away my drawing for to-day, and finish the copy of papa's quarterly cash-account for those dreadful Board of Trade people; then we shall go to the pier and have a walk, and on our way we will call on that poor old bedridden woman whom papa has ferreted out, and give her some tea and sugar.   Isn't it strange that papa should have discovered one so soon?   I suppose you are aware of his *penchant* for old women, Fan?"

" No, I was not aware of it," said·Fan, smiling.

Whatever Fan said, she accompanied with a smile. Indeed a smile was the necessary result of the opeuing of her little mouth for whatever purpose —not an affected smile, but a merry one—which always had the effect, her face being plump, of half shutting her eyes.

" Yes," continued Katie, with animation, " papa is *so* fond of old women, particularly if they are *very* old, and *very* little, and thin; they *must* be thin, though. I don't think he cares much for them if they are fat. He says that fat people are so jolly that they don't need to be cared for, but he dotes upon the little thin ones."

Fanny smiled, and observed that that was curious.

" So it is," observed Katie; " now *my* taste lies in the direction of old men. I like to visit poor old men much better than poor old women, and the older and more helpless they are the more I like them."

Fanny smiled again, and observed that that was curious too.

" So it is," said Katie, " very odd that papa should like the old women and I should like the old men; but so it is. Now, Fan, we'll get ready and—oh how provoking! That must be another visitor! People find papa out so soon wherever we go, and then they give him no rest."

" A boy wishes to see you, miss," said Mrs. Cackles.

" Me ? " exclaimed Katie in surprise.

" Yes, miss, and he says he wants to see you alone on important business."

Katie looked at Fanny and smiled. Fanny returned the smile, and immediately left the room.

" Show him in, Mrs. Cackles."

The landlady withdrew, and ushered in no less a personage than Billy Towler himself, who stopped at the door, and stood with his hat in his hand, and an unusually confused expression in his looks. " Please, miss," said Billy, " you knows me, I think ? "

Katie admitted that she knew him, and, knowing in her heart that she meant to befriend him, it suddenly occurred to her that it would be well to begin with a little salutary severity by way of punishment for his former misdeeds.

" Last time I saw you, miss, I *did* you," said Billy with a slight grin.

" You did," replied Katie with a slight frown, " and I hope you have come to apologize for your naughty conduct."

" Well, I can't 'xactly say as I have come to do that, but I dessay I may as well begin that way. I'm very sorry, miss, for havin' *did* you, an' I've called now to see if I can't *do* you again."

Katie could not restrain a laugh at the impudence

of this remark, but she immediately regretted it, because Billy took encouragement and laughed too; she therefore frowned with intense severity, and, still remembering that she meant ultimately to befriend the boy, resolved to make him in the meantime feel the consequences of his former misdeeds.

"Come, boy," she said sharply, "don't add impertinence to your wickedness, but let me know at once what you want with me."

Billy was evidently taken aback by this rebuff. He looked surprised, and did not seem to know how to proceed. At length he put strong constraint upon himself, and said, in rather a gruff tone—

"Well, miss, I—a—the fact is—you know a gal named Nora Jones, don't you? Anyhow, she knows you, an' has said to me so often that you was a parfect angel, that—that—"

"That you came to see," interrupted Katie, glancing at her shoulders, "whether I really had wings, or not, eh?"

Katie said this with a still darker frown; for she thought that the urchin was jesting. Nothing was further from his intention. Knowing this, and, not finding the angelic looks and tones which he had been led to expect, Billy felt still more puzzled and inclined to be cross.

"Seems to me that there's a screw loose somewheres," said Billy, scratching the point of his nose in his vexation. "Hows'ever, I came here to ax your advice, and although you cer'nly don't 'ave wings nor the style o' looks wot's usual in 'eavenly wisiters, I'll make a clean breast of it—so here goes."

Hereupon the poor boy related how he had been decoyed from the Grotto—of which establishment he gave a graphic and glowing account—and said that he was resolved to have nothing more to do with Morley Jones, but meant to return to the Grotto without delay—that evening if possible. He had a difficulty, however, which was, that he could not speak freely to Nora about her father, for fear of hurting her feelings or enlightening her too much as to his true character, in regard to which she did not yet know the worst. One evil result of this was that she had begun to suspect there was something wrong as to his own affection for herself— which was altogether a mistake. Billy made the last remark with a flush of earnest indignation and a blow of his small hand on his diminutive knee! He then said that another evil result was that he could not see his way to explain to Nora why he wished to be off in such a hurry, and, worst of all, he had not a sixpence in the world wherewith to pay his fare to London, and had no means of getting one.

"And so," said Katie, still keeping up her fictitious indignation, "you come to beg money from me?"

" Not to beg, Miss—to borrer."

" Ah! and thus to do me a second time," said Katie.

It must not be supposed that Katie's sympathetic heart had suddenly become adamantine. On the contrary, she had listened with deep interest to all that her youthful visitor had to say, and rejoiced in the thought that she had given to her such a splendid opportunity of doing good and frustrating evil; but the little spice of mischief in her character induced her still to keep up the fiction of being suspicious, in order to give Billy a salutary lesson. In addition to this, she had not quite got over the supposed insult of being mistaken for an angel! She therefore declined, in the meantime, to advance the required sum—ten-and-sixpence— although the boy earnestly promised to repay her with his first earnings.

" No," she said, with a gravity which she found it difficult to maintain, "I cannot give you such a sum until I have seen and consulted with my father on the subject; but I may tell you that I respect your sentiments regarding Nora and your intention to forsake your evil ways. If you will call here again in the evening I will see what can be done for you."

Saying this, and meditating in her heart that she

would not only give Billy the ten-and-sixpence to enable him to return to the Grotto, but would induce her father to give him permanent employment in one of his ships, she showed Billy to the door, and bade him be a good boy and take care of himself.

Thereafter she recalled Fanny, and, for her benefit, re-enacted the whole scene between herself and Billy Towler, in a manner so graphic and enthusiastic, as to throw that amiable creature into convulsions of laughter, which bade fair to terminate her career in a premature fit of juvenile apoplexy.

CHAPTER XX.

MYSTERIOUS DOINGS.

DISAPPOINTED, displeased, and sorely puzzled, Billy Towler took his way towards the harbour, with his hands thrust desperately into his pockets, and an unwonted expression of discontent on his countenance. So deeply did he take the matter to heart, that he suffered one small boy to inquire pathetically " if 'ed bin long in that state o' grumps?" and another to suggest that "if 'e couldn't be 'appier than that, 'ed better go an' drown hisself," without vouchsafing a retort, or even a glance of recognition.

Passing the harbour, he went down to the beach, and there unexpectedly met with Mr. Morley Jones.

" Hallo! my young bantam," exclaimed Morley, with a look of surprise.

" Well, old Cochin-china, wot's up?" replied Billy, in a gruff tone. " Drunk as usual, I see."

Being somewhat desperate, the boy did not see, or did not mind the savage glance with which Mr.

Jones favoured him.   The glance was, however, ex-
changed quickly for an idiotic smile, as he retorted—

" Well, I ain't so drunk but I can see to steer
my course, lad.   Come, I 've got a noo boat, what
d' ye say to go an' have a sail?   The fact is, Billy, I
was just on my way up to the house to ax you to
go with me, so it 's good luck that I didn't miss
you.   Will 'ee go, lad ? "

At any other time the boy would have refused ;
but his recent disappointment in regard to the
angelic nature of Katie still rankled so powerfully
in his breast, that he swung round and said—

" Get along, then—I 'm your man—it 's all up now
—never say die—in for a penny in for a pound,"
and a variety of similar expressions, all of which
tended to convince Mr. Jones that Billy Towler
happened to be in a humour that was extremely
suitable to his purposes.   He therefore led him
towards his boat, which, he said, was lying on the
beach at Broadstairs all ready to shove off.

The distance to Broadstairs was about two miles,
and the walk thither was enlivened by a drunken
commentary on the fallacy of human hopes in general
on the part of Mr. Jones, and a brisk fire of caustic
repartee on the part of Master Towler.

A close observer might have noticed that, while
these two were passing along the beach, at the base
of the high cliffs of chalk running between Ramsgate

and Broadstairs, two heads were thrust cautiously out of one of the small caverns or recesses which have been made in these cliffs by the action of the waves. The one head bore a striking resemblance to that of Robert Queeker, Esq., and the other to that of Mr. Larks.

How these two came to be together, and to be there, it is not our business to say. Authors are fortunately not bound to account for everything they relate. All that we know is, that Mr. Queeker was there in the furtherance, probably, of his secret mission, and that Mr. Larks' missions appeared to be always more or less secret. At all events, there they were together; fellow-students, apparently, of the geology or conchology of that region, if one might judge from the earnest manner in which they stooped and gazed at the sands, and picked up bits of flint or small shells, over which they held frequent, and, no doubt, learned discussions of an intensely engrossing nature.

It might have been also noticed by a close observer, that these stoopings to pick up specimens, and these stoppages to discuss, invariably occurred when Mr. Jones and Master Billy chanced to pause or to look behind them. At last the boat was reached. It lay on the beach not far from the small harbour of Broadstairs, already surrounded by the rising tide. About the same time the geological and conchological studies of Messrs. Queeker and Larks coming to an end, these scientific men betook themselves suddenly to the shelter of a small cave, whence they sat watching, with intense interest, the movements of the man and boy, thus proving themselves gifted with a truly Baconian spirit of general inquiry into simple facts, with a view to future inductions.

"Jump in, Billy," said Jones, "and don't wet your feet; I can easily shove her off alone."

Billy obeyed.

"Hallo! wot have 'ee got here?" he cried, touching a large tarpaulin bag with his foot.

"Only some grub," answered Jones, putting his shoulder to the bow of the boat.

"And a compass too!" cried Billy, looking round in surprise.

"Ay, it may come on thick, you know," said Jones, as the boat's keel grated over the sand.

"I say, stop!" cried Billy; "you're up to some mischief; come, let me ashore."

Mr. Jones made no reply, but continued to push off the boat. Seeing this, the boy leaped overboard, but Jones caught him. For one instant there was a struggle; then poor Billy was lifted in the strong man's arms, and hurled back into the boat. Next moment it was afloat, and Jones leaped inboard. Billy was not to be overcome so easily, however.

He sprang up, and again made a leap over the gunwale, but Jones caught him by the collar, and, after
a severe struggle, dragged him into the boat, and
gave him a blow on the head with his clenched fist,
which stunned him. Then, seizing the oars, he
pulled off. After getting well away from the beach
he hoisted a small lug-sail, and stood out to sea.

All this was witnessed by the scientific men in
the cave through a couple of small pocket-telescopes,
which brought the expression of Jones's and Billy's
countenances clearly into view. At first Mr.
Queeker, with poetic fervour, started up, intent on
rushing to the rescue of the oppressed; but Mr.
Larks, with prosaic hardness of heart, held him
forcibly back, and told him to make his mind easy,
adding that Mr. Jones had no intention of doing
the boy any further harm. Whereupon Queeker
submitted with a sigh. The two friends then issued
from the cave, shook hands, and bade each other
goodbye with a laugh—the man with the keen grey
eyes following the path that led to Broadstairs, while
the lawyer's clerk returned to Ramsgate by the
beach.

Meanwhile the sun went down, and the lanterns
of the *Goodwin*, the *Gull*, and the *South sandhead*
floating lights went up. The shades of evening fell,
and the stars came out—one by one at first; then
by twos and threes; at last by bursts of constella-

tious, until the whole heavens glowed with a galaxy of distant worlds. During all this time Mr. Jones sat at the helm of his little boat, and held steadily out to sea. The wind being light, he made small progress, but that circumstance did not seem to trouble him much.

" You 'd better have a bit supper, lad," said Jones in a careless way. " Of course you 're welcome to starve yourself, if 'ee choose, but by so doin' you 'll only make yourself uncomfortable for nothing. You 're in for it now, an' can't help yourself."

Billy was seated on one of the thwarts, looking very savage, with his right eye nearly closed by the blow which had caused him to succumb.

" P'r'aps I mayn't be able to help myself," he replied, " but I can peach upon *you*, anyhow."

" So you can, my lad, if you want to spend eight or ten years in limbo," retorted Jones, spitting out his quid of tobacco, and supplying its place with a new one. " You and I are in the same boat, Billy, whether ashore or afloat; we sink or swim together."

No more was said for some time. Jones knew that the boy was in his power, and resolved to bide his time. Billy felt that he had at least the chance of being revenged if he chose to sacrifice himself, so he " nursed his wrath to keep it warm."

About an hour afterwards a squall struck the boat,

and nearly capsized it; but Jones, who was quite sobered by that time, threw her head quickly into the wind, and Billy, forgetting everything else, leaped up with his wonted activity, loosened the sail, and reefed it. The squall soon passed away, and left them almost becalmed, as before.

"That was well done, Billy," said Jones, in a cheerful tone ; "you 'd make a smart sailor, my lad."

Billy made no reply; and, despite his efforts to the contrary, felt highly flattered. He also felt the pangs of hunger, and, after resisting them for some time, resolved to eat, as it were, under protest. With a reckless, wilful air, therefore, he opened the tarpaulin bag, and helped himself to a large " hunk " of bread and a piece of cheese. Whereupon Mr. Jones smiled grimly, and remarked that there was nothing like grub for giving a man heart—except grog, he added, producing a case-bottle from his pocket and applying it to his mouth.

"Have a pull, lad? No! well, please yourself. I ain't goin' to join the temperance move myself yet," said Jones, replacing the bottle in his pocket.

The short squall having carried the boat nearer to the Gull lightship than was desirable, Mr. Jones tried to keep as far off from her as possible, while the tide should sweep them past; but the wind having almost died away, he did not succeed in this ; however, he knew that darkness would prevent recognition, so he thought it best not to take to the oars, but to hold on, intending to slip quietly by, not supposing that Billy would think it of any use to hail the vessel; but Billy happened to think otherwise.

" Gull ahoy ! hoy !" he shouted at the top of his shrill voice.

" Boat ahoy !" responded Jack Shales, who happened to be on duty ; but no response was given to Jack, for the good reason that Jones had instantly clapped his hand on Billy's mouth, and half-choked him.

" That 's odd," remarked Jack, after repeating his cry twice.   " I could swear it was the voice of that sharp little rascal Billy Towler."

" If it wasn't it was his ghost," replied Jerry Mac-Gowl, who chanced to be on deck at the time.

" Sure enough it 's very ghost-like," said Shales, as the boat glided silently and slowly out of the circle of the lantern's light, and faded from their vision.

Mr. Jones did not follow up his act with further violence.   He merely assured Billy that he was a foolish fellow, and that it was of no use to struggle against his fate.

.As time wore on, poor Billy felt dreadfully sleepy, and would have given a good deal for some of the grog in his companion's case-bottle, but, resolving to stand upon his dignity, would not condescend to ask for it. At length he lay down and slept, and Jones covered him with a pilot-coat.

No soft spot in the scoundrel's heart induced him to perform this act of apparent kindness. He knew the poor boy's temperament, and resolved to attack him on his weakest point.

When Billy awoke the day was just breaking. He stretched himself, yawned, sat up, and looked about him with the confused air of one not quite awake.

" Hallo !" he cried gaily, " where on earth am I ?"

" You ain't on earth, lad ; you 're afloat," replied Jones, who still sat at the helm.

At once the boy remembered everything, and shrank within himself. As he did so, he observed the pilot-coat which covered him, and knew that it must have been placed where it was by Jones. His resolution to hold out was shaken ; still he did not give in.

Mr. Jones now began to comment in a quiet good-natured way upon the weather and the prospects of the voyage (which excited Billy's curiosity very much), and suggested that breakfast would not be a bad thing, and that a drop o' rum might be agreeable, but took care never to make his remarks so pointed as to call for an answer. Just as the sun was rising he got up slowly, cast loose the stays and halyards of mast and sail, lifted the mast out of its place, and deliberately hove the whole affair overboard, remarking in a quiet tone that, having served his purpose, he didn't want mast or sail any longer. In the same deliberate way he unshipped the rudder and cast it away. He followed this up by throwing overboard one of the oars, and then taking the only remaining oar, he sculled and steered the boat therewith gently.

Billy, who thought his companion must be either drunk or mad, could contain himself no longer.

"I say, old fellow," he remarked, "you're comin' it pretty strong! Wot on earth *are* you up to, and where in all the world are 'ee goin' to?"

"Oh come, you know," answered Jones in a remonstrative tone, "I *may* be an easy-goin' chap, but I can't be expected to tell all my secrets except to friends."

"Well, well," said Billy, with a sigh, "it's no use tryin' to hold out. I'll be as friendly as I can; only I tells you candid, I'll mizzle whenever I gits ashore. I'm not agoin' to tell no end o' lies to please you any longer, so I give 'ee fair warning," said Billy stoutly.

"All right, my lad," said the wily Jones, who felt that having subdued the boy thus far, he would have little difficulty in subduing him still further, in course of time, and by dint of judicious treatment;

"I don't want 'ee to tell lies on my account, an' I'll let you go free as soon as ever we get ashore. So now, let's shake hands over it, and have a glass o' grog and a bit o' breakfast."

Billy shook hands, and took a sip out of the case-bottle, by way of clenching the reconciliation. The two then had breakfast together, and, while this meal was in progress, Jones informed his little friend of the nature of the "game" he was engaged in playing out.

"You must know, my lad," said Mr. Jones, "that you and I have been wrecked. We are the only survivors of the brig Skylark, which was run down in a fog by a large three-masted screw steamer on the night of the thirteenth—that's three nights ago, Billy. The Skylark sank immediately, and every soul on board was lost except you and me, because the steamer, as is too often the case in such accidents, passed on and left us to our fate. You and I was saved by consequence of bein' smart and gettin' into this here small boat—which is one o' the Skylark's boats—only just in time to save ourselves; but she had only one oar in her, and no mast, or sail, or rudder, as you see, Billy; nevertheless we managed to keep her goin' with the one oar up to this time, and no doubt," said Mr. Jones with a grin, "we'll manage to keep her goin' till we're picked up and carried safe into port."

Billy's eyes had opened very wide and very round as Mr. Jones's description proceeded; gradually, as his surprise increased, his mouth also opened and elongated, but he said never a word, though he breathed hard.

" Now, Billy, my boy," pursued Mr. Jones, " I tell 'ee all this, of course, in strict confidence. The Skylark, you must know, was loaded with a valuable cargo of fine herrings, worth about £200. There was 780 barrels of 'em, and 800 boxes. The brig was worth £100, so the whole affair was valued at £300 sterling."

" You don't mean to tell me," said Billy, catching his breath, " that there warn't never no such a wessel as the Skylark ? "

" Never that I know of," replied Jones with a smile, " except in my brain, and on the books o' several insurance companies."

Billy's eyes and mouth grew visibly rounder, but he said nothing more, and Mr. Jones, renewing his quid, went on—

" Well, my lad, before this here Skylark left the port of London for Cherbourg, I insured her in no fewer than five insurance Companies. You 'll understand that that ain't regular, my boy, but at each office I said that the vessel was not insured in any other, and they believed me. You must know that a good deal of business is done by these Companies in good faith, which gives a chance to smart fellows like me and you to turn an honest penny, d' ye see? They are pretty soft, luckily."

Mr. Jones happened to be mistaken in this opinion, as the sequel will show, but Billy believed him at the time, and wondered that they were " so green."

" Yes," continued Jones, counting on his fingers, " I 'm in for £300 with the *Advance* Company, and £300 with the *Tied Harbours* Company, and £225 with the *Home and Abroad* Company, and £200 with the *Submarine* Company, and £300 with the *Friend-in-need* Company—the whole makin' a snug little sum of £1325. 'In for a penny, in for a pound,' is my motto, you see ; so, lad, you and I shall make our fortunes, if all goes well, and you only continue game and clever."

This last remark was a feeler, and Mr. Jones paused to observe its effect; but he could scarce refrain from laughter, for Billy's eyes and mouth now resembled three extremely round O's with his nose like a fat mark of admiration in the midst.

A gusty sigh was all the response he gave, however, so Mr. Jones continued—

"We've been out about thirty hours, starvin' in this here little boat, you and I, so now it 's about time we wos picked up ; and as I see a vessel on our larboard-beam that looks like a foreigner, we 'll throw the grub overboard, have another pull at the grog-bottle, and hoist a signal of distress."

In pursuance of these intentions Jones applied the case-bottle to his lips, and took a long pull, after which he offered it to Billy, who however declined. He then threw the bread-bag into the sea, and tying his handkerchief to the oar after the manner of a flag, set it up on end and awaited the result.

The vessel alluded to was presently observed to alter its course and bear down on the boat, and now Billy felt that the deciding time had come. He sat gazing at the approaching vessel in silence. Was he to give in to his fate and agree to tell lies through thick and thin in order to further the designs of Mr. Jones, or was he to reveal all the moment he should get on board the vessel, and take the consequences? He thought of Katie, and resolved to give up the struggle against evil. Then Nora rose up in his mind's eye, and he determined to do the right. Then he thought of transportation for a prolonged term of years, with which Jones threatened him, and he felt inclined to turn again into the wrong road to escape from that; presently he remembered the Grotto, and the lessons of truth to God and man that he had learned there, and he made up his mind to fight in the cause of truth to the last gasp.

Mr. Jones watched his face keenly, and came to

the conclusion that he had quelled the boy, and should now find him a willing and useful tool, but in order to make still more sure, he employed the few minutes that remained to him in commenting on the great discomfort of a convict's life, and the great satisfaction that accrued from making one's fortune at a single stroke.

This talk was not without its effect. Billy wavered. Before he could make up his mind they were alongside the strange vessel, and next moment on her deck. Mr. Jones quickly explained the circumstances of the loss of the Skylark to the sympathetic captain. Billy listened in silence, and, by silence, had assented to the falsehood. It was too late now to mend matters, so he gave way to despair, which in him frequently, if not usually, assumed the form of reckless joviality.

While this spirit was strong upon him he swore to anything. He not only admitted the truth of all that his tempter advanced, but entertained the seamen with a lively and graphic account of the running down of the Skylark, and entered into minute particulars—chiefly of a comical nature—with such recklessness that the cause of Mr. Jones bade fair to resemble many a roast which is totally ruined by being overdone. Jones gave him a salutary check, however, on being landed next day at a certain town on the Kentish coast, so that when

Billy was taken before the authorities, his statements were brought somewhat more into accord with those of his tempter.

The wily Mr. Jones went at once with Billy to the chief officer of the coast-guard on that station, and reported the loss of his vessel with much minuteness of detail—to the effect that she had sailed from London at noon of a certain date, at the quarter ebb tide, the sky being cloudy and wind sou'-west; that the casualty occurred at five P.M. on the day following near the North Foreland Light, at half flood tide, the sky being cloudy and wind west-sou'-west; that the vessel had sunk, and all the crew had perished excepting himself and the boy. This report, with full particulars, was sent to the Board of Trade. Mr. Jones then went to the agent for the Shipwrecked Mariners' Society and related his pitiful tale to him. That gentleman happening to be an astute man, observed some discrepancies in the accounts given respectively by Billy and his master. He therefore put a variety of puzzling questions, and 'took down a good many notes. Mr. Jones, however, had laid his plans so well, and gave such a satisfactory and plausible account of himself, that the agent felt constrained to extend to him the aid of the noble Society which he represented, and by which so much good is done to sailors directly, and indirectly to the community at large. He paid their passage to London, but resolved to make some further inquiries with a view either to confirming or allaying his suspicions.

These little matters settled, and the loss having been duly advertised in the newspapers, Mr. Jones set out for London with the intention of presenting his claims to the Insurance Companies.

In the train Billy had time to reflect on the wickedness of which he had been guilty, and his heart was torn with conflicting emotions, among which repentance was perhaps the most powerful. But what, he thought, was the use of repentance now? The thing was done and could not be undone.

Could it not? Was it too late to mend? At the Grotto he had been taught that it was "never too late to mend"—but that it was sinful as well as dangerous to delay on the strength of that fact; that "*now* was the accepted time, *now* the day of salvation." When Billy thought of these things, and then looked at the stern inexorable face of the man by whom he had been enslaved, he began to give way to despair. When he thought of his good angel Nora, he felt inclined to leap out of the carriage window and escape or die! He restrained himself, however, and did nothing until the train arrived in London. Then he suddenly burst away from his captor, dived between the legs of a magnificent railway guard, whose dignity and person were overthrown by the shock, eluded the ticket-collector and several policemen, and used his active little legs so well that in a few minutes his pursuers lost him in a labyrinth of low streets not far distant from the station.

From this point he proceeded at a rapid though less furious pace direct to the Grotto, where he presented himself to the superintendent with the remark that he had " come back to 'make a clean breast of it."

CHAPTER XXI.

ON THE SCENT.

LET us change the scene and put back the clock. Ah, how many hearts would rejoice if it were as easy to return on the track of Time in real life as it is to do so in a tale!

It was the evening of the day in which Jones and Billy went to sea in the little boat. Ramsgate, Mr. Durant's supper-table, with Stanley Hall and Robert Queeker as guests.

They were all very happy and merry, for Stanley was recounting with graphic power some of the incidents of his recent voyage. Mr. Durant was rich enough to take the loss of his vessel with great equanimity—all the more so that it had been fully insured. Mr. Queeker was in a state of bliss in consequence of having been received graciously by Fanny, whose soul was aflame with sentiment so powerful that she could not express it except through the medium of a giggle. Only once had Fanny been enabled to do full justice to herself, and that was when, alone with Katie in the mysterious gloom of a midnight confabulation, she suddenly observed that size and looks in men were absolutely nothing—less than nothing—and that in her estimation heart and intellect were everything!

In the midst of his mirth Mr. Durant suddenly turned to Queeker and said—

"By the way, what made you so late of coming to-night, Queeker? I thought you had promised to come to tea."

"Well, yes, but—a—that is," stammered Queeker in confusion, "in fact I was obliged to keep an appointment in connection with the—the particular business—"

"The secret mission, in short," observed Katie, with a peculiar smile.

"Well, secret mission if you choose," laughed Queeker; "at all events it was that which prevented my getting here sooner. In truth, I did not expect to have managed to come so soon, but we came to the boat—"

Queeker stopped short and blushed violently, feeling that he had slightly, though unintentionally, committed himself.

Fanny looked at him, blushed in sympathy, and giggled.

"Oh, there's a *boat* in the secret mission, is there?"

cried Stanley; "come, let us make a game of it. Was it an iron boat?"

"No," replied Queeker, laughing, for he felt that at all events he was safe in answering that question.

"Was it a wooden one?" asked Katie.

"Well—ye—"

"Was it a big one?" demanded Mr. Durant, entering into the spirit of the game.

"No, it was a little one," said Queeker, still feeling safe, although anxious to evade reply.

"Was there a man in it?" said Katie.

Queeker hesitated.

"And a boy?" cried Stanley.

The question was put unwittingly, but being so put Queeker stammered, and again blushed.

Katie on the contrary turned pale, for her previously expressed hope that there might be some connection between Queeker's mission and Billy Towler's troubles flashed into her mind.

"But *was* there a boy in it?" she said, with a sudden earnestness that induced every one to look at her in surprise.

"Really, I pray—I must beg," said Queeker, "that you won't make this a matter of even jocular inquiry. Of course I know that no one here would make improper use of any information that I might give, but I have been pledged to secrecy by my employers."

"But," continued Katie in the same anxious way

as before, "it will not surely be a breach of confidence merely to tell me if the boy was a small, active, good-looking little fellow, with bright eyes and curly hair."

"I am bound to admit," said Queeker, "that your description is correct."

To the amazement, not to say consternation, of every one, Katie covered her face with her hands and burst into tears, exclaiming in an agony of distress that she knew it; she had feared it after sending him away; that she had ruined him, and that it was too late now to do anything.

"No, not too late, perhaps," she repeated, suddenly raising her large beautiful eyes, which swam in tears; "oh papa, come with me up-stairs, I must speak with you alone at once."

She seized her astonished father by the hand and led him unresisting from the room.

Having hurriedly related all she knew about Billy Towler, Morley Jones, and Nora, she looked up in his face and demanded to know what *was* to be done.

"Done, my dear child," he replied, looking perplexed, "we must go at once and see how much can be *un*done. You tell me you have Nora's address. Well, we 'll go there at once.

"But—but," said Katie, "Nora does not know the full extent of her father's wickedness, and we want to keep it from her if possible."

"A very proper desire to spare her pain, Katie, but in the circumstances we cannot help ourselves; we must do what we can to frustrate this man's designs and save the boy."

So saying Mr. Durant descended to the dining-room. He explained that some suspicious facts had come to his daughter's knowledge which necessitated instant action; said that he was sorry Mr. Quecker felt it incumbent on him to maintain secrecy in regard to his mission, but that he could not think of pressing him to act in opposition to his convictions, and, dismissing his guests with many apologies, went out with Katie in search of the abode of Nora Jones.

Stanley Hall, whose curiosity was aroused by all that had passed, went down to take a walk on the pier by way of wearing it off in a philosophical manner. He succeeded easily in getting rid of this feeling, but he could not so easily get rid of the image of Katie Durant. He had suspected himself in love with her before he sailed for India; his suspicions were increased on his return to England, and when he saw the burst of deep feeling to which she had so recently given way, and heard the genuine expressions of remorse, and beheld her sweet face bedewed with tears of regret and pity, suspicion was swallowed up in certainty.

He resolved then and there to win her, if he could,

and marry her! Here a touch of perplexity assailed him, but he fought it off nobly.

He was young, no doubt, and had no money, but what then?—he was strong, had good abilities, a father in a lucrative practice, with the prospect of assisting and ultimately succeeding him. That was enough, surely.

The lodging which he had taken for a few days was retaken that night for an indefinite period, and he resolved to lay siege to her heart in due form.

But that uncertainty which is proverbial in human affairs stepped within the circle of his life and overturned his plans. On returning to his rooms he found a telegram on the table. His father, it informed him, was dangerously ill. By the next train he started for home, and arrived to find that his father was dead.

A true narrative of any portion of this world's doings must of necessity be as varied as the world itself, and equally abrupt in its transitions. From the lively supper-table Stanley Hall passed to the deathbed of his father. In like manner we must ask the reader to turn with us from the contemplation of Stanley's deep sorrow to the observation of Queeker's poetic despair.

Maddened between the desire to tell all he knew regarding the secret mission to Mr. Durant, and

the command laid on him by his employers to be
silent, the miserable youth rushed frantically to his
lodgings, without any definite intentions, but more
than half inclined to sink on his knees before his
desk, and look up to the moon, or stars, or, failing
these, to the floating light for inspiration, and pen
the direful dirge of something dreadful and desperate!
He had even got the length of the first line, and had
burst like a thunderbolt into his room muttering— ·

"Great blazing wonder of illimitable spheres,"

when he became suddenly aware of the fact that his
chair was occupied by the conchological friend with
whom he had spent the earlier part of that day, who
was no other than the man with the keen grey eyes.

"What! still in the poetic vein?" he said, with
a grave smile.

"Why—I—thought you were off, to London!"
exclaimed Queeker, with a very red face.

"I have seen cause to change my plan," said Mr.
Larks quietly.

"I'm *very* glad of it," replied Queeker, running
his fingers through his hair and sitting down opposite
his friend with a deep sigh, "because I'm in the
most horrible state of perplexity. It is quite evident
to me that the boy is known to Miss Durant, for she
went off into *such* a state when I mentioned him
. and described him exactly."

"Indeed," said Mr. Larks; "h'm ! I know the boy too."

"Do you ? Why didn't you tell me that ?"

"There was no occasion to," said the imperturbable Mr. Larks, whose visage never by any chance conveyed any expression whatever, except when he pleased, and then it conveyed only and exactly the expression that he intended. "But come," he continued, "let's hear all about it, and don't quote any poetry till you have done with the facts."

Thus exhorted Queeker described the scene at the supper-table with faithful minuteness, and, on concluding, demanded what was to be done.

"H'm !" grunted Mr. Larks. "They've gone to visit Nora Jones, so you and I shall go and keep them company.   Come along."

He put on his hat and went out, followed by his little friend.

In a lowly ill-furnished room in one of the poorest streets of the town, where rats and dogs and cats seemed to divide the district with poverty-stricken human beings, they found Nora sitting by the bedside of her grandmother, who appeared to be dying. A large Family Bible, from which she had been reading, was open on her knee.

Mr. Larks had opened the door and entered without knocking. He and Queeker stood in the passage and saw the bed, the invalid, and the watcher through an inner door which stood ajar. They could hear the murmurings of the old woman's voice. She appeared to wander in her mind, for sometimes her words were coherent, at other times she merely babbled.

"O Morley, Morley, give it up," she said, during one of her lucid intervals; "it has been the curse of our family. Your grandfather died of it; your father—ah! he *was* a man, tall and straight, and *so* kind, till he took to it; oh me! how it changed him! But the Lord saved his soul, though he let the body fall to the dust. Blessed be His holy name for that. Give it up, Morley, my darling boy; give it up, give it up—oh, for God's sake give it up!"

She raised her voice at each entreaty until it almost reached a shriek, and then her whole frame seemed to sink down into the bed from exhaustion.

"Why don't 'ee speak to me, Morley?" she resumed after a short time, endeavouring to turn her head round.

"Dearest granny," said Nora, gently stroking one of her withered hands, which lay on the counterpane, "father is away just now. No doubt he will be back ere long."

"Ay, ay, he's always away; always away," she murmured in a querulous tone; "always coming back too, but he never comes. Oh, if he would give it up—give it up—"

She repeated this several times, and gradually dwindled off into unintelligible mutterings.

By this time Mr. Larks had become aware of whispering voices in a part of the room which he could not see. Pushing the door a little farther open he entered softly, and in a darkened corner of the apartment beheld Mr. Durant and Katie in close conversation with James Welton. They all rose, and Nora, seeing that the old woman had fallen into a slumber, also rose and advanced towards the strangers. Mr. Durant at once explained to her who Queeker was, and Queeker introduced Mr. Larks as a friend who had come to see them on important business.

"I think we know pretty well what the business is about," said Jim Welton, advancing and addressing himself to Mr. Larks, "but you see," he added, glancing towards the bed, "that this is neither the time nor place to prosecute your inquiries, sir."

Mr. Larks, who was by no means an unfeeling man, though very stern, said that he had no intention of intruding; he had not been aware that any one was ill in the house, and he would take it as a favour if Mr. Welton would go outside and allow him the pleasure of a few words with him. Of course Jim agreed, but before going took Nora aside.

"I'll not be back to-night, dearest," he said in a low whisper. "To-morrow, early, I'll return."

"You will leave no stone unturned?" said Nora.

"Not one. I'll do my best to save him."

"And you have told me the worst—told me *all*?" asked Nora, with a look of intense grief mingled with anxiety on her pale face.

"I have," said Jim, in a tone and with a look so earnest and truthful that Nora required no further assurance. She gave him a kindly but inexpressibly sad smile, and returned to her stool beside the bed. Her lover and Mr. Larks went out, followed by Queeker.

"We won't intrude on you longer to-night," said Katie, going up to Nora and laying her hand quietly on her shoulder.

"Your visit is no intrusion," said Nora, looking up with a quiet smile. "It was love that brought you here, I know. May our dear Lord bless you and your father for wishing to comfort the heart of one who needs it so much—oh, so much." She put her hands before her face and was silent. Katie tried in vain to speak. The tears coursed freely down her cheeks, but never a word could she utter. She put her arm round the neck of the poor girl and kissed her. This was a language which Nora understood;—many words could not have expressed so much; no words could have expressed more.

CHAPTER XXII.

MR. JONES IS OUTWITTED, AND NORA IS LEFT DESOLATE.

WHEN Morley Jones found himself suddenly deserted by his ally Billy Towler, he retired to the privacy of a box in a low public-house in Thames Street, and there, under the stimulus of a stiff glass of grog, consulted with himself as to the best mode of procedure under the trying circumstances in which he found himself placed. He thought it probable, after half an hour of severe meditation, that Billy would return to the Grotto, but that, for his own sake, he would give a false account of his absence, and say nothing about the loss of the Skylark. Feeling somewhat relieved in mind by his conclusions on this head, he drank off his grog, called for another glass, and then set himself to the consideration of how far the disappearance of the boy would interfere with his obtaining payment of the various sums due by the Insurance Offices. This point was either more knotty and difficult to unravel than the previous one, or the grog began to render his intellect less capable of grappling with it. At all events it cost him an hour to determine his course of action, and required another glass of grog to enable him to put the whole matter fairly before his mental vision in one comprehensive view. This, however, accomplished, he called for a fourth glass of grog " for luck," and reeled out of the house to carry out his deep-laid plans.

His first act was to proceed to Greenwich, where a branch of his fish-curing business existed, or was supposed to exist. Here he met a friend who offered to treat him. Unfortunately for the success of his schemes he accepted this offer, and, in the course of a debauch, revealed so much of his private affairs that the friend, after seeing him safely to his lodging, and bidding him an affectionate farewell, went up to London by the first boat on the following morning, and presented himself to the managers of various Insurance Companies, to whom he made revelations which were variously received by these gentlemen; some of them opening their eyes in amazement, while others opened their mouths in amusement, and gave him to understand that he was very much in the position of a man who should carry coals to Newcastle—they being then in possession of all the information given, and a great deal more besides.

The manager of the Submarine Insurance Com-

pany was the most facetious among these gentlemen
on hearing the revelations of Mr. Jones's "friend."

"Can you tell me," said that gentleman, when
he had pumped the "friend" dry, "which of us is
likely to receive the distinguished honour of the
first visit from Mr. Jones?"

"He said summat about your own office, sir,"
replied the informer; "leastwise I think he did, but
I ain't quite sartin."

"H'm! not unlikely," observed the manager; "we
have had the pleasure of paying him something
before to-day. Come here, I will introduce you to
an acquaintance of Mr. Jones, who takes a deep interest in him. He has just arrived from Ramsgate."

Opening a door, the manager ushered the informer
into a small room where a stout man with peculiarly
keen grey eyes was warming himself at the fire.

"Allow me to introduce you, Mr. Larks, to a friend
of Mr. Jones, who may be of some use. I will leave
you together for a little," said the manager, with a
laugh, as he retired and shut the door.

It is not necessary that we should enter into
details as to how Mr. Jones went about the business
of drawing his nets ashore—so to speak,—and how
those who took a special interest in Mr. Jones
carefully assisted him, and, up to a certain point,
furthered all his proceedings. It is sufficient to
say that, about a fortnight after his arrival in Lon-

don—all the preliminary steps having been taken—
he presented himself one fine forenoon at the office
of the Submarine Insurance Company.

He was received very graciously, and, much to his
satisfaction, was told that the claim could now be
settled without further delay. Former experience
had taught him that such a piece of business was
not unusually difficult of settlement, but he was
quite charmed by the unwonted facilities which
seemed to be thrown in his way in regard to the
present affair. He congratulated himself internally,
and the manager congratulated him externally, so to
speak, by referring to his good fortune in having
insured the vessel and cargo to the full amount.

Even the clerks of the establishment appeared to
manifest unwonted interest in the case, which gratified while it somewhat surprised Mr. Jones. Indeed, the interest deepened to such an extent, and
was so obtrusive, that it became almost alarming,
so that feelings of considerable relief were experienced by the adventurous man when he at length
received a cheque for £300 and left the office with
it in his pocket.

In the outer lobby he felt a touch on his arm, and,
looking round, met the gaze of a gentleman with
peculiarly keen grey eyes. This gentleman made
some quiet remarks with reference to Mr. Jones
being "wanted," and when Mr. Jones, not relishing

the tone or looks of this gentleman, made a rush at the outer glass door of the office, an official stepped promptly in front of it, put one hand on the handle, and held up the other with the air of one who should say, " Excuse me, there is no thoroughfare this way." Turning abruptly to the left, Mr. Jones found himself confronted by another grave gentleman of powerful frame and resolute aspect, who, by a species of magic or sleight of hand known only to the initiated, slipped a pair of steel bracelets on Mr. Jones's wrists, and finally, almost before he knew where he was, Mr. Jones found himself seated in a cab with the strong gentleman by his side, and the keen grey-eyed gentleman in front of him.

Soon afterwards he found himself standing alone in the midst of an apartment, the chief characteristics of which were, that the furniture was scanty, the size inconveniently little, and the window unusually high up, besides being heavily barred, and ridiculously small.

Here let us leave him to his meditations.

One fine forenoon—many weeks after the capture of Morley Jones—Dick Moy, Jack Shales, and Jerry MacGowl were engaged in painting and repairing buoys in the Trinity store on the pier at Ramsgate. The two former were enjoying their month of service on shore, the latter was on sick-leave, but convalescent. Jack was painting squares of alternate

black and white on a buoy of a conical shape. Dick
was vigorously scraping sea-weed and barnacles off
a buoy of a round form. The store, or big shed, was
full of buoys of all shapes; some new and fresh,
others old and rugged; all of them would have
appeared surprisingly gigantic to any one accustomed
to see buoys only in their native element. The
invalid sat on the shank of a mushroom anchor, and
smoked his pipe while he affected to superintend
the work.

"Sure I pity the poor craturs as is always sick.
The mouth o' man can niver tell the blessedness of
bein' well, as the pote says," observed Jerry, with a
sigh, as he shook the ashes out of his pipe and proceeded to refill it. "Come now, Jack Shales," he
added, after a short pause, "ye don't call that square,
do 'ee?"

"I'll paint yer nose black if you don't shut up,"
said Jack, drawing the edge of a black square with
intense caution, in order to avoid invading the
domain of a white one.

"Ah! you reminds me of the owld proverb
that says somethin' about asses gittin impudent an'
becomin' free with their heels when lions grow sick."

"Well, Jerry," retorted Jack, with a smile, as he
leaned back and regarded his work with his head
very much on one side, and his eyes partially closed,
after the manner of knights of the brush, "I'm not

offended, because I 'm just as much of an ass as you are of a lion."

" I say, mates," remarked Dick Moy, pausing in his work, and wiping his brow, "are 'ee aweer that the cap'n has ordered us to be ready to start wi' the first o' the tide at half after five to-morrow ?"

" I knows it," replied Jack Shales, laying down the black brush and taking up the white one.

" I knows it too," said Jerry MacGowl, "but it don't make no manner of odds to me, 'cause I means to stop ashore and enjoy meself. I mean to amoose meself with the trial o' that black thief Morley Jones."

Dick Moy resumed his work with a grunt, and said that Jerry was a lucky fellow to be so long on sick-leave, and Jack said he wished he had been called up as a witness in Jones's case, for he would have cut a better figure than Jim Welton did.

" Ay, boy," said Dick Moy, "but there wos a reason for that. You know the poor feller is in love wi' Jones's daughter, an' he didn't like for to help to convict his own father-in-law *to be*, d' ye see ? That 's where it is. The boy Billy Towler was a'most as bad. He 's got a weakness for the gal too, an' no wonder, for she 's bin as good as a mother to 'im. They say that Billy nigh broke the hearts o' the lawyers, he wos so stoopid at sometimes, an' so oncommon 'cute at others. But it warn't o' no use.

Jim's father was strong in his evidence agin him, an' that Mr. Larks, as comed aboard of the Gull, you remember, he had been watching an' ferreting about the matter to that extent that he turned Jones's former life inside out. It seems he's bin up to dodges o' that kind for a long time past."

" No! has he ?" said Jack Shales.

" Arrah, didn't ye read of it?" exclaimed Jerry MacGowl.

"No," replied Jack drily; "not bein' on the sick-list I han't got time to read the papers, d' ye see?"

" Well," resumed Dick Moy, "it seems he has more than once set fire to his premises in Gravesend, and got the insurance money. Hows'ever, he has got fourteen years' transportation now, an' that 'll take the shine pretty well out of him before he comes back."

"How did the poor gal take it?" asked Jack.

Dick replied that she was very bad at first, but that she got somewhat comforted by the way her father behaved to her and listened to her readin' o' the Bible after he was condemned. It might be that the death of his old mother had softened him a bit, for she died with his name on her lips, her last words being, "Oh Morley, give it up, my darling boy, give it up ; it's your only chance to give it up, for you inherit it, my poor boy; the passion and the poison are in your blood; oh, give it up, Morley, give it up!"

"They do say," continued Dick, "that Jones broke down altogether w'en he heard that, an' fell on his gal's neck an' cried like a babby. But for my part I don't much believe in them deathbed repent-ances—for it's much the same thing wi' Jones now, he bein' as good as dead. It's not wot a man *says*, but how a man *lives*, as 'll weigh for or against him in the end."

"An' what more did he say?" asked Jerry Mac-Gowl, stopping down the tobacco in his pipe with one of his fire-proof fingers; "you see, havin' bin on the sick-list so long, I haven't got up all the details o' this business."

"He didn't say much more," replied Dick, scraping away at the sea-weed and barnacles with renewed vigour, "only he made his darter promise that she'd marry Jim Welton as soon after he was gone as possible. She did nothing but cry, poor thing, and wouldn't hear of it at first, but he was so strong about it, saying that the thought of her being so well married was the only thing as would comfort him w'en he was gone, that she gave in at last."

"Sure then she'll have to make up her mind," said Jerry, "to live on air, which is too light food intirely for any wan excep' hummin'-birds and potes."

"She'll do better than that, mate," returned Dick, "for Jim 'as got appointed to be assistant-keeper to a light'ouse, through that fust-rate gen'leman Mr. Durant, who is 'and an' glove, I'm told, wi' the Elder Brethren up at the Trinity 'ouse. It's said that they are to be spliced in a week or two, but, owin' to the circumstances, the weddin' is to be kep' quite priwate."

"Good luck to 'em!" cried Jerry. "Talkin' of the Durants, I s'pose ye've heard that there's goin' to be a weddin' in that family soon?"

"Oh, yes, I've heard on it," cried Dick; "Miss Durant—Katie, they calls her—she's agoin' to be spliced to the young doctor that was wrecked in the Wellington. A smart man that. They say 'ee has stepped into 'is father's shoes, an' is so much liked that 'ee's had to git an assistant to help him to get through the work o' curin' people—or killin' of 'em. I never feel rightly sure in my own mind which it is that the doctors does for us."

"Och, don't ye know?" said Jerry, removing his pipe for a moment, "they keeps curin' of us as long as we've got any tin, an' when that's done they kills us off quietly. If it warn't for the doctors we'd all live to the age of Methoosamel, excep', of coorse, w'en we was cut off by accident or drink."

"Well, I don't know as to that," said Jack Shales, in a hearty manner; "but I'm right glad to hear that Miss Durant is gettin' a good husband, for she's the sweetest gal in England, I think, always exceptin' one whom I don't mean for to name just now. Hasn't she been a perfect angel to the poor —especially to poor old men—since she come to Ramsgate ? and didn't she, before goin' back to Yarmouth, where she b'longs to, make a beautiful paintin' o' the lifeboat, and present it in a gold frame, with tears in her sweet eyes, to the coxswain o' the boat, an' took his big fist in her two soft little hands, an' shook an' squeezed it, an' begged him to keep the pictur' as a very slight mark of the gratitude an' esteem of Dr. Hall an' herself—that was after they was engaged, you know ? Ah ! there ain't many gals like *her*," said Jack, with a sigh, " always exceptin' *one*."

" Humph !" said Dick Moy, " I wouldn't give my old 'ooman for six dozen of 'er."

" Just so," observed Jerry, with a grin, " an' I 've no manner of doubt that Dr. Hall wouldn't give *her* for sixty dozen o' your old 'ooman. It 's human natur', lad,—that 's where it is, mates. But what has come o' Billy Towler ? Has he gone back to the what 's-'is-name—the Cavern, eh ?"

" The Grotto, you mean," said Jack Shales.

" Well, the Grotto—'tan't much differ."

" He 's gone back for a time," said Dick; " but Mr. Durant has prowided for *him* too. He has given him a berth aboord one of his East-Indiamen ; so if

Billy behaves hisself his fortin's as good as made. Leastwise he has got his futt on the first round, an' the ladder 's all clear before him."

" By the way, what 's that I 've heard," said Jack Shales, " about Mr. Durant findin' out that he 'd know'd Billy Towler some years ago ? "

" I don't rightly know," replied Dick. " I 've 'eerd it said that the old gentleman recognised him as a beggar boy 'e 'd tuck a fancy to an' putt to school long ago; but Billy didn't like the school, it seems, an' runn'd away—w'ich I don't regard as wery sur-prisin'—an' Mr. Durant could never find out where 'e 'd run to. That 's how I 'eerd the story, but wot 's true of it I dun know."

" There goes the dinner-bell ! " exclaimed Jack Shales, rising with alacrity on hearing a neighbour-ing clock strike noon.

Jerry rose with a sigh, and remarked, as he shook the ashes out of his pipe, and put it into his waist-coat pocket, that his appetite had quite left him; that he didn't believe he was fit for more than two chickens at one meal, whereas he had seen the day when he would have thought nothing of a whole leg of mutton to his own cheek.

" Ah," remarked Dick Moy, " Irish mutton, I s'pose. Well, I don't know 'ow you feels, but I feels so hungry that I could snap at a ring-bolt; and I know of a lot o' child'n, big an' small, as won't look sweet on their daddy if he keeps 'em waitin' for dinner, so come along, mates."

Saying this, Dick and his friends left the buoy-store, and walked smartly off to their several places of abode in the town.

In a darkened apartment of that same town sat Nora Jones, the very personification of despair, on a low stool, with her head resting on the side of a poor bed. She was alone, and perfectly silent; for some sorrows, like some thoughts, are too deep for utterance. Everything around her suggested absolute desolation. The bed was that in which not long ago she had been wont to smooth the pillow and soothe the heart of her old grandmother. It was empty now. The fire in the rusty grate had been allowed to die out, and its cold grey ashes strewed the hearth. Among them lay the fragments of a black bottle. It would be difficult to say what it was in the peculiar aspect of these fragments that rendered them so suggestive, but there was that about them which conveyed irresistibly the idea that the bottle had been dashed down there with the vehemence of uncontrollable passion. The little table which used to stand at the patient's bedside was covered with a few crumbs and fragments of a meal that must, to judge from their state and appearance, have been eaten a considerable time ago; and the confusion of the furniture, as well as the dust that covered everything, was strangely out of keeping with the character of the poor girl, who reclined by the side of the bed, so pale and still that, but for the slight twitching movement of her clasped hands, one might have supposed she had already passed from the scene of her woe. Even the old-fashioned timepiece that hung upon a nail in the wall seemed to be smitten with the pervading spell, for its pendulum was motionless, and its feeble pulse had ceased to tick.

A soft tap at the door broke the deathlike silence. Nora looked up but did not answer, as it slowly opened, and a man entered. On seeing who it was, she uttered a low wail, and buried her face in the bed-clothes. Without speaking, or moving from her position, she held out her hand to Jim Welton, who advanced with a quick but quiet step, and, going down on his knees beside her, took the little hand in both of his. The attitude and the silence were suggestive. Without having intended it the young sailor began to pray, and in a few short broken sentences poured out his soul before God.

A flood of tears came to Nora's relief. After a few minutes she looked up.

"Oh! thank you, thank you, Jim. I believe that in the selfishness of my grief I had forgotten God ; but oh! I feel as if my heart was crushed beyond the power of recovery. *She* is gone" (glancing at the empty bed), "and *he* is gone—gone *for ever.*"

Jim wished to comfort her, and tried to speak, but his voice was choked. He could only draw her to him, and laying her head on his breast, smooth her fair soft hair with his hard but gentle hand.

" Not gone for ever, dearest," he said at length with a great effort. "It is indeed a long long time, but—"

He could not go further, for it seemed to him like mockery to suggest by way of comfort that fourteen years would come to an end.

For some minutes the silence was broken only by an occasional sob from poor Nora.

"Oh! he was so different *once,*" she said, raising herself and looking at her lover with tearful, earnest eyes; "you have seen him at his worst, Jim. There was a time, before he took to—"

She stopped abruptly, as if unable to find words, and pointed, with a fierce expression, that seemed strange and awful on her gentle face, to the fragments of the broken bottle on the hearth. Jim nodded. She saw that he understood, and went on in her own calm voice :—

"There was a time when he was kind and gentle and loving; when he had no drunken companions, and no mysterious goings to sea; when he was the joy as well as the support of his mother, and *so* fond of me—but he was always that; even after he had—"

Again Nora paused, and, drooping her head, uttered the low wail of desolation that went like cold steel to the young sailor's heart.

"Nora," he said earnestly, "he will get no drink where he is going. At all events he will be cured of *that* before he returns home."

"Oh, I bless the Lord for that," said Nora, with fervour. "I have thought of that before now, and I have thought, too, that there are men of God where he is going, who think of, and pray for, and strive to recover, the souls of those who—that is—; but oh, Jim, Jim, it is a long, long, weary time. I feel that I shall never see my father more in this world—never, never more!"

"We cannot tell, Nora," said Jim, with a desperate effort to appear hopeful. "I know well enough that it may seem foolish to try to comfort you with the hope of seein' him again in this life; and yet even this may come to pass. He may escape, or he may be forgiven, and let off before the end of his time. But come, cheer up, my darling. You remember what his last request was?"

"How can you talk of such a thing at such a time?" exclaimed Nora, drawing away from him and rising.

"Be not angry, Nora," said Jim, also rising. "I did but remind you of it for the purpose of sayin' that as you agreed to what he wished, you have

2 A

given me a sort of right or privilege, dear Nora, at least to help and look after you in your distress. Your own unselfish heart has never thought of telling me that you have neither money nor home; this poor place being yours only till term-day, which is to-morrow; but I know all this without requiring to be told, and I have come to say that there is an old woman—a sort of relation of mine—who lives in this town, and will give you board and lodging gladly till I can get arrangements made at the lighthouse for our—that is to say—till you choose, in your own good time, to let me be your rightful protector and supporter, as well as your comforter."

"Thank you, Jim. It is like yourself to be so thoughtful. Forgive me; I judged you hastily. It is true I am poor—I have nothing in the world, but, thanks be to God, I have health. I can work; and there are some kind friends," she added, with a sad smile, "who will throw work in my way, I know."

"Well, we will talk about these things afterwards, Nora, but you won't refuse to take advantage of my old friend's offer—at least for a night or two?"

"No, I won't refuse that, Jim; see, I am prepared to go," she said, pointing to a wooden sea-chest which stood in the middle of the room; "my box is packed. Everything I own is in it. The furniture, clock, and bedding belong to the landlord."

"Come then, my own poor lamb," said the young sailor tenderly, "let us go."

Nora rose and glanced slowly round the room. Few rooms in Ramsgate could have looked more poverty-stricken and cheerless, nevertheless, being associated in her mind with those whom she had lost, she was loath to leave it. Falling suddenly on her knees beside the bed, she kissed the old counterpane that had covered the dead form she had loved so well, and then went hastily out and leaned her head against the wall of the narrow court before the door.

Jim lifted the chest, placed it on his broad shoulders and followed her. Locking the door behind him and putting the key in his pocket, he gave his disengaged arm to Nora, and led her slowly away.

CHAPTER XXIII.

TELLS OF AN UNLOOKED-FOR RETURN, AND DESCRIBES A GREAT FEAST.

IF, as we have elsewhere observed in this narrative, time and tide wait for no man, it is not less true that time and tide work wonderful changes in man and his affairs and fortunes. Some of those changes we will now glance at, premising that seven years have passed away since the occurrence of the events recorded in our last chapter.

On the evening of a somewhat gloomy day in the month of sunny showers, four men of rough aspect, and clad in coarse but not disreputable garments, stopped in front of a public-house in one of the lowest localities of London, and looked about them. There was something quite peculiar in their aspect. They seemed to be filled with mingled curiosity and surprise, and looked somewhat scared, as a bird does when suddenly set free from its cage.

Two of the men were of an extremely low type of humanity—low-browed and scowling—and their

language betokened that their minds were in keeping with their faces. The other two were better-
looking and better-spoken, one of them having evidently been a handsome man in his day. His hair
was blanched as white as snow although it still
retained the curls of youth. His figure was much
bent, and he appeared like one who had been smitten
with premature old age.

"Well, uncommon queer changes bin goin' on
here," said one of the men, gazing round him.

One of the others admitted that there certainly
had been wonderful changes, and expressed a fear
that if the change in himself was as great, his old
pals wouldn't know him.

"Hows'ever," observed he who had spoken first,
"they won't see such a difference as they would
have seen if we'd got the whole fourteen. Good
luck to the ticket-of-leave system, say I."

The others laughed at this, and one of them suggested that they should enter the public-house and
have a glass of grog in memory of old times. Three
of the men at once agreed to this proposal, and said
that as it would not be long before they were in the
stone jug again it behoved them to make the most
of their freedom while it lasted. The man with
white hair, however, objected, and it was not until
his companions had chaffed and rallied him a good
deal that he consented to enter the house, observing,

as he followed them slowly, that he had not tasted a drop for seven years.

"Well, well," replied one of the others, "it don't matter; you'll relish it all the more now, old feller. It'll go down like oil, an' call up the memory of old times—"

"The memory of old times!" cried the white-haired man, stopping short, with a sudden blaze of ferocity which amazed his companions.

He stood glaring at them for a few moments, with his hands tightly clenched; then, without uttering another word, he turned round and rushed from the house.

"Mad!" exclaimed one of the other three, looking at his companions when they had recovered from their surprise, "mad as a March hare. Hows'ever, that don't consarn us. Come along, my hearties.— Hallo! landlord, fetch drink here—your best, and plenty of it. Now, boys, fill up and I'll give 'ee a toast."

Saying this the man filled his glass, the others followed his example—the toast was given and drunk—more toasts were given and drunk—the three men returned to their drink and their old ways, and haunts and comrades, as the sow returns to her wallowing in the mire.

Meanwhile the white-haired man wandered away as if he had no settled purpose. Day after day he moved on through towns and villages and fields, offering to work, but seldom being employed, begging his bread from door to door, but carefully avoiding the taverns; sleeping where he could, or where he was permitted—sometimes in the barn of a kindly farmer, sometimes under a hay-stack, not unfrequently under a hedge—until at last he found himself in the town of Ramsgate.

Here he made inquiries of various people, and immediately set forth again on his travels through the land until he reached a remote part of the coast of England, where he found his further progress checked by the sea, but, by dint of begging a free passage from fishermen here and there, he managed at last to reach one of our outlying reefs, where, on a small islet, a magnificent lighthouse reared its white and stately column, and looked abroad upon the ocean, with its glowing eye. There was a small village on the islet, in which dwelt a few families of fishermen. They were a hard-working community, and appeared to be contented and happy.

The lighthouse occupied an elevated plateau above the cliffs at the sea-ward extremity of the isle, about quarter of a mile distant from the fishing village. Thither the old man wended his way. The tower, rising high above shrubs and intervening rocks, rendered a guide unnecessary. It was a calm evening. The path, which was narrow and rugged, wound its serpentine course amid grey rocks, luxuriant brambles, grasses, and flowering shrubs.   There were no trees. The want of shelter on that exposed spot rendered their growth impossible.   The few that had been planted had been cut down by the nor'-west wind as with a scythe.

As he drew near to the lighthouse, the old man observed a woman sitting on a stool in front of the door, busily engaged with her needle, while three children—two girls and a boy—were romping on the grass plat beside her.   The boy was just old enough to walk with the steadiness of an exceedingly drunk man, and betrayed a wonderful tendency to sit down suddenly and gaze—astonished !   The girls, apparently though not really twins, were just wild enough to enjoy their brother's tumbles, and helped him to accomplish more of them than would have resulted from his own incapacity to walk.

A magnificent black Newfoundland dog, with grey paws and a benignant countenance, couched beside the woman and watched the children at play. He frequently betrayed a desire to join them in their gambols, but either laziness or a sense of his own dignity induced him to sit still.

" Nora," called the mother, who was a young and exceedingly beautiful mother, " Nora, come here ; go tell your father that I see a stranger coming up the path. Quick, darling."

Little Nora bounded away like a small fairy, with her fair curls streaming in the wind which her own speed created.

"Katie," said the mother, turning to her second daughter, "don't rumple him up *quite* so violently. You must remember that he is a tiny fellow yet, and can't stand such rough treatment."

"But he likes it, ma," objected Katie, with a look of glee, although she obeyed the order at once. "Don't you, Morley?"

Little Morley stopped in the middle of an ecstatic laugh, scrambled upon his fat legs and staggered towards his mother, with his fists doubled, as if to take summary vengeance on her for having stopped the fun.

"Oh, baby boy; my little Morley, what a wild fellow you are!" cried the mother, catching up her child and tossing him in the air.

The old man had approached near enough to overhear the words and recognise the face. Tears sprang to his eyes and ran down his cheeks, as he fell forward on the path with his face in the dust.

At the same moment the lighthouse-keeper issued from the door of the building. Running towards the old man, he and his wife quickly raised him and loosened his neckcloth. His face had been slightly cut by the fall. Blood and dust besmeared it and soiled his white locks.

"Poor old man!" said the keeper, as his mate, the assistant light-keeper, joined him. "Lend a hand, Billy, to carry him in. He ain't very heavy."

The assistant—a strapping young fellow, with a powerful, well-made frame, sparkling eyes and a handsome face, on which at that moment there was a look of intense pity—assisted his comrade to raise the old man. They carried him with tender care into the lighthouse and laid him on a couch which at that time, owing to lack of room in the building, happened to be little Nora's bed.

For a few moments he lay apparently in a state of insensibility, while the mother of the family brought a basin of water and began carefully to remove the blood and dust which rendered his face unrecognisable. The first touch of the cold sponge caused him to open his eyes and gaze earnestly in the woman's face—so earnestly that she was constrained to pause and return the gaze inquiringly.

"You seem to know me," she said.

The old man made no reply, but, slowly clasping his hands and closing his eyes, exclaimed "Thank God!" fervently.

*   *   *   *   *

Let us glance, now, at a few more of the changes which had been wrought in the condition and circumstances of several of the actors in this tale by the wonder-working hand of time.

On another evening of another month in this same year, Mr. Robert Queeker—having just completed an ode to a star which had been recently discovered by the Astronomer-Royal—walked from the door of the Fortress Hotel, Ramsgate, and, wending his way leisurely along Harbour Street, directed his steps towards St. James's Hall.

Seven years had wrought a great change for the better in Mr. Robert Queeker. His once smooth face was decorated with a superb pair of light-brown whiskers of the stamp now styled Dundreary. His clothes fitted him well, and displayed to advantage a figure which, although short, was well made and athletic. It was evident that time had not caused his shadow to grow less. There was a jaunty, confident air about him, too, which might have been thought quite in keeping with a red coat and top-boots by his friends in Jenkinsjoy, and would have induced hospitable Mr. Stoutheart to let him once more try his fortune on the back of Slapover without much anxiety as to the result; ay, even although the sweet but reckless Amy were to be his leader in the field! Nevertheless there was nothing of the coxcomb about Queeker—no self-assertion; nothing but amiableness, self-satisfaction, and enthusiasm.

Queeker smiled and hummed a tune to himself as he walked along drawing on his gloves, which were lavender kid and exceedingly tight.

"It will be a great night," he murmured; "a grand, a glorious night."

As there was nothing peculiarly grand in the aspect of the weather, it is to be presumed that he referred to something else, but he said nothing more at the time, although he smiled a good deal and hummed a good many snatches of popular airs as he walked along, still struggling with the refractory fingers of the lavender kid gloves.

Arrived at St. James's Hall, he took up a position outside the door, and remained there as if waiting for some one.

It was evident that Mr. Queeker's brief remark had reference to the proceedings that were going on at the hall, because everything in and around it, on that occasion, gave unquestionable evidence that there was to be a "great night" there. The lobby blazed with light, and resounded with voices and bustle, as people streamed in continuously. The interior of the hall itself glowed like a red-hot chamber of gold, and was tastefully decorated with flowers and flags and evergreens; while the floor of the room was covered with long tables, which groaned under the glittering accessories of an approaching feast. Fair ladies were among the assembling company, and busy gentlemen, who acted the part of stewards, hurried to and fro, giving directions and keeping order. A large portion of the company consisted of men whose hard hands, powerful frames, and bronzed faces, proclaimed them the sons of toil, and whose manly tones and holiday garments smacked of gales and salt water.

"What be goin' on here, measter?" inquired a country fellow, nudging Mr. Queeker with his elbow.

Queeker looked at his questioner in surprise, and told him that it was a supper which was about to be given to the lifeboat-men by the people of the town.

"An' who be the lifeboat-men, measter?"

"'Shades of the mighty dead;' not to mention the glorious living!" exclaimed Queeker, aghast; "have you never heard of the noble fellows who man the lifeboats all round the coasts of this great country, and save hundreds of lives every year? Have you not read of their daring exploits in the newspapers? Have you never heard of the famous Ramsgate lifeboat?"

"Well, now 'ee mention it, I doos remember summat about loifboats," replied the country fellow, after pondering a moment or two; "but, bless 'ee, I never read nothin' about 'em, not bein' able to read; an' as I've lived all my loif fur inland, an' on'y comed here to-day, it ain't to be thow't as I knows much about yer Ramsgate loifboats. Be there mony loifboat men in Ramsgate, measter?"

"My good fellow," said Queeker, taking the man

by the sleeve, and gazing at him with a look of earnest pity, "there are dozens of 'em. Splendid fellows, who have saved hundreds of men, women, and children from the raging deep; and they are all to be assembled in this hall to-night, to the number of nearly a hundred—for there are to be present not only the men who now constitute the crew of the Ramsgate boat, but all the men who have formed part of her crew in time past. Every man among them is a hero," continued Queeker, warming as he went on, and shaking the country fellow's arm in his earnestness, "and every man to-night will— "

He stopped short abruptly, for at that moment a carriage drove up to the door, and a gentleman jumping out assisted a lady to alight.

Without a word of explanation to the astonished country fellow, Queeker thrust him aside, dashed forward, presented himself before the lady, and, holding out his hand, exclaimed—

"How *do* you do, Miss Hennings? I'm *so* glad to have been fortunate enough to meet you."

"Mr. Quee—Queeker," exclaimed Fanny, blushing scarlet; "I—I was not aware—so very unexpected—I thought—dear me!—but, pardon me—allow me to introduce my uncle, Mr. Hennings. Mr. Queeker, uncle, whom you have often heard mamma speak about."

Mr. Hennings, a six-feet-two man, stooped to

shake Queeker by the hand. An impatient cabman shouted " Move on." Fanny seized her uncle's arm, and was led away. Queeker followed close, and all three were wedged together in the crowd, and swept towards the banquet-hall.

" Are you one of the stewards?" asked Fanny, during a momentary pause.

How exquisite she looks ! thought Queeker, as she glanced over her shoulder at him. He felt inclined to call her an angel, or something of that sort, but restrained himself, and replied that he was not a steward, but a guest—an honoured guest—and that he would have no objection to be a *dis*honoured guest, if only, by being expelled from the festive board, he could manage to find an excuse to sit beside her in the ladies' gallery.

" But that may not be," he said, with a sigh. " I shall not be able to see you from my allotted position. Alas ! we separate here—though—though—lost to sight, to memory dear !"

The latter part of this remark was said hurriedly and in desperation, in consequence of a sudden rush of the crowd, rendering abrupt separation unavoidable. But, although parted from his lady-love, and unable to gaze upon her, Queeker kept her steadily in his mind's eye all that evening, made all his speeches to her, sang all his songs to her, and finally —but hold ! we must not anticipate.

As we have said—or, rather, as we have recorded that Queeker said—all the lifeboat men of the town of Ramsgate sat down to that supper, to the number of nearly one hundred men. All sturdy men of tried courage. Some were old, with none of the fire that had nerved them to rescue lives in days gone by, save that which still gleamed in their eyes; some were young, with the glow of irrepressible enthusiasm on their smooth faces, and the intense wish to have a chance to dare and do swelling their bold hearts; others were middle-aged, iron-moulded; as able and as bold to the full as the younger men, with the coolness and self-restraint of the old ones; but all, old, middle-aged, and young, looking proud and pleased, and so gentle in their demeanour (owing, no doubt, to the presence of the fair sex), that it seemed as if a small breeze of wind would have made them all turn tail and run away,—especially if the breeze were raised by the women !

That the reception of these lion-like men (converted into lambs that night) was hearty, was evinced by the thunders of applause which greeted every reference to their brave deeds. That their reception was intensely earnest, was made plain by the scroll, emblazoned on a huge banner that spanned the upper end of the room, bearing the words, " God bless the Lifeboat Crews."

We need not refer to the viands set forth on that great occasion. Of course they were of the best. We may just mention that they included "baccy and grog!" We merely record the fact. Whether buns and tea would have been equally effective is a question not now under consideration. We refrain from expressing an opinion on that point here.

Of course the first toast was the Queen, and as Jack always does everything heartily, it need scarcely be said that this toast was utterly divested of its usual formality of character. The chairman's appropriate reference to her Majesty's well-known sympathy with the distressed, especially with those who had suffered from shipwreck, intensified the enthusiasm of the loyal lifeboat-men.

A band of amateur Christy Minstrels (the "genuine original" amateur band, of course) enlivened the evening with appropriate songs, to the immense delight of all present, especially of Mr. Robert Queeker, whose passionate love for music, ever since his attendance at the singing-class, long long ago, had strengthened with time to such an extent that language fails to convey any idea of it. It mattered not to Queeker whether the music were good or bad. Sufficient for him that it carried him back, with a *gush*, to that dear temple of music in Yarmouth where the learners were perpetually checked at critical points. and told by their callous teacher (tormentor, we had almost written) to "try it again!" and where he first beheld the perplexing and beautiful Fanny.

When the toast of the evening was given—"Success to the Ramsgate Lifeboat,"—it was, as a matter of course, received with deafening cheers and enthusiastic waving of handkerchiefs from the gallery in which the fair sex were accommodated, among which handkerchiefs Quecker, by turning his head very much round, tried to see, and believed that he saw, the precious bit of cambric wherewith Fanny Hennings was accustomed to salute her transcendental nose. The chairman spoke with enthusiasm of the noble deeds accomplished by the Ramsgate lifeboat in time past, and referred with pride, and with a touch of feeling, to the brave old coxswain, then present (loud cheers), who had been compelled, by increasing years, to resign a service which, they all knew better than he did, taxed the energies, courage, and endurance of the stoutest and youngest man among them to the uttermost. He expressed a firm belief in the courage and prowess of the coxswain who had succeeded him (renewed cheers), and felt assured that the success of the boat in time to come would at the least fully equal its successes in time past. He then referred to some of the more prominent achievements of the boat, especially to a night which all of them must remember, seven years ago, when the

Ramsgate boat, with the aid of the steam-tug, was the means of saving so many lives—not to mention property—and among others the life of their brave townsman, James Welton (cheers), and a young doctor, the friend, and now the son-in-law, of one whose genial spirit and extensive charities were well known and highly appreciated—he referred to Mr. George Durant (renewed cheers), whose niece at that moment graced the gallery with her presence.

At this there was a burst of loud and prolonged applause which terminated in a roar of laughter, owing to the fact that Mr. Queeker, cheering and waving his hands in a state of wild enthusiasm, knocked the neck off a bottle of wine and flooded the table in his immediate vicinity! Covered with confusion, Queeker sat down amid continued laughter and rapturous applause.

The chairman then went on to say that the event to which he had referred—the rescue of. the crew and passengers of the Wellington on the night of the great storm—had been eclipsed by some of the more recent doings of the same boat; and, after touching upon some of these, said that, although they had met there to do honour to the crews of their own lifeboat, they must not forget other and neighbouring lifeboats, which did their work nobly—the brave crews of which were represented by the coxswains of the Margate and Broadstairs

lifeboats, who sat at that board that night as honoured guests (loud cheers, during which several of
the men nearest to them shook hands with the coxswains referred to). He could not—the chairman
went on to say—sit down without making special
reference to the steam-tug, without which, and the
courage as well as knowledge of her master, mate,
and crew (renewed cheers), the lifeboat could not
overtake a tenth part of the noble work which she
annually accomplished. He concluded by praying
that a kind Providence would continue to watch
over and bless the Ramsgate lifeboat and her crew.

We need scarcely add that this toast was drunk
with enthusiastic applause, and that it was followed
up by the amateur minstrels with admirable effect.

Many songs were sung, and many toasts were
proposed that night, and warm was the expression of
feeling towards the men who were ever so ready to
imperil their lives in the hope of saving those of
their fellow-creatures, and who had already, often-
times, given such ample proof that they were
thoroughly able to do, as well as to dare, almost
anything. Several singers with good, and one or
two with splendid, voices, gave a variety of
songs which greatly enhanced the brilliancy of the
evening, and were highly appreciated in the gallery;
and a few bad singers with miserable voices (who
volunteered their songs) did really good service by

impressing on the audience very forcibly the immense difference between good and bad music, and thus kindly acted as shadows to the vocal lights of the evening—as useful touches of discord in the general harmony which by contrast rendered the latter all the sweeter.

But of all the solos sung that night none afforded such delight as a national melody sung by our friend Jerry MacGowl, in a voice that rang out like the voices of three first-class bo's'ns rolled into one. That worthy son of the Emerald Isle, and Dick Moy, and Jack Shales, happened to be enjoying their month on shore when the supper to the lifeboat-men was planned, and they were all there in virtue of their having been instrumental in saving life on more than one occasion during their residence in Ramsgate. Jerry's song was, as we have said, highly appreciated, but the applause with which it was greeted was as nothing compared with the shouts and cheers that shook the roof of St. James's Hall, when, on being asked to repeat it, Jerry, modestly said that he "would prefer to give them a duet—perhaps it was a trayo—av his mates Jack Shales and Dick Moy would only strike in wid bass and tenor."

The men of the floating light then sang "The Minute-Gun at Sea" magnificently, each taking the part that suited him best or struck his fancy at the moment, and Jerry varying from tenor to bass and bass to treble according to taste.

"Now, Mister Chairman," said the bold Jerry MacGowl, when the cheers had subsided, "it's my turn to call for a song, so I ax Mr. Queeker to favour the company wid—" Thunders of applause drowned the remainder of the sentence.

Poor Queeker was thrown into great confusion, and sought to explain that he could not sing, even in private—much less in public.

"Oh yes, you can, sir. Try it, sir, no fear of 'ee. Sure it's yourself as can do it, an' no mistake," were the remarks with which his explanation was interrupted.

"I assure you honestly," cried Queeker, "that I cannot sing, *but*" (here breathless silence ensued) "if the chairman will kindly permit me, I will give you a toast."

Loud cheers from all sides, and a good-humoured nod from the chairman greeted this announcement.

"Mr. Chairman and Friends," said Queeker, "the ladies have—" A perfect storm of laughter and cheers interrupted him for at least two minutes.

"Yes," resumed Queeker, suddenly blazing up with enthusiasm, "I repeat—the ladies—"

"That's the girls, blissin's on the swate darlints," murmured Jerry in a tone which set the whole table again in a roar.

"I echo the sentiment; blessings on them," said Queeker, with a good-humoured glance at Jerry. "Yes, as I was going to say, I propose the Ladies, who are, always were, and ever will be, the solace of man's life, the sweet drops in his otherwise bitter cup, the lights in his otherwise dark dwelling, the jewels in his—in his—crown, and the bright stars that glitter in the otherwise dark firmament of his destiny (vociferous cheering). Yes," continued Queeker, waxing more and more energetic, and striking the table with his fist, whereby he over-turned his neighbour's glass of grog, "yes, I re-assert it—the ladies are all that, and *much more!* (Hear, hear.) I propose their health—and, after all, I may be said to have some sort of claim to do so, having already unintentionally poured a whole bottle of wine on the tablecloth as a libation to them! (Laughter and applause.) What, I ask," continued Queeker, raising his voice and hand at the same moment, and setting his hair straight upon end, "what, I ask, would man be *without* the ladies?" ("What indeed?" said a voice near the foot of the table, which called forth another burst of laughter.) "Just try to think, my friends, what would be the hideous gloom of this terrestrial ball if there were no girls! Oh woman! softener of man's rugged nature! What—in the words of the poet (he carefully re-frained from saying what poet!)—

" What were earth and all its joys ;
What were wealth with all its toys ;
What the life of men and boys
          But for lovely woman ?

What if mothers were no more ;
If wives and sisters fled our shore,
And left no sweethearts to the fore—
          No sign of darling woman ?

What dreary darkness would ensue—
What moral wastes devoid of dew—
If no strong hearts of men like you
          Beat for charming woman ?

Who would rise at duty's call ;
Who would fight to win or fall ;
Who would care to live at all,
          Were it not for woman ?"

Prolonged and rapturous cheers greeted this effusion, in the midst of which the enthusiastic Jerry Mac-Gowl sprang to his feet, waved his glass above his head—spilling half of its contents on the pate of a bald skipper who sat next to him—and cheered lustily.

" Men of the Ramsgate lifeboat," shouted Queeker, " I call on you to pledge the ladies—with all the honours !"

It is unnecessary to say that the call was responded to with a degree of enthusiasm that threatened, as Dick Moy said to Jack Shales, " to smash all the glasses an' blow the roof off." In the midst of the noise and confusion Queeker left the hall, ascended to the gallery, and sat himself down beside Fanny Hennings, with an air of intense decision.

"Oh, Mr. Queeker!" exclaimed Fanny.

"Listen, Fanny," said the tall uncle at that moment, "they are giving one of the most important toasts of the evening—The Royal National Lifeboat Institution."

Fanny tried to listen, and had caught a few words, when she felt her hand suddenly seized and held fast. Turning her head quickly, she beheld the face of Queeker turned to bright scarlet.

What more she heard or saw after that it would be extremely difficult to tell. Perhaps the best way of conveying an idea of it is to lay before the reader the short epistle which Fanny penned that same night to her old friend Katie Hall. It ran thus :—

"RAMSGATE.

"OH, KATIE! DARLING KATIE!—He has done it *at last!* Dear fellow! And so like himself too— so romantically, so poetically! They were toasting the Lifeboat Institution at the time. He seized my hand. 'Fanny,' he said, in the deep manly tones in which he had just made the most brilliant speech of the evening, 'Fanny, my love—my life—my *lifeboat*—will you have me? will you *save* me? There was a dreadful noise at the time—a very storm of cheering. The whole room seemed in a whirl. My head was in a whirl too; and oh! *how* my heart beat! I don't know what I said. I fear I burst into a fit of laughter, and then cried, and dear uncle carried me out—but it's all over now. That *darling* Lifeboat Institution, I shall never forget it; for they were sounding its praises at the very moment when my Queeker and I got into the same boat—for life!—Your happy

"FANNY."

To this the next post brought the following reply :—

"YARMOUTH.

"MY DEAREST FANNY,—Is it necessary for me to say that your last short letter has filled my heart with joy? It has cleared up a mystery too! On Tuesday last, in the forenoon, Mr. Queeker came by appointment to take lunch with us, and Stanley happened to mention that a supper was to be given to the Ramsgate lifeboat-men, and that he had heard *you* were to be there. During lunch, Mr. Queeker was very absent and restless, and appeared to be unhappy. At last he started up, made some hurried apology about the train for the south, and having urgent business to transact, looked at his watch, and rushed out of the house! We could not understand it at the time, but I knew that he had only a few minutes left to catch the train for the south, and I *now* know that he caught it—and why! Ah, Fanny, did I not always assure you that he would do it in desperation at last! My earnest prayer is, that your wedded life may be as happy as mine has hitherto been.

"When your honeymoon is over, you must promise to pay us a visit. You know that our villa is sufficiently far out of town to warrant your regarding us in the light of country friends ; and Stanley bids me say that he will take no denial. Papa— who is at present romping round the room with my eldest boy on his shoulders, so that I scarce know what I write—bids me tell you, with his kind love and hearty congratulations, that he thinks you are 'not throwing yourself away, for that Queeker is a first-rate little fellow, and a rising man !' Observe, please, that I quote papa's own words.

"I *must* stop abruptly, because a tiny cry from the nursery informs me that King Baby is awake, and demands instant attention !—With kindest love and congratulations, your ever affectionate,

"KATIE HALL."

· CHAPTER XXIV.

CONCLUSION.

ONCE again, and for the last time, we visit the floating light.

It was a calm sunny evening, about the end of autumn, when the Trinity tender, having effected "the relief" of the old Gull, left her in order to perform the same service for her sister light-vessels.

"Good-bye, Welton, good-bye, lads," cried the superintendent, waving his hand as the tender's boat pushed off and left them, for another period of duty, in their floating home.

"Good-bye, sir," replied the mate and men, touching their caps.

"Now, sir," said Dick Moy to the mate, shortly after, when they were all, except the watch, assembled below round the galley stove, "are you goin' to let us 'ave a bit o' that there letter, accordin' to promise?"

"What letter?" inquired Jack Shales, who having

only accomplished half of his period of service on board—one month—had not come off with his comrades, and knew little or nothing of what had occurred on shore.

"A letter from the lighthouse from Jim," said the mate, lighting his pipe; "received it this forenoon just as we were gettin' ready to come off."

"All well and hearty, I hope?" asked Jerry MacGowl, seating himself on a bench, and rolling some tobacco between his palms, preparatory to filling his pipe.

"All well," replied the mate, pulling out the letter in question, and regarding the address with much interest; "an' strange news in it."

"Well, then, let's 'ear wot it's all about," said Dick Moy; "there's time to read it afore sunset, an' it ain't fair to keep fellers in all the hagonies of hexpectation."

"That's true enough," said Jerry with a grin. "Arrah! it's bustin I am already wid kooriosity. Heave ahead, sir, an' be marciful."

Thus entreated, Mr. Welton glanced at his watch, sat down, and, opening his letter, read as follows :—

"DEAR FATHER,—Here we are, thank God, comfortably settled in the new lighthouse, and Nora and I both agree that although it is more outlandish, it is much more cheerful in every way than our last abode, although it *is* very wild-like, and far from the mainland. Billy Towler, my assistant,—who has become such a strapping fellow that you'd scarce know him,—is also much pleased with it. The children, too, give a decided opinion in favour of the place, and even the baby, little Morley, seems to know that he has made a change for the better !

" Baby's name brings me to the news that I've got to tell you. Morley Jones has come back ! You'll be surprised to hear that, I daresay, but it's a fact. He got a ticket-of-leave, and never rested till he found out where Nora was. He came to us one evening some time ago, and fell down in a sort of fit close to the lighthouse-door, while Nora was sitting in front of it, and the children were romping with Neptune beside her. Poor fellow ! he was so changed, so old, and so white-haired and worn, that we did not know him at first; but after we had washed the blood off his face—for he had cut himself when he fell—I recognised the old features.

" But he is changed in other respects too, in a way that has filled my dear wife's heart with joy. Of course you are aware that he got no drink during the seven years of his imprisonment. Now that he is free he refuses to let a drop of anything stronger than water pass his lips. He thinks it is his only chance, and I believe he is right. He says that no-thing but the thought of Nora, and the hope of one day being permitted to return to ask her forgiveness on his knees, enabled him to endure his long captivity with resignation. I do assure you, father, that it almost brings tears to my eyes to see the way in which that man humbles himself before his daughter. Nora's joy is far too deep for words, but it is written plainly in her face. She spent all her spare time with him at first, reading the Bible to him, and trying to convince him that it was not the thought of *her*, but God's mercy and love that had put it into his heart to repent, and desire to reform. He does not seem quite inclined to take that view of it, but he will come to it, sooner or later, for we have the sure promise that the Lord will finish the good work He has begun. We have hired a room for him in a little village within half a mile of us. It is small, but comfortable enough, and he seems to be quite content with it—as well he may be, with Nora and the children going constantly about him !

"I tell you what, father, the longer I live with Nora, the more I feel that I have got the truest-hearted and most loveable wife in all the wide world ! The people of the village would go any length to serve her ; and as to their children, I believe they worship the ground she walks on, as Jerry Mac-Gowl used to say."

"Och, the idolatrous haythens !" growled Jerry.

"And the way she manages our dear youngsters,"

continued the mate, reading on, without noticing
Jerry's interruption, " would do your heart good to
see.   It reminds me of Dick Moy's wife, who is
about the best mother I ever met with—next to
Nora, of course !"

"Humph !" said Dick, with a grim smile; " wery
complimentary.   I wonder wot my old ooman will
say to that ?"

"She 'll say, no doubt, that she 'll expect you to
take. example by Jim Welton when speaking of
your wife," observed Jack Shales.   " I wonder, Dick,
what ever could have induced Mrs. Moy to marry
such a fellow as you ?"

" I s'pose," retorted Dick, lighting his pipe, " that
it was to escape the chance o' bein' tempted, in a
moment of weakness, to marry the likes o' *you*."

"Hear, hear," cried MacGowl, " that's not unlikely, Dick.   An', sure, she might have gone farther
an' fared worse.   You 're a good lump of a man, anyhow ; though you haven't much to boast of in the
way of looks.   Howsever, it seems to me that looks
don't go far wid sensible girls.   Faix, the uglier a
man is, it 's the better chance he has o' gittin' a
purty wife.   I have a brother, myself, who 's a dale
uglier than the figurhead of an owld Dutch galliot,
an' he 's married the purtiest little girl in Ireland,
he has."

" If ye want to hear the end of Jim's letter, boys,

you'd better shut up your potato-traps," interposed Mr. Welton.

"That's true—fire away," said Shales.

The mate continued to read.

"You'll be glad to hear that the old dog Neptune is well and hearty. He is a great favourite here, especially with the children. Billy Towler has taught him a number of tricks—among other things he can dive like a seal, and has no objection whatever to let little Morley choke him or half punch out his eyes. Tell mother not to be uneasy on that point, for though Neptune has the heart of a lion he has the temper of a lamb.

"There is an excellent preacher, belonging to the Wesleyan body, who comes here occasionally on Sundays, and has worship in the village. He is not much of a preacher, but he's an earnest, God-fearing man, and has made the name of Jesus dear to some of the people here, who, not long ago, were quite careless about their souls. Careless about their souls! Oh, father, how often I think of that, now. How strange it seems that we should ever be thus careless! What should we say of the jeweller who would devote all his time and care to the case that held his largest diamond, and neglect the gem itself? Nora has got up a Sunday school at the village, and Billy helps her with it. The Grotto did wonders for *him*—so he says himself.

"I must close this letter sooner than I intended, for I hear Nora's voice, like sweet music in the distance, singing out that dinner is ready; and if I keep the youngsters waiting long, they 'll sing out in a sharper strain of melody!

"So now, father, good-bye for the present. We all unite in sending our warmest love to dear mother and yourself. Kindest remembrances also to my friends in the floating light. As much of my heart as Nora and the children can spare is on board of the old Gull. May God bless you all.—Your affectionate son,   JAMES WELTON."

"The sun will be down in a few minutes, sir," said the watch, looking down the hatchway, while the men were engaged in commenting on Jim's letter.

"I know that," replied the mate, glancing at his timepiece, as he went on deck.

The upper edge of the sun was just visible above the horizon, gleaming through the haze like a speck of ruddy fire. The shipping in the Downs rested on a sea so calm that each rope and mast and yard was faithfully reflected. Ramsgate—with the exception of its highest spires—was overshadowed by the wing of approaching night. The Goodwin Sands were partially uncovered; looking calm and harmless enough, with only a snowy ripple on their northern extremity, where they were gently kissed by the swell of the North Sea, and with nothing, save a riven stump or a half-buried stem-post, to tell of the storms and wrecks with which their name is so sadly associated.

All around breathed of peace and tranquillity when the mate, having cast a searching glance round the horizon, leaned over the hatchway and shouted—

"Lights up!"

The customary "Ay, ay, sir," was followed by the prompt appearance of the crew. The winch was manned, the signal given, and, just as the sun went down, the floating light went up, to scatter its guiding and warning beams far and wide across the darkening waste of water.

May our little volume prove a truthful reflector to catch up a few of those beams, and, diverting them from their legitimate direction, turn them in upon the shore to enlighten the mind and tickle the fancy of those who dwell upon the land—and thus, perchance, add another thread to the bond of sympathy already existing between them and those whose lot it is to battle with the winds, and live upon the sea.

www.ingramcontent.com/pod-product-compliance
Lightning Source LLC
Chambersburg PA
CBHW030812110726
47900CB00006B/1594